D1706633

TRIALS OF POWER

FORCES OF POWER BOOK 1

BEN CROW

ISBN-13: 979-8-5717-4892-6

Exclusive Launch Edition

Published by Ben Crow

Cover design by Joan Crow

Original cover image by ArtTower from Pixabay

Printed in the United States of America

For more information visit www.benjamincrow.com

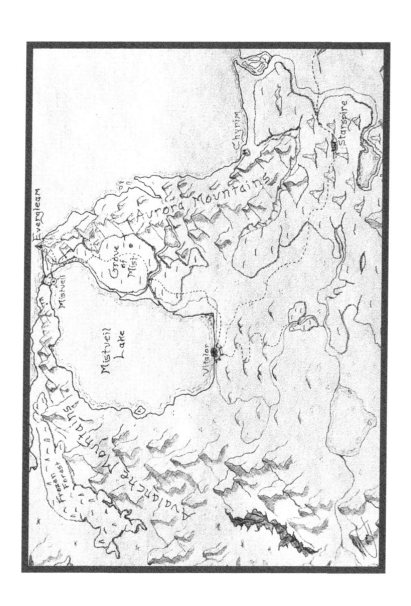

To Dad,
Who fostered my love for fantasy through my youth, and taught me to use my creativity for good instead of evil.

To Viv,
The inspiration for the mighty Sage, whose courage, passion, and ample dash of sass compelled me to press on when I felt I couldn't.

And to Mom,
Who has read the novel more times than I have, and whose unfailing support brought me light in the darkest days.

Your powers may not be visible to all, but to me, they are boundless.

This is for you.

TABLE OF CONTENTS

PROLOGUE

THE FORCES AND THE FOUNDERS

This'll never work . . .

Arkon shook his head as the seven other regal dignitaries bickered relentlessly at the large table before him.

"You don't belong on my land!"

"You couldn't outwit my hounds!"

"I'll crush you like the vermin you are!"

Arkon had called the meeting to prevent war on eight fronts. But despite his best intentions, the others showed no signs of cooperation. Coaxing them into the same room had been an unprecedented feat. He wasn't sure how much more his fraying mind could take, not after what he'd gone through to get them all here. But this was their one chance at peace. If he couldn't persuade them to understand, more than just his sanity would be lost.

But it has to work . . .

"Silence!" Arkon bellowed.

Much to his surprise, the others obeyed. Their eyes turned to the grizzled commander.

Arkon cleared his throat. "Enough of these petty quarrels. Do you not recall why we agreed to convene this night? We are to put an end to this madness before we claim the lives of each and every man, woman, and child in Physos."

"And how do you propose we do that, Lord Arkon?" said a bald, slender Lord.

"That, Lord Cyndus, is why we are here. If we do not cease these squabbles between ourselves, and between our people, we will surely perish in a great war—"

"All of you may die, but my warriors would paint the rivers red with yer blood!" the Lord beside him barked, slamming his meaty fist emphatically on the table.

"Lord Rodran, if I hear one more word about your impenetrable army—" *Peace,* Arkon reminded himself. He exhaled a slow breath. "It is known you care greatly for your people—we all do. But the futures we envision will forever remain a distant fantasy if we do not find a way to end our differences."

A low murmur of agreement resounded across the table. Finally, Arkon could feel the tides of persuasion churning. "Lady Tephra, you had mentioned a plan for trade?"

"Indeed," Tephra said, her brown skin gleaming in the candlelight. "When acting as independent regions, we each struggle to provide all that our people desire. But each of our lands produce resources others need. We've been fools not to take advantage of our unique wealth. Lord Cyndus, your waters and shores are teeming with fish. And Lady Celosia, your bountiful grain harvests produce more wheat than the rest of our lands combined. Why fight for each other's lands when we could share the abundance of resources Physos provides for us?"

"It's true," said Celosia, the youthful woman seated beside Tephra. "Our reserves are often full not days after harvest begins. We have plenty to spare."

"Of course you have more than enough, your land is twice the size of ours. Trades of this sort warrant no personal hardship when you monopolize all the food!" shouted another Lord.

"What's the matter, Lord Aoric?" Rodran taunted. "Still lamenting yer measly spigot of land after I smashed yer petty excuse for an army years ago?"

"Lord Rodran, mark my words," Arkon fumed, "one more quip from you and I'll toss you from the damned window!"

"Not if I toss yeh first!" Rodran shot back.

"Still resorting to violence to solve your problems, are we, Arkon?" hissed an older, balding Lord who hadn't spoken a word since arriving. "Though I'm not surprised. Your conflicts off the battlefield were resolved the same way."

"Mind your tongue, Lord Lussiek. Let us not dwell on the events of our past," Arkon seethed. "Consider yourself fortunate to have been invited. You're fortunate to be alive at all."

"They don't call you the *Dragon* for nothing, now do they?" Lussiek taunted. "I must say that title is quite suiting for someone of your . . . demeanor."

Arkon gripped the lip of the table. *Peace*, he reminded himself again. *We are here to bring peace.*

To his relief, he felt Lady Illara's hand on his shoulder, calming the storm inside him. "Enough of this!" she shouted, piercing the others with her wise, maternal gaze. "Recurring disputes of our pasts will not lead to the bright future we all desire. There is no future in war; only in harmony. The sooner we can set our pasts behind us, the sooner we can build a new future."

The debate continued well into the night as they waged a war of negotiation. After seemingly endless onslaughts of arguments and compromises, they had finally arrived on a treaty that benefited all parties.

"Are we in agreement, then?" Arkon said wearily.

The other seven leaders all muttered in unison.

Arkon stood and declared, "By the decree of the eight, we rightfully proclaim this land to be the allied realm of Physos. May we all live in harmony and flourish in the days to come; not as enemies, but as allies."

A collective sigh rose from the eight leaders. Slowly, they rose from their seats, eager to leave the musty room. Just as

Rodran reached the door, a brilliant, blinding light burst through the lone window in the castle wall.

The eight leaders recoiled in momentary agony.

An angelic voice echoed against the stone walls. "My children," soothed the voice. "I am known as the Mother. Long have I watched the growth of your lands and your people, the futures of which were clouded in mystery. But now, after your initiatives to bring peace to your realm, I foresee your future will no longer be of death and war, but of peace and tranquility."

"Wha—what do you want from us?" Rodran sputtered.

"You have all done a great service on this day, not only for your people, but for your world. It will thrive, as you will, for centuries to come. As reward, I have come with a gift. From this day forth, you shall each be blessed with powers, dictated by the forces of nature present in your world. When you return to your lands, you will teach these powers to your people; use them to improve the lives of your own, the lives of your allies, and the world around you." The voice grew louder. "But be warned, for if the temptations of the lone sparrow sing louder than the songs of the flock, the only future that exists is one of war."

The voice dissipated as quickly as it had come. The light funneled back through the window, returning the room to the dim glow of candlelight.

The eight leaders stood mute for several moments. Then came the uproar.

"Did she—that voice—say we will have . . . powers?" questioned a baffled Celosia.

"I don't feel any different—"

"She said we have to return to our lands first—"

"Did no one find it odd the voice called us her 'children'?"

"How will we share these powers with our people? With everyone?"

"And what's this about a damned flock o' sparra's?"

Questions and musings flooded from the eight leaders, each of them thrilled and perplexed by the mystery of the divine voice.

Departing from Arkon's castle, they each returned to their lands to discover a new world ahead of them; a world with powers beyond their wildest dreams, filled with the hope of a new dawn, living as one with the forces of nature.

TRIALS OF POWER

FORCES OF POWER BOOK 1

CHAPTER 1

THE ARENA

Dane should've been listening, but he couldn't stop thinking about the Trials of Power.

How could he? Everything was about to change. The Trials were to be the defining moment of his life, the ultimate test that bridged him into adulthood. He'd be assigned to a new city, meet new people, and could finally begin living the life he'd dreamt of for ten years.

Even thinking about the Trials sent another wave of jitters through his body. There was no telling which obstacles awaited him in the arena this year. Would he have to fight a warrior made of living vines and thorns? Or maybe swim up a waterfall? Navigate a pitch-black maze? And he'd have nothing but his bare fists. That, and his power . . . once he discovered how to use it.

He shifted his focus back to Elder Chrysanthe as she addressed the crowd of initiates. Her white hair was pulled back in a tight bun, exposing her pale face that deceived her growing age. Her robes of mossy green seemed to slither in the dim glow of the room's luminescent torches, as if the decorative vines wrapping around her had minds of their own.

"After finding your power in the arena today," she was saying, "you will all embark on a lifelong journey to fulfill the wishes of the Mother and provide for this wonderful world She has given us. Whether a Biophage, a Tempus, a Geomancer, or any power, there will always be a place for you to make your mark, to make a difference." Her soft expression turned serious. "But the Trials were not created to be a simple feat. They were designed to test your cunning intellect, natural survival instinct, and combat prowess. Most of you have witnessed the Trials as spectators. Today, you will learn how dangerous the Trials can be. They will tear you down. They will push you beyond your limits. But only then will the Mother's light shine upon you and grant your power, as She has done since the Trials began five centuries ago."

She dove into a retelling of the first Trials of Power, when the founders had first created them. Normally, Dane would've been sitting in the front row, gobbling up every word. He loved the founders. Ever since he was a boy, he'd wanted to be just like them. Now at eighteen, his boyhood dream still seemed a tangible reality. But he'd heard the story at least a hundred times before. And Elder Chrysanthe never did it justice.

It wasn't that she was boring. She spoke with passion and purpose, as if every word was of equal importance to its predecessor. Her soothing voice purred off the earthen walls. It was no wonder she had been chosen as elder. To her, the Trials and its traditions seemed as sacred as the Mother herself. In any other circumstance, her speech would've been nothing short of enchanting.

But the Trials were no ordinary circumstance.

Dane straightened, the wooden bench creaking loudly beneath him. He glanced around the room. Despite the flickering shadows, he could see other initiates fidgeting in their seats, wringing their hands and shifting uncomfortably.

At least I'm not the only one.

"Can't focus?" Sage whispered beside him.

Dane turned to face her. Her blonde ponytail glinted in the dim green light, and her eyes shone beneath her furrowed brow. Again came that tug of sadness, an empty longing that had plagued him more than ever in the days leading up to the Trials. Sage's hair sparkled as white as the sun's reflection—his more closely resembled that of dried autumn leaves—but they shared the same sea-blue eyes, the same as their mother's. Or so they'd been told.

Dane shook his head.

"Me neither," Sage said. "It's only the most defining moment of our lives. Nothing to worry about, right?" She let out a small laugh, then her lips curved into a frown. She gazed longingly at her hands clasped in her lap. "I wish mom and dad were here." Her voice cracked with emotion. "They would've been proud."

Dane squeezed her hand. Their parents had died nearly sixteen years ago, before either he or Sage had formed lasting memories of them. They had lived with their grandfather ever since in a small village immersed among the forest treetops outside the Vitalor city limits. They'd asked Grandfather Horas about their parents on countless occasions, but the old man would only press a hand to his temples, unable to remember anything about them—his own daughter, not even her name.

Dane wondered how long it would be until his grandfather forgot everything all together. Aside from Sage, he was the only family Dane had left. The thought of losing him too . . .

Dane pushed the thought aside. *Focus on the Trials.*

"I wish they were here too," he said. He offered a small smile. "But they're still watching over us . . . they always will be."

A sound like rolling thunder boomed overhead. The entire room shook. Dane inhaled sharply. He released Sage's hand and stared beyond Elder Chrysanthe, eyes fixed on the giant wooden door behind her. The arena was awake.

Just then an initiate from the crowd blurted, "Question!"

Dane searched the sea of faces and found a thin young man, one hand raised high above his wiry, disheveled black hair. His face was contorted with skepticism.

"Yes?" Elder Chrysanthe asked, clearly peeved by the interruption.

"Well, a scholarly pondering, rather," the initiate said. "Let's say I find out I'm a Chemocyte. Will I be—how do I put this— *put out of my misery* on sight, or will I be punished for my exogenous behavior and banished immediately to the Shrouded Isle?"

An eerie hush fell over the room. Shortly after the Council of the Founders, Founder Lussiek, the first Chemocyte, had betrayed the others. He'd attempted to steal their powers for himself. War had broken out, but Lussiek's threat had been quickly extinguished at the hands of the other seven founders. As punishment, he had been banished to the Shrouded Isle with his Chemocyte devotees—along with any other Chemocytes since—fearing they might pursue their Founder's nefarious wishes.

Rumors had it that Lussiek had been killed centuries ago by his own followers after a deadly infection mutated them into ravenous creatures. Some said those creatures still dwelled beneath the island's black cliffs, preying on unsuspecting travelers, sucking the power from their bodies before devouring them whole.

Dane shuddered at the thought. With the mystery of his parents' deaths, his mind often strayed to the Shrouded Isle. He hoped his parents would have known better than to venture near the island's treacherous shores.

Elder Chrysanthe's eyes were slits, her mouth a hard line. "Young man, the Trials haven't produced a Chemocyte in well over a century. The mere *idea* that such an event might disgrace *my Trials* is an insult to myself and the entire city of Vitalor. Not only have you tainted the thoughts of everyone in this room, but you have also rudely interrupted the most sacred ceremony in all of Physos. You would do well to mind your manners and respect that which the Mother has given us. Do I make myself clear?"

The young man said nothing as he shrank into himself, disappearing into the crowd.

"Now," the Elder continued, "you should know that there are three different trials you will face: The Trial of the Observer, the Trial of the Adventurer, and the Trial of the Warrior. For each trial you complete, you will receive one energy stone." She produced a translucent, gem-like stone from her pocket. "Upon completion of your Trials, you will present your stones to the energy well of your power. You will then receive your mark and have full use of your power."

She rolled up her right sleeve, exposing a series of twisting, dark green vines that ran up the length of her forearm.

"This is the mark of a Biophage. Each energy well provides you with a unique mark indicative of your power. Obtaining all three energy stones shows a masterful control over all aspects of your power. Most years will not produce any initiates who complete all three trials, so it is a . . . *remarkable* occurrence indeed to collect all three."

Dane noticed the hint of bitterness in the Elder's tone as she pulled her sleeve back down. Her mark was similar to others Dane had seen around the Biophage capital of Vitalor. *Even she hadn't collected all three stones . . .*

"However, the Mother does not discriminate on the energy stones you collect. Her blessing may fall on anyone who is willing to perform Her biddings and make this world better for all."

The tension in her face eased as she donned her usual comforting smile. She gestured to the door behind her. "In a moment, Boran will begin calling names. You will accompany him through this door and commence your first trial. You are granted one attempt per trial before proceeding to the next." She held her arms wide, as if enclosing the entire room in her warm embrace. "I wish you all the best of luck. May the Mother bless you and your journey as you discover your power." Then she turned and disappeared behind the giant door.

Silence settled over the room. Dane could already feel his hands trembling again. It was no wonder the initiates he'd watched in years prior had seemed so rigid and disoriented. The anticipation was maddening.

Desperately seeking to keep his mind occupied, Dane turned to Vilik seated beside him. Vilik was still, staring at the door, hands clasped to his knees. His dark skin gleamed in the torchlight, beads of sweat matting his brow.

Dane relaxed a little. The Trials had been on his mind for so long. It was all he ever thought about. But at least his entire family dynamic wasn't in the balance. He and Vilik had grown up in the same village, daydreaming about the founders as they went about their daily tasks. Once old enough, they'd become apprentices at a craftsmithing shop, spending their days learning to craft the intricate weapons and armor of the Vitalor guard, often discussing the powers they hoped to have.

Dane could never decide, but Vilik had always wanted to be a Geomancer. He had family in Stonehelm, the Geomancer capital. They were all Geomancers, but his Biophage parents claimed they were a poor influence on Vilik. His parents thought Geomancer ways were undisciplined, chaotic, a poor influence on their growing son. Vilik felt the opposite. He wanted to be like the rest of his family, to live with them in Stonehelm. And his parents resented him for it.

"Can you believe we're finally here?" Dane said to him. He looked around the dim anteroom and wrinkled his nose. "Though I did expect something a bit less . . . dismal."

Vilik said nothing, only nodded briefly.

Dane put a hand on his best friend's shoulder. "Look, whatever happens in there, you don't have to go back to your parents. Even if you're not a Geomancer, you can still go to Stonehelm. You can see your family."

Vilik let out a heavy sigh. "I know. I just . . . I wish things were different. I don't want to hate them. I wish they could accept the person I want to be. If only I could prove to them—"

"You don't owe your parents anything," Sage said, leaning over. "Vilik, they've treated you horribly. So what if you don't become a Biophage like they want? These are *your* Trials. You're not becoming who they want you to be. You'll become who *you* want you to be. Besides, you're our family too. You always will be."

Dane nodded his agreement. Though he was older than Sage—by a small margin, but older nonetheless—and tried to consider himself the wiser of the two, she never failed to surprise him with her maturity.

"I know you'll be great," Dane said. "We all will."

"You're right," Vilik decided. He loosened his grip on his knees. "Thank you. I don't know how I would've made it through any of this without you both."

"Well, we're not through it yet." Sage drummed her fingers across her thigh. She shifted in her seat, trying for a look at the door. It remained closed. She clenched her fists. "If that damned door doesn't open soon, I'm going over there to open it my—"

She stopped abruptly as Elder Chrysanthe's shadow fell over the three of them. Sage stared up, wide eyed.

"You heard that?" Sage asked, wincing. Even in the dim lighting, her face was bright red.

Elder Chrysanthe chuckled to herself. "I was the same way at your age, so eager to complete my Trials and serve the Mother's wishes." She knelt down, placing a hand on Sage's cheek. "Patience. I have nothing but confidence in you, my dear. You will be magnificent."

Sage managed a lopsided smile.

While Dane and Vilik had been craftsmith apprentices in the Vitalor market, Sage had been taken in as Elder Chrysanthe's personal apprentice, one of the highest honors in the entire city. Sage would shadow the Elder during meetings, inspect market trading and supplies, and care for the less fortunate. In recent years, Dane had even heard rumors that the Elder might one day choose Sage to be her successor.

But Dane couldn't wrap his head around why Elder Chrysanthe had chosen Sage as her apprentice in the first place. Despite his sister's undisputed accolades, she had no connection to the Elder. She didn't even have her power yet. But Elder Chrysanthe, the most powerful Biophage in Vitalor, had chosen Sage over dozens of other more qualified Biophages. He was happy for his sister nonetheless, but still . . . something about it had always left him uneasy.

Elder Chrysanthe broke her gaze from Sage, turning to Dane and Vilik. "And I have the highest of faith in the both of you as well. Nervous?"

"A bit," Dane managed. The understatement of his life.

Vilik merely bobbed his head.

"I'm sure you are. The Trials will be the hardest task you'll ever face. But it's all worth it. That's the greatest feeling in the world, discovering your power and finding your place." She smiled at the three of them. "It won't be long now. It's imperative you stay focused, but don't force anything in the arena. Your power will come naturally, when you least expect it. Have faith in the Mother's design."

With that she turned and disappeared once more behind the giant door.

"What do you think it'll be this year?" Dane asked, anything to break the silence.

"I like the ones where they fight elemental warriors," Vilik said, "but I'm not so sure about fighting one myself."

"I hope the Aquadorians designed the Trial of the Adventurer again," Sage said. "Those are always my favorite. Something like we saw in—"

She stopped abruptly and straightened, muscles tensing.

"Like we saw in . . ." Dane prompted.

"Oh—nothing. Forget I said anything." Her eyes darted around the room, as if purposefully avoiding his gaze. "Vilik, what were you saying?"

Vilik opened his mouth, but Dane cut him off. "Hold on. Sage, forget what?"

"I said it was nothing. It'd be better if you didn't hear it anyways." She winced again, as if she'd said something wrong.

Dane's expression hardened. "What don't I want to hear?"

Sage waved a dismissive hand. "It's *nothing*," she insisted. "Really—the Trials are more important."

Vilik pushed Dane's hand aside. "Come to think of it . . ." Sage shot him a withering look, like they'd both agreed to keep something secret, but Vilik didn't notice. "I did enjoy that Trial of the Adventurer a couple years ago, the one where Quinn—"

Sage leapt from her seat and clapped a hand to Vilik's mouth, stopping any more words from spewing forth. But it was too late. Dane had already heard.

Thoughts of Quinn had plagued Dane's mind over the past year. Every night he tried to convince himself that he hadn't done anything wrong, that it wasn't his fault. He couldn't remember the last time he'd had a good night's sleep.

The anticipation of the Trials had provided a welcome distraction. Somehow, he'd managed to bury the moments he and Quinn had shared: watching the Trials together every year, her visiting Vitalor more frequently to see him, them laying in the fields outside the city walls and gazing up at the mountainous Elderwood tree. Even now he felt the soft touch of her lips on his cheek, where she'd kissed him after her Trials two years ago.

That was before she'd disappeared.

He tried to quell the thoughts, but the efforts only made it worse. The last memory he had of her came to full focus; her dark, chestnut hair licking at her shoulders, gleaming in the late afternoon sun; her luminous, forest green eyes, filled with such hope and promise. His heart ached with renewed pain, worse than anything he'd felt before. It had been bad enough the year before, attending a Trials Festival without her. But now it was his turn in the arena. And she wouldn't be there for him.

Sage slapped Vilik on the arm. "I *told* you not to mention her!" she hissed.

Vilik winced apologetically.

Sage turned to Dane. "Please, you have to focus on the Trials. I'm worried about Quinn too. We all are. But it wasn't your fault. You know that, right?"

Dane stared vacantly at his clenched fists. "Sure."

"Good." She paused, looking at him with that all-too-familiar sympathetic frown.

The giant door finally creaked open, the sound of groaning wood reverberating off the walls. A tall, portly man with white and green robes emerged holding a scroll.

The tension in the room heightened instantly. Dane pressed his clenched fists to his stomach. *Focus,* he told himself. *You've waited ten years for this moment. Finally you'll discover your power.*

And Quinn won't be here to see it . . .

The man, whom Elder Chrysanthe had introduced as Boran, unfurled the scroll and cleared his throat. His gruff voice shattered the silence. "Hollis Hazelden."

A few seats over, a girl rose to her feet. She shuffled over to the door and followed Boran inside. The room was quiet for a long while before the ceiling shook to another wave of thunderous applause.

A moment later, Boran called "Tobias Thorn", then escorted a tall, muscled boy through the door.

Time progressed like dripping sap as the room of initiates slowly dwindled until only Dane, Vilik, Sage, and a handful of others remained.

Boran returned, glanced at his scroll, and called out: "Sage Willows."

Sage inhaled sharply and sprang to her feet. She whispered, "Wish me luck," then she, too, was gone.

A few more names were called, then Dane and Vilik were all that remained.

Boran made his penultimate return. "Vilik Amaranth."

Vilik exhaled a long, steady breath. He rose steadily, muscles tense, and accompanied Boran through the door.

Dane glanced at the empty room. He tried to take a calming breath, but the air around him suddenly seemed thick and heavy. His heart thudded relentlessly in his chest. His head throbbed. Thoughts of Quinn threatened to wedge through his withering mental blockade. He squeezed his eyes shut, forcing the thoughts away.

"Focus on the Trials," he repeated aloud. "Only the Trials."

He recalled the first time he'd ever seen the Trials. It seemed so much different then. The mere idea of having his chance in the arena, of finding his power—it had felt like a distant dream, a faraway place sitting on the perpetual horizon. Part of him wanted to believe he was still living that dream. At any moment, he would wake as a young boy, watching the Trials for his first time, with Quinn by his side.

The ceiling rumbled again. Dane could vaguely hear the muffled boom of the announcer's voice. Soon it would be him up there, fighting his way through the Trials to find his power.

His thoughts strayed to his parents as he stared up at the ceiling. A lump stuck in his throat. *I wish you were here,* he thought. *I wish we didn't have to do this without you.* Tears stung at his eyes, but he blinked them away. *I'll make you proud.*

The door creaked open for the final time, the low, groaning sound echoing like thunder.

Dane clenched his fists. *Ten years of waiting,* he thought, a surge of determination flooding through him. *It's time to discover your power.*

Boran called the final name.

"Dane Willows."

CHAPTER 2

THE RIDDLE OF THE OBSERVER

Dane followed Boran through the door and into a small room. The man extended a hand, holding a type of bracelet.

"Wear this," he said.

"What is it?"

"It's an energy band. Wear it on your wrist." When Dane continued to stare at the band, Boran added, "Initiates can't use their powers without first presenting their energy stones to their energy well. In the arena, this band acts as your energy well. It contains enough energy for you to pull from once you discover your power."

Dane tightened the band around his wrist, fighting against his trembling hands.

Boran stepped aside, revealing a smaller door engraved with eight figures all kneeling before a heavenly figure.

"Your Trials will begin once you pass through that door," he said, voice scripted and monotone. "May the Mother bless your Trials."

Dane drew in a deep breath, pushed the ornate door open, and stepped into another room.

At once he was hit with a waft of fresh air that smelled of sap and pine needles. The walls were covered in creeping vines. The ground resembled a forest floor, covered in a smattering of earth and grasses. Eight small, green orbs hung in a circle above a stone table at the center of the room, several small lumps set on its earthen surface.

For a moment Dane stood there, waiting for something to happen, a signal that his trial had begun. He could see no one else—the curved walls created a sort of corralled enclosure that offered no blanket of concealing shadow. His pulse quickened.

Is this the trial? He thought, almost voicing the words aloud. He glanced at the closed door behind him. *What am I supposed to do?*

He looked once more at the stone table and, bereft of better options, approached it with caution. The dirt floor crunched beneath his feet as he crept forward and stopped beside the table.

A thick layer of dirt and grass caked the table's surface. In its center rested six identical clay bowls, all circling a small pool of water. The bowls were each flipped over, as if protecting an object underneath.

That's when he noticed a small stone tablet engraved with writing. It was a riddle.

UPON THE TABLE RESTS THE FIRST TRIAL,
AN OBSERVATION OF SKILL, WIT, AND DENIAL.
TO FIND THE POWER YOU SO DESIRE,
THE BOWLS MUST LIFT HIGHER AND HIGHER.
ALAS, IT IS NO TEST TO CHOOSE FROM MANY,
ONLY ONE MAY FEEL THE WARMTH OF ANY.
BUT BEWARE, FOR EVEN IF YOUR CHOICE IS SOUND,
THE DARKNESS HIDES WHAT MUST BE FOUND.

Dane stared at the tablet, reread it. He looked at the bowls, trying to make sense of it.

Initiates of years past were forbidden from revealing the nature of the Trial of the Observer, but that hadn't stopped rumors from spreading. From the whisperings he'd heard at the Trials Festivals, Dane had grasped that the trial was taken in solitude, possibly in near darkness. But he'd been expecting a room packed with spare supplies, where he'd have to sift through detritus to find the energy stone. A hunt of sorts. He hadn't expected a riddle.

He drummed his fingers on the stone table. *How hard could it be?* He thought to himself. *Just lift each bowl until you find the energy stone.*

He reached for the nearest bowl, fingers outstretched, ready to peer underneath. Within a hair of touching the bowl, he jerked his hand back. Something was off. It couldn't be that simple.

He read the riddle again, hoping for further clarity, but he only became more agitated. Nothing was clear. The riddle was both astoundingly simple yet impossibly complex. The energy stone had to be under one of the bowls. *But which?*

Dane blew out a controlled breath and focused on each line of the riddle.

The first four lines were obvious. In this trial he must lift the bowls to find the energy stone. He moved to the next line.

Alas, it is no test to choose from many . . .

He chided himself at that line. The trial would be easy if he could simply lift every bowl and reveal the energy stone. There had to be more to it.

Only one may feel the warmth of any . . .

A sudden chill ran up Dane's arms. He glanced around, squinting at the walls. Nothing had changed about the room, but the air was now cold, much colder than it had been when he'd begun. Reflexively, Dane rubbed his hands together for warmth. Then it came to him.

Only one may feel the warmth of any . . .

He could only touch one bowl. *Or what? The trial would end if he touched more than one?* He wanted to believe that the thought was too drastic a conclusion, but he had a sneaking suspicion he was exactly right. So he'd only touch one bowl. *But which one?*

Dane inspected the table more closely. Aside from the six bowls surrounding the pool of water, the table only consisted of miniature plants and piles of dirt; nothing at first glance that was of any significance.

There has to be a way.

Then he saw something in the pool of water, nearly indiscernible to his eye—but it was definitely there. The water next to the middle left bowl was slightly receded, as if retreating from the bowl. *Maybe it's a sign,* he thought. *Don't choose that bowl.* The detail seemed too minute to pose any significance, but this trial had been designed to test initiates' skills in observation. Maybe this was what he was supposed to look for.

The agitation he'd felt a moment earlier waned, replaced with momentous excitement as he continued observing. Now he understood. *This* was the trial, focusing on the smallest, most seemingly insignificant of details. He found another. A small yellow flower grew next to every bowl except for the bowl in the bottom right.

That's it! It must be another one I can eliminate. Only four bowls left.

Dane squinted at the table, darkness narrowing in. He looked around. The lights in the room were dimming, almost as if—

He read the last two lines of the riddle. *Even if your choice is sound, the darkness hides what must be found . . .*

Then he understood. The longer he took, the darker the room would become. He wouldn't be able to see, wouldn't be able to choose correctly. He broke into a cold sweat as the full realization took hold. *The lights—I'm running out of time.*

Urgency flashed through him. Dane scoured the table for more clues, eyes scanning wildly. Each bowl had a small mound of dirt piled up around the edges except for the top left bowl.

Three to go . . .

The room was growing darker. Dane's eyes weren't adjusting fast enough—he could barely see the shapes of the bowls in front of him. He bent closer to the table.

Another thorough scan revealed a small cross carved only into the surface of the bottom right bowl. Surely that had to be another clue.

Two . . .

Dane could barely see his hands. Only two bowls remained—the middle and upper bowls to his right—but there were no differences between them. Dane leaned over as far as he could, stretching his neck over the table. His feet slid from under him and he had to arch his back to avoid smacking his head on the bowls. He started to panic. He would have to choose a bowl at random.

His mind went into a frenzy, thoughts churning faster than ever. Either bowl could contain the energy stone, but there was no telling which. All the practice, all the training he'd done, and it was all down to fate, to pure luck. Dane inhaled sharply and reached his hand into the darkness toward the middle bowl.

Then something caught his eye. A very faint glow was reflecting off the top bowl, but there was nothing of the sort on any of the other bowls. Maybe—just maybe—it was the final clue he needed; one that could only be seen at the last moment, when the room was at its darkest.

He froze with indecision. Bu what if he'd made it up? What if his eyes had simply played a trick on him? He shook his head. There was no better option. He had to choose.

He shifted his hand to the top right bowl and grasped its surface just as total darkness consumed his vision. When nothing happened, he tossed the bowl aside, fondled for what lay underneath, and squeezed his hand tight.

I've done it! He nearly exclaimed. He could feel it in his hand.

Then a cold liquid oozed across his palm. He lifted his hand to his face and inhaled a pungent, fruit-like smell.

The lights in the room suddenly sprang back to life, illuminating the bowls and the table. Crushed in the palm of his hand were the sticky remains of a prune.

No energy stone? Dane could hardly wrap his head around it as he stared at his prune-stained palm. *What did I do wrong?*

The table shook. Dane stumbled back as dozens of thick vines sprouted from the ground. The vines slithered up the table and over its surface until there was no trace of the table beneath.

"That's it?" Dane blurted aloud. He tugged at the vines, but they didn't budge. He stepped back and looked around the room. *There has to be more.*

A door opened on the other side of the circular room, all but confirming the trial's end.

Dane could only stare in disbelief. All his preparation—years of hope and longing for this opportunity—and the first trial was over in the blink of an eye.

It's fine, he told himself, trying to accept the realization. Each year there were hundreds of initiates who didn't complete the Trial of the Observer either. And he still had two trials ahead.

Taking a deep breath, Dane walked across the circular room and through the open door. He entered into another small, cramped room. No one awaited him, but the doors opposite him towered overhead. A stone plaque on the door read:

> ALL EMBRACE THE ADVENTURER,
> THE HARBINGER OF NATURE'S CALL,
> BUT WHEN ALL ARE SUMMONED,
> EVEN THE MIGHTY MAY FALL.
> THROUGH RIGOR AND PERIL,
> FEAR CLOUDS THE SECOND TRIAL,
> BUT WHEN CHALLENGE AWAITS,
> THE ADVENTURER WEARS ONLY A SMILE.

Dane stared at the doors, the muffled roar of the crowd erupting on the other side. A knot settled in his stomach as reality set in. He knew these doors. He'd seen them before—the doors to the arena pit itself.

Dane placed both hands on the smooth, oaken surface and thrust the doors open.

CHAPTER 3

THE CLIMB OF THE ADVENTURER

Dane shielded his eyes as harsh sunlight streamed through the open doors. He took a step forward and was immediately bombarded by a roar of applause.

He was in the arena, but no longer a spectator.

The announcer's voice bellowed across the arena, "And now, our final participant of this year's Trials Festival! Attempting his Trial of the Adventurer, Dane Willows!"

A cacophony of cheers erupted from the stands. All Dane could hear was a solitary barrage of noise. The wall surrounding the arena pit was nearly twice his height. Spectators were on their feet, whooping and chanting. High above the arena's open-air ceiling were the ever-present branches of the Elderwood tree, seeming to scrape the sky itself. Dane felt some of the tension in his body lift. The Elderwood never failed to calm his nerves, even now when he needed it most.

He allowed himself a brief respite as the cool breeze washed across his sweat-mottled brow, but his breath caught as he looked to the center of the arena. Suspended in the air were at least a dozen floating rocks and flat-topped boulders; some covered with small trees and hanging vines, others spilling water over their edges. They orbited a towering floating spire of slick, hardened rock. At the spire's peak was a small pedestal supporting a tiny object that glinted in the sunlight.

The energy stone. All I have to do is summit that spire.

He pushed the sounds of the crowd to the back of his mind, focusing on the floating rocks, plotting a path.

One by one, he told himself. *I can do this.*

Suddenly Dane's foot plunged into a thick substance. He tried to right himself, but lost balance as his other foot sank in beside the first. It felt as though the ground itself was gripping at his feet, pulling him down.

The announcer's voice blared overhead. "Watch out for that quicksand, Initiate. Don't want to find yourself stuck in there."

Quicksand?

Dane's gaze snapped downward. The ground beneath the floating rocks rippled, a slight shimmer in its surface.

Dane lurched back. His feet sprang free and he stumbled backward onto solid ground. He'd almost been swallowed by quicksand. Just like that, his second trial would have been over. Panic clouded his mind.

How do I get to the rocks without—

Something in the corner of his eye caught his attention. A narrow boulder was orbiting toward him, overflowing with ferns and plants. A thick vine trailed behind, its tip slithering across the quicksand surface.

Dane planted his feet, the tips of his boots barely distanced from the quicksand. When the boulder was directly ahead, he leapt.

For a moment he hung suspended in the air, his entire body outstretched, reaching desperately for the thick vine.

Then he felt it in his grasp and his fingers closed around it. The rest of his body whiplashed behind, nearly ripping his hands from the vine as his legs began to sink. His fingers burned, his palms turning slick. He could feel the vine sliding from his grasp.

Not like this!

With what strength he could muster, Dane climbed hand over hand up the vine until his legs pulled free from the quicksand's clutches. He gripped the top of the boulder and thrust his body onto the rock surface, rolling safely onto his back. Triumph resonated inside him as the crowd erupted with cheers.

"One . . . down . . ." Dane breathed aloud. He heaved several gulps of air, shook his burning hands, then glanced up to the central spire and the orbiting boulders above him. The brief pulse of triumph withered away. "And many more to go . . ."

Dane braced himself for the next leap, but the central spire was rising higher. He spun frantically, preparing to leap to any boulder within reach, but they were also rising away from him. He looked down in horror at the quicksand. It was rising toward him. He turned to look at the crowd, eyes wide with fear, hoping for an answer to what was happening. They, too, were rising.

No, they're not rising, Dane thought with sickening clarity. He was falling. The boulder he was on was slowly sinking into the quicksand.

A burst of adrenaline surged through him. He looked up just as another boulder passed overhead and he leapt without hesitation, hands outstretched.

Though void of assistive vines, Dane's fingers sought the jagged rock beneath. He cried out in a mixture of anger and torment as the rock dug into his fingertips, but he refused to let the pain triumph. He clawed up the jagged rock surface and heaved his body over the top, inducing another wave of cheers.

Dane sat on his heels and stared at his hands, wincing at the small cuts and bruises scattered across his palms and fingertips. He wasn't sure how much more his hands could take, but he had no choice. He had to reach the energy stone and find his power.

Clenching his fists to suppress the pain, Dane scrambled to his feet and spotted the next boulder. The nearest was orbiting overhead well out of his reach, but a trail of smaller rocks curved from its base, stretching outward like stepping-stones.

With a deft leap, Dane landed onto the first small rock. He could feel the rock sinking the instant his foot contacted, and he leapt again, then again. Before he knew it, the large boulder was within reach, and he thrust off the final rock toward it. He crashed on its surface, landing squarely on his chest. He gasped for air, black spots blooming before his eyes.

He desperately wanted to rest, if only to catch his breath and think clearly for a moment. But there was no time. He had to keep moving. The small rocks behind him had disappeared. Only the spire remained.

Dane staggered to his feet, nearly stumbling over the edge of the boulder as he fought for balance.

I'm close, he thought, his breaths coming in stunted, wheezing rasps. *Any moment now . . . I'll discover my power . . . I'm so close.*

He glanced up. The top of the spire was close, only a short climb away. But his hands ached. His legs burned with fatigue. Time wouldn't be on his side.

He peered over the edge of the boulder, then down at the rows of cheering crowds.

"You won't fall," he muttered to himself. "You *won't* fall. You have to do this."

He summoned a controlled breath and backed to the far edge of the boulder. Nothing short of a tremendous leap would position him close enough to the spire to secure his feet and hands. He had no choice. He *had* to make it.

Mother, Father . . . this is for you.

In two giant steps, Dane surged across the top of the boulder and catapulted himself at the central spire. He crashed into the rock face, his arms and legs flailing outward, seeking for anything to grasp. Just as he felt his body begin to slip downward, his foot pressed on a jutting rock, securing his fragile balance.

Rejuvenated by his good fortune, Dane pressed his body against the spire and craned his head upward. The top was within reach; soon he would have his first energy stone.

The rock supporting his foot crumbled. His fingers slipped from the jagged surface and he fell backward, plummeting toward the quicksand.

NO! Dane screamed in his mind. *Not again! I won't fail again!*

With a howl of rage, Dane thrust his legs outward. His feet hit the spire, catapulting him away.

For a moment, he was falling again, falling toward the ground to his imminent demise, falling away from the energy stone.

Then his body crashed into something hard. Excruciating pain lanced through his back as he splashed into a shallow pool of water. With a cry of agony, he rolled onto his stomach. He'd landed on another boulder. Everything hurt. His head spun. But there was still a chance. He pressed his hands into the water and thrust his body upwards, reveling in the cool liquid that soaked his clothes and soothed his aching limbs.

His hands were bleeding, his clothes were sopping wet, his back hurt, his legs wobbled uncontrollably under his own weight, and his lungs ached for air. But he had to make another jump—the energy stone was right there. He could still make it.

He charged forward with a primal yell of raw emotion. He took one step, his foot bracing against the boulder's edge.

Then his foot slipped.

The world became a blur as Dane spiraled downward and plunged into the quicksand. His legs sank so deep into the muck that only his head and arms remained above the surface. He thrashed wildly, scrambling and scraping for something—any-thing—in his reach. But his hands only met air.

It was too late.

Dane watched in horror, helpless, as the last of the boulders, the spire, and the energy stone sunk into the quicksand.

His hand closed around a thick vine—one of many spaced around the edge of the quicksand, tethered to a rock near the arena wall. Bewilderment and frustration filled his mind as Dane pulled himself to solid ground. His limbs screamed in protest as he struggled to his feet, but it was nothing compared to the fire that had suddenly lit inside him.

There was still one trial left.

"What a performance that was," the announcer boomed as a resounding groan of sympathy echoed through the crowd. "A true display of will and determination. A shame he was not rewarded with his power or the energy stone. But fret not! In just a moment's time, it's on to the finale, the Trial of the Warrior!"

The arena burst into its usual jubilant cheers as Dane hobbled toward the open door at the opposite end of the arena pit. An elderly woman wearing drab green robes stood beside the door, wet cloths and wraps in hand.

"That was quite a nasty fall, young man. Are you all right?" she asked, her voice laced with endearment.

Dane took one of the cloths, wincing as he dabbed at his hands and face. The water was invigorating, subsiding the stinging pain.

"I'm fine," he muttered, handing the cloth back. "Thank you."

The Elderly woman wrapped his palms in cloth anyways, her Biophage powers seeping through the fabric. The burning subsided greatly, and when she removed the cloth, the swelling and bruising had partially receded. "You're all set, my dear. Your power awaits you."

Dane entered the final anteroom, identical to its predecessor. The door closed behind him, muffling the noise from the arena, finally allowing him a coherent thought. He shook the excess muck from his boots, wiped his damp hands on his trousers, then looked to the massive doors ahead and read the third engraved tablet.

ONE TRIAL REMAINS,
IN TRADITION MOST SACRED,
DEFEAT THE FINAL FOE,
WITH HUNGER NEVER SATED.
SHOULD THE WARRIOR FALL,
THE VILLAIN OF THIS STORY,
LET THE TRUE WARRIOR EMERGE,
TO REVEL IN GLORY.

Dane closed his eyes and drew a deep breath. The fire inside him kindled, spreading through his tired limbs. This was the final trial. This was the moment he'd been dreaming of his entire childhood. The Trial of the Warrior had always been his favorite, the trial he felt most prepared for. It only made sense this was the trial in which he'd discover his power. Giddy, childish excitement ran through him, just like he'd felt watching his first Trials, and every year thereafter. But now it was his turn.

Dane flung the doors open. He was once again greeted by the thunderous applause of the crowd, this time chanting his name.

He shielded his gaze from the beating sun, squinting at the stands. Every seat was filled, overflowing back through the columned archways surrounding the giant arena. Everyone had come to watch the last initiate perform, the final act in this year's Trials.

At the far end, Elder Chrysanthe and a few others Dane didn't recognize sat beneath a shaded awning. Elder Chrysanthe wore a pleased smile and gave a prompting nod as Dane's eyes met hers.

He dropped his gaze to the arena pit, eager to analyze his surroundings. Based on his past knowledge of trials, Vilik's assumption of an elemental warrior seemed—

Then something in the crowd caught his eye. No, some*one*.

At once the dark, vacant emptiness inside him began to wane. His heart skipped a beat. He tried to focus once more on the arena, on his final trial, but his eyes were pulled back to the crowd, pulled back to her.

It—it can't be . . .

Standing beneath the Elders' booth, hands tightly clutching the front railing, was Quinn. Her beautiful chestnut hair swayed with the gentle breeze as it brushed her bare shoulders. Her brilliant eyes sparkled just as he remembered, gleaming as green as the leaves that reminded him so much of home. Her elegant, dark blue robes hugged her form and shimmered with colorful auroras that sparkled in the sunlight. She was more radiant than ever.

It was all he could do to keep from bursting into tears. All the worries and fears he'd had about her vanished instantly. She had come to his Trials. She hadn't forgotten. She was here, just like she'd promised. She still cared about him.

Then his heart plummeted into the pit of his stomach like he was falling from the top of the Elderwood tree. An uncontrollable wave of nausea boiled up from deep inside, consuming that determined fire.

Quinn wasn't alone. Someone was standing beside her, arm around her shoulder, looking at her in a way only Dane thought possible.

She was standing with another man.

CHAPTER 4

THE BLADE OF THE WARRIOR

While waiting to watch Quinn on the day of her Trials two years ago, Dane, Vilik, and Sage had entered the Trials Arena to the sound of raucous applause, funneling their attention to the arena pit. The initiate, a tall young man with broad shoulders, was striding purposefully toward a small grove of stout trees, hands balled in tight fists at his side. His composure was calm, determined, unlike that of any initiate Dane had seen. He even resisted the formulaic urge to wave clumsily at the sea of howling onlookers.

The initiate stopped at the edge of the grove and readied himself. The announcer formally welcomed the initiate, inducing a thunderous wave of cheers even louder than before.

"What's going on?" Sage had asked a nearby woman after they had found their seats in the stands.

The woman's eyes were wild with excitement. "He's already completed his first two trials! If he completes his Trial of the Warrior, he'll be the first initiate in decades to collect all three energy stones! Isn't that exciting?"

Dane had turned his attention to the arena, excitement matching the buzz around him. He'd watched as initiates in past years entered their final trial with the same prospects, only to fall short of completing the final trial. But something about this initiate was different, and the crowd sensed it too.

Dane analyzed the grove in the arena pit. There didn't seem to be anything special about the trees. Their leafless branches merely swayed in the wind—their stiff, thick branches . . .

Then Dane realized. There was no breeze in the arena; the trees were moving themselves.

The branches suddenly sprang to life, as if matching the crowds' energy, whipping through the air and colliding into adjacent aged, demented trunks with resonating cracks that echoed throughout the arena. A small pedestal rose on the other side of the grove, the final energy stone for this initiate to claim.

The announcer's booming voice commenced the trial. The young man surged forward immediately, skidding to a halt beside one of the trunks as a branch sailed past his neck. The man attempted to dart through once more but was forced to retreat to avoid the branches.

A wave of commotion spread through the crowd. The initiate tried again, but was once more buffeted by the flailing branches. Everyone was on their feet, yelling and hollering louder than ever before.

Then, all at once, the branches had stopped, pointing toward the grove's center. The crowd fell silent, suspense thick in the air. The young man held one hand out, his fingers curled as if gripping a large invisible fruit, aiming at the same spot where the branches were pointing. The young man was a Gravitus, Dane had realized, using his power to pull the branches in, effectively immobilizing them. One by one, the initiate snapped the branches from their stumps with his free hand, littering the ground with their dried, cracked remains until a clear path had been carved through the grove.

The crowd reacted immediately, erupting with a deafening roar as the young man gently bowed, walked to the pedestal to secure his third and final energy stone, and strode out of the arena.

At the time, Dane had wanted nothing more than to be just like him. But now that same man was standing beside Quinn, leaning close to her, whispering in her ear.

A barrage of clashing emotions hit Dane at once. Relief came first. Quinn was alive. Despite the fears he'd had of her falling victim to the creatures of the Shrouded Isle, she was alive and more beautiful than he remembered.

Then came the anger, complete, consuming, boiling and frothing in the pit of his stomach. Why hadn't she returned earlier like she'd promised? Where had she been for the past two years?

Dane glared at the man beside her. Without realizing it, his mind fetched the man's name from the deep recesses of his memory: Cayde Jerwood. The crowd had chanted the name after Cayde had collected all three energy stones. Dane's jaw tightened, his teeth grinding.

Where had she been . . .

A sharp pain radiated in his hands. He glanced down to see red stains pooling beneath the cloth on his wrapped palms. He unfurled his fingers

Focus on the Trials, Sage had told him. *The Trials . . .*

He tore his attention away from the stands and back to the arena pit. The walls surrounding the pit were made of rugged stone that jutted out in all directions. The ground was a mixture of dirt and stone. Tall ferns sprouted from the ground in sporadic patches. A shallow pond spanned the right side of the pit, and a large pile of stones sat in the arena's center.

He moved toward the rocks. They began to shift and crumble as he watched, only they didn't tumble down. The rocks rolled up the pile, sprouting upward like a tree trunk, piling on top of one another until Dane was eclipsed in their shadow. The rocks rolled outward, extending like branches. One final, large rock rolled up and perched atop the sculpture of stone.

Dane felt the blood drain from his face as the rocks solidified into hulking creature made entirely of stone. In one hand it held a blunt stone sword, in the other a flat earthen shield. Large stone plates layered its body like armor. Its head was covered in a smooth, faceless stone helmet with dark, narrow slits where its eyes would have been.

The chants changed to cheers, and echoing howls filled the arena.

The stone warrior finally seemed to notice Dane beneath it and swung. Dane dove, narrowly evading the warrior's cascading blow as the sword sliced through the vacant air where he had just been.

A small movement in the corner of his eye pulled Dane's attention away from the warrior once more. Beneath where Quinn was standing, the energy stone and its pedestal had slowly started sinking into the ground.

I have to defeat the warrior before the pedestal disappears, he realized. *I need to discover my power . . .*

Dane scoured the area around him. Everything in the arena was at his disposal, his power waiting to come out. His eyes landed on the pond.

Dane skirted the edge of the pond, skimmed a hand along the water's surface, keeping one eye on the warrior as it shuffled after him, its body hunched and prepared to charge. Dane's legs tensed beneath him, coiled like a serpent about to strike.

Once the warrior touches the water, he thought, *I'll grab its legs and drag it under, just like an Aquadorian would.*

The warrior charged, stampeding into the pond. Dane sprung from its path. The warrior twisted, groping in Dane's direction, but swiped uselessly at the air as its massive weight carried it headfirst into the water.

Dane spun in place and focused his mind, his hands submerged, reaching out to the water to hold the warrior down. The warrior lay motionless for several moments as the small lapping tides soaked its stone armor.

I've done it! Dane nearly shouted aloud. *I—*

The warrior burst upward with a gravelly, sputtering roar. Dane stumbled backward and landed on firm ground.

Not an Aquadorian . . .

Dane staggered to his feet as the warrior turned toward him, water dripping from its soaked body. His eyes drifted to the warrior's sword.

That's it!

Dane sprinted straight for the warrior before it could recover. He latched his hands onto the warrior—one hand on the sword hilt, and the other on the warrior's wrist—and kept running, willing the stone to crack beneath his grip, just like a Geomancer would.

But the sword didn't budge. Dane heaved downward with all his strength. Nothing. The stone warrior stared down at him, its stone helmet dripping cold water onto his forehead. The warrior growled and thrust its sword arm upward. Inexplicably, Dane's hands tightened in fear and the warrior pulled him off his feet. The next thing he knew he hit the ground hard, his back slamming against the arena wall.

The warrior charged. Dane shook the black stars from his vision and placed both trembling hands to the ground, desperately willing the earth beneath the warrior to swallow its feet and anchor it in place.

But he felt nothing. The warrior only charged faster.

Not a Geomancer . . .

Panic started to creep in. He shoved himself to his feet and turned to face the arena wall as the warrior's massive strides thundered directly behind him.

He kicked upward, planted his feet on the wall, and launched himself into the air and over the warrior's head. His hands fumbled over the warrior's head, his fingers hooking in the warrior's eye slits. Once his grip was secure, he wrapped his legs around the warrior's hulking frame.

The warrior flailed uncontrollably. Its arms battered against the wall, sending shards of stone flying in all directions. It flailed again, then began to tip, set to crush Dane beneath its weight.

All thoughts of defeating the warrior fled Dane's mind as fear took over. If he held on much longer, the warrior would flatten him beneath its massive weight.

Dane pushed away from the warrior, hitting the ground hard. He scrambled to the side, clawing through the rough dirt of the arena just as the warrior smashed the ground where he'd just been.

Dane heaved himself upright and glanced toward the energy stone pedestal, now sunk halfway into the ground. The time had passed to think ahead, to plan his options; he had to act on instinct.

The warrior was pushing itself to its knees, using the stone shield as a brace against the ground. Adrenaline pumped through Dane. This was his chance.

He charged at the fallen warrior. He planted one foot on the warrior's shield hand, pinning it to the ground, then clutched both edges of the stone shield and pulled toward the warrior's body.

His efforts were met with the resounding crack of breaking stone. Dane ripped the shield upward, dislodging it and the warrior's hand from the rest of its body. The warrior let out another gravelly roar.

The shield was much heavier than Dane expected. He stumbled backward, trying to maintain balance, before gripping it with both hands. But that didn't stop the faintest spark of hope from injecting life into his fatigued body. Finally, the battle was turning in his favor.

A sharp pain suddenly flared through his right arm. While he had been adjusting his grip on the shield, the warrior had risen to its feet and slashed at him. The sword had sliced through his sleeve, hitting his upper arm. The skin was already swollen, and a trail of blood seeped from the wound.

The warrior had lost its balance with the effort. Dane tore the cloth wrappings off one hand and, using his teeth, tied the cloth around his bleeding arm. He let out a stifled groan as he pulled the bandage taut.

The warrior rose once more. Now only armed with the stone sword, it was even more menacing, could move much faster.

The warrior raised its sword and charged.

Dane raised the shield. He wasn't sure what he intended to do with it—he could barely lift the shield, let alone use it to his advantage. His mind was going blank. He could only stand there, watching as the warrior came closer with every thundering stride.

Then a single voice rose above the utter chaos and deafening screams from the crowd. Quinn's voice.

Dane risked a glance behind him. She was leaning far over the railing of the stands, hands cupped around her mouth. "The sword!" she was shouting. "*Block the sword!*"

He could sense the warrior directly behind him. Without a second thought, he whirled and thrust the shield over his head.

A deafening crack echoed throughout the arena. For a moment, Dane just stood there, eyes squeezed tight. He was aware of a jarring pain in his arms, tingling down from his fingers, but no other pain. Had he stopped the warrior? Had he died, and was now in the empty void between lives?

Then came an ear-splitting eruption of cheers. He wasn't done for, not yet anyway.

Hesitantly, Dane peered through one eye, expecting the warrior to thrash at him again. Instead, he could only stare in disbelief. The warrior's sword had lodged itself into the shield.

The warrior ripped the sword away. Dane's arms fell to his sides as the shield cracked and split into two narrow halves.

The warrior righted itself, then charged once more. Dane's exhausted arms felt akin to willow tree branches as he gripped the two shield halves. Despite his fatigue, he heaved one shield half up in defense.

The sword ricocheted off the shield, fragments of rock splintering all around as the sword tip deflected downward and buried into the ground at Dane's feet. With a cry of exertion, Dane smashed the shield over the warrior's head.

Rock exploded outward upon impact. The warrior recoiled in a partial daze and swung blindly at Dane's chest. Dane heaved the remaining shield half up just in time to intercept the blow.

The shield shattered into a dozen pieces. Dane staggered backward. He righted himself quickly, but the warrior was faster.

It launched an uppercut and grazed Dane's wrist, slicing his energy band. Dane watched in horror as the band soared through the air and clattered against the arena wall.

Dane couldn't move. He felt as though it was all a dream, that at any moment he would wake from the utter nightmare that unfolded before him. All he could do was stare blankly up into the warrior's slitted eyes as it advanced toward him.

The warrior swung its handless arm, smashing squarely into Dane's chest. He went sprawling to the ground, feeling as though he'd been struck by a falling tree trunk. He gulped for air, breaths hoarse and rasping.

Not . . . like . . . this . . .

He tried to push his body upward when the warrior's massive stone foot pressed down on him, pinning him to the ground beneath its engulfing shadow.

Dane felt the air squeeze from his lungs. He writhed and thrashed beneath the weight of the warrior's foot, but the warrior didn't budge. He only had moments of air left before the warrior would finish him off.

Dane concentrated all thought, all energy, on the warrior, his hands outstretched.

This is my time! I need my powers! Mother help me!

In desperation, he commanded the air around him to push the warrior away and free him from its weight.

The air remained calm.

He urged a nearby cluster of ferns and vines to spring to life and pull the warrior away.

The plants didn't move, only rustled in the light breeze.

He willed the light of the sun to blind and daze the warrior enough so he could slip from its clutches.

The warrior stood resolute.

He imagined summoning a field of gravity that would suspend the warrior in its place long enough for him to slip from its clutches.

But still, nothing happened. A ring of blackness narrowed his vision with every passing instant. His breaths were nothing more than shallow, shuddering wheezes as the warrior pressed its foot into his chest and raised its sword, preparing for one final, fatal blow.

Dane no longer felt the pain of his bruised and beaten body, the searing agony in his lungs. This was it. Ten years of waiting and dreaming, and he was about to die in the Trials of Power.

His thoughts fleeted to Sage and Vilik, to Grandfather Horas, to his parents . . . and to Quinn. All of them had believed in him. And he'd let them all down.

Overcome with unbearable sadness, Dane closed his eyes as the stone sword plunged toward his chest.

There was a scream, followed by the crunch of breaking stone. The arena went silent, not one voice rising above the eerie rustling of leaves through the city.

Only the sound of strained breathing broke the silence— only, the breathing wasn't his.

Dane cracked one eye open. The stone sword hovered above his head, unmoving, as if halted in time. But something else held it in place. A twin-bladed, transparent sword.

Dane's eyes snapped open.

Cayde stood over him, sword clutched in his grasp, his expression a mixture of strain and confusion as his eyes flicked between Dane and the warrior. In his periphery, Dane saw a man in brown robes sprint to the warrior and press both hands to the warrior's back. Immediately the pressure on Dane's chest dissipated as the warrior's foot lifted from his chest. He sucked in a huge breath, his body shuddering as air spilled back into his lungs.

He rolled to one side and watched the stone warrior walk to the center of the arena as if in a trance. Then it crumbled into a nondescript pile of rubble.

With great effort, Dane turned onto his stomach, supporting his weight on his knees and elbows. His arm was streaked with blood beneath his makeshift cloth wrapping. His clothes were tattered beyond repair. Then he remembered where he was.

His rasping breath quickened as his eyes glazed across the sea of spectators. Everyone was on their feet, mouth agape, staring down at him with expressions he couldn't understand.

Dane glanced across the pit to where the energy stone pedestal had been. It was nowhere to be seen.

His mind whirled in confusion. Only when he looked up and met Quinn's devastated gaze did the unthinkable realization finally sink in.

My Trials. I . . . failed.

"Dane?" Cayde said behind him, voice low and cautious. "Are—are you all right?"

Tears swelled in Dane's eyes, his stomach sinking like a rock through water.

I failed.

Cayde took another hesitant step toward him. Dane glared up, halting Cayde where he stood.

"Do I *look* all right?" he seethed. Dane leapt to his feet so quickly that Cayde took a step back, throwing his palms up like someone trying to calm a frenzied beast.

"That's not—I didn't mean to—"

"HOW IS THIS ALL RIGHT?" Dane yelled, his ragged cry echoing across the entire arena. "I *FAILED!*"

Before Cayde could utter another word, Dane turned and sprinted for the doors leading out of the arena. As he flung the doors wide and tore through the Vitalor market streets, one excruciating thought echoing through every corner of his mind:

Everyone found their power in the Trials. Everyone, except him.

CHAPTER 5

THE MAN WITH THE SWORD

Dane didn't stop running until he reached the willow overlook balcony. He threw himself into it, breaths coming in wheezing rasps as he pressed his weight into the waist-high stone railing.

He had hoped the overlook would have offered some relief. There was nothing special about it. Its half-moon terrace was flanked by the massive roots of the Elderwood tree looming high overhead, and a lone drooping willow tree sprouted from its center. It was tucked behind the Elderwood tree, perched atop the cliff acting as the natural wall for the back of the city, overlooking Mistveil Lake.

But the willow overlook held sentimental value. It was the only place in the bustling city he could be alone. He and Sage had found the overlook at the end of their first Trials Festival, after weaving the maze of tunnels through the Elderwood's roots. They'd practiced their combat skills, imagining they were in their own Trial of the Warrior—Sage using a whip-like willow branch, and Dane with a sturdy staff he'd carved from a fallen

Elderwood branch. They'd returned every year since, making a tradition of dueling beneath the calm majesty of the willow tree.

As he stared out at the distant snow-capped mountains framing the lake before him, the brisk bite of the cold lake air nipping at his face and hands, it only made him feel worse. The world of Physos had been waiting for him all this time. All he had to do was discover his power. Then he could finally start living and exploring the wonders around him. But now that dream was nothing more than the stone warrior, reduced to rubble.

A spark of anger ignited inside him. He gripped the balcony until his fingers turned white. How could his Trials have gone so wrong? It had gone by in a blur, but he recalled every moment with perfect clarity. There was nothing he could have done differently, nothing he could have improved. He replayed it again. Every decision he made, every action he took—

The anger withered away, replaced once more by swallowing grief. There was *nothing* he could've done differently. Nothing at all. No matter what he could've done, *this* was who he was supposed to be. Nothing.

Mindlessly, Dane glanced at the massive Elderwood tree towering over him. With its mountainous height and vast canopy, the tree was so often a source of calm and awe for all who looked upon it. But even now, the tree's natural wonder could do nothing to ebb his grief.

With every blink, he saw the faces of the arena crowd, staring down at him like he was some sort of monster. But their faces weren't the worst part. It was *Quinn's* face, the way *she* had looked at him. Dane felt as though two clawed hands were tearing his heart in two. He clasped his ears, trying to purge the image. Everywhere he looked, he only saw her and the utter devastation in her limpid green eyes.

His head pounded with renewed agony and he let out a garbled cry. The pain was worse than anything he'd ever felt; tearing, ripping, and burning. His skin felt like fire. His entire body pulsed and throbbed, eager to shred itself limb from limb. All those years spent awaiting his Trials, all those nights spent dreaming about his powers, of seeing Quinn again . . . all of it had been for nothing.

His legs buckled and he collapsed on the railing, chest pressed to the cold stone. He blinked away tears as he stared down at the lake. Waves crashed against the cliffside below. Amongst them, he could see the dark silhouettes of rocks jutting from the lake waters.

He fastened his trembling grip on the railing, heart standing still.

It's a long way down, he found himself thinking, leaning further. *A very long way. A fall from this height . . .*

"Dane?"

Quinn's voice tore him from his thoughts. His arms stiffened, but he held silent, staring at the waves.

"Dane?" Quinn repeated, but her nurturing tone had disappeared, replaced with urgency. She took a cautious step toward him. "You're very close to the edge."

Dane realized his fingers were still curled to the railing. He released it and took a step back.

Quinn let out an audible sigh. "Sage said I might find you here."

Dane stared at his quivering palms. A lump formed in his throat. "Why did you come?"

"I . . . I was worried." She placed a tentative hand on his arm. "I wanted to see if you were all right—"

Dane wrenched his arm from her grasp. He didn't dare look at her, afraid her pitying, forest eyes would send him into a fit of sobs from which he'd never recover. "Do I *look* all right?"

Quinn withdrew her hand. She held silent for a long moment, then said, "I—I'm sorry. For everything. I didn't—I never wanted it to be this way."

Dane stared fixedly at the ground. He'd wanted this for the past two years; to hear her voice and be with her again. But now that it was happening, he felt nothing in return. He only wanted her to leave.

"I can't imagine what you're feeling right now," she said after another pause, "but please don't give up hope. There has to be a reason why this happened. Maybe you weren't meant to find your powers yet? Maybe there's a reason you didn't—"

"And what reason is that?" Dane blurted, a twist of anger coiling inside him. Her voice was filled with pity, and pity was the last thing he wanted from her.

"I-I don't know, but maybe—there has to be—"

"Am I supposed to believe that I'm *special*? That not having any powers is somehow *better*? That having *no future* is *better*?"

"Of course n—that's not what I meant. I don't know what you've been through—"

"HOW COULD YOU?" Dane cried, whirling to face her. "YOU WEREN'T HERE!"

Guilt crashed over him the instant the words left his mouth. She was only trying to help, and in return he had screamed at her.

He drooped over the balcony and cradled his head in his hands. "I—I'm sorry. I didn't—I didn't mean—"

"It's all right," she said. "Things have been hard for us all lately."

She placed a hand on his shoulder, squeezing lightly. Whatever thin barrier he'd fronted to restrain his emotions melted at her touch. A steady torrent of tears spilled down his cheeks, splattering on the cold stone of the railing.

"I just wish things could go back to the way they were," he croaked. "Back when we were children, when the Trials were only a distant dream. I just want this nightmare to end."

Quinn gripped his shoulders suddenly, spun him around. "Listen to me, Dane," she said, voice gentle yet firm. "I know it's hard. I can't imagine what you must be feeling. No one in the world can. But there's a reason this happened. There has to be. And you're the only one who can discover what that reason is." She raised her eyebrows and pressed a hand to his cheek, staring into his eyes. "This hasn't changed you. You're still that curious boy I first met, so full of life, so eager to learn. You'll find a way through this. I know you will."

Dane managed a nod. She flashed him a smile, then glanced over one shoulder, looking back toward the city. Her jaw tightened. The vein in her temple bulged slightly, the way it did when she was stressed.

"I have to go. I need to speak with Elder Chrysanthe about the—well, we have some catching up to do. Remember what I said, all right?"

"Mhmm," Dane mumbled.

"Good." She took a step away, making to leave, then turned and pulled Dane in for an embrace. "It was good to see you again," she said, squeezing him tightly.

"You too."

She let go too quickly for Dane's liking and hastened away from the balcony. She lingered at the far end of the overlook, then called back:

"One day people will hear the story of the great Dane Willows. But when they recall this story, they won't remember how you fell down in defeat. They'll remember how you rose back up."

And then she was gone, the faint sound of her footsteps fading with the wind.

Dane stared at the landscape in silence, bound to his thoughts, until the only traces of daylight were the soft, yellow streaks glowing from behind the mountains. She was right. There was a reason he didn't find his power. There had to be.

And you're the only one who can discover what that reason is . . .

Dane drew in a deep breath, buoying himself in that dark abyss lurking in his mind, and stared out across Mistveil lake. The air had turned cold, the darkness of night beckoning, and the lake's surface reflected the orange hue of the setting sun. He'd have to find somewhere to stay for the night, but that could wait. Now, he needed to walk.

He stuffed his hands in his pockets and meandered back through the twisting tunnels through the Elderwood roots until he reached the Elderwood market, the crowded marketplace contained within the giant tree's hollowed center. The market's usual bustle had died down to a dull mumble, only traces of the

40

day's excitement lingering amongst the remaining market goers and shopkeepers.

Dane skirted the edge of the market and made his way toward the temple staircase, the wide expanse of wooden stairs spiraling toward the Elder Temple Courtyard halfway up the Elderwood's trunk. He lowered his head as he walked, shrugging up his shoulders, trying to draw as little attention to himself as possible. He felt as though he were walking on a frozen lake, that at any moment, a rogue passerby would recognize him as that powerless boy from the Trials and start hurling insults, alerting everyone to Dane's location. The mere thought sent him into a cold sweat, and he picked up his pace.

He was practically running by the time he reached the base of the staircase. He crouched, hiding behind the wooden railing as he risked a glance back toward the marketplace. To his relief, his movements appeared to have gone unnoticed. People went about their business tearing down their stalls in preparation for the following morning, not one of them having glanced in his direction.

He made his way up the walkway, watching the market below grow smaller until the stands looked nothing more than fallen leaves, people milling around like ants.

After some time walking in silence, with nothing but the groaning bark of the Elderwood and memories of the arena consuming his thoughts, he emerged from the spiral walkway into the Elder Temple Courtyard.

The courtyard itself was a wide grassy dais dotted with pathways made from flattened stones. At the edges of the courtyard were at least a dozen narrow columns carved from the Elderwood's trunk, supporting the upper half of the gigantic tree while exposing the courtyard to open air on all sides. In all, it looked as though an entire slice of the Elderwood trunk had been removed, now only supported by a ring of smaller tree trunks.

A suspended network of huts and walkways had been built into the trunk overhead, acting as guest rooms for initiates who had traveled from the further reaches of Physos. Dane, Sage, and Vilik had shared one of them the night before. It reminded him of his Grandfather's house back at the village, nestled high in the canopy, suspended above the forest floor.

Dane walked to the edge of the courtyard and leaned against the railing, looking over Vitalor. Despite the diminishing light, he could still see the market streets as they carved through the residential district, connecting the arena and central market to the half-moon wall surrounding the city. Stone bridges spanned across the Celosian River that flowed just beyond the city borders, depositing the busy streets into the rolling hillside beyond. The hills spread into a vast valley of green farmland that stretched back to his village, now just a faint huddle of trees at the edge of his vision. To the west rose the foreboding, stormy peaks of the Avalanche Mountains; and to the east, the glistening, snow-capped peaks of the Aurora Mountains and the city of Evergleam—Quinn's home.

Dane's eyes drifted back to the market street below. A cluster of palm trees sprouted from the middle of a circular courtyard at the street's center, and the faint greenish hue of luminescent torches flickered like twinkling stars. On the right side of the courtyard, nestled tightly between two smaller stands, was a familiar flat-topped stone building. He could almost see the crude, half-worn letters lining the building's façade: Duxor's Craftsmithing Services. Duxor was the self-proclaimed best craftsmith in Vitalor, specializing in crafting weapons, armor, totems, and other energy-infused wares for ambitious Festival attendees. Dane and Vilik had apprenticed with Duxor for the better part of six years, learning to craft the weapons and armor of the Vitalor guards.

But Duxor had become much more than a mentor over the years. Though Dane didn't think of Duxor as a father figure—Duxor barely managed to keep his beard in order, let alone his own kin—Dane considered him family nonetheless. The master craftsmith had even shed a tear when Dane and Vilik had ended their apprenticeship the day before their Trials.

The tightness in his throat returned as he looked down at the little shop. Duxor believed in him. Others did too. Sage. Vilik.

Quinn. His failure in the arena wasn't the end; he could still find a way through this, find his power. He had to.

A light flickered at the edge of Dane's vision. He pulled his gaze away from the familiar streets below and glanced at the building on the far edge of the courtyard. The Elder Temple, while not known for its size, was widely regarded as the most stunning building in Vitalor. Its stained-glass exterior was emblazoned with intricate designs inspired by vegetation native to the city. When caught in the sunlight, the glass refracted dazzling color all across the courtyard. Eight white stone statues of the founders bordered its large triangular doors, each carved to such immaculate detail that Dane often mistook the statues for regular citizens from afar.

But now the temple was dark and deserted. At least, it would have been, except for the candlelight flickering in the second-floor window. Elder Chrysanthe's room.

I need to speak with Elder Chrysanthe, Quinn had said, *we have some catching up to do.*

Momentarily, Dane pushed his Trials to the back of his mind, allured by the scent of Quinn's secrecy. The way Quinn had said it, it was as if she had almost slipped up, said something she wasn't supposed to tell him.

Dane crept across the courtyard. The triangular doors of the temple groaned as he nudged them open and slipped inside. A long hallway stretched down the temple, leading to a large table set against a panoramic glass wall at the far end. Several smaller rooms lined the hallway to either side, most of which containing nothing more than bookshelves and archived texts of Physosi history, as he and Sage had discovered on their first visit to the temple.

Flanking the entryway were two spiral staircases, each blockaded by a tangle of twisting leafy vines, restricting passage to the Elder's chambers on the second floor. Dane moved to the staircase on the right and crouched beside it, seeking the cover of shadow. A moment later, he could hear voices from the room above—fragments, partial sentences at best. One was the soothing, motherly tone of Elder Chrysanthe. The other, unmistakably, belonged to Quinn.

"How many so far?" asked Elder Chrysanthe.

"Just the two," Quinn responded. "—tried to find more—ran out of options. We need more help."

"I understand—see what I can do. There are a few I have in mind."

"Thank you, Elder—do what we can. But . . . there's more."

"More?"

"He found one too. We tried to—he got away."

"You're certain?"

A long pause ensued, followed by the creaking of floorboards. Then came another voice, a low, husky voice that made Dane's blood boil.

Cayde. His fists tightened involuntarily. *What's he doing here?*

"He was too powerful, even for us." Another pause, then, "We think—headed this way."

"How long?"

"Not sure," Quinn said. "Maybe a few days. Can't be certain, but—"

Her voice trailed off as they moved deeper into the room. Dane shifted in place, trying to get closer. Without thinking, his hand closed around one of the vines. Its leaves crackled under his grip. Every hair on his body bristled. He may as well have smashed a pane of glass.

The voices stopped immediately. Dane crouched as low as he could, slinking deeper into the shadows. The sound of footsteps grew louder and stopped directly above him. Dane waited in suspended silence for a moment, then, curiosity getting the better of him, peeked through the vines.

Cayde stood at the top of the stairs. He wore a loose-fitting jacket both simple and elegant, covering his dark shirt and pants. His hair was a short tangle of orange curls. His murky brown eyes appeared unfocused, as if he wasn't staring at anything in particular, merely listening intently. That with his square jaw and chiseled features, he looked like one of the Founder statues, carved to painstaking perfection.

A coil of jealousy tightened in Dane's stomach. *This is why Quinn never returned?* He thought bitterly. *She found Cayde and never looked back?*

"What is it?" came Quinn's voice.

Cayde held silent a moment longer, staring down the staircase into the hallway, but showed no sign of noticing Dane. "Nothing." He finally said. "Probably just the wind."

Cayde disappeared. The door to the Elder's chambers shut a moment later, and Dane could hear nothing but meaningless reverberations of the floorboards.

Reluctantly, he slunk from the shadows and retreated from the temple. He slowly made his way across the courtyard, staring at his feet as he walked, trying to piece together what he'd just heard. Quinn and Cayde were looking for something, something they couldn't handle alone. *He found one too,* Quinn had said. Someone else was searching too, posing a significant threat to their cause. Dane sighed dejectedly. There was too much he didn't know, and what he'd overheard had only confused him further.

He stopped as he neared the initiate training grounds. A low fence enclosed a smattering of wooden figures outfit with worn pieces of armor. Dane and the other initiates had used these as training warriors for the Trials the day before. Now, in the low light, they looked like the remnants of a beaten and battered army, hobbling away from a narrow victory. Thinking back, Dane couldn't see how the training had been helpful; they'd used various blunted weapons against the so-called warriors in training yet hadn't been able to use weapons at all in the arena.

Dane walked past the row of training warriors, breathing a sigh of relief as he approached the warrior on the end. His Elderwood staff still rested against it; in the buildup to his Trials, he'd forgotten it the day before.

A flash of anger hit him as he grasped the staff. The fight would have gone much differently if he had been able to use it in the arena. The stone warrior might have even been able to land a hit on him, if it was fortunate. But no one was supposed to use weapons of any kind in the arena, only their power.

No one was supposed to fail the Trials of Power either.

He glared down at the dilapidated training warrior before him. Strands of straw poked from the sack clothing beneath its wooden chest piece. One wooden shoulder pad clung to its arm, drooping nearly to the ground. Straw burst through a large tear in its sack head from beneath its simple, rounded helm. Dane hadn't realized it the day before, but it was fitting he'd practiced on this particular warrior. It was the reject, the outcast. Just like him.

He struck the warrior's helmet. His staff connected with a satisfying knock, and the warrior's head slumped from one side to the other. He hit it again, harder, firing a barrage of repeated blows. His strikes were calculated at first, precise, but slowly turned more reckless as he let his frustration get the better of him. He didn't feel remorse any longer, only anger—anger at the Trials, at Cayde, at himself. Anger at the impossible situation he was now in. None of it made sense; there was no explanation. It was as if the Mother herself had plucked him from the crowd, declared him unworthy of Her divine blessing and cursed him to a fate he didn't deserve.

He gripped one end of his staff with both hands and swung at the warrior's neck. A loud crack filled the air as the warrior's pedestal snapped. It went sprawling to the ground, dusting the air with fragments of wood and straw.

Dane lowered the staff and wiped the sweat from his brow. For a moment he relished in the trivial triumph, then his shoulders slumped as reality set back in, and his anger was once more replaced by swallowing sadness. Beating on a hapless, mangled training warrior wouldn't gift him another chance in the arena. He still had no power.

"You fight well. I'm impressed."

The sudden voice nearly made Dane leap from the balcony. He whirled around, staff in hand, eyes wide with alarm. He immediately scowled.

Cayde was leaning against the nearest tree column, arms crossed in silent judgement, voice tainted with the subtle hint of amusement. His mere presence exuded a haughty confidence. For a reason unbeknownst to Dane, Quinn had chosen this man over him. It made Dane furious.

"Who trained you?" Cayde asked, all-too-genuinely. "Not many people have your level of combat prowess with a staff."

How long have you been standing there? Cayde must have heard Dane's strikes on the warrior after speaking with Quinn and Elder Chrysanthe. But the others weren't to be seen.

Briefly Dane thought about indulging Cayde's curiosity, but his bitterness got the better of him. "You wouldn't know him," he said. He turned his back to Cayde, readying himself as if to engage with the training warrior once more.

"Try me," said Cayde.

Dane sighed exhaustively; clearly Cayde couldn't take a hint.

"Duxor. Only the best craftsmith in all of Vitalor," he lied. In truth, he'd trained himself—granted sometimes in Duxor's shop. He'd taken to practicing more in recent years, often to the point of total exhaustion while trying to purge old, heart-aching memories of Quinn from his mind. But Cayde didn't need to know that.

"You don't say? Quinn and I talked with him the other day. He was very helpful. Spoke highly of his former apprentices."

Quinn's name was like poison coming from Cayde's mouth. Dane wanted nothing more than to smack the top of Cayde's head like he'd done to the dilapidated training warrior, but he managed to suppress the urge—barely. It was bad enough Cayde had stolen Quinn from him. Now Cayde was intruding and attempting to strike up casual conversation.

"That was you, wasn't it? His apprentice?"

"What do you want?" Dane said.

An uncomfortable silence ensued. Cayde cocked an eyebrow, a mysterious glint in his eyes. He pushed away from the tree column and walked toward Dane. He was at least a head taller and stood with impeccable posture. That with his broad shoulders, Dane got the feeling Cayde was much stronger than he looked—and he looked very strong.

Then Dane caught a glimpse of something on Cayde's back that glittered in the dim evening light. It looked like a sword handle.

Curiosity pushed his resentment aside. "What's on your back?"

Cayde halted. "This?" He gestured to the handle, looking genuinely taken aback—surprised even—at the Dane's interest in it. "It's a—well—it's—"

"It's a sword, isn't it?"

A strange look flashed across Cayde's face. "More or less."

"Can I see it?" Dane pestered. If Cayde was going to bother him unwillingly, the least Dane could do was return the favor.

Cayde opened his mouth then paused, glancing at his surroundings, as if expecting someone to be lurking nearby. After a moment's hesitation, Cayde sighed and withdrew the sword from its scabbard.

All the anger, sorrow, and disbelief of the day floated away as Dane stared incredulously at Cayde's sword. The blade was nearly transparent, its twin parallel blades shimmering in the reflected moonlight, each with a thin, orange light coursing through its center. Above the hilt—wrapped in ornate leather bindings—was a diamond-shaped hole about the size of Dane's fist. A thin gap separated the twin blades above the hole, extending two arm lengths before nearly converging at the sword's sharp point. In all his days apprenticing for Duxor, Dane had never seen a sword—or any weapon, for that matter—crafted as immaculately as the blade displayed before him.

"Is that . . . *glass*?" Dane managed, running his fingers along the blade's terrifyingly smooth surface.

Cayde stared down at the sword, pursing his lips in thought. "You could say that."

"It's a totem, isn't it," Dane said. He had learned about totems while apprenticing for Duxor—items infused with energy that allowed the wielder improved range and control of their power, though never enhancing that power. He'd crafted totems of his own on a few occasions.

"Well—no, actually. At one point, maybe, but I—*we*, rather—found it—"

"Does it do anything different? Anything special?"

Cayde's eyes traced from tip to hilt. His mouth twisted, brows lowering, as if he'd pondered that same question before. "Other than the material it was made from . . . no. It's just an ordinary sword."

Something about Cayde's hesitant tone left Dane feeling uneasy. He got the feeling Cayde knew more than he was sharing.

Then his anger resurfaced. Here Cayde was, showcasing his marvelous sword while withholding all detail about it, as if Dane wasn't worthy enough to understand. Luckily, Cayde was the perfect outlet.

Dane tightened the grip on his staff. "I want a duel."

Cayde blinked. "You . . . what?"

"You interrupted."

"I'm sorry?"

"In the arena. You didn't let me finish my Trial of the Warrior. You stopped the stone warrior before the fight was over." The warrior *had* been moments from ending Dane's life, but that was beside the point. Cayde had intervened. Besides, this was the best excuse he could offer for a duel. He'd make a fool of himself if he'd said, *Quinn is mine, I'll fight you for her affection.*

Cayde looked thoroughly confused. "You know this isn't the same as—"

"If you don't think you're good enough just say so."

"I didn't say that." Cayde eyed Dane's staff, then the sword. "Look . . . it's not that I doubt your abilities—" he stole a quick glance at the mangled training warrior, then returned his gaze to the sword. "But I've had quite a bit of practice with this. I don't really think you'd—"

"Try me."

Dane glanced at the sword after he spoke, then at his staff, then back at the sword. A seed of worry sprouted at the back of his mind. Had he even thought this through? Cayde had a masterfully crafted sword, honed for battle. Dane had a wooden stick.

He quickly doused his hesitation, replacing it with fierce determination. Cayde was a push-over; all talk and show. He needed to be put in his place.

"If you say so," Cayde said reluctantly. He raised the sword with one hand, readying for combat, then swung with alarming speed.

Dane launched his staff above his head, blocking Cayde's cascading blow. With a rapid flick of his wrists, Dane struck the side of the sword, nearly knocking it out of Cayde's grasp.

Cayde righted himself, rolled his shoulders. He smirked. "Elderwood, I'm impressed," he said, eyeing Dane's staff. "Stronger even than the finest of blades . . . but I'm sure you already knew that." Cayde wove the sword through the air with a dancer's grace before readying it at his side. His smirk grew wider. "Let's see how you really fight."

Cayde lunged again, once more alarming Dane with his speed. Dane barely recovered his footing before raising his staff to block another strike, leaving Cayde momentarily exposed. Dane seized the opportunity and knocked Cayde's sword arm outward before launching a deft kick to his stomach. Cayde grunted and stumbled backward, sword still in hand.

A maddening guilty sensation washed over Dane. Shouldn't kicking him have felt good? "Err—sorry—I didn't mean to—"

Cayde looked up, wincing slightly, but still grinning.

"It's all right . . . been some time since I last had a duel." He straightened. "You're good, did you know that? Really, I'm impressed."

Dane felt a surge of elation, but he forced it down. He didn't need Cayde's hollow praise.

"Show me what else you've got."

Cayde swung again, but this time Dane was prepared. He parried the sword downward, shifting Cayde's momentum with it. Dane spun his staff and brought it down behind Cayde's legs, wrenching Cayde's feet outward, sending him sprawling to the ground on his back.

Before Dane had a moment to revel in the minor victory, a stinging pain flared in his leg. He glanced down in time to see Cayde's sweeping leg beneath him before Dane, too, was sent crashing to the ground.

Determined not to let Cayde gain any advantage, Dane tumbled clumsily backward and sprung to his feet, staff at the ready. He whirled to face Cayde, expecting another blow from that wondrous glass sword.

But Cayde merely stood and stepped away from Dane, sword arm relaxed. He was smirking, staring as if in admiration, leaving Dane with a feeling of thorough confusion.

"You really are excellent with that staff," Cayde said, sheathing his sword before gesturing to Dane's weapon. The corners of his mouth twitched. "However, if we're being accurate to your Trials . . ." Cayde snatched the staff. "You won't be needing this."

Dane watched Cayde with increasing caution as Cayde inspected the staff, tossing it between his hands before gripping it firmly.

"What are you doing?" Dane said.

"Just because you didn't—err—because what happened, doesn't mean you can't learn from it," Cayde said. "You seem quite comfortable with this staff. One day, you may end up in a situation where you don't have it with you."

"I don't see how this is helping any—"

"Bear with me, all right?" There was a strange sternness in Cayde's voice. Dane wanted to believe otherwise, but it seemed like Cayde wasn't acting with malicious intent. It was as if he was genuinely interested in helping, like an older brother teaching the younger the secrets of life.

"Imagine I'm the stone warrior you faced in the arena." Cayde gestured to the staff. "This is my sword. See if you . . . can . . ."

Cayde trailed off, mouth parted slightly. His gaze settled on something behind Dane. His focused expression turned somber.

Dane turned and followed Cayde's gaze. A dark layer of clouds hovered over Vitalor, obscuring the night sky. But something was wrong. Clouds didn't billow from the ground up. And they most certainly didn't glow.

Dane broke into a cold sweat, heart pounding in his chest. He and Cayde sprinted for the across the courtyard.

Cayde's eyes bulged as they reached the railing. "By the Mother . . ."

Then Dane saw it too. Far below, a wall of flame bathed the market streets.

CHAPTER 6

TEARS OF THE ELDERWOOD

Vitalor was in chaos. The flames had doubled in size by the time Dane and Cayde emerged from the Elderwood. People screamed and ran from the market streets. Houses crackled and burned. The sun had already disappeared behind the Aurora Mountains, but the sky looked as though the sun had risen again, stained with the haunting glow of flame. The scene was disturbing to watch.

Dane found himself turning to Cayde. Despite Dane's resentment of the Gravitus, Cayde exuded a command far beyond his years. His mere presence suppressed Dane's swelling panic.

"What do we do?" Dane watched as a mother scooped up her child, face ashen with soot, before tearing down the street away from the market district. "How'd this happen?"

Cayde said nothing at first, merely stared in a trance at the unfolding tumult.

"Cayde?" Dane pressed.

"I don't know how," said Cayde, gaze locked on the burning streets. When he finally blinked from his stupor, fiery determination burned in his eyes. "We need to get everyone to safety."

Cayde leapt into action, barking commands to people as they passed. "Direct everyone toward the West Gate!" he called back. "Hurry!"

Dane turned his attention to the streets. Most of the market stands were now ablaze, and the fire was spreading deeper into the city. The only people heading toward the fire were the Vitalor guards, each hauling buckets of water.

A nearby house suddenly exploded, showering the street with burning chunks of wood and stone. Dane stumbled back, shielding his eyes from the intense light.

"Dane!"

The voice called to him through the howling flames and screaming crowds. Relief washed over him as he turned to the source. Sage had heeded Cayde's command, directing civilians away from the fire.

Dane rushed to his sister's side, ducking to avoid lashing flames. "What happened? What's going on?"

"This fire started out of nowhere!" she shouted back. "We have to clear the market streets and get everyone to safety! Quinn said this street leads to the—go on, this way, it's safe—it leads out of the city!"

A sudden thought struck Dane. He scanned the frantic crowds. His brow creased with worry.

"How long have you been here?" he asked. "Has everyone come this way?"

"Since the fires started. Guards started directing people this way shortly after. Elder Chrysanthe instructed the city's Aquadorians to try and control the flames."

"Have you seen Duxor?"

She paused too long for Dane's liking. "I—well—no, not yet. I guess he could have gone another—er—"

Vilik ran toward them against the flow of fleeing people. His face was blackened with ash, his clothes singed. "We have to control these flames!"

"Working on it!" Sage retorted. "We need to get everyone to safety first." She glanced at the guards rushing past, buckets in hand. She cursed under her breath. "Those buckets won't do anything to stop the flames. Not unless—" She craned her neck upward, staring through the smoke at the Elderwood branches. Her eyes widened. "I have an idea! I need to find Elder Chrysanthe!"

She started toward the tree, then halted mid-stride. She stared back at the fleeing crowds, desperation in her eyes.

"Go!" Vilik shouted to her. "We'll handle it!"

Sage hesitated a moment, then bolted for the Elderwood.

Roaring flames erupted nearby as several more market stands fell victim to the conflagration. Vilik snatched up a young boy as he made his way toward the West Gate. "Dane, let's go!"

"Vilik, wait!" Dane called out to him. He scanned the crowds, searching for a familiar face. He saw none.

"There's no time!" Vilik shouted. "We have to leave before—"

"What about Duxor?" It was possible his old mentor had already escaped, but something inside him said otherwise. "Have you seen him?"

Vilik stopped in his tracks. He stared down the central market street, his face a mask of worry and fear.

"Dane . . . we don't know for sure," Vilik said. He seemed to weigh his options as he glanced between the fleeing crowd, the market street, and the boy in his arms. Vilik feared for Duxor too, Dane could see it in his eyes. The man was as good as family.

"I have to find him," Dane said. "I have to try."

Vilik glared down the market street, his teeth gritted, as if willing Duxor to appear. Moments passed. No one else came. "Find him. But be quick. And be careful!"

Vilik turned and ran away with the others as Dane sprinted toward the inferno, following a narrow, unobstructed path that led down the middle of the street. Dane shielded his mouth from the smoke, ducking every few steps to avoid leaping flames until he was standing in front of Duxor's shop. A tree had fallen onto the roof. Another had fallen across the storefront, barricading the door. If Duxor was inside, he wouldn't last long.

Dane surveyed the fallen tree amidst the suffocating heat; the trunk was smaller than he expected, its exterior blackened and brittle. He stomped down hard and the trunk caved beneath his weight, spraying embers and wood into the air, clearing a path to the door. Dane pressed his weight into it. It didn't budge. He took a step back, closed his eyes in preparation, and thrust his shoulder into the door.

The door swung open with the jolting crack of breaking wood. Dane tumbled across the ash-ridden floor. He worked himself to hands and knees when a faint, unmistakable voice rose over the roaring fire.

"Help! Over here!"

Dane stumbled to the back of the shop. "Duxor!" he wheezed, choking on stray embers as he crouched beside his mentor. Duxor was lying on his back. Mild burns and lacerations scarred his meaty forearms, and a large ceiling beam had fallen across his portly mid-section, pinning Duxor beneath it.

"Dane, are yeh there?" Duxor coughed, craning his neck back.

"I'm here!" Dane shouted, blinking back stinging tears.

Duxor exhaled a laugh that quickly turned to a wracking cough. "I knew yeh'd find me, boy! Now help me out of here. I can't pry it loose!"

"Hold still. I'm going to lift the beam enough for you to—"

"Dane! What are you doing in here?"

Cayde burst through the broken doorway, his clothes and face charred and covered in ash. "What are you doing?" He threw his arms up as another ceiling beam crashed to the ground. "Get out of here!"

Dane motioned to Duxor. "He needs help! I won't leave him!"

Cayde, just now noticing Duxor, rushed to Dane's side and grasped the underside of the beam.

"I'll lift. You pull him out. I can only hold it for a moment, but that should be enough."

"Right." Dane hooked his arms under Duxor's shoulders. "Ready!"

"Now!" Cayde's muscles strained as he heaved the beam upward. Dane pulled the craftsmith's body free, his large belly barely scraping under before Cayde's grip failed. The beam tumbled to the floor with the rubble.

"This way!" Cayde shouted, his breath raspy as he helped Dane pull Duxor up.

They burst back through the collapsed doorway just as another burning tree destroyed what remained of the roof. Dane pulled one of Duxor's arms around his shoulder, Cayde grabbing the other, and hauled the large man to his feet before charging back through the street.

"Thanks, lads." Duxor patted his clothes wildly as they emerged from the dense flames, dousing the small embers that had erupted around his waist. "Thought I was done for. First those strange fella's from earlier, now the fire—"

Cayde stopped brushing the ash from his clothes. "What do you mean, strange fellows?"

"These two fella's came by earlier," Duxor said between labored breaths. "Normally I'd think nothin' of it, but they were wearing ridiculous clothes. Had hoods an' all too, as if tryin' to hide from somethin'. Didn't say much. Came in, glanced around, an' left without sayin' a word."

"What's odd about that?" Dane asked.

"That wasn't all." Duxor brushed the remaining burning embers from his grizzly beard. "I saw somethin' I knew I shouldn't 'ave as they were leavin'." His voice dropped to a conspiratorial whisper. "They were carryin' swords. *Metal* swords. And there I was about to close up and make my way to the Trials—"

"*Metal?*" Dane exclaimed. The material was so rare that only the largest establishments were deemed worthy of its use: door frames on sacred buildings, chandeliers in the Elder Temples. Most metal anyone had come across in the past few centuries had succumbed to rust and age, far beyond proper use. But never had Dane seen metal used to craft weapons, let alone weapons belonging to ordinary citizens. "Are you certain?"

"O'course I'm certain—I know what I saw! They were metal swords! And not that old rusted stuff, neither. Gleaming, genuine metal. Anyone carryin' weapons like that in the city is looking for trouble. But a mere coincidence that the fires started shortly after those men came 'round? Hah! I'd wager the whole shop they had somethin' to do with this—were it still standing, o'course."

"I don't understand," said Dane. "How can they have metal weapons? I thought—"

"It can't be," Cayde said suddenly.

Dane looked to him, confusion etching his brow. Then he saw Cayde's expression. Cayde's eyes bulged wide, his pupils a haunting reflection as he gazed into the fires. Beneath the streaks of ash, his face was ghostly white. It was as if he could see something in the flames—not a physical entity, but a memory. Something he'd seen before. And it terrified him.

"We have to warn Elder Chrysanthe. NOW!" Cayde grabbed Dane by the collar and whirled him toward the Elderwood. "The Elderwood is in grave danger."

"Why? What's happening? What's going on?"

"Avon."

Fear seized every bone in Dane's body. He'd heard that name before. Avon was a man of legend. Dane grew up hearing stories about how Avon had set the countryside ablaze for nothing but his own pleasure; how he'd tried to kill Elder Chrysanthe, torture her until she granted him the Elderwood's energy; how he could slay a dozen guards in the blink of an eye. And, most infamous of all, how he had leveled an entire city with nothing but his bare hands.

Dane didn't know which of the stories he believed. It didn't matter. Every one of them terrified him. But that terror had never truly manifested since he'd heard Avon perished with tens of thousands of others after destroying Starspire, the city of the Cosmonauts.

Now, according to Cayde, Avon wasn't only alive. He was in Vitalor.

Dane tried to swallow, but his throat had gone dry. "I-I thought—how did he—"

"No time to explain." Cayde ran toward the Elderwood tree, still gripping Dane's jacket. "We have to get to the Elderwood before—before . . ."

Cayde stopped abruptly, staring ahead at the tunnel leading to the Elderwood market, where a pulsing, unnatural white glow boiled from within.

"We're too late . . ."

Cayde sprinted for the tunnel without another word. Dane followed him through the tunnel leading into the Elderwood's hollowed interior, then recoiled the instant he entered the Elderwood market. It felt as if the skin on his face had ignited and burst into flame. He leapt back, pressing his body against the interior trunk in an effort to distance himself from the source.

A blinding maw of raging energy pulsed in the center of the market. Its ruthless white flares lashed out through the market stands and whipped against the interior walls of the Elderwood tree, searing the robust bark with its wicked white fire.

Dane had to peer through his fingers just to catch a glimpse of the horrific sight before him. It was unlike any fire he'd ever seen, fueled by visceral, untamed energy that threatened to burn the entire market. If left to wreak its havoc, the entire Elderwood would surely burn.

He registered a blur of movement in his periphery, and turned to see Elder Chrysanthe, followed by Sage, appear from the spiral walkway moments before the entire walkway succumbed to the blistering fire.

"I'll handle this," Elder Chrysanthe shouted. "Sage, do as we discussed. Now go, all of you!"

Sage grabbed Dane's arm, pulling him out of his horrified stupor and back out of the tunnel, Cayde following close behind.

"What—did Avon do that?" Dane gasped once relieved from the intense heat.

Cayde nodded, his face set with determined fury.

Dane turned to Sage. "I take it Elder Chrysanthe took your idea?"

"The Elderwood collects rainwater throughout the year, stores it in its branches." Sage pointed to the massive branches through a thick layer of smoke. "If we gather enough Biophages to offer their energy to the Elderwood, Elder Chrysanthe can divert it to the branches and release the water reserves. Once released, it'll be like a heavy rainstorm and extinguish the fire!"

"That's brilliant!" said Dane. "Let's gather—"

Her face grew pale. "But I saw him . . ." she said. "I was coming back from the temple with Elder Chrysanthe. I—I saw him."

Cayde grasped Sage's shoulders. His eyes looked wild. "Where? Which direction did he go? We can't let him escape!"

Sage nodded, her eyes wide with apprehension. "East entrance," she managed, gesturing beyond the Trials Arena.

"Gather the Biophages," Cayde told her. "Have Quinn help you. We'll stop Avon. He couldn't have gotten far . . ."

Dane froze and stared at Cayde.

"Wait . . . *we*? But I don't—"

Cayde was already sprinting toward the arena, pulling Dane with him.

"We have to get to the East Gate before Avon can escape." Cayde panted as he led Dane through the winding narrow streets. "He's not getting away this time."

Dane's head felt like the inside of the Elderwood. "How did you know he did this?"

"Avon and his followers are the only people in Physos who have access to metal weapons—it had to be his doing. I'll bet that fire in the market was a diversion so he could attack the Elderwood without Elder Chrysanthe in the way."

"H-how do you know this about him?"

"Quinn and I, we—we encountered him once before. But then—get down!"

Cayde thrust Dane against the wall of a dark, narrow passageway. He paused, listening in motionless silence. The only sound Dane could hear was the distant muffled screams and crackling of the fires—that and his own labored breaths. Then he heard it, faint voices echoing from the street ahead.

Cayde turned his head to the sound. "There's no way we can face him without an advantage."

"*Face* him?" Dane blurted in as low a voice as he could muster. "You expect me to—"

"Just shut up and listen," Cayde barked in a perfect whisper. "Avon is too powerful for us alone. We'll need to flank him, take him by surprise." Cayde knelt and began fiddling with something around his neck. He nodded to the end of the passageway. "I'll need a moment. Scout ahead, see if anyone is with him."

Dane hissed under his breath. "*What?* That's insane! What if he sees me? What if—"

"Do it, Dane! There's no time!"

Every bone in his body revolted, but Dane slunk along the wall, stopping behind a wooden barrel at the end of the passageway. He crouched down on hands and knees, cursed under his breath, and peered from behind the barrel.

A few paces away were two Vitalor guards flanking either side of a tall stone archway leading out of the city. Standing before them, their backs to Dane, were three hooded figures in triangular formation. The two forward figures concealed weapons that shone with the same the ominous red tinge suspended over the city.

The two men with metal swords . . .

Dane's gaze settled on the third hooded figure. He stood nearly a head taller than the others. He wore a cloak as dark as the smoke rising into the night sky, its length shredded and tattered. Other than his sleek black boots, the man looked like a reincarnate of some nightmarish conjuration.

The tallest man unsheathed two angled blades from his back, sliding them beneath his cloak as one of the guards held out a halting hand.

"I-I'm sorry s-sir, but this entrance is c-closed," the guard stammered.

"Anyone wishing to exit must undergo inspection," said the other, stepping defiantly forward. Dane's breath hitched, fearful for the guard's life. He held only a spear, its tip pointed to the sky. He wasn't prepared for what the hooded figures concealed.

"Step aside," said the tallest man, his voice hoarse and murderous. "There's no need for futile displays of courage tonight."

As if in protest, the guard stood taller. "I won't let you pass."

The two men in front stepped to the side, allowing the taller hooded man forward. "Let's try that again. If you value your life, step aside."

Do it! Dane wanted to scream. *Run!*

"I won't," the foolish guard said. "The consequence for harming a Vitalor guard is punishable—"

The hooded figure drew his blades, their lengths sizzling orange, as if ignited by the stars themselves, and slashed at both guards with terrifying speed. The guards shrieked in guttural agony as the blades sliced through their bodies. A moment later, both guards were mere heaps of dismembered body parts, blood oozing out over the cobblestones.

It took everything Dane had to keep from retching. Watching the hooded man slash at the guards had been horrific, but the smell of the guards' steaming bodies—if they could even be called bodies now—the putrid odor clung to his senses with burning flesh and blood.

Cayde's hand found Dane's shoulder and pulled him back into the passageway.

"This is our chance. You know how to use this, right?" He pushed his glass blade into Dane's hands.

Dane couldn't move. He stared blankly forward, shuddering as he replayed the massacre in his mind. He could scarcely breathe.

His hands shook violently around the sword's hilt. "I-I can't," he found himself saying. "I don't have any powers—how can I do anything against him? How—I don't—what do I—"

Cayde knelt beside him, his voice low but stern. "Listen to me, Dane. You can either drown in your own thoughts about what should have happened, or you can toughen up and deal with it." He balled one hand into a fist and pressed it against Dane's chest. "You don't need powers to be strong in here.

Right now, I need you out there with me. Avon has to pay for what he's done."

"How do you know he won't—" Dane gulped. "What if you end up like those guards? How do you know that won't happen?"

"I don't. But I *do* know that if I stand idly by and do nothing, he'll kill again and again—he won't stop, and I'll be *damned* if I allow that to happen. I have to stop him, and I will . . . because I *believe* I can. Do you?"

Dane nodded, swallowing hard. He staggered to his feet, clutching the sword with white knuckles.

"Stay here and wait for my signal. We take him together." Cayde peered around the corner. "Understand? Nod if you understand." Dane nodded. "Good." Cayde drew in a steady breath, then silently crept across the street before crouching in the shadows of another building.

Dane turned his attention to the hooded men, now crouching beside the downed guards.

"Hide their bodies and leave," the tall one said as he wiped his blades on the guard's tunic. "Their screams won't go unheard. It won't be long before—"

Across the street, Cayde gave the signal. He charged from hiding and screamed, "AVON!"

The tall hooded man rose and turned to Cayde. Before Cayde could take another step, a glowing orb of molten energy formed in Avon's hand. He tossed it at Cayde's feet.

Cayde swept a hand across his body, diving the opposite direction. The orb's path strayed as if mimicking Cayde's hand and exploded upon impact, sending chunks of stone and searing fire in all directions.

Cayde rolled out of his dive, springing toward Avon, but Avon had already tossed another orb in his direction. Cayde leapt backward at the last moment, narrowly evading the second explosion.

Then Avon turned his gaze on Dane, sending an icy shiver down his spine. He suddenly realized he had been watching all of this while standing in the open, defenseless, captivated by fear.

Avon was terrifying. His crazed eyes shone bright orange, accentuated by the reflection of the distant flames. A jagged, red scar ran from his scalp to his chin. The corners of his thin mouth curled into a sneer as he peered over his crooked, misshapen nose. With his black, tattered robes, he truly was a vision from a nightmare.

Dane's legs went useless and he fell to his back, immobilized under Avon's gaze. Avon scoffed and turned his attention back to Cayde.

"If it isn't the young Gravitus," Avon hissed, his voice plagued with both exasperation and amusement. "You never fail to intercede at the most . . . *opportune* of times."

"You did this!" Cayde shrieked, buffeted by the white flames that had sprouted from Avon's orbs. He tried to push through, but the flames seemed to swarm around him, blockading his way forward.

"Such a shame," Avon chuckled to himself, the sound a low, grating rumble in his throat. "Appears you're too late once again . . ."

Cayde howled and charged through the flames. But Avon paid him no mind. He clenched his serpentine fingers inward, creating yet another sphere of raw energy, and spilled it onto the downed guards. A raging white inferno erupted from the ground, nearly knocking Cayde off his feet.

Dane shielded his eyes and scrambled backward, blinded by the burst of energy. When white spots stopped flickering in his vision, Avon and the two hooded figures had disappeared.

Cayde reeled back, vigorously patting at the flames on his clothes. He glanced at the archway from which Avon had escaped, which was now wreathed in the same white flame that had burned inside the Elderwood. Cayde cursed loudly, then stormed toward Dane and hauled Dane to his feet.

"I-I'm sorry," Dane stammered. "I-I didn't know what t-to do but—"

Cayde's face was contorted with rage, but his voice was calm and surprisingly soothing.

"It's all right. It's not your fault." He placed a hand on Dane's shoulder and pried the glass blade from Dane's hands. "It wasn't fair of me to ask that of you." He turned his back to the archway and started back toward the Elderwood.

Dane stared at the wall of flame. "But—aren't we going after him?"

"Not this time," said Cayde. "We'd have to go around, and the next gate is too far away; he'd be long gone. This won't be the last we see of him." He glanced over his shoulder, gesturing for Dane to follow. "But next time, you'll need to be more prepared. Besides, we're needed elsewhere."

Dane's heart finally slowed its relentless thumping. He trotted to catch up to Cayde, eager to distance himself from Avon and his wake of destruction.

"That wasn't a very good plan," Dane said, his jitters finally ebbing.

Cayde chuckled at that. "I suppose it wasn't, in hindsight. I should have thought it through ahead of time, what I'd do the next time I encountered him. I guess it doesn't matter now." He shook his head, then raised an eyebrow at Dane. "How about you do the planning next time."

Dane shuddered at the thought of seeing Avon again, but quickly pushed the thought aside. "What was that—that—*energy* in his hands? I've never seen anything like it. Was that the same power he used in the Elderwood market?"

"Yes, that was a cosmic flare. A very powerful one, too. Avon is a Cosmonaut—one of the last of them, come to think of it. He damn near killed them all when he destroyed Starspire decades ago."

Dane's eyes widened as if he had seen a Chemocyte. "So it's true, then?"

"Afraid so. We're lucky Vitalor is still in one piece, really."

Dane silently nodded in agreement. If the stories held true—which it appears they did—Vitalor was quite lucky indeed.

A large drop of water smacked Dane's head and he looked up. A heavy mist rained down from the Elderwood branches as they swayed over the city. Dane watched as the smoke and ash hovering over the market streets slowly dissipated with the ebbing flames.

"Seems there was enough water reserved in those branches after all," Cayde said. "That was a quick decision on your sister's part. I'm sure you know she's very gifted—she might very well be the strongest Biophage from this year's Trials."

"She's a Biophage?"

Guilt washed over Cayde's expression. "Oh—I thought you already knew."

"No, I didn't. That's . . . that's great," Dane said, trying to force enthusiasm into his words. He wanted to feel happy for Sage, with all his heart he wanted to. Sage had always talked about becoming a Biophage—of following in Elder Chrysanthe's footsteps, helping as many people as she could with her powers. That was her dream, and now she'd achieved it. But even as Dane thought it, memories of his own Trials, of his failure, squeezed their way into his mind. Again, he saw the look in Quinn's eyes as he had fled the arena.

Quinn . . .

Dane eyed the path ahead. They still had some distance to cover before reaching the Elderwood. Now was as good a time as any. He looked to Cayde.

"So," Dane said, trying to keep his voice level. "How'd you meet Quinn?"

He cringed inwardly the instant the words left his mouth. *Who was he to pry into their relationship?* Yes, it had pained him seeing her with Cayde in the arena, after all Dane and Quinn had been through. But now he was stooping to a new level, an embarrassing attempt at subtle espionage.

To his relief, Cayde answered promptly and without hesitation. "It was after I completed my Trials, actually," he said thoughtfully. "Elder Yarrin came to congratulate me, then asked me to meet him and his daughter in Evergleam after I pledged my power." He rolled up his sleeve to reveal his Mark of the

Gravitus—a helix of floating stones—on his right arm. "He and my mentor, Elder Durkanis, taught us how to improve our powers . . . among other things."

Dane cocked his head. "Elder Durkanis? I've never heard of him before."

"He's the Elder of Alto-Baros. He came to watch my Trials that day; he's always looking for an excuse to visit Elder Yarrin. Once I learned to control my power, they sent Quinn and me on—well . . . we've been traveling together ever since."

Dane shuddered involuntarily at the thought; them traveling together alone, nothing but each other's company. Fortunately, Cayde didn't seem to notice.

"She talks about you often, though—about how she bumped into this young boy when she was younger and had to teach him everything about the Trials, because it was 'so outrageous that he hadn't heard of it before.'"

Cayde smiled and laughed to himself. Dane frowned, unamused.

"She really thinks highly of you, Dane. Missing the Festival last year really impacted her—I could tell how much she enjoyed it from her youth. You're a great friend to her."

"Yes." Dane let his gaze fall to the ground. "Friend . . ."

A solemn serenity hung in the air as Dane and Cayde returned to the Elderwood tree. With the threat of the fire gone, people had already started flocking back to the market streets, some carrying burnt rubble, others hauling overflowing buckets for the residual flames. Dane felt a surge of pride as he watched. Avon's attack had been horrible. Though the fires hadn't reached the residential areas, the market streets had suffered major damage, and Avon's cosmic flare had nearly destroyed the Elderwood from the inside out. But still people returned at first opportunity, already mending the damage that had been done, their love for the city transcending the threat of danger they so narrowly escaped. Dane realized the citizens of Vitalor would do anything for this city, risk their own lives if it came to it. And he was only witnessing a part of it. He wondered how many other minor victories had been won this day, how many others had charged into a burning building, saved the ones they loved.

"Cayde! Dane!" Quinn parted through the crowd and ran at them with open arms. "Oh, I'm so glad you're safe!" She flung her arms around Cayde and kissed him. Dane forced himself to look away.

"I was so worried!" she said. "Sage said you both went to stop Avon. What happened? I heard screams!"

Cayde exhaled deeply. "He escaped . . . again."

Quinn released Cayde and clenched her fists. "I don't understand. How is he always one step ahead? I should've known he would attack the Elderwood—"

"There's no way you could have. Besides, the next time we see him—" Cayde glanced meaningfully at Dane "—we'll be ready."

Quinn looked to Dane. Her eyes were filled with endearment. Her lips quirked into a smile. Despite himself, he couldn't help but smile back.

"I'm relieved neither of you were harmed—everyone's safe now." She gestured to the mass of people shuttling across the streets. "The Elderwood will recover, but it sustained near irreparable damage from Avon's flare. I don't know what would've happened without Sage's quick thinking."

Dane scanned the passing crowds. "Where is she?"

"She left for the overlook after the fires died down. She was brilliant, really—but she seemed quite upset."

"Thanks. I'll be back."

Cayde started detailing the encounter to Quinn as Dane weaved through the crowd toward the overlook. It was true he wanted to check on Sage, make sure she hadn't been injured in the fire, but he couldn't stand another moment with Quinn and Cayde. His feelings for Quinn were more muddled than ever, and the mere sight of Cayde still made Dane's hair stand on end, though the Gravitus wasn't as repulsive as he originally seemed. But seeing them together made Dane's blood curdle.

He pushed the thought from his mind, focusing instead on the people around him. Much to his relief, none of them stared or leapt in revulsion as Dane passed. After the atrocities that had happened to the Elderwood tree and the city, no one seemed to care about his failure at the Trials—at least, no one else did.

Dane snuck into the hidden tunnel unnoticed, eventually depositing into the overlook. Sage was kneeling beside a charred stump, facing the spot where the willow tree once stood. A pile of charred wood lay strewn about the ground around Sage.

"It's gone," she muttered, tracing her fingers along the stump's jagged edges. "I can't believe it's gone."

"Sage . . . you just saved the entire city," Dane said. "Without you—"

"The Elderwood was *crying*, Dane. Those flames—they were burning its life force. It was crying. I—I could *feel* it."

Dane knelt beside her. "Elder Chrysanthe knows how to heal it, doesn't she?"

"In time, yes. But the willow . . ." She shook her head, tears catching in her throat. "I used to sit here every morning, watching as the sun rose over the mountains. After completing my tasks for Elder Chrysanthe, I'd come back and watch the sunset. Right here with this tree." Her hand fell limp at her side. "Now it's gone."

The charred stump split as her hand trailed away, blackened chunks of wood crumbling around her. A tear dripped down her face, carving a thin, pale streak on her ash-ridden cheek.

Dane opened his mouth but said nothing, unable to find any words that would comfort his sister. He dropped his gaze to the remains of the willow and found himself choking back tears of his own. He and Sage had spent a lot of time together on this overlook. Discovering it for the first time, dueling beneath the willow branches—it was a part of them.

The blackened wood settled, and a strip of vibrant green caught Dane's attention.

He sifted through the charred wood. "What's that?"

Sage looked up. "What's what?"

"In here." Dane parted the remains, revealing a thin, wisp-like branch. Sage cradled it in both hands and lifted it free. It was characteristically thin and elongated, not unlike the former willow branches. But it was completely unscathed by the fire, still lush green and smooth to the touch.

Dane stared, bewildered, as Sage unfurled the branch. "Was that branch . . . *inside* the tree?"

"I—I think so."

"How is that possible?"

"I don't know." Sage stood, weighing the branch in her palms. Its tip coiled beside her foot. "It feels different though," she mused. "Strange it wasn't burned." She peered even closer at the branch, lifting it up to a nearby light before waving the stem back and forth.

"Quite limber, too. I wonder if—"

Sage whipped her hand to the side. The branch sprang to life like a tree snake, slithering through the air before flicking with a resounding crack.

Dane shoved backward to avoid the whiplash. "Watch it!"

"Fascinating," said Sage. "Such strength and flexibility . . . nothing like normal willow branches."

"But how is this possible?" Dane repeated. "I'm no expert on trees, but branches usually sprout *from* the trunk, not *inside* it."

"It must have been a gift from the Elderwood tree."

Dane stared at her. "A *what?*"

"Do you have any better ideas? I did help save it, after all . . ."

"A gift?" Dane mocked. Sage nodded decisively. He rolled his eyes. "Let's ask Elder Chrysanthe. Maybe she knows why a willow branch was in an old stump."

"Perhaps. But I'll worry about that later." Sage coiled the branch into a tight loop around her waist and covered it with her shirt. Her grim expression from before had faded, her spirits heightened by her discovery.

"I heard about your Trials," Dane said. "Biophage. That's—that's wonderful."

Her face immediately brightened. "Isn't it? You should've seen the look on Elder Chrysanthe's face when I saw her after. It's just what I wanted—" She glanced at Dane and her excitement withered. "I didn't mean—your Trials—"

Dane shook his head, afraid his voice might crack if he were to speak. Seeing her enthusiasm die just looking at him . . . that brought a whole new pain. Instead he wrapped his arms around her. "You deserve it, Sage," he managed. He forced a smile. "Don't worry about me."

She returned the smile. She studied him with clouded, scrupulous eyes. Finally, she said, "Come here. I want to show you something."

She walked to the edge of the overlook, gazing out across the landscape. "Look out there."

Dane squinted through the dark. He could make out the rough shapes of the snow-capped mountains framing Mistveil lake. The night obscured the rest.

After a moment of silence, he let out a sigh. "Is this what you wanted to show me?"

"Look across the lake."

"It's great, but I've seen it before."

"Just . . . humor me, will you?"

He relented, resting his elbows on the balcony, same as he had earlier that day, after the Trials. He held his gaze forward, not wanting to look down into the dark waves below. Far below.

No, he chided himself, shoving the thoughts aside. *That's not the answer.*

You'll find a way through this, Quinn had told him. *I know you will.*

"No matter what happens," Sage said, "the waters will still flow with the gentle currents. The snowy mountaintops will still sparkle under the light of the sun. The trees will still stand tall amidst storms and mighty winds. Regardless of what happened, or of what is yet to come, the world will still be the same. We'll always have each other, through good times and bad. And we'll always find a way through it."

She placed a gentle hand on his back and Dane was surprised to find tears forming in his eyes. He blinked them away and slung his arm around her.

"Thanks," he mumbled.

"Of course." She held him at arm's length, fixing him with her sea-blue gaze. "You're not alone in this. I promise I'll do everything I can to help you find your power. And you *will* find it. It's only a matter of time."

"I hope so." Dane still had his reservations, but the confidence in her voice did wonders for his spirits.

Sage squinted up at the Elderwood. Her lips tightened into a thin line. "We should get back to the market. I'm sure they could use the help."

Quinn and Cayde had joined the others in the restoration of the market streets as Dane and Sage returned. The crowd had thinned from before, many likely having turned in for the night, but those who remained were as diligent as ever.

Sage immediately joined in and was soon swallowed by the crowd. Vilik emerged a moment later, his expression a mix of terror and childish awe.

"Is it true?" he whispered to Dane. "You *saw* Avon?"

Dane nodded silently and told Vilik what had happened.

Vilik gave a low whistle. He stared ahead, eyes glazed. "And he killed guards too? We're lucky he didn't cause more harm, if you ask me. That fire he started in the Elderwood—I thought the whole tree would burn down."

Dane recalled the frightening speed at which Avon had dispatched the guards and conjured those cosmic flares. A shiver ran down his spine. "I've never seen anyone so powerful."

"What if he attacks again? Attacks somewhere else? Vitalor can't withstand another assault like that."

"I don't know . . . but Cayde seems to have a plan."

They both stared at the ground for a long moment, letting reality sink in.

Dane broke the silence, eager to change the subject.

"Your Trials . . . did you—"

"Find my power?" Vilik shifted uncomfortably. "Geomancer," he said quickly.

Dane had to inject excitement into his voice once more. "Vilik . . . that's great! Just what you wanted." When Vilik didn't answer right away, Dane amended, "That *is* what you wanted, isn't it?"

"Yes . . . yes, it is." Vilik's mouth curved into a light smile. "I've been both dreading and dreaming for this outcome for some time. But—" He hesitated. "I heard what happened with your—well, you know. I—I don't know what—"

Dane shook his head and waved dismissively. For now, he wanted to forget his Trials ever happened. Vilik looked just as uneasy bringing it up.

"We've had a rather . . . *interesting* day today, haven't we?"

Elder Chrysanthe appeared behind them with a visibly exhausted Sage at her side. "Why don't you all get some rest. I'll handle the rest of the reconstruction. The fire looked much worse than it was; the markets took the brunt of the damage, but it's nothing we can't fix."

"But we're not done," Sage rebutted, gesturing to the crowds. Dane and Vilik nodded their agreement. "We can still help."

Elder Chrysanthe gave her an affectionate smile. "It's more important that you rest, dear child. After all, you only just finished your trials earlier today. I imagine you're exhausted." She gave Sage's shoulders a gentle squeeze. "Don't forget, you have your pledge ceremony in the morning. You'll need your rest."

Sage looked ready to argue, then huffed an exhausted sigh. "I suppose I am a bit tired."

"Very good. I've made the necessary arrangements with Patrice. She'll have a room ready for the three of you for tonight."

Then Elder Chrysanthe bid farewell.

Once she was out of earshot, Vilik let out a groan. "She got us a room with Old Lady Fern?"

Dane stifled a laugh. Patrice Fern—or Old Lady Fern, as Dane, Sage, Vilik, and all the other youth from their village liked to call her—used to be the oldest member in the village before she'd moved to Vitalor a few years ago; so old, in fact, that Dane used to think she was old enough to be his own grandfather's grandmother. For all he knew, she was the oldest person in all of Physos. According to the village rumors and gossip Dane heard throughout his youth, Old Lady Fern had built her first hut—the first of its kind in the village—on the forest floor surrounding the sapling that was now the tallest tree in his village. And since Grandfather Horas hadn't been able to travel to Vitalor in his condition, Dane and Sage had had the pleasure of Old Lady Fern's company on their trips to Vitalor until they were old enough to travel without supervision.

Despite her unfathomable age, Old Lady Fern was undoubtedly the loudest, crankiest, and most peculiar woman Dane had ever met. Most peculiar of all was her obsession with prune pies. It was no secret she craved the Vitalor delicacy above most anything else; she'd plotted her own orchard of plum trees on the forest floor of the village. Dane presumed her eventual move to Vitalor was ultimately fueled by her never-ending quest of creating the perfect prune pie.

And as far as Old Lady Fern was concerned, her quest would've been achieved years ago if not for Vilik.

"It's not *that* bad," Dane said. In all fairness, Old Lady Fern arguably ran the best inn in Vitalor. "At least it's warm."

Vilik folded his arms over his chest. "No way. I'd rather sleep *anywhere* else."

"Anywhere?" Sage asked. "Even the streets?"

Vilik brushed aside a pile of charred rubble and sat. "Right here looks great."

Sage kicked the charred wood at her feet. "Oh, quit your complaining. It's a free bed for the night. It's not our fault you nearly destroyed her orchard."

"I never—" Vilik threw his hands in the air. "She *has* to know that was an accident."

Sage bit her lip to mask a growing smile. "I'm sure she's forgotten about it by now. Come on, I'll fall asleep if we stand around much longer."

Dane trotted to Sage's side as she started away from the Elderwood. "Did you ask Elder Chrysanthe about that branch?"

Sage touched her waist, brushing her fingers against the branch. She shook her head. "Time didn't seem right. Not yet, anyway. I'll ask once everything has calmed down."

Vilik must have seen the branch before Sage concealed it again, because he rushed to her side and asked, "Now *what* is that?"

Sage told him about the branch as they made their way through the narrow back streets away from the market. Dane followed behind, eying the rows of finely crafted huts, decorated with countless ornate plants and flowers encompassing their entire exteriors. Small statues were displayed on occasional porches, people kneeling beside them. The statues were all the same: a penitent woman with long hair, hands steepled at her chest. Sage had told him the statues depicted the Mother in human form. Those kneeling beside the statues seemed to mimic Her statuesque figure; their heads bent and hands clasped, muttering prayers under their breath. They'd press a hand to the statue's forehead when finished, offering a portion of their own energy in thanks for the Mother's divine blessing.

Such practice wasn't observed much in his village. He had only ever grown up hearing and reading stories about the Mother. Part of him wondered if all of it *was* just a story. But displays like this reminded him what the Mother had done for them, of what She'd done for Physos.

They weaved through the narrow residential streets until arriving at a small clearing amongst the dense population of huts. Before them stood a stone building with long, snaking vines creeping up the exterior. A solitary light shone through the vine-covered entryway.

Dane looked up at the large sign posted above the low-hanging branches, lit by the glow from inside the inn: *The Pruned Prune.*

Sage brushed aside the branches covering the entryway. From behind a large wooden counter, a hunched, bony woman forced herself into the light. Dane found it a miracle the old woman was still living; the wrinkles in her face could have given the bark of the Elderwood tree a run for its name. Her back arched like that of a slouching tree, and her long, wisp-like limbs could have swayed in the gentlest breeze. Her dwindling wisps of wiry, white hair framed her face, only accentuating her wrinkles; a look that would have aged anyone else by decades.

Old Lady Fern's small, beady eyes darted across the room and narrowed on Dane. He shuddered inwardly. Those beady eyes always seemed to stare straight through him, like she could dissect his every thought before the thought even formed.

"Hello Ol—er—Missus Fern," said Sage.

Old Lady Fern nodded in acknowledgement.

"I know it's late, but Elder Chrysanthe—"

"No matter," the woman croaked, shuffling back toward the counter. "I hardly sleep nowadays. Are you watching my plum trees like I asked?"

"Yes, and they're all growing just fine. Even better than last year."

Old Lady Fern nodded repeatedly, mumbling to herself. She jabbed one of her bony fingers at Vilik. "You haven't let this one touch anything, have you? I don't want him touching my prunes again. You know what he did the last time I let him touch them."

"That was one time," Vilik muttered.

Sage sucked on her lip. "No, the prunes are safe. And I'm the only one who has touched them."

Old Lady Fern squinted at Sage, then her wrinkled lips curved into a smile. "Good. The Mother has done Her duty guiding me to the ingredients of my precious prune pies, but I'm still missing that secret ingredient. I can only ask so many questions before the bakers slam their doors in my face. You can understand my frustrations." She stared at Dane as she said this, beady eyes peering expectantly. Dane forced a sympathetic nod.

"But I still need my prunes. A year is too long to wait for the next Festival." She turned to Sage. "So, I thank you for watching after my trees, sugarplum."

She shuffled away from the counter and down a darkened corridor with several adjoining rooms, beckoning them with her twig-like fingers. Dane, Sage, and Vilik followed her upstairs to a moderately sized room with three small beds.

"I hope you can manage the rest on your own," she said from the doorway. Her fragile form cast a withering shadow across the floor. It reminded Dane of a barren tree in the dead of winter, rustling and creaking and planting fearful thoughts in young minds. "I'm leaving early in the morning. It's due time that baker gave me his final ingredient." She crinkled her eye in what Dane assumed was a wink, then disappeared into the corridor.

CHAPTER 7

THE MARK OF THE BIOPHAGE

Aside from a few burnt overhangs and charred tree trunks, the market street appeared largely unscathed the following morning. People were still shuttling piles of burnt rubble in and out of various market stands. Duxor was busy rummaging through the wreckage for salvageable items, shouting at the waves of children gathering displaced weapons and armor. In all, everyone seemed to be in good spirits.

"Wonderful sight, isn't it?" Elder Chrysanthe said, joining them. "People coming together in a time of crisis—there's no greater strength than that of communal unity." She inhaled deeply and turned to Sage. "Well, my dear, are you ready to pledge to the powers of a Biophage?"

Sage exhaled a steady breath. "I am."

Elder Chrysanthe led Sage into the Elderwood market, Dane and Vilik following close behind. Dane bowed his head in reverence as they passed through the damaged interior of the Elderwood trunk and entered a small tunnel on the far side of the market area. The tunnel carved through the large roots of the Elderwood, weaving in and out of the exposed sunlight much like the passage to the willow overlook, and deposited into a small enclosure where a handful of other anxious Biophage initiates stood waiting.

Twisting vines and roots—some as thick as Dane's legs, others as thin as his hair—bordered the small enclosure. Opposite them rose a tangled mass of roots reaching out from the wall like an open hand. Elder Chrysanthe guided Sage to the outstretched roots and beckoned the other initiates to do the same. Dane slid along the back wall, keeping to the shadows, not wanting to catch the attention of the initiates for fear of what they might say. Vilik slid next to him as Elder Chrysanthe addressed the small group.

"Today marks a very special occasion," she said, gaze lifting to the Elderwood branches soaring overhead. "Today you will fully embrace your power and step into a whole new world of possibility. From this day forth, you shall use your powers of the Biophage to enrich the lives of everyone around you, to grow toward a more peaceful future for generations to come. May the Mother guide you on every step of your new journey as you embrace your full potential—your true power—as a Biophage." Elder Chrysanthe looked to the initiates. "Are you prepared to fulfill your pledge and harness your power?"

Sage and the other initiates nodded silently, standing tall and proud. Elder Chrysanthe gestured to Sage with a sweeping hand.

"If you please, Sage Willows, present your stones to the Roots of Life."

Sage strode toward the tangle of roots, grasping her two energy stones in her palm. She held her hand in offering. The roots sprang to life, slithering over her palm, tightening around the stones—now pulsing with brilliant shades of green. The stones cracked, dissolving into a glowing green mist that seeped into her palm. The roots crept up the length of her forearm and circled her elbow.

Sage's face contorted, wincing as the roots solidified and tightened on her arm. But she held her composure, breaths slow and controlled, gritting her teeth through the apparent pain.

"Repeat after me," said Elder Chrysanthe. "By the grace of the Mother, I pledge to devote my power to enriching all life, from now until my dying breath."

Sage repeated each word with astounding valor, as if commanding the roots herself. The roots receded, and Sage lifted her arm into the sunlight. A small tangle of green leaves and vines was now engraved in her palm. Smaller leafy vines spread over her hand, twisting up her forearm to her elbow. When she clenched her fist, a faint green pulse surged through her veins.

"Congratulations, my dear," said Elder Chrysanthe, beaming with unrivalled pride.

Sage beamed back, then pushed her way through the other initiates to rejoin Dane and Vilik.

"That was incredible!" Vilik said. He prodded her arm. "What did it feel like?"

Sage stared at her mark, looking both perplexed and amused. "It was the strangest thing! The roots were rather constricting at first. They began to burn—but not a heat burn. It was freezing cold, like standing barefoot in a river in the middle of winter."

"So what happens now?" asked Dane.

She smiled and traced her fingers along the weaving vines. "I'll have to test my powers," she said with a smirk. "Elder Chrysanthe said she'd teach me a thing or two."

She looked ready to go on, giddy with excitement, then seemed to see through Dane's hopeful expression, glimpsing the pain underneath. They watched the rest of the ceremony in silence.

Once the last initiate received her mark, Elder Chrysanthe pulled Dane, Sage, and Vilik aside as the other initiates exited the enclosure. Her gaze looked troubled, like that of a Geomancer trying to move water.

"I know we discussed training, my dearest," she told Sage with a sigh. "But regretfully, our time today has been cut short. Cayde has requested your presence in the Elder Temple—Vilik too."

A seed of anger sprouted in Dane's stomach. What did Cayde want with Sage and Vilik? Dane had wanted to talk with them both, help them realize their powers. He couldn't stand the thought of seeing Cayde again, not after the look Quinn had given Cayde after the fight with Avon.

"What does he want?" Sage asked.

Elder Chrysanthe turned her gaze skyward. "Oh, they wouldn't say for certain. But I have a few thoughts. I presume a few questions is all we can see to your training."

"They?"

"Ah, yes. Quinn as well."

"What about me?" Dane asked, trying to control his rising hysteria. What would Quinn and Cayde want with Sage and Vilik, but not him? He gritted his teeth in defiance as he stared at the Elder, trying to avoid the obvious response.

"They did stress the importance of speaking with Sage and Vilik in particular," Elder Chrysanthe mused. She waved a dismissive hand. "I suppose they wouldn't mind. Come, I'll escort you there now."

Cayde and Quinn were both waiting by the panoramic glass wall of the temple as Elder Chrysanthe pushed open the giant triangular doors and ushered Sage, Dane, and Vilik inside.

"I'll be upstairs if you need me," Elder Chrysanthe sighed. She retreated up a spiral staircase to the second floor, displacing the barricading vines with a sweep of her hand.

Quinn glanced at Sage's arm and pulled her in for an embrace. Her eyes flicked momentarily to Dane, but as she did, her whole posture changed. Her movements turned rigid and clumsy. She hesitated, then went on asking questions about Sage's Trials—small talk. Something was off. She kept rubbing at her left eyebrow, her eye twitching beneath. She was nervous. It was as if she hadn't expected him to be here. *But why?*

"I know you all just discovered your—well, most of—er—" Her gaze drifted once more to Dane and he saw a look of pity there he hadn't seen since his Trials. While no one had said as much, he'd seen occasional glares shot his way while walking through the city, heard the mumbling undertones of conspiratorial whispers. *It's the boy with no powers,* he imagined these onlookers saying. *It's the boy who doesn't belong here.* And the look

Quinn gave him now wasn't much different. He forced himself to look away.

"I'm sorry—" Quinn mumbled. She looked to Sage and Vilik. "I meant to say Cayde and I—we'd like you—err—" her voice lowered considerably, just above a whisper. "We'd to accompany us to Evergleam. My father needs to hear—" She fell silent suddenly, and Dane could feel her watching him again.

Then he understood. *She doesn't want my help.* And he couldn't blame her. What good was the boy with no powers against a murderous man like Avon? *She doesn't need me.*

Cayde intervened in her silence. "Elder Yarrin has been our primary point of contact of late, he'll need to hear what happened so we can create a plan to stop Avon. We don't know his motives, but if history can teach us anything—that with his attack last night—other cities might be in danger. And if his strength has returned, we have to spread the word, try to stay one step ahead before he attacks again."

"We could really use the extra help," Quinn offered.

"I'm in," Sage said. "Avon's crimes here can't go unpunished. And it seems we were lucky to escape with our lives." Her stern expression brightened. "Besides, I've always wanted to visit Evergleam."

Dane's heart sank. He too had long dreamed of visiting Quinn's home city. It seemed too prime an opportunity to squander. Traveling to Evergleam also meant seeing Quinn's father, Elder Yarrin. Dane had always thought very highly of the Elder and his insight. Elder Yarrin might even know why Dane didn't find his powers. Now he only needed to convince Quinn and Cayde he was worth taking along.

"Good. Wonderful." Quinn smiled, but it looked forced. There was something she wasn't telling them—something they didn't want to hear. Her gaze flicked between Sage and Vilik. "The both of you were among the top performers at this year's Trials, that's why we need your help. What we're asking of you won't be easy, but—"

"And what about me?" Dane blurted before he could stop himself. The thought sounded selfish, stealing focus from Sage's and Vilik's accomplishments in the arena, but he was tired of Quinn's pity, of her deception. He needed answers.

She paused too long for Dane's liking. "I—err—of course! We need your help too."

"Why?" Dane countered. He could have fabricated a response to indulge his fragile sense of self-worth, but he didn't want to. He wanted to hear it from her.

Quinn looked taken aback, startled even. "Wh—what do you mean?" she stammered.

"Why do you need my help?" The words came out more desperate than he'd intended, but he didn't stop. "Why do you need me?"

She hesitated, watching him with wide, petrified eyes. Dane stared back, hoping—pleading—for her answer. But she said nothing, her body deflating.

"Of course you can join." Cayde said, intervening in her stead yet again. "You're the only one who saw what Avon can do first-hand. That information is more valuable than you think." Cayde put his huge hand on Dane's shoulder, but Dane didn't shrug away. The conviction in Cayde's voice bolstered Dane's spirits more than he thought possible. He had to admit it was a little reassuring. "We *do* need you, Dane," Cayde continued. "We need all the help we can get to end Avon's tyranny."

Dane wanted to argue, to ask why Quinn had failed to produce any response, any reason why she needed him, but he forced the urge down. "Then how are *we* supposed to stop Avon?" he asked, clinging to this new purpose. "Even together, he's just too powerful for us."

"Let's just say that we have the right—er—resources," Cayde said carefully.

Though unsatisfied with Cayde's insubstantial response, it didn't change the fact that Dane wanted to go with them. There was nothing left for him in Vitalor, only painful memories. And at least fighting back against Avon was a noble cause.

"So you'll join us, then?" Cayde prompted.

Dane paused a moment, feigning indecision, then nodded.

Quinn expelled a heavy breath. "Great—good—yes, Dane, I—*we*—need you with us." She glanced at Cayde, her eyes expressing her appreciation.

She turned to Vilik. "Vilik? Will you come with us?"

The Geomancer hadn't said a word since Quinn's initial request. Now his mouth was a hard line, his gaze unreadable. After a moment's silence, he shook his head.

Dane recoiled as if he'd been struck. He stared at his friend in disbelief. "What? You're not coming?"

"No," Vilik mumbled. "I—I can't."

"Of course you can," Sage exclaimed. "This is important, Vilik. There are other lives at stake too. We need you."

Vilik pressed his fists to his temples. "I know. I just—there's something I have to do first."

"I don't understand," Dane said. "You don't want to—"

"Of course I *want* to! But—" Vilik heaved a sigh and combed his fingers through his dark hair. "This is my chance to meet my family. My *real* family—the ones who will accept me for being a Geomancer. My parents raised me to believe the rest of my family is full of bad people. I need to know my parents were wrong about them, that I still have family out there who cares for me, who will accept me. After I pledge my power in Stonehelm I—I want to stay and find them. If I don't take this chance now, I know I'll regret it forever."

Dane wanted to argue, to tell Vilik that he had to go with them to Evergleam. He and Vilik finally had the chance to travel to a new city together like they'd always dreamed. But he knew how important this was to Vilik, finding his real family—it was all Vilik ever talked about. As much as it pained him, Dane couldn't take that away.

"Vilik . . . are you certain?" Sage asked, crestfallen. "It won't be the same without you."

Vilik looked at her, solemn but resolute. "I'm certain. I need to do this. But I won't take long. Once I find them, I'll return here and join you. Promise."

"Very well." She forced a smile. "But know that you'll always have family here, too."

"I was hoping you too would join us after pledging your power, but we respect your decision, Vilik," said Cayde. "Seek out Elder Rogdar in Stonehelm and tell him what happened here. The city may be a defensive stronghold, but no place is safe from Avon now. The more prepared they are, the better."

Vilik nodded. "I will."

"When do you have to leave?" Dane asked, suddenly aware of their limited time together.

"Midday tomorrow, with the other Geomancer initiates. It'll be safer in a group, in case we encounter anything . . . odd." He smirked. "What, miss me already?"

"Good luck to you, Vilik," said Quinn, stealing Vilik away with a light embrace. "I do hope we'll see you again after you find your family." She turned to Dane and Sage, urgency returning to her voice. "As for you two, we'll be leaving before sunrise. It's a two-day journey to Evergleam. We won't make it if we don't leave early. And pack warm clothing. This time of year, the mountain pass will—"

"Leaving so soon?" Elder Chrysanthe descended the staircase behind them and strode through the hall. A hint of fear dwelled beneath her steady voice.

"I'm afraid we must, Elder," Quinn said automatically. "My father needs to know what happened. And it—err—may be some time before we are able to return." She shared a meaningful glance with the Elder, then added, "You know that as well as I do if we are to prevail."

"Of course I understand, but—why, you've only just arrived!" Elder Chrysanthe sputtered. "What if Avon returns? How will Vitalor fare then?"

"We didn't notice he was in the city until the market went up in flames," Cayde said. "The guards are on high alert—you said so yourself. Besides, Dane and I only saw two other men with him. If he wanted to return, he would've brought more. I think he meant to go unnoticed, escape before anyone could stop him."

"He's right," said Quinn. "And even if he did return with a larger force, there's not much we could do to help. If Avon *wanted* to go unnoticed, he'll know not to return anytime soon, not when the entire city is on lookout. We must spread word to prevent further attacks and stop him before more innocent lives are lost. He grows more powerful every day. We have to stay one step ahead if we ever hope to stop him. I'm sorry, Elder, but we don't have a choice."

Elder Chrysanthe pressed a hand to her forehead and released a long, reluctant sigh. "If you must, then you have my blessing on your journey to Evergleam. At least let me send someone with you. With Avon on the loose, I have plenty of capable Biophages who—"

"That won't be necessary, Elder," Cayde said. "We already have our Biophage."

Elder Chrysanthe furrowed her brow and stared blankly at Cayde. Her eyes bulged when the realization hit her. She whirled to face Sage.

"You're staying, aren't you, my dear?" Elder Chrysanthe said, a new panic riddling her voice. "Don't tell me you're leaving."

Sage merely stared at her feet, pale-faced.

Elder Chrysanthe shook her head, mouth agape. "But I—you're supposed to stay here and learn to use your powers with other Biophages. You haven't had proper training! I—I need you here! There's so much more I—"

"I know," Sage muttered. "I know I'm supposed to stay and learn about my power here, but I feel I'm meant to do this."

"She's certainly proven herself worthy," Quinn offered. "You saw her quick thinking during the fire, not to mention her Trials. She's brilliant. We need her with us."

Elder Chrysanthe ignored Quinn and stared at Sage, eyes swimming with longing and disbelief. "Sage . . . you really wish to leave? Tell me it's not true."

Sage nodded feebly. "I've wanted to see the world for as long as I can remember. This is my chance. I can help more people than if I stayed." She stared at the ground. "I—I hope you can understand."

Elder Chrysanthe merely stared, horror-stricken, for a long moment. Finally, she offered a soft smile. "I felt the same way at your age, my dear." She let out a reluctant sigh. "Yes, I do understand. And I suppose we have the rest of the day to begin on your training. But promise me you'll return as soon as you're able. You've done a great deal for this city and its people, but there's still so much more you can become."

Sage looked up as if a heavy burden had been lifted from her shoulders. "Of course, Elder. I promise. And I'll return as soon as I can. We all will."

"*All* of you?"

Elder Chrysanthe's eyes narrowed. She stared at Dane, her gaze scrutinizing. With the mere inflection of her voice, she had placed him right back in the arena, moments from the stone warrior's sword cleaving into him. Though the rest of the city seemed to have forgotten what happened at his Trials—at least momentarily—Elder Chrysanthe still regarded him with disdain. He'd created a disturbance in her perfect city, a blight in her sacred Trials.

"Dane saw what Avon could do with his own eyes," Cayde interjected. "That's more than you or anyone else can say about him. We need him."

Elder Chrysanthe's gaze softened. She turned to Quinn. "I must oversee the progress of the Elderwood market restoration. May the Mother bless you on your journey." Her eyes flicked to Sage. "Come see me once you're through here."

Sage nodded, sparking a smile from Elder Chrysanthe before the Elder retreated from the temple.

Dane, still reeling from the look Elder Chrysanthe had given him, turned his attention back to Quinn and Cayde. Quinn had that same pitying, sympathetic look in her eyes, but Cayde stepped in front of her. "Ignore what Elder Chrysanthe said— about you joining us. What happened to you in the arena surprised everyone. As the Vitalor elder, she feels responsible to some degree. But trust me, you *are* needed here."

Dane wished he could believe Cayde. But he couldn't forget the way Elder Chrysanthe had looked at him, like he was inferior in every way. He feigned a smile. "Of course."

Quinn clapped her hands together. "That's all for now. Cayde and I have other matters to attend to, so you can enjoy the rest of your day in Vitalor. Remember to pack this evening and to bring warm clothing—we'll be spending the first night in the woods near the mountain pass. Meet us near the East Gate before sunrise."

৽ ৶

They returned to the Pruned Prune that evening. Old Lady Fern was nowhere to be seen, but their beds had been made with fresh linens. A welcoming aroma hung the air, that of freshly baked pies. Soon enough, Dane dozed off.

That night, Dane dreamt of his Trials. He was in the Trials Arena, but it was nothing like he remembered. The ground was pitch black, smoking tendrils of fog seeping upward like rising smoke. The crowd roared around him, but instead of people, a sea of dim lights occupied the stands, all glowing shades of orange and purple. But they were all eclipsed by a pulsing white light emanating from the center of the arena pit.

Dane walked toward it. The light brightened with every step until his entire vision was encompassed by its glow.

A hand appeared from the light, reaching toward him. Dane extended his own. He was so close. He could almost touch it. Then a face appeared; a face that was completely foreign, yet somehow familiar. He squinted as the light continued to overpower his vision. He could almost make it out. The face was calling to him, calling his name. No words came, but he felt the voice more than heard it, reverberating inside him, screaming his name ever louder.

The light flashed, forcing his eyes shut. When he opened them again, the face had disappeared. The light dwindled away into darkness, leaving only the dim lights of the crowd. Just before everything faded into darkness, a faint whisper sliced through the silence.

Your time will come.

Sleep eluded Dane for the rest of the night. He lay still, staring at the ceiling boards, listening to them settle and groan as night pressed onward. He couldn't stop thinking about the dream. It was more real than any dream he'd ever had: the lights, the crowds, the hand, the mysterious face. It had felt as if he was actually there, wherever that had been. And the final words still echoed through his mind, a trapped flame trying to ignite. *Your time will come.* It had to be a message from the Mother. He'd heard of people having peculiar dreams, claiming the Mother had blessed them with Her divine presence. Part of him wanted to believe it, if not merely to offer explanation for the dream in the first place. He tried convincing himself the dream was a product of his exhaustion. After all, he'd had his Trials and encountered Avon only the day before. But another part of him couldn't help but wonder if it meant something more.

His thoughts soon diverted to the terrifying encounter with Avon and the shrill, guttural shrieks of the dismembered guards. The smell of their seared bodies still clung to his nose. Eventually he pushed those thoughts away, making way for memories of his Trials. His heart ached at how Elder Chrysanthe had scrutinized him, at the look on Quinn's face as he fled the arena. They saw him as an outcast, the only initiate in the history of Physos who hadn't been worthy enough to discover his power in the Trials of Power. When he'd finally managed to sweep those thoughts aside, all he could think of was Quinn.

He abandoned his pitiful attempt at sleep and glanced around the room. Sage had uprooted her blankets and was curled in a tight ball, snoring loudly. Vilik lay stiff as a plank, face buried in his pillow. Dane crept out of the room and exited the inn.

A calming mist hung over the city as he traversed the deserted streets. He had walked through Vitalor at night only a few times before; but now, watching the green luminescent lights flicker all along the market street, the city was more serene than ever. A few merchants were still repairing the burnt walls and collapsed ceilings of their market stands. Rogue grasses and vines had already begun to sprout through the thin layer of ash that still covered the stone street. The sky was void of the suffocating smoke from the night before. The city was healing.

A smile tugged at Dane's lips as he approached Duxor's shop. Despite the nonexistent roof and walls charred with soot, the shop still invoked fond memories. He recalled the first time he'd seen the shop. It had been his third year attending the Trials Festival. He and Vilik had been meandering through the market when they happened across a low stone building. Racks of ornate armor and weapons had been displayed out front, all too inviting for their young and eager minds. Through the open windows, the walls boasted rows of small forging hammers, each radiating a dim, colorful haze.

But entering Duxor's shop had been no easy feat. To the left of the entrance was a cramped, disorganized market stall where an ostentatious man shouted maniacally, gripping fistfuls of bright orange fruits attached to wiry stems, swinging them dangerously close to passing market goers. To the right was a miserable excuse for a market stall, only considered as such by its owner: a ragged, screeching elderly woman whose name Dane so often forgot. Dane had accidentally glanced at her once, which since had led her to believe Dane was eternally interested in what she had to offer. Beneath the shamble of loose sticks and stray billowing canvases, the woman would sit eagerly, vigorously stroking one of several small, ugly rodents skittering around in a jumble of twigs that loosely resembled a cage, ready to pounce in Dane's direction should he wander too close.

As Dane had quickly learned, to enter Duxor's shop unscathed, one simply kept their head down and plowed forward. He would shoulder past the screeching woman and her hairy monstrosities, simultaneously evading the man's swinging orange fruits before stumbling through the doorway into Duxor's craftsmithing shop.

Now, Dane was almost sad to see that the two flanking stalls had burned down in the fire. Granted they had been unpleasant, and by no means profitable for Duxor's business, but they were a part of his memories here, part of his history.

Dane gave the busted doorframe a gentle tap and peered through the doorway. The small, stone building was lit only by the orange glow emanating from the forge in the far corner of the room. Duxor was filtering through piles of the rubble, muttering obscenities under his breath.

"I like what you've done with the place," Dane said.

"Oh, didn't see yeh there, Dane." Duxor straightened his pants around his hefty waist. "Shop's a mess, ain't it?"

Dane looked around. "Sure is."

Duxor let out a crisp chuckle. "I've been meanin' to thank yeh for savin' me the other night. If yeh didn't come to help . . . well, I'd be nothin' but ash and bone."

Dane shrugged. "You'd have done the same."

Duxor smiled briefly, then wiped his palms on his blackened apron. "What are yeh doin' up this time of night anyhow?"

"Couldn't sleep," Dane said.

"I saw yeh gatherin' yer things earlier. Are yeh headed somewhere?"

"Evergleam. We're leaving in the morning."

"Ah." Duxor stroked his beard. "Off with those two who came to the Trials, are yeh? I 'member talkin' with that Cayde fella' the other day. I made sure to talk yeh up, let 'im know who he was dealing with." Duxor barked a laugh, then gave Dane a longing glance. "I s'pose you're here to say your goodbyes, then."

Dane nodded. "I wanted to thank you for—well, for everything."

"Oh, hush now. Yer the one who deserves thanks! The shop's had more success than ever with yer help." Duxor scanned the improving remains of his shop and sighed remorsefully. "I'll miss yeh around here—might even have to train up a couple more runts to take yer place. I reckon I'll need a good four or five of 'em to make up for it." He let out hearty laugh. "Just promise yeh'll at least come visit when yer in Vitalor again. I want to hear all about yer travels. There are some mighty good craftsmiths out there—none better than me, o'course."

"I will," Dane said. He wrapped his arms around Duxor—never an easy feat—then turned to leave.

"One more thing," Duxor called out. He scratched the back of his neck. "I—err—don't know what yer feelin' right now—

about yer Trials an' all—but know that I still believe in yeh. Others do too. Yer not alone out there, and yeh never will be. Remember that."

Dane smiled back at his mentor and ducked out of the shop. He replayed Duxor's parting words as he meandered back through the streets to the inn. *You're not alone out there, and you never will be.* He still didn't know what to do about his power. At the moment, it was easier not to waste thought on it. But Duxor was right—there were still people who cared about him: Sage, Vilik, Duxor, Quinn, and even Cayde. And Evergleam was at least a start. The path ahead was clouded in uncertainty, but his friends were going to help him through it. It was only a matter of time. It had to be.

Soon enough, he closed his eyes and drifted off to sleep.

୨ ଓ

Dane woke feeling rejuvenated despite his late-night excursion. The sky was still dark, but the air was crisp and cool, and thin waves of morning light peeked over the distant mountains. He prodded Sage and Vilik awake and they gathered their belongings. After bidding farewell to Vilik, who promised he'd see them again soon, Dane and a groggy Sage parted for the East Gate where Quinn and Cayde were waiting for them.

"You both ready for an adventure?" said Quinn, tightening the straps of her pack, a youthful smile on her lips.

Dane returned the smile, nodding succinctly. Sage grumbled something incomprehensible.

"Wonderful." Quinn reached in her pack and pulled out two loaves of bread. "Here, eat these." She tossed them to Dane and Sage. "We have a full day ahead of us. You'll want to keep your energy up if we're to make it to the mountain pass before dark."

With that she turned and passed through the archway leading out of Vitalor, the others following in her wake, their sights set on the City of Light.

CHAPTER 8

THE GREEN-EYED GIRL

"Remind me again why we had to leave so early?" Sage said, shielding her eyes and glancing toward the snow-capped mountains as the first rays of sunlight illuminated the sky. She paused and gazed longingly at Vitalor far behind them.

Quinn, leading several paces ahead, called back, "I wanted to leave before the new Aquadorian and Luminarus initiates." She slowed and motioned to the stone path they were following. "This path leads to Mistveil if you stay along the lake, but it also splits and leads to Evergleam through the mountain pass. If we waited until sunrise, the road would be crowded with initiates traveling to their respective cities to pledge their powers—Vilik will be doing the same, but he'll be headed South to Stonehelm. In any case, it's best we travel alone—less chance of being seen."

"Where the road splits," Dane mused. "That's where we'll follow the path through the mountains?"

Quinn gave him a nurturing smile. "Exactly. We'll set up camp once off the main path."

Sage mumbled something between mouthfuls of bread, then, reinvigorated, trotted to Quinn's side as they continued.

Dane stared out across Mistveil Lake on his left. The path ahead sloped downward with the descending cliffside, only a short distance from the lake's gentle shores. To his right, a sprawling grass meadow preluded a dense thicket of trees back dropped by the looming, snow-capped slopes of the Aurora Mountains. Despite the storm of emotions still swirling in his mind, Dane allowed himself to relax as he gazed out at the beautiful scenery before him, the cool, morning breeze wafting through his hair and clothes.

No matter what happens, Dane thought, recalling what Sage had said to him before his Trials, *the waters will still flow with the gentle currents. The snowy mountaintops will still sparkle under the light of the sun. The trees will still stand tall amidst the storms and mighty winds. No matter what happens, the world will still be the same . . .*

Once the path plateaued along the lake shore, Dane turned to look at the cliff from which they had just come. He nearly stumbled as he took the sight in.

Vitalor was perched atop the cliff high above the southern-most point of the lake, completely dwarfed by the towering Elderwood tree. He had thought the tree was massive before, but now, viewing it from the backside, Dane was utterly dumbfounded. The giant roots that wove through the city were mere twigs compared to the tangle of colossal roots digging in and out of the cliffside, stretching to either side of the cliff face— nearly as wide as the lake itself—before plunging far beneath the water's surface.

"Is that Evergleam?"

Sage was pointing to the farthest peak in the Aurora Mountains where a distant building reflected the morning sun.

Quinn nodded. "It's hard to tell from this distance, but the reflection is coming from Evergleam Castle." When she looked back, her eyes were sparkling. "I'll show you around once we arrive. My room is on the highest floor. The view of the city is breathtaking."

Dane's heart raced as she spoke. For a moment, he was at his first Trials Festival again, listening to Quinn talk about her home and her city. Her joy and adoration had been palpable then. Even now—ten years later—her voice still carried the same elation.

An inexplicable throb of sadness tightened in his chest. They had been so close then. He had grown so fond of her company that he imagined spending every day with her, talking and laughing as they shared their powers and explored their world of wonder together. But now that dream couldn't be further from reality.

Dane let his gaze slide down to the base of the mountain, which seemed to merge with the thick layer of fog that hung over Mistveil at the far end of the lake.

"How far is Mistveil from Evergleam?" Dane asked, recalling the excitement he'd felt that first day in Vitalor. "I'd love to visit there after we meet with Elder Yarrin."

"Not far at all," said Cayde. "There's a path leading from Evergleam to the East Bridge of Mistveil—if it weren't for the occasional snow cover, you could walk to Mistveil and back before morning's half over."

"Are any other cities in such close proximity?"

Cayde stared ahead, running a hand through his hair. Quinn said, "Stonehelm *used* to be close to Starspire—the city of the Cosmonauts. That was before Avon destroyed Starspire and left it in ruin. Most other cities are several days' walk apart. But from what you've told me, the distance between Evergleam and Mistveil seems quite similar to that of Vitalor and your village."

Dane nodded speculatively, then halted and whirled to Sage.

"The village! What about Grandfather? We didn't tell him about our Trials, or that we're leaving, or—"

Sage twisted her mouth to one side. "It's . . . taken care of." Her face contorted in a pained expression. She attempted a smile, but it looked more like a grimace. "I asked Elder Chrysanthe before we left. She said she'd send Old Lady Fern to notify Grandfather. We could have gone ourselves, but as Quinn said, we'd waste too much time walking to the village and back, especially if we are to stop Avon before it's too late." She paused, worry lines creasing her forehead. "He'll understand, won't he? He was our age too once. He should know what it's like to discover—" She stole a worried glance at Dane. "Well . . . to start life on your own."

Dane nodded and looked at his feet. "Yes, he'll understand," he repeated.

They continued onward, only the sound of their pattering footsteps disturbing the natural ambiance around them, until Vitalor was no larger than an acorn in the distance. But Mistveil and Evergleam seemed no closer.

Quinn broke the silence. "Sage, I've been wondering . . . Cayde and I watched your other two trials, but how did you complete the Trial of the Observer? I always love hearing how others succeeded."

Sage rubbed the back of her neck. "I didn't think I could do it at first," she said. "I was so caught up trying to decipher the riddle, I didn't see the room dimming until I could barely read. Eventually, I became so lost in thought I almost didn't notice that one of the bowls had tilted open. I was so confused until I looked down at my hands—I must have clenched my fists and buried them into the dirt on the table without thinking—but there were small vines sprouting from the ground, raising one side of the bowl. When I released my grip, the bowl fell back. I tried it again, clenching the dirt with my hands, and concentrated on the same bowl. Sure enough, the little vines came back and tilted the bowl up. The first one had a prune underneath, so I did the same to the other bowls until I found the energy stone." She exhaled as if she'd just experienced the trial again. "I'm nervous just thinking about it."

"Fascinating," Quinn said. "I was wondering if that's how Biophages did it."

Sage broke into a fit of giggles. "I wish I could've seen Vilik's though. He was so frustrated by the riddle he accidentally smashed three of the bowls at once." She let out an infectious laugh, then added, "What about you, Quinn? How did you complete yours?"

"Mine? Oh, it was nothing special really."

"Nothing special?" Cayde blurted with wild enthusiasm. "It was incredible! Can I tell it?" Quinn shrugged and gave Cayde a small nod.

Cayde beamed. "She's sitting there trying to decipher the riddle when she notices the lights dimming—I didn't notice the lights myself for quite some time either—but she notices the lights, glances at the table, and just stands there! She waits until the room is pitch black—can't see a thing. Then she focuses her hands toward the center of the table, and the smallest flicker of light appears. Mind you, the energy stones emit a faint gravitational field, pulling energy toward them at all times. It's impossible to see on your own, but with that small flicker of light in the darkest setting, you can see the light pulled in by the energy stone in close proximity. Brilliantly, Quinn moves the little light over each bowl, waiting for that gravitational pull. Sure enough, there was the energy stone."

Cayde let out a satisfactory sigh. "I wish I could've seen it. The Elders in attendance were baffled when they first heard— your father had the proudest smile I'd ever seen. Elder Chrysanthe was speechless!"

Quinn's cheeks had flushed red. "I'm sure it wasn't *that* exciting."

Cayde stopped and turned to her. "Quinn, it was incredible. You can't keep cutting yourself short. What you did had never been done before. You were truly remarkable."

Sage nodded vigorously in agreement with Cayde. Quinn's blush deepened.

Dane feigned a smile, but there was nothing behind it. He had always thought Quinn was brilliant, even for someone of her background. Her other trials had been nothing short of remarkable.

Dane fell behind as Quinn, Sage, and Cayde reminisced on their Trials while comparing the marks on their arms. Watching them reminded Dane of the first time he'd ever seen the Trials: the pure, consuming awe in everything the Trials had to offer, the tantalizing prospect of who he would one day become.

It had been nearly ten years ago, his first day at the Trials Festival. Before attending the festivities in the arena, Dane had been drawn to the Elderwood market, the bustling communal marketplace inside the trunk of the Elderwood tree. Like any children his age, Dane had stared in absolute wonder as he tried to comprehend the enormity of the massive tree while staring up into its hollowed interior.

It was also where he'd first seen a mark of power. A man in the marketplace had pulled a dying flower from his pocket, displayed it to the children massed around him. He caressed the flower with his right hand, inducing a blooming wave of orange into its petals, ushering in a collective gasp from the children.

The man's sleeve had rolled up then, exposing a tangle of vines that spread up his forearm and disappeared beneath the sleeve. He had worried for the man then, confused why real vines were constricting the man's arm, only to realize the vines were etched into the man's skin.

Captivated by the mystery of the strange markings and invigorated with energy like the man's rejuvenated flower, Dane had started searching the hands and arms of other citizens from afar. To his surprise, nearly every adult walking past bore the same markings.

Most people appeared to be marked by the familiar vines, though no two markings were identical. The few without the vines had different markings entirely, from twisting rivers to swirling gusts of wind. He even saw one woman with the marking of a colorful aurora radiating from her elbow to her fingers.

That was when Dane collided into something and was sent sprawling to the ground. He clutched his head to remedy the sudden onslaught of dizziness, trying to comprehend what force had just thrown him down, when a small, pale hand extended down to him.

A young girl stood over him. She looked only a few years older than he, with her head cocked to one side, gazing curiously down with luminous green eyes. Sunlight shone from behind her, nearly blinding Dane as it shimmered through her dark brown hair.

"I'm terribly sorry!" she asked. "Are you all right?"

"I was—err—vines—and rivers—" Dane stuttered, still stupefied by his sudden twist of circumstance.

The girl laughed and reached for his limp hand, pulled him to his feet.

"I must have bumped you harder than I thought," she giggled. "What were you doing?"

Dane gestured to his arm, running his finger up and down its length, and pointed to the arms of people passing by. To his surprise, the girl's face lifted in understanding.

"Oh, you're curious about the mark? Father says that's what happens to everyone after their Trials of Power."

"Yes, those marks . . . what are they for?" Dane said, the excitement returning to his voice. "And what are the Trials of Power?"

"You don't *know*?" the girl asked, astonished, as if she'd never even considered the idea that someone hadn't heard of these Trials of Power. "That's the reason everyone gathers here! This is the Trials Festival!" She gestured her arms skyward and twirled in place before returning her gaze to Dane.

"Every year, people journey to Vitalor to watch and celebrate the Trials of Power. Then, after the Festival, there's a special ceremony at each of the energy wells. That's how people receive their marks and are finally able to control their powers. It's so exciting, isn't it?"

Enthralled by her unbridled enthusiasm, Dane nodded his head vigorously in response.

"Energy wells?" he asked. "What are those?"

"You really don't know very much, do you?" the girl said, furrowing her brow and cocking her head with the same curious expression she had met him with. "That's fine! I don't mind." She straightened proudly. "Father says I'm quite good at talking. But . . . it *is* a bit hard to explain. Here, give me your hand." Dane obliged, and the girl's brows furrowed with concentration as she splayed his fingers wide. She traced a finger along his palm. "Father says the energy wells are like a lake—your palm—and people are the lake's rivers—your fingers. One river can never take all the water from the lake, otherwise the lake would dry up, and the river would overflow. But if each river only takes the water it needs to continue flowing and nourish its lands, then the lake will always stay full and supply all rivers with the water they need." She paused and stared upward, tapping a finger to her lips. "At least, I think that's what he says . . ." She waved a dismissive hand. "But there are eight energy wells spread throughout Physos, one in each capital city."

Dane pushed a hand through his tangle of hair. "Does that mean Vitalor is a capital city? What is its energy well?"

The girl adorned a wide, toothy grin. "You're standing in it," she said plainly.

Dane stared at the girl, perplexed. He opened his mouth to speak, wanting to question her candid response, but paused when she craned her head back and stared upward.

"The Elderwood tree . . ." he gasped. He watched as she gestured to the crowds and markets nestled in the massive tree interior.

"The energy wells can take any form," she continued, "as long as they're connected to nature. The energy well where I'm from—Evergleam—is a giant ice crystal filled with spectacular auroras. Here, like this—"

She took a step closer and pulled a small gem from around her neck, holding it into the light. It was a tiny crystal, speckled with green, pink, and yellow auroras swirling harmoniously inside, glowing with soft, soothing light.

"Each capital city has a different energy well, but Father hasn't discussed what they all are yet. One day he'll tell me. He always says they'll be important when I'm older." She gave a wistful sigh, then straightened as if remembering something important.

"I'm sorry, how could I be so rude?" she said. "Here I am talking away, and I don't even know your name." She stared expectantly at Dane, her eyes soft with a welcoming glow.

"Oh—I'm Dane Willows. What's yours?"

The girl stuck out one of her pale hands and grabbed Dane's.

"Quinn. Quinn Evergleam. It's nice to meet you, Dane," she said. "Now that that's taken care of, I *must* know . . . how is it that you've never noticed the marks before? I thought everyone knew that—I don't mean to say that you—err . . ." She paused, struggling for words. "Don't people use their powers where you're from?"

In truth, Dane had never noticed the strange marks on anyone from his village, nor had he known to look for them. There weren't many people in his village to begin with. When he and Sage would go about their daily duties, most of the adults were busy tending to their crops and fields. Not only that, but they also wore long sleeves and gloves while working, so Dane never had reason to suspect any strange marks in the first place.

Certainly, Grandfather must have the markings too, he thought. *But why doesn't he use his powers? Or does he, and we've never noticed? Do the markings fade away?*

"Dane? People do use their powers where you're from, don't they?" Quinn repeated gently.

Dane's cheeks flushed as he realized he'd just been standing there mute. He lifted his shoulders.

"Sometimes it can be hard to notice," she said with a smile. "Do you . . . have any other questions?"

"So . . . what are the Trials, and why—"

Before he could finish his thought, a great smile broke across Quinn's face. She grabbed his hand, gripping tighter than before.

"Come with me," she beamed. "I'll show you!"

Dane hurried behind as Quinn pulled him into the crowd. She led him out of the Elderwood Market and into the bustling city streets, weaving through the masses as she ventured forward with uncharacteristic silence.

"So, Quinn, how do you know—"

A thunderous roar drowned the rest of his words.

Dane nearly crashed into Quinn as he looked up, his vision suddenly eclipsed by a giant shadow. Quinn had led him to an enormous rounded structure, filled to the brim with jeering, jubilant crowds.

"This . . ." Quinn said, staring dreamily at the structure, "is the Trials Arena. This is why everyone comes to the Festival every year; to watch and cheer as the new initiates discover their powers." She cupped her hands to her heart, swaying gently from side to side. "I can't wait to discover my power when I'm old enough. I hope I have the same power as my Father. He's a Luminarus—my mother too." Quinn paused, staring at Dane's perplexed expression. "That means they draw their power from light. You know . . . sunlight, auroras, reflections? It's quite majestic." Quinn's eyes sparkled as she spoke. "What about you, Dane? What powers do you hope to have?"

What powers do I hope to have? Grandfather Horas had told him many tales of the founders, how they'd use their powers to enrich the world and defeat the corrupt founder Lussiek. But his grandfather had never told him the names of the powers themselves.

"I suppose you don't actually know what powers there are?" Quinn guessed, eyeing him curiously. "Because you don't—" she stuttered, shifting her eyes to the ground as she twisted her fingers in her robes. She shook her head, as if clearing her thoughts. "Come, let me show you."

"Yes, please!" Dane shouted, far louder than he anticipated.

Quinn gave a nervous smile, then took his hand and led him into the arena.

The large crowds slowed their forward movement, but Dane could still see what they were all cheering for. Beyond the rows of stone steps where people sat pumping their arms and shouting in jubilation, two figures stood in the middle of a large, sunken pit.

Quinn led Dane through the crowd until the entire arena pit was in view. His eyes nearly bulged from their sockets. On one side of the pit stood a thin young man, arms raised and poised for battle. On the other side stood a hulking, emotionless warrior made entirely of roots and vines. The warrior brandished a barbed stone sword in one hand, and a massive wooden shield in the other. The young man wielded nothing but his bare fists, yet he stood resolute, ready to face the imposing figure before him.

A horn blared overhead. The earth beneath the root warrior suddenly sank inward, swallowing up its feet and rooting it in place. The next moment, the young man sprinted forward and lunged for the warrior's sword. With a deafening crack that echoed through the entire arena, the young man dislodged the sword from the warrior, taking its hand with it. Without missing a stride, he leapt for the closest wall. A slab of earth jutted out the instant the young man's foot hit the rocky surface and, thrusting off the newly formed foothold, he twisted and launched himself into the air, stone sword raised high above his head.

In one swift, expertly executed movement, the young man brought the sword down, plunging it through the top of the warrior's head, sending its body crumbling to pieces as he deftly planted both feet on the ground.

Dane stared, his gaze transfixed at the arena's center, and hollered with the crowd as the young man walked to the edge of the arena pit, picked up a stone-shaped object on the pedestal there, and thrust both hands into the air: one hand showcasing the peculiar stone, and the other still gripping the warrior's sword.

"How did he *do* that?" Dane shouted, trying to raise his voice above the roars of the crowd as the man trotted out of the arena.

"He discovered he's a Geomancer!" Quinn shouted back, jumping in place and clapping her hands fervently. "He used his powers to anchor the warrior's feet, so he could take its sword! Spectacular, isn't it?"

They continued to watch in excitement, Dane unable to divert his eyes from the wondrous displays of power as Quinn narrated beside him. The next man, an Aquadorian ("they draw power from water"), trapped his root warrior in a small pond after turning the water's surface—and the warrior's legs—to ice. One woman suspended parts of her warrior midair, slowly pulling apart its limbs until it crumbled to the ground ("she's a Gravitus—she manipulates gravity"). The final initiate was a pale, scrawny young man who tricked his root warrior into charging headfirst at him. As he jumped out of the way, he raised a hand and emitted a flash of light. The dazed warrior collided with the arena wall before collapsing into a heap of rubble ("And he's a Luminarus! I told you it was incredible!").

The crowds dissipated after the final initiate raised his small stone, moving the celebrations from the arena into the streets.

"That was unbelievable!" Dane gushed as they flooded into the streets. "And this happens every year? And one day *we* get to do that?"

"Of course! Everyone takes part in the Trials of Power," she said. "Father says you must be eighteen years old to participate. I can't remember why—something about being mature enough to handle your powers—or maybe . . ."

Quinn paused and noiselessly moved her lips for several moments, lost in her own thoughts.

Dane pondered what she'd said. Though disappointed he'd have to wait so long for his chance, Dane made a silent vow that he would learn everything he could about the different powers and return to the Festival every year. He might even get to see Quinn again.

"Do you come here every year?" he asked her.

She blinked from her stupor. "Yes, I have to—well, I don't *have* to." She sighed. "Not that it's an inconvenience, of course. It's just—my Father has to come, to represent Evergleam, and I love the Festival so much that I always join him. During our journey here, he teaches me stories of how the founders discovered their powers, how they shared their powers with the people of Physos, and—"

"You know about the founders too?" Dane blurted.

Quinn gave him a funny look and tilted her head to one side.

"Of course. How—how do *you* know about the founders?"

"My grandfather tells me those stories all the time! My favorite is the one where Founder Arkon and Founder Rodran fight against that—" He stopped abruptly, his eyes growing wide. "Wait—does that mean Founder Rodran . . . was a *Geomancer*?" Quietly, he added, "It all makes sense now."

Quinn laughed and nodded her approval. "I take it you like Founder Rodran? Did you know that his people often called him by an entirely different—Father!"

She stopped abruptly and ran to greet a tall, bearded man walking toward them.

Dane couldn't help but notice the intricate robes the man wore; a thick, wooly cloak, adorned with many small gems, similar to the one Quinn wore as a necklace, and laced with many colorful aurora patterns. He also had one of the strange aurora marks on his right arm.

"I was wondering where you had run off to," the man said, kneeling down to embrace his daughter. Despite his intimidatingly large cloak and scruffy brown beard, the man's smile was warm and comforting. His eyes glistened with the same piercing green as Quinn's.

He lifted his eyebrows in Dane's direction. "And who is this?"

Before Dane could introduce himself, Quinn said, "This is Dane Willows, Father. It's his first time at the Festival." She leaned to her father's ear and, in a voice meant as a whisper, said, "And I told him about the lakes and the rivers, just like you showed me." She smiled triumphantly, swaying back and forth, hands clasped behind her back.

The man gave a hearty chuckle. "Is that so?"

Quinn nodded eagerly.

"He didn't know very much, though," she continued, "so I had to tell him *everything.*"

The man placed a hand on her shoulder. "Not everyone has the privilege of learning so much at a young age, Quinn. Please don't lose sight of that."

Quinn's ears turned bright red. She scrunched her nose and mumbled, "Oh. Right."

The man turned to Dane. "Well, young man, I presume Quinn escorted you to the Trials Arena?"

Dane nodded, the exhilaration from the arena flowing back through him. "It was unbelievable—the powers, the arena, all of it! I can't wait until I'm old enough!"

Quinn's father gave him a big smile. "I remember when I first discovered my power. The most exciting day of my life. Well, one of the most exciting." He stole a glance at Quinn, and went on, "The Trials are a truly remarkable experience. You can never predict what will happen, but by the end of it all, you are certain about the power that lives inside you." The man knelt to one knee and tapped a finger to Dane's chest. "Everyone is born with a power, but your body has to mature before your power reveals itself. The Trials were created to test your limits under intense pressure, forcing you to adapt to your situation using your instincts."

Dane's heart sank a little, but Elder Yarrin offered him a cheerful smile. "Fret not, young man. You'll be old enough in due time. I sense a bright future ahead of you."

Dane's spirits lifted. "Thank you, sir."

"Elder Yarrin!" A voice called out from behind, and the man stood up to greet an elderly woman walking toward them.

"Elder Chrysanthe! What a fine trial we witnessed today—certainly a strong gathering of promising young men and women, don't you agree?"

"Oh, quite true, quite true indeed. They'll all grow to become marvelous additions to the community."

The two delved into conversation about the recent events at the arena, much of which Dane didn't understand. Instead, he inspected the Elderly woman with intrigue. Her dark green robes were ornately decorated and adorned with small vines and leaves. Though not similar in appearance, her robes were quite similar to those Quinn's father wore; both crafted with an ornateness and intricacy far superior to any Dane had ever seen.

"Who's that?" Dane whispered in Quinn's ear.

"Elder Chrysanthe. She's the Elder of Vitalor."

"Elder?"

"Right, you don't—that means she watches over everyone in the city, makes sure they're happy. She's the strongest Biophage in the city, which makes her the leader here."

Dane had begun to understand most of Quinn's jargon throughout their day together, but this left him lost once more. Quinn took in his puzzled look and continued.

"The Elder of each capital city is the person with the strongest control over their powers. My father, Yarrin, is the Elder of Evergleam—that's where I'm from. Members of my family have been elders for many generations, ever since Founder Illara first created the city. Father says it's likely I'll become the next Elder of Evergleam when I grow up, but . . ." Her voice trailed off as her gaze shifted to the ground. "I'm not sure if I want that."

Dane got the feeling this was something she thought of often, something her parents frequently discussed. He decided to change the subject. "Is Evergleam similar to Vitalor? Where is it?"

Just as he had hoped, Quinn immediately brightened, her green eyes alight with splendor.

"Evergleam isn't quite as large as Vitalor, since it's on top of a mountain—you can almost see it from here." She pointed to a mountain range to the east. At the top of the farthest peak, Dane could see the faint outline of a tall, shimmering structure canvased against the mountains. Even in the daylight, the sky above the city was dotted with dancing auroras, shimmering with the same greens, pinks, and yellows that shone in Quinn's necklace.

"We live at the very top—in Evergleam castle. In the wintertime, I like to watch the city from the balcony as the snow covers the rooftops like a soft white blanket. The night sky is always full of beautiful lights, too, with dozens of bright colors. It's quite cold most days—with the snow and all."

Dane drew in breath for another question when Elder Yarrin returned.

"Quinn, it's due time we started our journey back," he said. "We don't want your mother worrying about us again, do we?"

"Oh! Of course. I just need a moment." Quinn turned back to Dane, wearing a farewell smile. "I have to go, but thank you for listening to me today. It's nice to have someone to talk with now and then—someone close to my age, that is."

"Well . . . you did most of the talking," Dane said, blushing.

Quinn giggled. "But I sure did enjoy myself. I hope you did too."

"I did! I can't wait to see everything again next year!" he said, barely managing to restrain the excitement of the day. Then, in a shy, inquisitive voice, he added, "You'll be back too, won't you? At the Festival?"

Quinn looked at him strangely, and then grinned. "I come every year, remember? I'll see you then!"

She grabbed Dane by the shoulders and embraced him tightly before returning to her father's side. Quinn recited the rest of her day to her father, who reacted with an occasional hearty laugh, until they turned a corner and disappeared from view.

❧ ☙

Dane found the Trials Festival the following year just as exciting as his first. This time, joined by a curious Sage and Vilik, Dane returned to the Elderwood market in search of his Festival friend. As if it had been planned, Quinn stood waiting for him in the very spot where they had first met.

"I thought I'd find you here," Quinn said.

Dane introduced her to Sage and Vilik, then playfully punched her arm and said, "You never told me there were *more* trials!" In the year after his first Festival, Dane had taken to learning as much as he could about the Trials. He'd learned there were three trials in total: the Trial of the Observer, the Trial of the Adventurer, and the trial he and Quinn had first attended, the Trial of the Warrior. He guessed she'd gotten so caught up in the day's festivities that telling him about the other trials had slipped her mind, but that didn't mean he couldn't tease her for it.

Quinn flashed an apologetic smile. "There was a lot going on last year. Besides," she punched him back. "I *did* have to start from the beginning." She paused a moment, smiling at him, then said, "That's what I had planned today though, watching the

Trial of the Adventurer." She teetered back and forth, hands clasped. "If you're interested, of course."

Dane beamed. "Lead the way."

The air was filled with chatter and enthusiasm as they passed crowds of jubilant people on their way to the Trials Arena. Quinn's gaze kept shifting from Dane to people in the crowd as they walked.

When she stole yet another furtive glance, her mouth skewed to one side, Dane asked, "What? Do I have something on my face?"

Quinn cracked a sympathetic smile and stifled a laugh. "No, it's not that. I was just—why haven't I seen your parents here? You surely didn't come here by yourself. They have to be around somewhere . . . right?"

Dane dropped his gaze. "They died shortly after Sage and I were born. I . . . never knew them."

The color immediately drained from Quinn's cheeks. Her expression turned solemn.

"Oh, I—I'm sorry. I can't imagine what that feels like. I hope you know I didn't mean to—"

"No, that's all right," he said, a hollow ache burrowing into his chest. "It was a long time ago. I don't remember anything about them anyways."

"Do you know what happened to them?"

Dane pondered this for a long moment. The truth was, he knew about as little as she did. According to their senile Grandfather Horas, his parents had died the year after Dane's birth. He'd asked around the village on numerous occasions, trying to find someone else who knew anything about his parents—their whereabouts, what they looked like, even their names—but his grandfather's remorseful, "I just can't seem to remember anything else about them," was the height of his findings.

That hadn't stopped others from joining in on the mysterious fates of Mother and Father Willows. Some people Dane asked seemed to remember his parents were often preoccupied with their travels, rarely glimpsed throughout the year. Others rumored that, in their lengthy travels, his parents had ventured too close to the Shrouded Isle—the isolated island far out at sea where Founders Arkon and Rodran had banished Founder Lussiek and his dreaded Chemocyte followers. According to most, the Isle was plagued with a mutant disease that turned Lussiek's followers into revolting creatures that dragged their victims into the dark caves beneath the island, snatching any nearby traveler that voyaged too close to their shores. Some even thought the creatures ate their victims alive, sucking the power from their bodies. What Dane found most unsettling was the fact that he hadn't been able to find recounts of anyone, living or deceased, who had ventured to the Isle and lived to tell the tale, including the Chemocytes banished after Founder Lussiek's reign. Dane preferred to believe his parents were smart enough to avoid such a place, assuming it even existed.

Dane told Quinn what he knew. Part of it felt liberating, finally sharing the thoughts with someone other than himself or Sage. Quinn listened intently to his every word. By the end of his musings, it felt as though some invisible string had been cut, freeing his mind from its prison of uncertainty.

"I will say," Quinn said once he'd finished, her voice calm and nurturing. "It's rare that anyone in Physos could have such mystery surrounding them. From what you've told me, I'd think they were involved in something important . . . or at least very secretive."

"Something involving the Shrouded Isle?" Dane asked in a conspiratorial whisper.

"I hope not, but I just don't know."

"What about Lussiek? Did his followers kill him like the stories say?" Dane asked.

She lifted her shoulders. "No one really knows. But I wish I did. That place has been a mystery ever since." She grabbed his arm, pulling him close as they neared the arena and whispered, "Some say he went mad from the isolation. Others think he was killed by some other ancient creature living there. But Father thinks something still lives in the labyrinth of tunnels beneath the island. He said he dreamt of a sinister force that threatened to conquer all of Physos. He doesn't have dreams like that very often . . ."

Quinn shuddered, then her voice returned to normal. "I'm not sure what to believe though. Chemocytes aren't very powerful to begin with—or so I'm told. There's no way they could defeat the unified people of Physos. My mother always says, 'the strongest force in all of Physos doesn't come from our individual powers, but from the strength of unity'. I'd like to believe that too, but I can't see the Geomancers and the Tempi ever agreeing on anything, not to mention the whole of Physos. I think she likes to reassure me there's nothing to worry about." Quinn exhaled a tired breath. "I'm sure your parents wouldn't have gone near that place either. They would have known better."

The rest of the journey to the arena was taken in silence as they weaved through the passing crowd, and soon Dane felt the familiar surge of excitement as cheers echoed overhead.

He started toward the grand entrance and its towering, embroidered archways, but Quinn pulled him down a different path, leading around the outside of the arena. Vaguely, he recalled hearing about the Trials Arena actually consisting of two arenas, one for each of the latter two trials.

Quinn continued until they had reached another set of archways leading into the other arena, which, from the outside, looked identical to that of the Trial of the Warrior arena. They hurried inside and found their seats in the stands.

Everything was the same, from the circular arena pit, to the many rows of seating that slowly filled as people poured in. But there was one unmistakable difference: there was no stone warrior waiting in the center of the arena. In its place was a huge stone pillar, surrounded on all sides by rocks and exotic plant life. At the top of the pillar was a familiar small object that glinted in the sunlight streaming through the arena's open ceiling.

"Why are there two arenas?" Dane asked.

"Right," she said, drawing her gaze away from the pillar. "There aren't actually *two* Trials Arenas—just this one building—but there are two different arena pits. This one is for the Trial of the Adventurer." She pointed to the opposite side of the seating area. "But if you go through there, you'll be where we were last year for the Trial of the Warrior. I can see how it would be confusing for your first time—aside from the Trials themselves, both areas look exactly alike."

"I thought we were going to see the root warrior you told us about," Sage shouted as Quinn finished. She eyed the stone pillar skeptically. "That doesn't look like a root warrior . . ."

"This is the Trial of the Adventurer," Quinn said. She thought for a moment, then added, "It's like an obstacle course, but much more dangerous."

Sage's eyes widened hungrily. Dane would often race his sister through the treetops in their village. More often than not, she left him in the dust.

"But we'll be able to see the root warrior too, right?" asked Vilik eagerly.

"The Trials change every year. The Trial of the Warrior will be something different today."

Vilik frowned, his shoulders sinking, but his mood flipped as the announcer's voice boomed across the arena.

Quinn leapt to her feet, clapping wildly. "It's starting!"

The applause commenced as a scrawny young man entered the arena. He summited the nearest rock with some difficulty. Then the entire arena rumbled. Water poured in from the walls, flooding the arena pit. The man cried out, body shivering as the water engulfed his feet. He leapt to the adjacent rock, barely out of reach of the water, repeating the process until nothing stood between him and the central pillar. He swung his arms in a futile attempt to grasp the pillar's surface, barely keeping from falling into the icy depths. But the water continued to rise, lapping at the man's feet.

Out of time, the man faced the pillar, planted his feet, and leapt. But his leap was clumsy, and he was on course to plummet into the frigid water.

Then an audible resonance of gasps erupted throughout the arena. Dane jumped from his seat as the man's body shifted midair, as if a sudden breeze was pushing him toward the pillar. The man latched his body to the stone surface and focused his efforts upward, climbing with incredible speed. Once at the summit, he grabbed the small object atop the pedestal and thrust his hand into the air to the sound of surging applause.

"Did you see that?" Quinn shouted, jumping in place, her hand on Dane's shoulder. "He created a gust of wind midair to avoid falling in the water, just like a true Tempus! And then to create another gust to propel himself while climbing? *Brilliant!*"

For the rest of the day, they watched as other initiates attempted the Trial of the Adventurer. After the festivities concluded and they had left the arena, Quinn stopped amongst the crowd and turned to Dane.

"I had a wonderful time talking with you again this year. I don't have many friends back home—none close to my age, that is." She sighed, her cheeks turning a rosy red. "I guess what I'm trying to say is . . . I really enjoy your company."

Dane was suddenly taken aback. He had been so caught up with the excitement of the Festival, he hadn't once thought that Quinn, the daughter of an elder, didn't always have someone to talk with. The thought warmed his heart.

"You're not so bad yourself," he said, nudging her with his shoulder.

Quinn broke into a fit of giggles. "I guess you're right," she said playfully. She smiled her wide, infectious smile, and Dane couldn't help but do the same as she turned away and waved with the promise to return in a year's time.

Dane had met with Quinn at subsequent Trials Festivals, spending the day cheering in the arena, perusing the crowded Festival streets, sharing stories of the founders and the powers he and Quinn hoped to have, until the year had finally arrived when Quinn was old enough to participate in her own Trials of Power. Dane couldn't have been more excited. He eagerly awaited the next Festival, counting down the days until he'd be able to see Quinn again.

But when Dane finally saw her the day of her Trials, something changed.

It was as if he was looking at her for the first time—only, he no longer saw the same curious girl with the green eyes he had met on his first visit to Vitalor. Instead, his heart raced faster than it ever had, pounding with such force that it could have leapt from his chest.

On that day, she was perfect.

Her dark brown hair danced delicately across her bare shoulders, swaying with the warm, spring breeze. Her radiant eyes, sparkling with the purest shade of forest green, shone in the soft glow of the afternoon sun. Her form-fitting robes glimmered with a deep blue that mirrored the night sky, decorated with green and pink auroras that wove across her sleeves and waist.

Dane stared speechless as Quinn raised a hand to her face, trying to cover her own blush as her lips curved into a beaming smile.

"Do you like it?" she said, holding the edges of her robes, twirling gently. "My father had it made for my Trials tomorrow. You'll be there to watch, won't you?" She eyed Dane curiously, eyebrows raised.

Dane nodded reactively, unsure whether he was agreeing to watch her Trials, or whether he liked her stunning robes. Luckily, Quinn didn't seem to notice.

"I'm actually quite nervous," she admitted, knotting her fingers in her robes. "My parents both say they'll be happy with whichever power I discover, but I know they want me to be a Luminarus like them. Everyone in Evergleam is hoping I'll be a Luminarus too. I even hope I'll be a Luminarus . . ." She paused, lowering her gaze to her trembling hands. She let out a shaky breath. "They never say it, but I know they expect a lot from me. What if my power is different? What if I'm not strong enough, and—" She shook her head violently, clearing her head of the unfinished thought. "I'm sorry. I don't mean to burden you with my own problems."

Dane cleared his throat, regaining control of his voice. "You'll be great." He placed a comforting hand on her shoulder, fingers touching her smooth skin. His body flushed with warmth and he dropped his hand to his side. "And of course I'll be there tomorrow. I wouldn't miss it for the world."

Quinn glanced up at him with a soft, conciliatory smile.

"Just remember, no matter what happens tomorrow, you'll still have your family and friends beside you—even if you discover you're a Chemocyte."

At that Quinn let out a laugh. "You're too kind," she teased. "But . . . thank you." She breathed a sigh. "I still have some preparations to finish before my Trials. I'll see you after?"

"See you after," Dane said.

She had—quite literally—flown through her Trial of the Adventurer. A ring of cascading waterfalls had surrounded the arena pit, the energy stone pedestal perched atop a central pillar that spouted water in all directions. After a moment's hesitation, Quinn ran around the arena, one hand extended, tracing her fingers along the exterior ring of waterfalls. Inexplicably, she jumped, landing mid-air beside the waterfall, seeming to levitate off the ground. She jumped again, her hand still caressing the water, and levitated even higher. She continued jumping and levitating until she had reached the top of the outer ring of waterfalls, then stepped out and walked across thin air toward the pedestal. Dane's grasp on reality was finally put to ease when she later told him that a series of camouflaged rocks led up the waterfall and bridged toward the central pillar, and that the camouflage could only be revealed using her Luminarus powers to distort the rocks' reflection.

During her Trial of the Warrior, with the grove of trees where he had first seen Cayde, she had sprinted to the first trunk and crouched beneath its swinging limbs. The crowd had gasped in unanimous surprise as she traced the brittle bark—one hand methodically along the trunk and the other balled in a fist against her temple. She brought her face close to the trunk, as if peering through the wood itself, and thrust a deft kick to the spot she last touched. The trunk caved inward, creating a high-pitched squeal as it tipped toward the ground and shattering into a dozen wooden splinters. With meticulous yet expedited care, she performed the same, peculiar action on the other trunks and cleared a path to the energy stone pedestal. Vicarious elation surged through Dane as Quinn thrust one hand into the air—the other clasped tightly to her mouth—tears of joy swelling in her eyes as she claimed her third and final energy stone.

Quinn had rushed into Dane's open arms after the Festival had concluded. Her body was still shaking, but he'd never seen her so happy.

"Thank you all for coming!" she gushed. She released Dane and patted the folds of her robes. "I can still hardly breathe—my heart was pounding relentlessly!"

"That was incredible!" said Sage, wrapping her arms around Quinn. "How exciting to complete all three trials. And a Luminarus? You must be so relieved!"

"You were wonderful!" said Dane, "I knew you could do it."

Quinn beamed at him, her face as radiant as her dazzling robes in the sunlight.

"Can we see the stones?" Vilik asked.

Quinn reached in her robe and pulled out three transparent stones, each smooth and glowing with a dim, colorless light.

Dane stared at her open palm. Three stones, but they had only seen two of her trials. Quinn had told him of the other trial—the Trial of the Observer—but he had never seen it at the Festival. "The first trial—what was it like?"

"Hard. And really tense. But I'm not supposed to elaborate on it," Quinn admitted. "Before the trial you must swear on the Mother never to mention it, which I understand—it's the only trial that hardly changes each year—but it takes place in a solitary room as Elder Chrysanthe watches. It was very clever, though. I actually quite enjoyed it."

Quinn cut herself short and glanced over Dane's shoulder, adopting a wide, humble smile.

Elder Chrysanthe strode toward them, arms spread wide. "Congratulations, dear child!" The Elder exclaimed. "What a marvelous performance! And your Trial of the Observer . . .

well, that was nothing short of remarkable." She gripped Quinn's shoulders, tilting her head affectionately. "Your family should be very proud."

Quinn beamed as tears welled in her eyes.

Elder Chrysanthe turned to the others. "And you three, are you excited for your own Trials? It's only a matter of a year or two before you will have your chance, yes?"

"Two years," Sage said.

"Counting down the days," Dane added.

"I look forward to it. Who knows, maybe you'll perform as well as dear Quinn here," the Elder said, eyeing Quinn one last time before waving and turning back toward the arena.

"Well, I'm going to swing through the markets one last time before they all close up," Sage said. Dane? Vilik? Care to join?"

"I'll catch up in a bit," Dane said. Sage shrugged, then she and Vilik sped off.

Once they had rounded the street corner, Quinn turned back to Dane and, without warning, wrapped her arms around his back and pulled herself to him. Dane stood stunned, his heart thudding in his chest. After a moment, his body relaxed under her soothing touch and he slid his arms around her.

"I couldn't have done any of this without your support, Dane," she whispered, hugging him tighter. "Thank you."

Dane smiled and held her for several long moments. Her hair smelled of fresh dew on morning leaves. Her nervousness from before the Trials had all but disappeared, her heart beating in time with his. For the briefest instant, he felt completely at peace, wishing this moment would last forever.

Then Quinn leaned toward him and pressed her lips to his cheek. Dane's face surged with soothing, sensational warmth. It felt as though the sun itself had reached down from above, blessing him with its warm touch, cradling his body and soul in a pool of endless euphoria.

All too soon, Quinn pulled away, her hands gently sliding down his limp arms. Still in a blissful daze, his entire face warm and flushed, Dane gently placed a hand to his cheek. A silent moment passed between them as he stared into her glistening green eyes. For the first time, he glimpsed something else there, something beyond the memories of their time together—memories of times to come.

Quinn's smile faded, but only slightly, "I'm afraid I must join the other new Luminari back in Evergleam. But now that I've proven myself—well, after I pledge my powers and convince my father, of course—I want to travel on my own, see the world." Her lips curved into a smile. "Vitalor is quite the centralized location, you know. I'll need to return here often." Dane's heart fluttered as she looked at him, her eyes brimming with hope and possibility. "You'll be here, won't you?"

An uncontrollable grin spread across Dane's face. "I will, every day."

She grinned back. "Promise?"

"Promise."

And he'd meant it. Every day thereafter he ventured to Vitalor, waiting, dreaming, of the day he could see Quinn once more.

But after nearly two years of waiting, Quinn had never returned.

Now, looking back, Dane felt a fool. He had wanted to kiss her that day. He wished he could've dragged himself from his amorous stupor and confessed his affection for her, taken her in his arms and never let go. Maybe things would've turned out differently. Maybe she wouldn't have disappeared after discovering her power. Or maybe she still would have disappeared anyways, making the pain of her absence worse than it already had been.

But hearing Cayde talk about her Trials with such enthusiasm and love burned Dane's heart like one of Avon's cosmic flares. He'd heard it in Cayde's voice before, when he'd told them of her Trial of the Observer. Quinn had obviously retold the story of her Trials to Cayde many times, if not the other way around. They'd shared many memories together—memories Dane wished *he* had shared with her.

And it wasn't as if she'd forgotten about him. Though she hadn't said as much, he'd seen it in her gaze, a strange longing whenever she looked at him. She still cared for him—maybe not as much as he cared for her, but she still cared. He could see it. But she hadn't chosen him. She'd chosen Cayde. And despite how much Dane hated himself for it, he couldn't stop the spiteful anger from resurfacing every time he laid eyes on her.

A tide of rage and despair swept through Dane's body. His breathing escalated, coming in short, shallow bursts. He didn't want to feel this way toward Quinn—or anyone, Cayde included. Even if he let himself believe there was still hope, he couldn't stop thinking about his failed Trials, about Quinn. His head felt ready to burst.

Why hadn't she returned after her Trials? Why hadn't she returned to see me? She promised she would. She promised . . .

The trees, sky, and ground blurred into one, and everything went black.

CHAPTER 9

THE ABUSER AND HIS TERRORS

"Dane, is everything all right?"

He was kneeling on the stone path, hands clutched to his throbbing head. His skin felt cold and wet. His limbs trembled. *Did I faint?* He realized he was being watched and looked up to see Quinn's beautiful, concerned eyes staring down at him. Cayde and Sage looked on from behind her.

"I'm fine," he managed. He pushed himself to his feet. The world spun and he thought he'd black out again, but he forced himself upright. "Just a headache. It's nothing. We should keep moving."

Quinn watched him a moment longer, lips pursed in thought, then continued forward. After a brief silence, Cayde eyed Sage and said, "What's that around your waist?"

She had just tightened the straps on her carrying pack, lifting her shirt enough to expose the peculiar willow branch still coiled around her waist. "What, this?"

Cayde's eyes bulged.

She uncoiled the branch from her waist and held it with open palms. "It's my Willow Whip. I found it after—"

"You gave it a *name*?" Dane blurted.

Sage glared at him. "Of course. It's a branch, it looks like a whip, it's from a willow tree; what else would I call it, a *tree branch*?" She scoffed, as if its name wasn't an obvious conclusion. "I *found* it after the willow tree on the overlook burned down. The trunk split open. This branch was buried inside, but it wasn't burned or damaged at all." She gazed affectionately at the branch. "Could it be a gift from the willow tree—maybe even from the Elderwood?"

Relieved to keep the conversation off him, Dane retorted, "That's absurd. Trees can't give gifts."

Sage folded her arms over her chest. "And you know this because you're an expert on trees?"

Cayde whispered something to Quinn. She nodded, eyes growing wide. "I believe it."

"You do?" said Dane, incredulous.

"You do?" repeated Sage. "I mean—yes, of course you do, because that's what happened."

Quinn nodded speculatively. "These sorts of oddities aren't impossible—certainly rare—but not impossible. I've heard of a few such occurrences when studying Physosi history. It's possible someone hid it centuries ago, but it's impossible to know for certain without evidence." Her gaze flicked to the branch. "May I?"

Sage offered her the Willow Whip.

"Fascinating," Quinn said, cradling the branch, running her palm along its surface. "Does it do anything . . . unique?"

"I—well, not exactly. As I said, after the rest of the tree had burned, this branch was completely unharmed. It's quite strong, nothing like other willow tree branches. Other than that . . . well, it's only proven useful as a belt."

Sage continued to detail the strange encounter with the Willow Whip to Quinn as they pressed onward. Dane followed, Cayde walking beside him. He recalled something from the night before, and Avon's dreadful voice filled his thoughts. *If it isn't the young Gravitus . . . it appears you're too late once again.*

Dane shuddered inwardly. He turned to Cayde.

"Can I ask you something?"

"Sure. Anything."

"It's about Avon. He seemed to know you from before. But . . . how?"

Cayde glanced sidelong at Dane. "You don't miss much, do you?" When Dane said nothing, only stared back, Cayde said, "I suppose it's only fair you know what you're up against." He slowed his pace, separating further from Quinn and Sage. "Quinn and I had a run-in with him once before, in a grotto tucked in the mountains west of Mistveil. We were just entering when he emerged from the shadows. I tried using my powers to pull him back, but he was quick to retaliate, igniting the cave floor with white flame, leaving us trapped behind the cosmic flare as he escaped." Cayde blew out a sigh. "I wish I could have done more to stop him, but I had just recently harnessed my abilities. I wasn't ready, neither was Quinn."

Dane stared forward, astonished. "What was he doing there?"

Cayde pursed his lips in thought. "I wish I knew. But we've tried to find him since, predict where he'll be next, but he always seems to stay one step ahead. I don't understand it."

Dane's brow furrowed in thought. "Avon was alone in the grotto? But there were those two other men with him in Vitalor—the ones with metal swords. Are there more of them?"

"I'm not certain, but I don't doubt it. From what I've been told, there are very few places in Physos that have access to metal resources, none of which are pleasant." He paused and scanned either side of the path. He lowered his voice. "That's enough for now. And—err—let's keep this between us. Elder Yarrin instructed us to keep information about Avon to ourselves, but I think you've earned it."

༄ ༄

The sun beamed down as they neared a dense forest encompassing the path ahead. Dane glanced over his shoulder, then squinted through the upcoming trees. Vitalor was barely visible behind them, but Mistveil was still no larger than a drop of water at the opposite end of the lake. Dane sighed, then pressed on into the forest with the others.

The stone path curved deep into the forest. The only light was that of the narrow shafts that peered through the dense canopy. Thick branches arched overhead, creating a kind of tunnel around the path.

"Are you sure this is the right way?" Dane asked warily. "It seems like we're straying away from the lake."

"We're still on course," Quinn replied automatically. "The split between Mistveil and Evergleam is just beyond this forest."

Dane nodded, but his hesitance remained unchanged. The path was lit well enough from the rays of sunlight dotting the road ahead, but the usual melodies from chirping birds had dissipated, and the wind no longer rustled through the leaves overhead. A thin fog had started creeping in from the right, settling into the forest.

"I don't like the look of this place. Where exactly are we?" said Sage, tightly gripping the straps of her pack.

"We're in the Grove of Mist," said Cayde.

"Clever," she said dryly. "So where is this mist coming from?"

Cayde gestured to his right. "We can't see it from here, but the base of the Aurora Mountains is just beyond those trees. Cold air from the sea flows down the slopes and into this grove. Since the air here is warmer than on top of the mountain, the cold air creates a thick layer of mist as it passes through the trees and pools above the lake. Hence why it's the Grove of Mist."

"Makes sense," Sage admitted. "I would've been much more creative with the name though."

"And we're certain this place isn't haunted?" Dane asked as a branch cracked in the distance, breaking the ominous silence, sending a prickle of fear up his spine.

"I can see how you'd think so," said Cayde. "I thought the same the first time I came through here, but my mentor told me the mist has a strange effect on sounds and there's nothing to worry about. We've been through here many times since. It *is* rather ominous, I'll give you that. But I can assure you it's quite normal."

They continued through the forest until reaching a small clearing where several small boulders disrupted the monotony of trees. The lake and sky were no longer visible through the thick mist and dense foliage, and an eerie silence still filled the gray misty air.

"Let's stop here," said Quinn, offering a smile. "I thought it would take longer to reach this point—we could use a short rest."

"Good, I'm starving," said Sage. She sat contently on a boulder, rummaging through her pack for another loaf of bread.

Dane pulled out a loaf of his own, about to take a bite something moved in the corner of his vision. He stopped, mouth open, and stared into the forest mist. In the distance, a dark shadow emerged from beyond the last row of visible trees.

"What do you see, Dane?" Quinn asked, sensing his unease. "Is something wrong?"

Dane froze, breathing shallow, rapid breaths. Anything could be out there. Any*one*. Watching, lurking, waiting to strike. He stared, straining his eyes, trying to see through the thick mist.

"There's something out there," he whispered. As he said it, the mist seemed to recede until Dane could see a large shape emerge from the fog. His breathing eased slightly.

"It looks like . . . a hut."

"Where?" asked Cayde.

Dane pointed through the trees. By now he was sure the ominous shape was indeed a hut of some sort, barely visible at the edge of his vision.

"I'll be damned," said Cayde. "Usually the mist is so thick we can't see past the first few trees. I bet that's the Abuser's hut."

"The *what?*" Sage shouted through a mouthful of bread. Her eyes bulged. "I thought you said this place was safe!"

"We're fine, don't worry—his title is very misleading. That hut belongs to Varic Tumulus. His tale is well-known in the eastern parts of Physos. He was banished here for misusing his powers and given the title, The Abuser, so everyone would know what he did."

Dane's fear dissipated, replaced by intrigue. "What do you mean, banished? Like Founder Lussiek centuries ago?"

"Definitely not like that, no. He was just banished from Alto-Baros, the City of Storms."

Sage swallowed her mouthful of bread and leaned in. "What'd he do?"

"It started about thirty years ago," Cayde began. "The former Elder of Alto-Baros had grown very old. As is custom among Tempi, the next most powerful Tempus in the city was to be his successor. In the years leading to the Elder's death, that honor belonged to Varic. But as the Elder neared his final days, another man, Durkanis, had become Varic's equal. But Durkanis understood the city and its people better than Varic, so when the Elder took his final breaths, Durkanis was named Elder of Alto-Baros—rightfully so, if you ask me. But Varic was furious, and he became consumed by rage.

"When he was younger, shortly after his Trials, Varic became fascinated with the city, devoting his time to studying its foundations and creation. You see, Alto-Baros was built atop a narrow cliff, bordered by ocean on either side. Through the years, the waters carved through the cliff, and now all that remains are several massive columns of natural stone and earth suspending the city high above the ocean currents below.

"Outraged at his snub for the position of elder, Varic decided he would use his power to topple the entire city. If he couldn't be the next elder, no one could. Varic went to the furthest edge of the city and conjured an enormous maelstrom—something no Tempus should ever be capable of doing.

"But Varic had a brother, Atax. He too was a powerful Tempus—not as powerful as Varic or Durkanis, but gifted nonetheless. Atax foresaw Varic's plot to destroy the city and confronted his brother that day on the city outskirts. What ensued was a violent surge of energy between the two brothers, Varic trying to create a storm to destroy the city, Atax using all his power to save it."

Cayde looked to Dane and Sage. "Now, I don't know what you've heard about overexerting your power, but the energy wells only offer so much energy to their people. If too much energy is drawn for someone's power—say, for creating a maelstrom to engulf an entire city—the well must find a way to refuel its energy source. When the maelstrom grew too large, the Sacred Cyclone—the Tempus energy well—began to drain the very life from the brothers.

"The damage started in their hands. Their skin dried and cracked like scorched earth in the hot sun, spreading up their arms and over their entire bodies. Varic released his hold on the maelstrom a moment before exhaling his last breath. He crumpled to the ground, weaker and frailer than the oldest man to ever live in Physos. But his brother was not so lucky. To prevent the storm from manifesting, Atax overexerted his power until his life force was completely drained. He defended the city to his dying breath, sacrificing his life to save thousands more.

"After that, Varic was shamed and titled, the Abuser, as a living reminder to the consequences of abusing the energy wells' gifts. He was banished to the Grove of Mist to live out the rest of his days in solitude. Nothing has been heard of him since, except that he's too afraid to ever leave that hut."

Dane looked back to the hut, still shrouded in mist. He squirmed as an uneasy feeling washed over him.

"Is he there now? Is he still dangerous?"

"I suppose he's there now, but dangerous? Not in the slightest. The damage to his skin may have partially healed over the decades, but his days of abusing his power are over—I'd bet he can barely conjure enough wind to lift a leaf from the ground. The damage he sustained can't be healed."

"And it serves him right," Sage said, her fists clenched in frustration. "Why would someone do that? Our powers are a gift. They're supposed to help the world, not destroy it."

"It makes me sick," Quinn muttered. "This world has so much to offer, and most give everything they have to make it a better place for all. But then there are people like Varic—like Avon—who just want to take it away."

Quinn shuddered then glanced to the others before rising to her feet.

"We should keep moving. We're halfway through the forest. Once we're out it's only a short detour to where we'll make camp for the night."

They had just risen to their feet when a strong breeze rustled through the trees. Dane watched as the mist receded with the wind, granting him a clearer view of the hut.

At once, the wind stopped, and an eerie, chilling silence swept over the forest. Dane looked to the others, equally unsure, before glancing once more at the hut.

His eyes widened, his heart racing. Something was wrong. Cayde had noticed it too.

"Hold on," Cayde said. "Something isn't right."

"What's wrong?" asked Quinn. She had already started walking. She failed to hide the urgency in her voice. "I'm sure it was nothing. We really should keep moving."

Cayde stared fixedly at the hut. "The front door looks broken. The windows are shattered."

"I'm sure it's normal," said Dane shakily, trying to convince both Cayde and himself that there was nothing to fear. "He probably just broke them on accident . . . or something."

"He was a frail, decrepit man," Cayde insisted. "He couldn't have done that on his own. Something's wrong."

"Cayde, we don't owe that man anything," Quinn said, her voice suddenly stern. "You don't need to—"

But Cayde had already left the path and was pacing toward the hut.

"What are you doing?" Sage hissed after him. She stared dully after him when he didn't respond, then turned to Quinn. "What is he doing?"

"Off to save someone in need," Quinn grumbled. "Come on."

Quinn dashed after Cayde, Dane and Sage following reluctantly. Cayde stopped as he neared and knelt behind a tree, unsheathed his sword, staring ahead.

Quinn knelt beside him and whispered, "Do you hear anything?"

Cayde shook his head nearly imperceptibly.

"Is that good or bad?" whispered Dane.

Cayde squinted, unmoving, staring intently at the broken hut door. His grip tightened on his sword. "Definitely bad. Stay close. Be ready for anything."

Cayde crept silently forward, staying low to the damp forest floor. Dane unlatched his staff from his pack and clenched it with shaking fists; he hoped he wouldn't have to use it. Heart pounding, he gulped down his fear and followed Cayde's footsteps.

Cayde flattened his body against the side of the hut, the others following his lead. Cautiously, he eased into the mangled doorway, sword at the ready. He stood there a moment, staring into the doorway, then disappeared inside.

Dane held his breath, straining for any sound of struggle. He could feel Quinn and Sage behind him, but he didn't dare look away from the doorway.

Cayde appeared a moment later and beckoned the others to follow. Dane released a shaky sigh. Quinn did the same.

They entered into a small room, lit only by a faint, orange glow from the dying embers of a fireplace. The room was relatively bare if not for the broken remains of a chair and table scattered across the floor. A tattered, undisturbed bookshelf clung to the far wall.

Dane's eyes locked on the floor. Long, jagged lines had been clawed into the wooden surface, raking across the room as if some feral beast had taken residence in the hut. Dane listened for the source of the destruction, but all he could hear was the others' rapid breaths.

Cayde crouched and inspected the fireplace.

"These embers are fresh." He glanced around the room then inspected the embers again. Quinn eyed the ruined door—it had been smashed against the wall and was barely hanging by its wooden hinges—and ran her fingers along the frame. Sage stepped lightly across the room and gripped the Willow Whip with one hand, her squinted eyes focused on the tattered books.

But Dane still stared at the claw marks across the floor, following them as they led beneath the debris toward a dark corner of the hut. Slowly and quietly, he stalked across the room, his eyes trained on the ground.

The markings stopped in front of another doorway obscured by shadow and remnants of the broken table. Dane froze, staring into the dark doorway, then glanced at the others.

None of them seemed to notice.

A rancid odor filled the air when he turned back toward the hidden room. He had never smelled anything so horrid in his life, but somehow, inexplicably, the smell was familiar. He thought for a moment, trying to conjure the memory.

Then a cold shiver ran through his spine. His stomach lurched to his throat. The odor was that of the mutilated Vitalor guards; it was the smell of death.

Dane held his breath and forced his head through the doorway. When he saw the body, his stomach nearly lurched from his mouth.

The motionless body of a man lay crumpled in the corner of the room beside a bed, partly masked by shadow. His chest glistened a dark crimson, his torso riddled with violent slash marks. His head had slumped to one shoulder, drenched in the blood that oozed from the man's mutilated face.

Horrified, Dane tracked the vicious gashes to the man's limbs. The skin on his arms looked cracked and dry, almost brittle, that of sunbaked earth. Dane froze. It was the body of the Abuser, Varic Tumulus.

Dane took a step back and nearly collapsed to the ground. His limbs felt encased in ice. His mouth had gone completely dry. He swallowed hard, forcing down the rising bile as he stumbled into the other room. When he looked up, Sage, Quinn, and Cayde were all staring at him, concern riddling their features.

"Dane . . . you're so pale. Are you all right?" Quinn said, trepidation lacing her voice. Her gaze fell on the doorway and she lifted a hand to her mouth. "What did you see?"

Dane pushed his hands into the wooden floorboards, finally finding his voice again. "Dead," he muttered.

Cayde surged into the small room, sword at the ready, only to clasp a hand over his mouth and nose as he registered the scene. He knelt beside the mangled corpse. Quinn gasped and clamped both hands to her mouth. Sage stared wide-eyed, transfixed by the body.

"Avon did this, didn't he?" Dane managed.

But Cayde didn't answer. His face had turned a ghostly pale. His hands trembled as his grip tightened on the sword. When Cayde finally spoke, his voice was nearly inaudible, "This was not Avon . . ."

Dane's insides writhed. Even against Avon, Cayde had held his stoic composure, defiant in the face of danger. But now, Cayde looked truly afraid. Whatever had killed Varic was worse than Avon . . . *much* worse.

Cayde stood, his entire body rigid. "We're not alone."

The orange glow from the fireplace extinguished. An eerie silence penetrated the room. Dane held his breath, paralyzed with fear as Cayde's ominous last words replayed his mind.

A loud crack echoed outside the hut. Petrified, Dane frantically scanned the room. Quinn and Sage were also unmoving, eyes darting wildly. Cayde was nowhere to be seen.

Then a cold hand clasped over Dane's mouth. He nearly jumped to the ceiling as Cayde appeared beside him, one finger raised to his lips in a silent gesture. Breathing heavily, Dane nodded in understanding as Cayde slowly withdrew his hand, sword at the ready, and crept toward the hut's exit. The fingers of his free hand were curled, as if grasping an invisible bowl, just as they had when Dane had watched Cayde's Trial of the Warrior.

Cayde reached the door, paused a moment, then took a long look at Quinn. They seemed to hold a silent conversation before Quinn, pale and trembling, nodded succinctly.

Cayde stepped out of the hut and stood in the doorway, head swiveling slowly to either side. Then he stepped out of sight, and an eerie, penetrating silence filled the air.

Dane held his breath, his heart pounding in his throat, straining for an inevitable scream or cry of terror. Any moment, something would charge into the hut—a beast, a man, a shadow—and kill them all.

But nothing came.

He breathed a sigh of relief as Cayde reappeared in the doorway, sword sheathed behind his back. Dane mopped the cold sweat from his brow.

"It was just a raven," Cayde said, his voice still hushed.

"We need to leave," Quinn said, panic rising in her voice. "We need to get as far away as we can before the sun sets."

"Wait," Dane managed, swallowing hard. "What did you think—"

Cayde turned and stared at him, his face stern yet stricken with fear.

"Dane, we need to leave. *Now.*"

Abruptly, Cayde strode out the door, the others following close behind. Dane didn't need a second invitation. His heart raced as they returned to the path, leaving the hut far behind them. Dane didn't spare any parting glances as the mist once more settled in around them. The thing that had killed Varic could still be lurking nearby. He didn't want to be there when it returned.

Not another word was spoken for the remainder of the journey through the Grove of Mist. Dane walked with Sage, who stared blankly ahead with glazed eyes, while Quinn and Cayde walked several paces ahead of them, eyes wide and alert as they scanned the mist-shrouded forest for the slightest of sounds or traces of movement.

Even though the hut and the mutilated corpse of Varic the Abuser was far behind them, Dane couldn't quell the growing knot in his stomach. He got the feeling Quinn and Cayde knew what had killed Varic. The fear in Cayde's eyes had been unmistakable. He'd find out what they knew soon enough. For now, it could wait.

ॐ ॐ

The sky was a warm sunset orange when they emerged from the grove. The wind rustled through the trees as melodious bird songs filled the dusk air, easing Dane's suspicions of imminent danger.

They followed the stone path through an open grass field populated until reaching a wooden signpost at the base of a looming mountain slope. On the signpost were two engraved planks: one read *Mistveil*, the other *Evergleam*.

Dane looked ahead. The path continued to his left along Mistveil Lake. To their right, the path wound gradually upward, carving deeper into the mountains.

"We're almost there," Quinn said, gesturing to the right. "There's a cave just beyond that ridge. We'll spend the night there and follow the mountain pass in the morning."

Now that the dense shroud of mist was far behind them, everyone seemed to be in better spirits. Dane could finally think straight, his questions from earlier percolating back in.

"So what *did* kill Varic?" he said hesitantly as they had approached the first curve in the path. "If it wasn't Avon, then what was it? A bear? Wolves?" He swallowed. "Was it another person? Someone else like Avon?"

Quinn exchanged a nervous glance with Cayde, who nodded reluctantly. She took a deep breath and looked at Dane, her green eyes filled with worry.

"We're not entirely certain. But those slash marks . . ." She let out a long, controlled sigh. "We think it was a Chemocyte."

Dane's knees buckled. He swallowed hard. "A Chemocyte? How is that possible? Wha—was it there? At the hut? How can you be sure?"

Cayde winced, placing one hand to his forehead. Dane waited on bated breath, and Sage stared with equal horrified curiosity.

"I wish we were wrong," Cayde said, "but I can't see any alternative. No other creature alive could have done that. The way Varic was slashed—it wasn't out of defense, or some animal hunting him for food. He was killed simply for being alive. It had to be a Chemocyte."

"But the stories—the rumors—" Dane stuttered. "Chemocytes only live on the Shrouded Isle. No one has ever seen them and lived. How can one be here?"

"That's what has me worried," Quinn mumbled, "I don't know how one arrived on the mainland—if it even was a Chemocyte. But if our suspicions are true, then Avon isn't the only threat to Physos."

"But we can stop it, right? We—" Dane cut himself short, wrought with a disheartening thought. What could *he* do against a Chemocyte? He had no powers to defend himself. He'd end up no different than Varic.

His expression somber, Dane glanced up to meet Quinn's bleary gaze. She kneaded her temples with her knuckles, her eyes glassy.

"I don't know. For now, we need rest."

Silence fell between them a moment, then Sage said, "What if the Chemocyte comes back?"

Quinn shook her head and quickened her pace. "Let's hope it doesn't."

They followed the path as it wound up the steep mountain slopes, surrounded on both sides by jagged rocks and boulders, littered with the occasional small trees and foliage.

Quinn paused and stared ahead as they summited the first cliff. The path opened onto a small meadow bordered by more slopes. Ahead of them, Dane could see the opening to a small cave hidden behind a grove of pine trees.

"We'll set up here," Quinn said as they had ducked under the low-hanging branches and into the shadows of the cave. The walls were damp and spattered with moss. A series of small, worn rocks circled a charred patch of ground in the cave's center.

Dane sat on one of the rocks, heaving his pack onto the ground before rubbing at his aching feet.

Sage did the same, letting out a sigh that echoed softly off the walls. She eyed the shallow cave and wrinkled her nose. "It's a bit . . . cozy . . . don't you think?"

Quinn gave an emotionless smile but said nothing. Solemnly, Sage added, "Will we be safe?"

A moment passed, then Quinn said, "From the elements, yes." She glanced to Cayde as she began unpacking the contents of her bag, but he was already headed for the cave opening.

"We need to make a fire if we hope to stay warm," Cayde said. "I'll be back soon."

Sage sprung to her feet. "I'll come too. I might go insane if I sit here worrying much longer."

Cayde nodded indifferently, and Sage followed him out of the cave.

Dane watched them go, his body flushing with anticipation as they disappeared from view. He was alone with Quinn. He glanced around the cave, eyes periodically landing on Quinn as he too began unpacking, but she only stared unflinching at the cave entrance. Her face was creased with worry. She looped a lock of hair around one finger, tugging nervously, her chest heaving with shallow breaths.

Dane parted his mouth to speak, but no words came. For several moments he tried to muster something—anything—to say to her. But his mind was blank. No words came. Instead, he sighed resignedly and stared at his hands.

Why didn't you come back? But he couldn't ask that of her, not now, so sudden and without warning.

They sat in tense silence as the night sky slowly darkened and bloomed with sparkling starlight.

"They should've been back by now." Quinn said suddenly, breaking from her trance. She looked at Dane. "Stay here. I'm going to—"

She gasped as Cayde and Sage pushed aside the branches blocking the cave entrance, each carrying a bundle of loose sticks.

Quinn exhaled like she'd been holding her breath since Cayde and Sage had left. "What took you so long? I thought you—"

"We're fine," Cayde said. He tossed his sticks to Sage, who caught them with ease and placed them on the patch of charred ground. "We had to search a bit farther—there weren't many branches left after last time."

Cayde kindled the fire, and the cave walls were soon painted with dancing flame. Dane thought of the burning Elderwood as he watched—the charred market street, and of Av—

He closed his eyes, trying to shut out the memory. It worked for a moment, but then he saw the hut, the vicious marks raking across the floor, and the body.

Resignedly, he opened his eyes and stared pensively into the flames with the others.

"We should get some rest," said Quinn, prodding the fire with a small stick.

She moved to her makeshift bedding—spare blankets with a balled-up jacket for a pillow. Sage had already tucked herself in, both hands under her cheek as she stared at the flames. Cayde remained seated by the fire, prodding it mindlessly.

Dane didn't move, only stared into the fire. In a voice that sounded too foreign, vulnerable, and afraid to be his own, he said, "What if it comes back?"

No one said anything in response. Dane looked up to see Cayde, Quinn, and Sage all looking back at him, their faces pale and uncertain.

Cayde tossed the prodding stick into the fire. "I'll take first watch."

"Cayde, no," Quinn protested, "I can—"

"It's all right, I can do it. It'll be safer. I won't be able to sleep much anyways."

"Neither will we. But you need rest too."

Cayde smiled lightly, then unfurled a blanket from his pack and spread it beside the fire.

"Fine," Quinn said. She squeezed his shoulder as he propped himself against a rock, facing the cave entrance. "Wake me if you hear anything, promise?"

"Sure," Cayde said.

Quinn regarded him with uncertainty for a moment, then she pulled her blanket over her shoulders and lay down facing the cave wall.

Dane wrapped himself in his blanket and stared into the fire. The rotting stench of the corpse still stained his smell. The piercing silence of the hut's haunting air still rang in his ears. He saw Varic's mutilated body every time he closed his eyes. When he finally diverted his thoughts, all he could think of was Quinn and her broken promise, only making him feel worse. And deep down, forever plastered at the back of his mind, were the tainted memories of his Trials—of his failure.

Overwhelmed and utterly exhausted, Dane lay, focusing on the soft crackling of the aging fire until his eyelids were too heavy to hold open, and he drifted into slumber.

∽ ∾

An anguished howl startled Dane awake. He forced his eyes open.

He immediately assumed the worst. His worst nightmare was unfolding before him and the dreaded Chemocyte was lurking just outside the cave—or worse, in the cave—waiting for the moment to leap on him and tear his body to pieces.

Dane fumbled at his chest, probing over his skin as the terrorizing thought flashed through his mind. He released an exhausted sigh when his fingers didn't come away with blood.

It wasn't real, he thought, reeling at the ridiculous trick his mind had played. *It wasn't real.*

Then the howl came again, a faint, guttural shriek barely audible over the crackling fire.

Dane sat upright, eyes darting around the cave. Sage was rolled up in her bedding, fast asleep. Quinn still had her back turned to him, her blanket slowly rising and receding with her calmed breaths.

Cayde was sitting on the rock nearest the cave entrance, his body rigid, face hard as stone, staring into the dark shroud of night. He held a stout, makeshift torch in one hand, his glass sword in the other, its transparent blade gleaming dark orange in the fire's reflection.

Dane kept his voice low, not wanting to disturb the others. "Did you hear—"

Cayde pressed a finger to his lips, then turned his gaze back to the cave entrance. Without making a sound, he stood and crept into the darkness.

In a panic, Dane pushed himself to his feet, fumbled for his staff and followed.

The night sky cloaked the landscape in wisps of darkness, the mountains barely visible through its shroud. The light from Cayde's torch lit the few trees in front of them before melting into shadow. Dane stood, straining for another sound, as sweat beaded and dripped down his forehead.

Nothing but silence filled the air.

Dane released a shaky breath. "Maybe it was just the wind," he whispered unconvincingly.

Then the faint sound penetrated the air again, seeping out of the blackness like the thick tendrils of mist that had lingered around the Abuser's hut.

Dane's fists clenched around his staff. He could sense something was near—something bad. Cayde's firm hand pressed against his chest, stopping him where he stood.

Inexplicably, Cayde tossed the torch to the ground, doused it with his boot, and pointed into the darkness. Dane squinted, letting his eyes adjust, and noticed a soft, orange prick of light through the trees. The light from another torch.

Cayde crept forward silently, easing toward the distant light amidst the shelter of trees. All instincts told Dane to sprint back to the cave and hide in the darkest corner. Instead he followed, not daring to breathe.

In an agonizingly slow crawl, they drew closer and closer until Dane could see the outline of a torch handle attached to the flame. It flickered on the ground, projecting wavering shadows on nearby foliage.

Cautiously, Dane moved forward and bent to pick up the torch. He stopped, hand hovering over the handle, as a reflection from the shadows captured his gaze. A sword lay at the base of a small bush, gleaming in the torchlight. *Metal.*

Dane's eyes widened with equal fear and fascination. It was a metal sword—rather, it *used* to be a metal sword. The hilt lay beside the blade, torn in half like a sheet of parchment. He moved to pick it up when he noticed a dark, glistening stain trailing away from the bush, into the darkness. *Blood.*

A cold shiver trickled down his spine as his eyes tracked the crimson trail. A thick, dark puddle had pooled at the base of a bush. Protruding from the bush, drenched in blood, was a motionless pair of legs.

Dane averted his gaze from the gruesome sight, forcing down the bile in his throat.

Cayde crouched beside the body. "These gashes—they're the same as before," he said, his voice as monotone as the eerie ring of silence piercing the night sky. He stood slowly, gaze unwavering from the body. When Cayde spoke again, Dane felt as though the very ground beneath him quaked with fear.

"It's here."

A strong gust whistled through the trees. The dying flames of the abandoned torch flickered, then extinguished. Shadows closed in, enveloping everything in darkness.

Dane stood petrified. His heart leapt into his throat, pounding incessantly, as if trying to claw out of a collapsing tunnel. The black cloak of night obscured his vision. He couldn't see Cayde, the body, or the metal sword.

Instinctively he threw his arms up in defense, certain that something was leaping toward him, claws outstretched and poised for the kill.

But there was nothing.

He squinted through the darkness, trying to discern any sign of movement. Something stirred to his left. He turned, peering into the shadows. The rough outline of a tree trunk took shape in front of him. He squinted harder. Maybe Cayde was trying to find the torch.

Dane opened his mouth to call to him. Then his breath hitched in his throat.

The darkness blinked. A pair of gleaming, crimson eyes stared back at him.

Dane toppled backward as something huge and dark lunged from the shadows and soared through the air where he had been standing. There was a crackling thud as the creature collided with a tree trunk and let out a horrific, chilling screech.

Dane scrambled across the ground, searching blindly. His hands clasped around his Elderwood staff. He heaved himself to his feet and whirled around. The dark clouds of night parted, and a thin beam of moonlight shone into the forest.

Then he saw the creature. Only, it wasn't a creature—it was a monster. Its skin was black as night. It stood on two legs, with jagged, red protrusions—some mix between crystal and bone—jutting out of its hunched back and shoulders. Its beady red eyes shone from their sockets. Its mouth was a gaping hole of blackened teeth. More protrusions framed its sunken face, looking like some mutilated, bloody crown. Its long, pincer-like claws dripped dark liquid, forking out of each hand like five small daggers carved from bone.

Dane tried to scream, but he had no voice, could utter no sound.

The creature turned, piercing Dane with its hungry, crimson gaze. It shrieked—the sound like fingernails raking glass—and tore through the underbrush toward Dane.

Dane turned to run but his legs fell from under him. He crashed through a thick bramble of branches. Pain flared in his upper arm as a sharp branch ripped his skin. His head slammed into the ground, clouding his vision with blooming black spots. He fought back the pain and clambered blindly across the muddy forest floor. One hand closed around the handle of his staff as the thicket behind him exploded with cracking branches and wood splinters.

Dane flipped onto his back with a rasping, garbled cry. The creature lunged. He thrust his staff over his chest. It collided with the staff in a sickening crunch. A jarring pain splintered down Dane's arms to his shoulders. The creature's long arms flailed, raking through the air right in front of Dane's face.

The cords of his neck bulged as he tried to escape, pressing his head into the liquid ground as the creature's claws lashed at him again. Mud oozed into his hair and seeped through his clothes. Once more he was in the arena, quicksand swallowing his body whole. He could feel his strength failing, arms quivering under the creature's thrashing body.

NO! Dane screamed in his mind, gritting his teeth and willing the strength into his wilting limbs. *Not like this! NOT LIKE THIS!*

He wriggled and writhed, pushing his sweating palms into the steadfast staff.

He thrust his arms upward, pushing against air as the creature reared back. Dane seized the chance. He curled his legs to his chest and kicked at the creature.

At least, that's what he'd planned to do. But his legs didn't budge.

For a moment he could only stare in stupefied bewilderment. He lifted his head to see why his legs hadn't moved, but the creature was on him again. He barely managed to sink back into the mud to evade its ripping claws.

A wild, frantic fear took control of Dane's body. He tried to move his legs again, still pushing the creature with all his strength, but something—a branch or tangle of roots—pinned his legs down. He wanted to scream but air had become a stranger to him, as if his mind had forgotten how to breathe.

The creature's weight was overpowering. His grip was failing. His arms screamed in protest. But he was only delaying the inevitable. He was helpless, pinned by the creature's onslaught. The creature was in control. Soon it would claim his life.

Move! Dane urged his limbs. *MOVE!*

Dane summoned what little strength remained and lurched the staff upward in one final effort to heave the creature off of him.

Then his hand slipped. Dane watched in slow, agonizing horror as the staff fell from his grasp, cascading through the dark void between the creature and his exhausted body and thudded against his chest.

A wave of hopelessness crashed down as the air was pulled from his lungs.

I failed . . . again.

His arms fell limply to his side, casualties to exhaustion. He closed his eyes, waiting for the creature's claws to tear into his flesh.

Then darkness enveloped him.

"NOOOOOOO!!"

A piercing howl shattered the silence. In a daze, Dane opened his eyes to see the creature suspended above him, hovering, as if still impeded by his staff. It thrashed through the air, its claws narrowly missing Dane's chest.

Cayde burst through the shadows, hand outstretched and surging with power, aimed straight at the creature. The dim starlight reflected a faint halo around Cayde's head. His eyes were gleaming slits of pure resilience and determination. Tears of desperation and overwhelming relief pooled in Dane's eyes. His life had been over; he had failed. Then, as if sent by the Mother herself, there was Cayde; a beacon of light and hope to pierce the darkness.

Cayde rammed into the creature at full speed and threw his arms around its horribly disfigured body. In a mix of enraged cries and wretched shrieks, Cayde and the creature sailed through the air and crashed into a thicket.

Dane wrenched his feet free. He shook all over, but he grabbed his staff and staggered upright.

He heard a cry of pain and spun to face where Cayde and the creature had landed. Their darkened shapes converged as one for several moments before the creature tumbled backward. It crashed against a nearby trunk, emitting a primal screech.

Dane started to hobble forward when he saw the reflection of Cayde's glass sword at the base of a tree.

The sword!

"Dane, don't move!"

Dane looked up. Cayde was running toward him, toward the sword, the creature only moments behind him. Dane could only watch in petrified fear.

Cayde skidded to a halt. He didn't reach for the sword, instead pivoted, back pressed against the tree, and faced the creature. He raised both hands toward it, fingers arched and straining. Dane waited for the creature's movement to slow, but it only ran faster, *gaining* speed with rampant, barbarian intensity.

Dane watched in bewilderment a moment. Then it came to him. Cayde wasn't trying to slow the creature's charge—he was using his power to *pull* the creature forward.

When merely a body length away from Cayde, the creature leapt with claws at full extension.

Cayde spun away from the tree. The creature smashed into the trunk with a sickening crunch. Without missing a beat, Cayde shoved one boot under the sword and kicked up. The sword levitated perfectly upward, gleaming in the moonlight. With the fluidity and execution of a master swordfighter, Cayde snatched the hilt of the sword from the air. He swept his arm across his body with such terrifying force that the sword whistled through the air, cleaved clean through the creature's writhing torso, and buried itself into the trunk with a resounding thud.

The creature's two severed halves toppled to the ground. A calm silence—with the exception of Cayde's labored breathing—hung in the air.

Dane stared at Cayde. Whatever resentment he'd had of the man vanished. Cayde had just saved his life.

"Wha—" Dane started to say, but the words seized in his throat. He fell to one knee, head swimming as if in a distant dream, and wretched on the forest floor.

He felt Cayde's firm hand on his back as he wheezed several long, controlled breaths. The sharp yet welcome pain of the fresh night air rushed into his lungs, breathing life back into his spent limbs. He gathered himself and stared down at the unmoving halves of the creature's body.

"What . . . was . . . that thing?" he croaked.

Cayde wrenched the sword from the tree, its blade squealing against the oozing sap where it had split the trunk. He stared down at the body, then looked to Dane, staring with dreading, fearful certainty.

You know what it was, Cayde's eyes said. *Chemocyte.*

The creature's body shifted. Dane scrambled back, only to realize it was crumbling apart, splitting like a shattered rock. Cayde knelt to inspect the body and stood holding something Dane could only describe as a hardened piece of black stone streaked with red veins, one of dozens that were now piled where the creature's body halves had been.

Cayde pocketed the stone and turned to Dane.

"Did it get you?" he asked.

Reflexively, Dane's hand shot to the wound on his arm; he had forgotten about it until now. He dabbled his fingers at the wound. There was some blood, mixed with dried mud, but he felt no pain.

"It—it's fine—a branch cut me, that's all," he said. Then his eyes tracked down Cayde's shirt to a dark red stain near his stomach.

"Hit a branch while rolling, same as you. I've had worse." Cayde eyed Dane's arm more closely. "We should head back to the cave and get that cleaned." He spared another glance at the Chemocyte then stared up at the sky, watching, listening. After a moment, he shook his head and said, "Come on, the others are probably worried."

Quinn was sitting bolt upright, her body heaving and rigid in front of the fire when they stumbled back into the cave. She jumped to her feet as they entered and ran to Cayde with outstretched arms. Sage, who had been curled up facing the fire, ran to embrace Dane.

"What happened?" Quinn said, holding Cayde at arm's length. "Did you—"

"It's gone," Cayde said.

Quinn looked him over. "You're bleeding," she stated matter-of-factly. She reached as if to touch his wound, but Cayde pulled back.

"It's nothing, I'm fine." He tilted his head to Dane's bloodied arm. "Dane's is worse." Quinn blew a shaky sigh, then released him and gingerly grasped Dane's arm, inspecting his wound.

Sage stared for a moment, then her eyes widened with sudden purpose. "Wait, I can help."

Dane eyed her skeptically.

"Trust me, will you? Here . . ." She pulled a cloth from her pocket and blotted the blood from his arm, exposing a long, shallow gash between his shoulder and elbow. Sage rolled up her sleeve and hovered a hand over the wound.

"Elder Chrysanthe taught me a few techniques before we left. This may hurt, but it should speed up the healing process."

Dane's skepticism waned. "What are you doing?"

"Healing you." She thought for a moment, then amended, "Aiding your body's natural healing. It's a discipline Biophages can learn." One corner of her mouth quirked into a lopsided smile. "Now hold still."

Cayde detailed the encounter with the Chemocyte as Sage worked at Dane's arm. He pulled the stone from his pocket. Its red veins glimmered in the firelight, and Dane could see now that it wasn't like a stone at all; more a charred, blackened piece of thick tree bark.

"And you're sure that was the only one?" Quinn asked.

Cayde shook his head solemnly. "We can only hope. But I think it was alone. We would've seen more by now if it wasn't."

After a long, contemplative silence, Quinn clapped her hands to her knees and said, "We really do need rest. The journey tomorrow isn't easy. We'll need our strength . . . especially now."

Without another word, she curled up under her blanket, her back facing the fire. The others did the same.

Dane tried to shut out the horror of the Chemocyte encounter for the rest of the night, but every time he closed his eyes, he no longer saw the mutilated body in the hut, only the Chemocyte's burning crimson eyes, their slow, predatory blink in the darkness. For a long time he stared at the mossy formations on the cave ceiling, listening to Quinn, Cayde, and Sage shift and twist in their own efforts of sleep.

Resignedly, Dane closed his eyes and focused on the sound of the crackling fire. For now, he was safe.

But the night was still young.

CHAPTER 10

THE MOUNTAIN PASS

A low rumbling reverberated off the cave walls.

Dane's eyes snapped open. He couldn't remember dozing off, but now it had cost him. His mind assumed the worst: another Chemocyte had found them and was in the cave. Any moment and—

The noise came again. A voice—Quinn's voice. His panic subsided. *It's just Quinn,* he thought. *There's no Chemocyte.*

Wrapped in his blanket, his back to the dwindling fire, Dane watched the soft, orange flames flicker across the walls. The cave entrance glowed with the slightest hint of blue amongst the darkness waiting outside. He'd slept through the night.

Then came another voice—Cayde's voice—but his tone was unfamiliar. When Quinn spoke again, her voice carried an unpleasant blend of agitation and resentment. Something was wrong, but Dane couldn't quite place it.

Then, with absurd and sickening satisfaction, he understood. *Is something wrong with . . . them?*

He dismissed the thought and closed his eyes, trying to drift back into sleep. But a little voice whispered at the back of his mind. *Listen,* it said.

Whatever they were saying, they weren't happy. It could be important. They might reveal what they've been hiding from him.

They think I'm asleep. If I lay still, they won't notice—

Then guilt sank its teeth in. Everything about it felt wrong. Quinn was his friend, one of his dearest in the world—more than a friend, at least to him. He would do anything for her. And Cayde was . . . well, Quinn trusted Cayde, and Dane trusted Quinn. Even now, after everything they'd been through, he couldn't possibly—

But a raw, selfish thought stirred deep in his mind, and again he heard that little voice. *Listen.* The honest part of him knew it was wrong, but still that little voice persisted. He didn't fight it. He *wanted* to know what had them at odds. He *had* to know.

With painful slowness, he brushed the hair from his exposed ear, closed his eyes, and focused on Quinn's voice.

"I just don't understand, Cayde. Don't you have any concern for your own safety?" she hissed.

"Quinn, can we please discuss this later? It's late. We're tired. I don't want to wake the others."

"We're talking about this now!" she nearly yelled. "Every time it's the same. You *have* to see that, right?" She let out a long, exasperated sigh. "I don't know how much more I can take."

"And what was I supposed to do? Pretend I heard nothing and let that—that—*thing* kill us all?"

"You *know* that's not what I meant."

"Someone needed help. I could've saved them if only—"

"What about Dane? What if something worse had happened to him?"

Cayde's voice was cold and unwavering. "I wasn't going to let anything happen to him."

Quinn's frustration rose. "You know how vulnerable he's been ever since his Trials. And to put him in danger? *Again?*"

Dane felt himself cringe, her words sending an aching pain through his heart. She knew he was outmatched, weak in the face of danger. And she wasn't wrong.

"He's stronger than you think," Cayde shot back. "So he hasn't found his power yet. That doesn't mean he can't defend himself. He's an excellent fighter, and not just with that staff. You saw him in the Trials. I've never seen *anyone* try so hard in my life. And to pull himself together after everything he's gone through? He's stronger than either of us." There was a short pause, then Cayde said, "And no, I don't regret what I did. The Chemocyte is dead now. Who knows what it could have done if I wasn't there to—"

"But you could have *died!*"

Quinn's words hung over the cave, as if caught in an invisible web.

Dane realized his heart was racing, making his chest throb like the beat of a drum. He held his breath, hanging on every word.

When Quinn spoke again, her voice was barely more than a whisper. "What am I supposed to do, Cayde? What happens then? My father entrusted *us* with this task. *Us.* I can't do this alone . . . I can't."

Cayde breathed a labored sigh. "I'm sorry. I—I didn't know that—"

"—that what? That I worry every time you do this? That I fear I'll have to go on alone if something happens to you? We've only found two—maybe three—so far . . . I can't do it alone." Her voice was desperate, pleading. "I *need* you."

Dane felt his face flush with heat, hearing the pain in her voice. She meant those words. Not for him, but for Cayde.

He cupped the blanket to his mouth, suddenly aware of his rapid breaths. He forced himself to breath slower, to quell the tide of anger swelling in his mind. Deep down, he knew thinking about it would only tear him apart.

We've only found two, she had said. *Two what? What are you looking for? And why do you need Cayde to do it?*

His thoughts strayed to the conversation he'd overheard between Quinn and Elder Chrysanthe in the Elder Temple. She'd mentioned the same thing then—she had found two of something, and she had to find more of whatever it was.

Quinn continued, her words pouring out with increasing speed.

"First Stonehelm, then the mishap in the grotto. And now this? Cayde, I fear for you every time. I know you want to help, but please, don't trivialize your own life to do so."

Cayde suddenly sounded on the brink of tears. "Stonehelm wasn't—I-I never meant for that to happen . . . not like that." There was a long, aching pause. When Cayde spoke again, the hurt in his voice was gone. "At least I'm doing something about all this. At least I'm trying to improve my powers."

"Now what is *that* supposed to mean?!"

"You know exactly what it means. You're an incredible Luminarus, Quinn—the best I've ever seen. Why don't you use your powers? You need to practice so you're prepared when—"

"Just because I don't *flaunt* them at every opportunity doesn't mean I'm afraid to use them, Cayde," she snapped. "I don't need another lecture on how to use my powers. You know I get that enough from my father."

"That's not—"

"No, you're right, we're done talking about this now. I've told you my reasons before and I don't need to again."

They fell silent for a long moment, the only sound that of the crackling fire.

In an irritated yet motherly tone, Quinn finally said, "Will you *please* let me look at that? It doesn't look good."

"I told you, it's nothing. It'll heal soon enough."

"Can you at least let me wrap it? Or have Sage heal it when she wakes up?"

"Quinn, I can handle it," Cayde insisted. "Sage has done enough. She was exhausted after healing Dane's arm. Healing like that is very draining on anyone's body, and for Sage, it being her first time . . ." He sighed. "We still have a long journey in the morning; she'll need her strength. I can't have her wasting energy on me. I understand your concern, but I don't need you to keep doting on me."

"Fine," Quinn said. "Forget I said anything. Keep throwing your life away. Just know that you're putting me through *agony* every time you do."

Blankets rustled as Quinn tucked herself in without another word. After a short while, Cayde rummaged through his pack, gave a short grunt of pain, then tucked under his own blankets.

The fire crackled and popped as the cave fell quiet once more.

Dane tried to process what he'd just heard. Clearly Quinn and Cayde had had this conversation before, about Cayde putting himself in harm's way. Dane could see it now, looking back: how Cayde had charged at Avon, how he'd marched toward Varic's hut, how he'd thrown himself at the Chemocyte to protect Dane. But it wasn't as if Cayde relished the danger he put himself in—it was almost as if Cayde hadn't had a choice, like he held himself responsible for anything that could've gone wrong, that it was his responsibility.

Dane's mind strayed to how Quinn had talked about him, like he couldn't defend himself, like he was some child needing constant supervision. A cold hand squeezed around his heart. She and Cayde had asked Sage to join them based on her performance in the arena, because she was a powerful Biophage. They hadn't asked him to join at all.

They . . . they don't need me.

He thought of the stone warrior, of Avon and the men with metal swords, of the Chemocyte. He was just a liability to them, another thing for them to worry about, to keep eyes on.

She doesn't need me. Why am I even here? Why—

A pained whimper escaped his mouth. He squeezed his eyes shut, fighting back tears.

Why didn't I discover my power?

๑ ๛

Quinn, Sage, and Cayde were all donning their winter clothes when Dane woke the next morning. Soft rays of yellow light parted the deep blue of waning night. The cave walls were abundant with morning dew. The fire had been reduced to a charred pile of wood.

Quinn and Cayde intentionally avoided the other's gaze, packing in rigid silence. Sage, oblivious to Quinn and Cayde's quarrel the night before, was fighting a losing battle against gravity as she tried to pull on her boot. She hissed as her leg kicked out, flinging the boot across the cave, before she fell to a sitting position on the cave floor. She huffed the hair from her face and flashed a smile to no one in particular before marching over to retrieve the disobedient boot.

Once Dane had packed, he pulled out a thick wool cloak given to him by Duxor before leaving Vitalor. He frowned, holding it up to his body, cursing himself for not trying it on before leaving.

At least I'll be warm, he thought, shaking his head at the huge cloak, smiling at the trivial inconvenience. Resignedly, he enveloped himself in his personal fireplace and, heaving his pack over his shoulders, met the others at the cave entrance.

Cayde wore a cloak similar to his, though naturally Cayde's fit to perfection. Quinn had wrapped a thick woolen scarf around her chest and shoulders, covering the top portion of her usual form-fitting robes. She'd pulled the scarf over her face, leaving only her hair and radiant green eyes uncovered.

Sage, however, had on a mere jacket, not unlike the one she often wore in the village, paired with a thin green scarf.

Quinn and Cayde eyed her skeptically.

"Don't worry, I don't get cold," Sage said. She flashed a toothy grin and walked out of the cave, "I don't know about you, but I plan on sleeping on a real bed tonight. You coming?"

Quinn smiled lightly and followed her out of the cave, Dane and Cayde following behind.

No sooner had they rejoined the stone path when Dane, suddenly aware that the Chemocyte's crumbled body was somewhere nearby, recalled the gash on his arm from the night before. He wrestled his injured arm from his massive cloak. His eyes grew wide as he inspected the wound. There was still a noticeable tear in the skin, but the wound had nearly halved in size, and the swelling had all but disappeared. Pleasantly satisfied, he looked up to see Sage eyeing his arm, admiring her handiwork.

"See?" she said with a triumphant-yet-subtly-smug smile. "Told you I could do it."

Quinn led the way as the path carved deeper into the mountains, only stopping as they approached the base of a rocky cliff. Dane followed Quinn's gaze up a vertical wall of boulders as tall as an aged oak tree. At the top were the remnants of another path leading along a mountainous ridge.

"*This* is the mountain pass?" he asked, peering up at the precarious pile of boulders.

"The start of it, yes," said Quinn nonchalantly, staring at the closest boulders, as if to start climbing. "As I said before, the path by the lake may be less treacherous, but this way is the fastest. If we hope to stop Avon, we need to take some risks."

"You'll be fine," Sage said dismissively, staring hungrily up the cliff. She rubbed her hands together and blurted, "Race you to the top!" She leapt to the first boulder and began to scale upward with startling ease.

"The trail is much more manageable once we summit these boulders—a bit colder, but straight forward," Quinn said. She put her hand on Dane's shoulder and gave him a reassuring smile. "You'll be fine."

Dane's stomach twisted bitterly, and he was reminded of what she'd said the night before.

She thinks I can't do it, that I'm somehow inferior because I don't have any powers.

Resisting the urge to say something he'd regret, Dane forced a smile and began to climb.

The air was noticeably colder as they neared the cliff's summit. Small snowflakes had begun sifting down from the dull gray sky overhead. Despite his best efforts, Dane still hadn't caught up with Sage, who was climbing three boulders above him and gaining speed with every reach.

"So, I've been thinking," Sage called down, peering through her dangling legs as she paused and sat on a jutting rock, "why haven't we crossed paths with the other Aquadorians and Luminari that were supposedly following behind us?" She eyed Quinn curiously. "Didn't you say they'd take the same path?"

"There's an inn . . . just off the path . . . along the lake's shore," said Quinn between labored breaths. She heaved herself atop a boulder and sat on her heels. "They always stop there . . . for the night."

Sage's expression turned sour. "You mean we could have slept in a warm and cozy bed instead of in some damp old cave?" She leapt to her feet, throwing her arms in the air and huffing exaggeratedly. She began climbing again, but Dane could see the sly grin spreading across her face.

Sage extended a hand to each of them as Quinn, Dane, and finally Cayde joined her at the summit. Mountains loomed across the landscape, their frosted peaks barely visible through the increasing snowfall. A narrow trail weaved through the rocky terrain and disappeared deeper into the mountains.

"All right, what gives?" Sage said suddenly. She was still standing near the cliff's edge, one hand thrust on her waist as the other waved dismissively through the air. She glanced at Dane, then scrutinized Quinn and Cayde, one eyebrow raised. "Everyone seems rather quiet since last night. Did I miss something?"

Quinn and Cayde exchanged an emotionless glance.

"I think we're just tired after the long day, that's all," said Quinn. She looked at Cayde again, then, with a hint of resentment, added, "some of us more than others."

"Not to mention the savage Chemocyte," Dane offered casually. "And everything else that's happened."

"I know that, it's just—" Sage's smile faded, and she looked genuinely hurt. "It pains me to see all of you like this—so tense and fearful. I'm scared too. I—I was just trying to lift your spirits a little."

Quinn exhaled a labored breath. "You are," she said gently. She managed a smile and hooked her elbow through Sage's arm. There was a gleam in her eyes Dane hadn't seen for a long time, as if a small weight had been lifted from her mental burden. For a moment, she even looked happy. "I knew it was a good decision to bring you along." Her smile widened. She pulled Sage forward along the trail. "We're getting close. I can't wait for you to see Evergleam."

The narrow path grew more and more treacherous as it curved along a ridge, and Dane could barely stand with both feet side-by-side as they plodded forward. At one point, he nearly slipped as the rocks crumbled beneath his foot, tumbling down the cliffside. He dropped to one knee and stared down the foreboding, rocky slopes, now freckled with patches of white powder, holding still to keep from plunging into the dark, mountainous ravine far below.

"Keep back from the edge!" Quinn called back over the rising howl of the wind. "Nothing will save you if you fall!"

Dane nodded frantically, trying to maintain his balance as he pushed himself to his feet. The only visible patches of trail left were those of their fading footprints, the rest obscured by a thick sheet of snow. Soon the mountains too were lost in the white haze, snow and ice enveloping everything around them.

Dane strained his ears as Quinn shouted again, trying to separate her words from the gusts whipping and biting at his face and ears. She was pointing ahead to a hazy mountain looming in the distance. A high, narrow canyon cut the mountain in two, intersecting the path ahead.

He buried his face in the thick cloak until only his eyes were exposed to the cold. He silently thanked his old mentor as the cloak bravely buffeted the increasingly harsh winds, protecting his body from a single invading breath of frigid air.

Dane broke into a run once the canyon was in sight. He filed in behind the others and fell to his hands and knees. Hundreds of the storm's icy tendrils pricked at his fingers and toes through his thick gloves and boots, and his face and nose had gone numb. Despite the cold, he smiled, heaved a deep breath, and recoiled into the warmth of his cloak as he gazed around.

The winds whistled overhead like a songbird in spring, gracing the cold canyon air with its soft melody. Flakes of snow cascaded down like leaves in autumn, gently swaying and pinwheeling. The ice layering the canyon walls sparkled and gleamed a bright, frosted blue; it was as if they'd wandered into a winter's dream.

"This is incredible," he said softly, his voice reverberating throughout the icy canyon.

Quinn dusted the snow from her hair and met Dane's gaze. She flashed an infectious, youthful smile that reminded him of the first time he saw her, full of discovery and wonder.

"Wait until you see Evergleam," she said.

She turned and trotted to Sage, who walked forward with her neck craned back, staring up in awe.

Dane watched Quinn and Sage curiously as they delved into conversation. His thoughts drifted to what he'd heard the night before.

Is she telling Sage about last night? About her argument with Cayde?

Suddenly aware that Quinn and Sage were out of earshot, he snuck a glance at Cayde walking beside him, staring forward with an unreadable expression. A curious anticipation took hold. He could ask Cayde about last night, about his argument with Quinn. Part of him didn't want to pry into their personal affairs, but the other part of him relished at this opportunity, the part governed by that little voice at the back of his mind. *Maybe he'll mention what he and Quinn are looking for, or why they started arguing in the first place, or—*

Cayde's voice parted the silence.

"Dane, can I ask you something?"

Dane's thoughts grinded to a halt. He eyed Cayde curiously.

Cayde stared ahead with glazed eyes, as if lost deep in his own thoughts. When he spoke, his voice was quiet and hauntingly calm.

"Did you ever feel you . . . weren't good enough for her?"

Dane's breath hitched in his throat. He'd prepared for a question about the Chemocyte, or perhaps his Trials. But this . . . he would have sooner expected Cayde to ask him for combat lessons before asking such a question.

He opened his mouth, but no words came. He'd thought the same thing during his Trials, that he wasn't good enough for Quinn, that he had to prove he was good enough for her. But to hear Cayde voice the same concern, after all they've been through together, after all he's accomplished—the thought wove deep into Dane's heart, burrowing in with suffocating pain. *If he doesn't feel good enough for her, then how can I—*

He squeezed his eyes shut, cleared his mind before more depressing thoughts could take hold.

Dane realized he still hadn't answered Cayde's question. He shook his head and conjured the most indifferent, casual tone he could muster. "I—well, I suppose I might've felt that way before." He stole another glance at Cayde, who was still staring forward with the same vacant expression. "Why do you ask?"

Cayde startled, as if realizing he'd spoken the thought aloud. He glanced around wildly until his eyes landed on Dane. "Oh, I—no . . . it's just—" he exhaled deeply "—she holds so much love and compassion—not just for her family and friends, but for everyone. She's always concerned with what's best for her people, for all people, putting their needs above hers. But recently—" He paused and released a long, pensive sigh, cradling his forehead with his gloved hand. "I just want Quinn to be happy. She deserves it—more than anything. But this journey, what we've been asked to do . . . I see it in her eyes, feel it with her touch. The burden is too much for her. She'll never admit it, even when I ask, but—" He sighed again, his breath a shaky torrent. "I know she's hurting, but . . . I feel like there's nothing I can do."

Dane tried to mask his surprise at Cayde's confession. He couldn't have said it any better, nor so eloquently. But he hadn't missed the kernel of secrecy Cayde had just divulged. *This journey, what we've been asked to do . . .*

Cayde's brow creased with worry. In a small, quiet voice, he said, "How'd you do it?"

Dane stared at Cayde like he'd just asked what power Dane had. "I . . . don't understand."

"I see the way she lights up when she mentions her childhood, the Trials Festivals . . . her days with you. Listening to her talk about it, I—I've never seen her so happy. What was so different back then?"

Dane stared at the ground, trying to formulate a response. "Well," he started, "every year she'd lead me through the markets and we'd watch the Trials. We would talk, laugh, cheer—she'd share her favorite stories from the year or tell me more about the Trials. We were free to do as we pleased."

Suddenly his eyes widened. His mind searched every memory he had with Quinn, replaying them all with vivid clarity, looking for the one connection, the reason why she'd been so happy. Then he found it. He slowed to a stop.

"What is it?" Cayde said, almost pleading, eyebrows raised in silent question.

"I think Quinn just wants to be free."

"Free . . ." Cayde repeated distantly. The tension eased from his face and his misty eyes brightening with sudden clarity. He started forward again, stroking his stubbled chin, staring longingly ahead at Quinn. He kept mouthing the word over and over, his lips moving noiselessly, his brow etched with deep thought.

Dane watched him curiously a moment, but his mind wandered back to the events of the night before.

"So," he prodded, perhaps too eagerly. "Is that all? There's . . . nothing else wrong?"

He cringed as the words echoed lightly off the canyon walls. Cayde was certain to see through his thinly veiled disguise of indifference.

To his relief, Cayde took no notice, merely blinked and shook his head, stirring himself from his thoughts.

"We don't always agree, Quinn and I," Cayde said. "But we—" He shook his head. "I apologize. I don't mean to bore you with my problems."

"No, it's fine, I don't mind," Dane said, feigning innocence, his voice more eager than he'd anticipated.

Cayde gave him a sideways glance, studied Dane a moment. He shrugged as if to say, *I warned you.*

"Quinn and I—we see our powers differently. I tell her she doesn't use her powers enough, but she insists on being more reserved, saving them for when the critical occasion arises. She's convinced I use mine too flagrantly, that I must show restraint unless it's absolutely necessary. But am I wrong for wanting to use my powers to save people?" Cayde winced as the words left his mouth, his voice catching in his throat. "She—she's not wrong though. Our powers can be dangerous if not controlled—I know that now." He sighed, staring down at clenched fists. "But our powers are a gift. I've saved more lives than I've lost in using mine to protect others." The corners of his mouth curved into a small, sad smile. "I suppose we're both right and we're both wrong . . . sometimes it's just hard to understand."

Dane dropped his gaze as a vacant expression washed over his face. He had been so preoccupied with thoughts of Quinn and Cayde that he'd almost forgotten about his Trials. But now, hearing Cayde talk about his own powers, the floodgates had opened, and Dane couldn't stop the onslaught of bitter thoughts. His throat constricted under the duress of ensuing tears, and he let out a nervous laugh in a feeble attempt to quell the rising pain.

"At least you have powers to argue about," he said shortly. "You could be like me."

"And what's so wrong with that?"

The sudden harshness in Cayde's response made Dane recoil. He stared up at Cayde, his words falling from his mouth like shattered glass. "I was useless against the Chemocyte. I tried, but I—if you didn't save me I would've—" He squeezed his eyes shut, focusing on his trembling breaths. "First my Trials, then Avon, and now the Chemocyte." He realized Cayde had been with him for each of those events, had watched him fail time and time again. The ache in his heart intensified. "If something else were to happen . . ."

Cayde turned abruptly, planted both hands firmly on Dane's shoulders and stared straight into his eyes.

"Listen to me, Dane. Pitying yourself won't fix anything. What happened to you was beyond the realms of anyone's wildest imagination. But that doesn't mean you're inferior. Your power doesn't control your actions or define who you are. It doesn't stride into the unknown with unrivaled curiosity. It doesn't exercise strength and compassion when needed most. It doesn't force you into harm's way to save the ones you love. *You* do that, not your power.

"After watching you in the Trials—how you refused to back down even when all seemed lost—you are truly destined for something great." Cayde offered a strong, reassuring smile. "I still see that greatness in you now. Maybe it's not your time yet. Maybe you were meant to fail your Trials so you could one day find your true calling. Whatever the reason, you must stay strong, so you're ready when that day comes."

Cayde pushed away, holding Dane at arm's length. His gaze was nurturing and kind.

Dane drew in deep breaths, compiling his thoughts.

"What do I do if there's another Chemocyte? How do I fight back?"

Cayde's smile widened into a lopsided grin. "When the time comes, you'll know, and nothing will be able to stop you. When all hope seems lost, when everything in this world is working against you, you know you'll stop at nothing to save the ones you love. If you can keep fighting back, keep pushing against the darkness until the day you find your power . . ." exhaled, the breath whistling from his mouth. "You'll be unstoppable."

Dane looked up at Cayde with pleading, hopeful eyes. He wanted to believe Cayde with all his heart.

"You're certain?"

Cayde gave a succinct nod. "One day you'll see. You're stronger than you look—inside and out—I think you'll be surprised what you can do once you stop putting yourself at a disadvantage."

Dane smiled reflexively. Something in Cayde's tone filled him with a calming certainty. Despite all that had happened, despite his failures, Cayde still believed in him, believed he was destined for something more. And if Cayde believed it, maybe Dane could too.

"I may not show it," Cayde continued, "but I fear for your safety all the time—everyone's safety, for that matter. If I'm physically able, then it's my duty to protect others—I *have* to." His eyes glazed over, as if replaying a memory. "I know it doesn't make sense, but I wasn't always like this. A couple years ago, after my Trials—it was my first time using my powers in combat—in *real* combat—and I—" A faint whimper resounded in his throat, then he breathed a long, shaky sigh. "When the time comes, promise me you won't give up, no matter what."

Dane stared at him with genuine interest. "Why are you telling me this?"

Cayde's expression had turned grim and solemn, and though he didn't show it, his eyes glistened with hidden tears. "I don't think I could stand losing anyone else."

Dane looked at him, glimpsing the veil of sorrow in the Gravitus' eyes, masking a troubled past Dane didn't understand. *Who else had Cayde lost?*

Ahead of them, Quinn stopped, seeming to notice Dane and Cayde's slowed pace, and called back, "Come on, we're nearing the bridge."

The winds had slowed to a mild breeze as they exited the canyon and followed the path around the steep mountainside. Though the gray, hazy air was still shrouded in heavy snowfall, something in the distance caught Dane's eye. A strange, multicolored light filtered through the snow directly ahead.

As they drew closer, Dane could see the outline of a narrow bridge. Waves of pink, green, and yellow light sparkled beneath its icy surface that spanned across the dark, bottomless chasm separating the cliffs ahead.

"Is that bridge made of ice?" Sage asked.

Quinn nodded, a child-like grin plastered across her face. "One of several on the outskirts of the city. Energy from the Aurora Crystal courses through the ice, forever illuminating the path despite any storm."

Cayde stiffened and gestured something to Quinn. Her smile faded. She whirled around to face the bridge, squinting through the thick snowfall.

"What's wrong?" asked Dane, his voice hushed but urgent. "What do you see?"

"Quiet. There's something moving ahead," Quinn said.

Dane shielded his eyes from the snow, squinting to follow Quinn's gaze across the bridge, trying to make out the source of her concern.

Two dark shapes emerged from the white backdrop of the snow from the other side of the bridge, heading toward them.

"Turn back." hissed Cayde. "*Turn back!*" Then Cayde was pulling Dane's arm, leading him back the way they came. Quinn followed, hooking her arm around Sage, retreating further away until their backs were pressed against the cliffside. Quinn fumbled her hands along the surface, then frantically beckoned to the others.

"Quick, in here," she said, gesturing to a small crevice in the cliffside. The four of them would barely fit inside, but it was large enough to shelter them from both the storm and the mysterious figures on the bridge.

"What was that?" Sage asked as she craned her neck to avoid smacking her head on the sharp rocky interior.

"Someone was on the other side of the bridge," Quinn whispered. "Or some*thing.*"

Dane shuddered. The figures had looked humanoid from afar, but that didn't mean the figures weren't Chemocytes.

"What if they're citizens of Evergleam?" Sage asked.

Quinn squeezed into the crevice last and crouched beside the others, clutching her pack with one hand and rifling through its contents with the other. "Any respectful Luminarus carries an aurora torch whenever venturing down this path, especially in these conditions," she mumbled. "Whoever was out there held nothing of the sort, and I'm in no mood for taking chances."

She pulled an orb from her pack, cradling it between her palm and curled fingers; it emitted the same colored lights that coursed through the bridge, clouded behind a haze of dark gray mist.

She clutched the orb with her left hand. "Stay silent and don't move. We can't be seen."

For a moment, Dane forgot about the two figures as Quinn began swirling her marked hand over the orb. Colorful wisps of light slithered from the orb, drawn to her hand as she caressed the small pocket of air around them. The wisps followed like a shadow, expanding into the space around them until the air was tinted with colored light, cascading through the air like morning mist.

Dane opened his mouth to speak, his curiosity nearly getting the better of him, but Quinn already had a finger to her lips, her eyes wide and glaring.

Quinn clenched her marked hand into a tight fist; the light shook and wavered in place. She opened her hand, splaying her fingers wide, and pressed her palm forward. At once the wisps and faint colors dissipated, and all Dane could see from the crevice's cramped shelter was the shroud of snowflakes dotting the outside air. Nothing appeared different, but Quinn still held her arm forward, fingers splayed, gaze unflinching from the crevice opening.

Then came the crunch of snow beneath a heavy foot, and a deep, rasping voice sliced through the air.

"Yes, I'm certain you fool. Someone was here. You heard Avon. We have to stop anyone else from interfering with—well, well, well . . . what have we here?"

There was a short, agonizing pause, then another voice hissed, "Footprints. Someone *is* close."

"These tracks are still fresh," the first voice said. Dane shuddered involuntarily. Even though he couldn't see it, he could almost hear the man's peeled, predatory grin. "Look . . . this way."

The footsteps drew nearer. Dane's heart leapt into his throat. His eyes darted between Quinn and Cayde. Quinn remained motionless, her gaze and concentration locked on the entrance. The veins in her outstretched arm were bulging from her skin, and trickles of sweat now dripped from her brow despite the bitter cold. Her entire face was tense. Cayde was staring at her, his face equally strained but creased with worry.

Dane wanted to scream at them both. *We're going to be seen! We're stuck here with no way out and they're going to see us! We have to do* something!

A metal boot plunged into the snow just outside. Dane wanted to push Quinn and Cayde forward, running with them to take the stranger by surprise. He didn't know whether the man was armed, but they had to do something. *Anything.*

But before he could move, the stranger crouched down and stared directly at him.

Dane was paralyzed. A thick grey hood framed the weathered, sullen skin on the man's face. His dark, beady eyes stabbed into Dane's, and his cracked, splitting lips carved a red smile between his bony cheeks. His arms and chest were coated in metal beneath his thick woolen cloak.

Dane grimaced and bared his teeth, bracing himself for the ensuing struggle with the metal man. But the man simply stared at him—rather, stared past him, through him, his gaze vacant and dreary. He craned his head slightly from side to side, glazing first past Quinn, then Cayde, then Sage.

He can't see us, Dane realized. *But . . . but how?*

A second pair of footsteps plodded through the snow and stopped beside the metal man.

"Well?" the other voice beckoned.

The metal man stared a moment longer, his gruesome grin now a hard, expressionless line. He rose to his feet, his face disappearing from the opening. "Check the canyon. They couldn't have gone far."

The two men headed toward the canyon and disappeared from view.

Dane, Quinn, Cayde, and Sage waited in aching silence, straining for any more sounds from the men. Several moments passed, the only sound that of the howling winds.

Quinn let out a pained gasp, her arm falling limply to her side. The wisps of light around them sparkled momentarily, then retreated back into the orb.

"Quinn . . . what *was* that?" Sage asked. "Why couldn't he see us?"

"No time . . . to explain," she said between labored breaths, moving toward the outside air on hands and knees, wincing as she spoke. "We have to . . . cross the bridge before—"

Her words were lost in the wind as she collapsed into the snow.

Cayde was at her side in a heartbeat. She tried pushing herself up, but her trembling arms failed and she fell into Cayde's supporting embrace.

"I'm fine, I just . . . my strength . . ." she said unconvincingly. Her face was as pale as the snow. Red lines streaked across the whites of her eyes.

"I know, we need to get you to safety." Cayde gently pulled her from the crevice, then flung one of her arms over his shoulder and started shuffling toward the bridge. "Dane, grab her other arm. Hurry!"

Dane scrambled out behind them and hurried to Quinn's side. With a pained whimper, she draped her weakened arm across his shoulder. Dane tightened one arm around her waist, lifting upward to support her weight, and gripped her limp hand in his. Her hand was freezing.

Dane squeezed her hand tighter, willing his warmth into her as they trudged through the snow. The bridge was barely wider than the path leading away from the canyon. A dark, foggy ravine stretched beneath it. When they drew closer, Dane kicked a hardened mound of snow over the edge, watching it fall until it was engulfed by the icy fog. He swallowed hard and stared ahead. He had to help Quinn across the bridge, help her to safety.

"There they are! Don't let them get away!"

Dane's breath halted in his throat as voices erupted behind them. He glanced over one shoulder. The two men were running straight toward the bridge, straight toward him.

Cayde scooped Quinn in his arms and shouted behind him, "I'll get Quinn across. You and Sage stall them until you can follow us across. Then I'll destroy the bridge."

Without another word, Cayde stepped onto the bridge, ice splintering beneath his feet as he ventured forward.

Dane could feel the claws of fear digging in once more as the two men charged toward them. Sage squeezed his shoulder. Despite the ensuing danger, her touch was reassuring and comforting. "We can do this," she said, her face contorted with determination. Dane nodded and she jerked the Willow Whip from around her waist. It swung free in a green blur, soaring elegantly through the air before coiling neatly at her feet.

The two men were running faster now. Snow sprayed behind them as they each reached into their dark, ragged cloaks and revealed gruesome metal blades. Their charging roars cascaded over the howling winds, enraged and murderous.

Dane pulled out his staff, gripping it with trembling hands.

When all hope seems lost, Cayde had told him, *when everything in this world is working against you, you know you'll stop at nothing to save the ones you love.*

Dane blinked away the fear that threatened to claim him, clinging to a new purpose. He needed to give Cayde time to cross the bridge. He had to protect them. He had to protect Quinn.

The men were now so close that Dane could see the refined edges of their metal frames protruding from beneath their dark cloaks. One man was running toward Sage, both hands grasping his sword. The other man—the same man who had narrowly caught them in the crevice, the man covered in metal—ran straight at Dane, arm held high above his head.

These men have powers, Dane thought. *They have metal swords.* He stood taller, clenching his staff, strengthened by its weight in his hands. *But they won't get through me.*

Dane let out a primal cry of rage, fear, and desperation. Clenching his staff in both fists, he thrust it into the air as the man's blade came crashing down toward him. His eyes shut involuntarily; he could only hope the sword wouldn't cleave through his staff and his body.

There was a suppressive thud and a sting of pain shot through Dane's locked arms. He peeked through one eye. The man's incredulous face was so close that Dane could smell his rotting breath.

Dane ventured a glance up at his staff. Though the man's sword looked as if it could slice through stone, the staff had intercepted his blow, soaking the blade's full force without a shred of visible damage. Dane felt his mouth curve in a satisfactory smirk. *Stronger than the sharpest of blades . . .*

The man pulled his arm away and swung a second time. Again, Dane thrust the staff upward, watching as the blade connected with the staff's resilient surface and bounced off without a scratch.

The man stumbled backward, looking between his deadly sword and the staff.

"How—how is this possible?" The man said, bewildered. "That's just a—it's just a stick!"

Dane's smirk widened. Fear still clouded the forefront of his mind, but now it was a revitalizing fear that filled him with renewed vigor and purpose. He wouldn't let this man win.

"It's not a stick," Dane said, letting his fear fuel him, making him stronger. Finally, he was fighting back. "It's an ELDERWOOD STAFF!"

Dane whirled the staff and leapt toward the man. The man, still in a daze, swung half-heartedly in response. Dane deflected the sword with ease and shoved the butt of his staff into the man's metal chest. A loud clang erupted and the man reeled back with a grunt of pain. Dane spun his staff around again and smashed its end against the man's upper arm. Another clang re-sounded from the metal, but the man didn't recoil, showed no sign of injury.

The metal—I can't damage him like this . . . but I don't need to. I don't have time. I just need to get across the bridge and leave him behind.

Dane took a step toward the bridge and readied his staff again.

The metal man growled and roared in anguish. He lunged at Dane, leading with the sword's jagged tip. Dane twisted to the side—channeling how Cayde had baited and twisted away from the Chemocyte—and brought the staff down on the man's hand. The man howled as the sword sprang from his hand and disappeared into the thick pile of snow. Allowing the man no time to recover, Dane fastened both hands around one end of the staff and swung it like a club at the man's head.

The clang of wood on metal rang again, but this time the impact violently jerked the man's head to one shoulder. The man toppled, landing on the edge of the icy cliff with a crack as the ground beneath him gave way, cascading into the ravine below. The man flailed his arms upward as he began to fall, scrambling for any handhold in a desperate attempt not to plummet into the ravine. His hand grasped the ledge, the man clinging for his life.

Dane watched the man a moment, frozen in place. He could end it. He could kick the man's hand free, send him to his death in the ravine.

But the thought passed through his mind in a heartbeat, and giddy triumph bubbled up inside him. He'd done what Cayde had asked. He'd beaten the metal man with nothing but his Elderwood staff and his bare hands. Now it was his chance to escape.

"Sage!" He called out, sprinting for the bridge, carefully stepping his way across. "We have to go!"

He reached the middle of the bridge when he heard an en-raged cry behind him. Not wanting to lose his balance on the icy surface, he glanced over one shoulder to see Sage with the Willow Whip in hand, her arm outstretched to the second metal man. She wrenched her arm backward and the whip jerked away. The man's sword sprung from his hands and sailed into the air, arcing away from Sage and the man, headed directly toward Dane.

Dane dove face first onto the bridge, sliding across the slick icy surface as the sword plunged into the ice where he had just been. For a moment, nothing happened. Then the ice splintered, long jagged cracks sprouting from where the sword had pierced the bridge, distorting the veins of color beneath like light shining through shattered glass.

The entire bridge groaned.

"*Sage!*" Dane called again, his voice tremulous with fear. "RUN!"

Sage's hair fanned through the air as she glanced at Dane then back to the confused man. With a cry of exertion, she jumped up and planted both feet on the man's chest. The man went sprawling onto his back, skidding toward the ledge as Sage fell, grunting in pain as she landed with a thud on the icy bridge.

Dane moved swiftly to the other side of the bridge, keeping his body as low as possible, his eyes never leaving Sage. She staggered to her feet, coiled the Willow Whip back around her waist, and began tiptoeing around the spreading cracks, her body straining against the wind, fighting for balance and her life.

Then a guttural roar filled the air. The man Sage had kicked was on his feet and plowing toward her.

Cayde's voice erupted behind them.

"DANE! SAGE! NOW!"

Sage disregarded all caution and sprinted across the bridge.

Infected by the sudden urgency and blinded by sheer mayhem, Dane turned, saw that the bank of snow on the other side of the bridge was within reach, and leapt.

He crashed to solid ground as snow sprayed into his face. He scrambled to his feet. Quinn had propped herself against a rock a short distance away and was shouting incoherently at Cayde, who was looking frantically between Quinn and the bridge.

Both were safe. Only Sage remained.

The world seemed to slow as he turned back to the bridge.

Sage lost her balance and fell to the cracking ice, her face narrowly evading the sword's blade. Before she could push herself to her feet, the man, who had bounded through the snow with blind rage, was on the bridge, one hand outstretched and reaching for the sword. His mouth was twisted in a maniacal grin. Strands of black, greasy hair clung to the sides of his bloodied face. The bridge groaned again beneath his weight as his hand edged closer to the hilt.

Fear consumed Dane. If the man removed the sword, the ice would surely shatter. Sage would plummet to her death.

MOVE! He screamed in his mind, urging himself toward the bridge and his frightened sister. *She needs you! You have to HELP HER!*

He started to move, but the air felt like water, his body like dripping sap. The man was moving faster.

Dane heard himself scream, but it sounded distant, detached from his own body. Everything, every part of himself that he could control, was focused solely on saving Sage.

But it was too late.

The man clasped the sword hilt and wrenched it from the ice. The cracks in the ice turned to giant fissures that spread the entire length of the bridge.

"SAGE!"

The bridge shattered into chunks of ice and frozen debris with a deafening crack. The man fell instantly, shrieking as the ground beneath him gave way, taking him with it. Then Sage began to fall. Dane dove for the bridge with both hands extended for his sister. He landed on his stomach, both arms reaching over the ledge where the bridge had been.

She saw him and flung one hand toward his. For a moment it looked as though he would catch her, clasp her desperate hand in his and pull her to safety.

Then the moment was gone. Her fingers swept through the air just out of his reach.

Sage fell into the ravine.

Dane couldn't breathe. His mind, his entire body, had gone numb.

This can't be—it's all a dream—Sage can't be gone—she isn't dead— it can't *be—SAGE NOOOO!!*

Then a hand shot out of the fog—a small, thin, green hand.

Dane stared in absolute confusion as it extended toward him. He blinked and stared harder.

The hand drew closer—only, it wasn't a hand—at least, not a normal hand. The Willow Whip was reaching toward him. The small, thin branches at its tip slithered through the air like grasping fingers, searching for Dane's dangling arms.

His heart sprang back to life as the finger-like branches coiled around his hand. The whip tightened, its end still lost beneath the fog. He felt something in his shoulder pop as the whip pulled taut, but he didn't care. He started pulling hand over hand, lifting the whip up until a shape emerged from the fog.

"Sage!" Dane cried, hot tears streaking down his frozen cheeks. "Sage, I've got you!"

Cayde was beside him a moment later, hands gripping the willow branch.

"Pull!" Cayde grunted.

Dane erupted with joyous laughter as Sage's hand found the edge of the cliff. He and Cayde grabbed under her arms and heaved her away from the ledge.

Sage looked dazedly at the others, gasping for air and stroking the fine snow beneath her.

"What . . . happened?"

"You fell," Dane said, throwing his arms around her, squeezing her with everything he had. "I thought you had—you disappeared beneath—" His face contorted in confusion. "Didn't you use the whip to grab my hand?"

Sage shook her head, bewildered. "No, I—that wasn't me. One moment I was falling—I thought I was done for—then my body jerked to a halt." She winced, rubbing her waist. "I thought *you* saved me."

Dane shook his head, equally perplexed. Then his eyes widened. "You don't suppose . . ."

Sage diverted her gaze to the whip half-coiled around her waist. With precise, motherly care she lifted the other half of the whip from the snow.

"Did *you* save me?" She said quietly, staring at it with her large, sea blue eyes.

The whip said nothing.

Sage smirked, smiling fondly. "That's all right, I know you did."

Quinn hobbled over and knelt down beside Sage, grimacing as she did so, pressing the fingers of her marked hand to her temple. Her eyes were no longer streaked red, and the rosy color had returned to her cheeks, but she looked exhausted.

She embraced Sage gently. "That was too close, Sage, but you were sensational fighting off those men." She looked at Dane. "You both were." She paused, exhaling a burdened sigh and grinned. "I think we've had enough close calls in the past couple days to last a lifetime, don't you?"

Sage nodded emphatically and exhaled sharply through her nose. "I don't know about all of you, but I'm staying on solid ground from now on." She barked her infectious laugh, and Dane couldn't help but join in. It felt good to laugh again after all that had happened.

"Now," Quinn said promptly, rising shakily to her feet. "Evergleam is just around that bend. We have to inform my father of those men, especially if they're involved with Avon."

"Yes, yes we do," said Cayde faintly. He pushed himself to his feet, breathing heavily as he staggered away from the ledge. A thin veil of sweat glistened on his forehead. His eyes suddenly looked dull and lifeless. "We need to—we—I—"

He took another step forward and fell face-first into the snow, unmoving.

"Cayde!" Quinn cried. She knelt beside him, cradling his head in her lap. "What happened? What's wrong?"

Cayde muttered something incomprehensible. His body was limp. One of his hands was stained red.

Dane's eyes widened. He knelt beside Quinn and lifted Cayde's cloak, exposing the wrapped wound Cayde had suffered the night before. The wrap was soaked with blood.

"Over there!"

A voice rang out behind them. Dane stood and spun to face where the voice had come from, expecting to see more men with metal swords running at them. Instead, he saw two figures approaching through the haze of snow, both adorned in white armored robes, each carrying a colorfully lighted torch.

"Lady Quinn!" One of them said. "What happened? We thought there was an avalanche."

"Guards!" Her voice turned stern, authoritative, masking the fear beneath. "He just collapsed; he's lost a lot of blood. He needs healing right away! Take him to the infirmary!"

The two guards heeded her command without question and lifted Cayde from the ground, supporting his body between them.

"I-I can try to heal him," stammered Sage. "I still have some strength left to—"

Quinn shook her head. "No, save your strength. You've done enough already. He'll be all right, but only if we move quickly."

She followed the guards as they turned back down the path they had entered from, Sage following close behind.

Dane gathered his belongings and started after them, but he only took a few steps before a strange feeling forced his gaze back to the ravine and the shattered bridge.

The metal man—the one Dane had nearly sent over the ledge into the ravine, the one whose life he could have ended—stood on the other side.

Dane felt his skin crawl as he stared back. For a moment he dreaded his decision to spare the man's life. The chance had been there, to kick the man's hands from the cliff and let him plummet into the ravine. But he didn't—couldn't. Deep down, he feared that taking the man's life would have been the final tipping point, propelling him down a dark path from which he'd never recover. Instead he'd vouched for mercy—possibly cow-ardice, running away like he had.

Staring at the man now, Dane got the sinking feeling that mercy would come back to haunt him. Though he couldn't see it through the thick haze of snowfall, he could feel the man's beady eyes staring into him, glimpsing the fear beneath; could see those thin red lips parting in a sinister grin. The man was memorizing his scent, a hunter on the prowl. And now, Dane was his prey.

Whoever the metal man was, wherever he'd come from, he'd be back. And next time, Dane knew mercy wasn't a luxury he'd be able to afford.

The man swept his tattered cloak across his face. He turned his back to Dane, retreated from the ravine, and disappeared into the storm.

CHAPTER 11

THE FESTIVAL OF LIGHT

"Hurry! It's not much farther!" Quinn shouted.

Sheer cliffs of magnificent ice eclipsed either side of the path as they hurried away from the bridge and through the mountains. The ice was now streaked with the same glowing greens and pinks they had seen in the bridge. Evergleam was close.

The guards were following Quinn around a curve in the path, Sage in pursuit, as Dane caught up to them. The snowfall hadn't let up, but the harsh wind had calmed to a mere whisper.

"Take him to the infirmary. Dane. Sage. Go with them," Quinn instructed. "I'll meet you there."

The guards heeded her command and continued toward a massive stone wall as Quinn ran to the left. When Dane didn't follow, one of the guards, trying to conceal his labored panting, called back, "Come on, then, it's this way!"

But Dane wasn't listening. He could only stare at the wall before him—Evergleam Castle. Quinn had told him stories of her home, but seeing it for himself was something else entirely. The castle's exterior stone wall protruded from the looming

174

mountain cliff behind it, circling the castle's towers as it disappeared out of view. Though void of snow, the wall shimmered with sparkling white light like the sun reflecting off fresh snowfall. Several stone parapets towered overhead like steadfast sentries against the cold winter nights. A single tower erupted from within the walled enclosure, nearly grazing the top of the cliff behind, and was topped with a magnificent sculpture of scintillating ice that reflected hundreds of colorful auroras into the dusk sky.

"You heard Lady Quinn, quickly now!"

The guards stopped at the base of a parapet where an open archway preceded a spiral staircase. Dane ran to their aid and helped carry Cayde up the staircase and over the fortuitous castle wall. They entered into a large stone courtyard that surrounded the castle's tower. Ahead, another archway beckoned, leading into a softly lit room. Dane followed the guards in.

The room was long and narrow, lined with dozens of beds, all fitted with clean, white linens. The walls were lit with rows of colorful torches, their handles short lengths of wood, each topped with a swirling, heatless flame of green, yellow and pink.

The guards holstered their torches into wall sconces flanking the entryway and hustled Cayde to the nearest bed.

"What is this place?" asked Dane, taken aback by the sheer wonder of the room and the castle.

"Evergleam castle. This is the infirmary," one guard said promptly, positioning a pillow under Cayde's head. "Doubles as the guard barracks when necessary."

Footsteps echoed from the far end of the room, reverberating off the walls in sharp taps. Quinn emerged from a large spiral staircase, followed by a stout woman in dark green robes adorned with a pattern of ivy leaves tipped in frost. She carried a large basket brimming with cloths and medicines under one arm, her rosy cheeks glistening in the torchlight.

"He just collapsed," Quinn was saying as she and the woman stood over Cayde. Her authoritative resolve from before faltered, panic finding its way through. "He—he was wounded in

the woods—a tree branch. Dilpha, please, I don't know if he—
"

The stout woman, Dilpha, squeezed Quinn's arm. Gently, she said, "Let's take a look." Dilpha lifted Cayde's seeping bandages between finger and thumb, peering underneath.

Cayde moaned and stirred slightly, his eyes no more than slits.

Dilpha rummaged through her basket and pulled out a roll of cloth. She traced her hand—marked with Biophage vines—around the edge of Cayde's wound, dabbing at the blood there. Once the skin around the wound was clean, she placed the cloth over it, pressing lightly.

"He'll require further attention, but he is stable," Dilpha said.

Quinn allowed herself a moment of respite, then her mind seemed to shift, eyes growing wide and urgent. "Where are my mother and father? We have to speak with them right away."

"Your father has been gone a few days. And your mother is attending to a few final preparations for the Festival."

"Festival?" asked Dane.

"Why, the Festival of Light," Dilpha said with a warm smile. "The night we welcome each Luminarus initiate into their new home. It's a joyous occasion for all."

Quinn went on unperturbed. "I need to see them now! We're all in danger! If we don't act soon Evergleam will—"

"Breathe, dear one. Breathe." Dilpha gripped Quinn's forearms in her hands, massaging her skin there. "Whatever it is can wait a few moments longer."

Quinn's jaw tightened. She closed her eyes, forcing several deep breaths.

"Your mother will be along shortly, don't you worry," Dilpha said, her voice low and soothing. She sniffed the air near Quinn's head, and, with a grin, said, "When was the last time you bathed? Your mother will want you presentable for the Festival tonight."

Quinn opened her eyes, releasing the breath she'd been holding. Her sense of urgency had dwindled. Now she just looked exhausted. "It's been a rough few days."

"I can only imagine." Dilpha's grin softened. She patted Quinn's cheek. "Go. Relax a little. You deserve it, my dear."

Quinn grasped Dilpha's hand in hers, leaning into the woman's touch. She inhaled deeply, gave a small nod, then turned and walked from the room.

Sage cleared her throat once Quinn had gone, teetering on the balls of her feet. "Excuse me, Miss Dilpha. You don't suppose . . . *we* could bathe too?"

Dilpha turned to Sage and let out a high-pitched chuckle. "Of course, you may. Come, come."

She led them out of the infirmary and down the hall to a set of adjoining rooms where she drew them each a bath. Dane undressed and lay in the bath a while, letting the steaming water soothe his tired and cold limbs.

He dried himself off once the water had lost its temperature. Fresh clothes lay on the table outside, various sizes of standard Luminari garb. He pulled on a white tunic hemmed with strips of blue and green, meant to mimic the aurora design so often paired with the Luminari, and pulled on a pair of black trousers with matching hemming.

Feeling thoroughly refreshed, he set out down the hall and returned to the infirmary.

Quinn was with Dilpha at Cayde's bedside, guards still stationed nearby. She had replaced her dark blue robes from before with a nearly identical set, only now the hemmed auroras seemed to shimmer and wave in the light. Her hair was still damp, like she'd dried off in a hurry.

"How is he?" Dane asked, mostly to fill the emptiness of the room.

"Better," Dilpha said. "He's resting now."

Sage appeared behind Dane a moment later. She eyed Dilpha with interest as the healer worked at Cayde's skin, just as Sage had done to Dane's arm the night before.

"Do you mind if I watch?" Sage asked.

Dilpha looked Sage up and down, gaze landing on her exposed mark. She beamed. "It's due time I had another Biophage around here. I have been rather lonesome of late."

The sharp tap of footsteps once more resonated from the spiral staircase. A tall, strikingly elegant woman approached, wearing white robes etched with brilliant, dancing auroras. Her hair billowed behind her in a lustrous shade of chestnut brown, the same shade as Quinn's.

"Lady Evergleam," the guards stated, bowing their torsos level with the ground.

The tall woman strode across the room with nonpareil grace, seeming to float across the white surface. Dilpha stepped aside as the woman approached Cayde's bed. When she spoke, the words rolled from her mouth like a warm summer breeze.

"That will be all, gentlemen. You are free to resume your duties," she said.

"Yes m'lady," the guards replied, and hustled out of the infirmary.

Lady Evergleam turned to Quinn, her voice composed, simultaneously stern and gentle. "Tell me what happened."

The words flew from Quinn's mouth. "He was wounded on our journey, Mother. He said it was nothing—that he was fine. But he wasn't. After we—he just collapsed. He was bleeding and he didn't tell me and I thought he was—"

Lady Evergleam tucked a hand behind Quinn's neck and pulled her in.

Quinn flung her arms around her mother, burying her face into her mother's shoulder, squeezing tightly. "I was so scared," she said.

Lady Evergleam held Quinn for a moment, then looked Cayde over, from his pale, clammy skin to the steady rise and fall of his chest. She put the back of her hand to Cayde's damp forehead, smoothed the hair from his face.

She looked to Quinn with a reassuring smile. "He'll be fine, don't you worry. I'm confident in Dilpha's healing abilities."

Quinn turned to her mother.

"Where is Father? We need to see him immediately. It's urgent."

"Off on diplomatic matters until morning. In the meantime, why don't we—"

Quinn's face contorted with strain. "There's no time for waiting, Mother! The city isn't safe! We have to prepare everyone before—"

Lady Evergleam squeezed Quinn's shoulders, staring deep into her eyes. A slight smile touched her lips. "Breathe, my dear. Just breathe. It's all right. When Yarrin returns, you may all speak with him then. What is it you wish to tell him?"

Quinn exhaled a deep, practiced breath. "We saw him—we saw Avon—in Vitalor. He tried to set the Elderwood ablaze. We only realized it was him when Cayde and Dane ran after him." Graveness swallowed her features. "He's back, Mother."

Lady Evergleam's expression turned bleak as Quinn spoke. She inhaled sharply, clasping a hand to her parted mouth, and glanced to Cayde with a look of concern.

"That isn't how he—"

"No, that was after. Avon didn't hurt him."

"Good. That's good. But dear me, I'm so relieved none of you were injured. I fear for what he could do to Evergleam if we were caught unprepared." Lady Evergleam breathed a long, calming sigh, her body visibly relaxing. "I'll talk with the captain of the guard tonight before the Festival and tell him to be on the watch for suspicious activity."

She turned to Dane as if noticing him for the first time. She adorned a wide, apologetic smile, offering her hand. "Oh my, where are my manners? You must be Dane Willows. Quinn has told me so much about you."

Dane took her hand, heat rushing to his face. *Quinn told her about me?*

"Yes, Lady Evergleam," he managed politely.

"Please, call me Zena." She turned to Sage with the same welcoming smile. "And you must be Sage. A Biophage, aren't you?" Zena smirked. "It's due time we found Dilpha some proper company."

"Proper company indeed," Dilpha added with a chuckle as she continued tending to Cayde's wound.

Zena smiled fondly, then turned her attention to Quinn, her expression suddenly clouded with concern.

"Now, would you enlighten me as to why you arrived so late today? We were expecting you at noon to welcome the new Luminari into the city. You had me quite worried."

Quinn's voice was steady, controlled, but Dane could see her body tense beneath her robes.

"We started later than expected this morning, that's all," she said shortly.

Dane furrowed his brow. *That's all? What about the Chemocyte?*

Zena stared at Quinn for a long moment, then sighed. "Very well, I'm sure you've all had a long day. In light of what happened in Vitalor, it would do well to keep the people of Evergleam in a festive mood. Why don't you open the gates and greet everyone into the temple."

Quinn's eyes twinkled momentarily, then locked nervously on Cayde.

"Don't worry," Zena said in her comforting, motherly tone, smiling gently, "Dilpha will have him better in no time. Now go, we don't want to keep everyone waiting in the cold."

"Of course, Mother," Quinn said. She started toward the staircase, then turned back, her eyes locking on Dane. Her entire complexion seemed to be glowing, and not from the glow of the room. Her eyes sparkled with excitement, as if all the stress and worry from the past couple days had been blown away by the cold mountain air.

"Dane, do you want to come with me?" Quinn asked. "Sage?"

"I'd like to stay with Dilpha. I'll join you later," Sage said.

"Dane?" Quinn repeated.

Dane's heart pounded. This was his chance to be alone with Quinn, his chance to share in her joy like he had done so many times at the Trials Festival, his chance to ask why she never returned like she'd promised.

Quinn flashed a smile and beckoned him to her.

Dane stepped forward but stopped when he felt Zena's calm touch on his shoulder. In a hushed voice, she said, "Before you go, Dane. I heard about—well, I'm sorry about what happened at your Trials. I want you to know that I will help you to the best of my ability. What happened at your Trials happened for a reason. I'm confident you'll find that reason soon enough." She smiled a strange, secretive smile. "Enjoy the Festival. Quinn is waiting."

"Thank you," he said genuinely, thinking how bitterly Elder Chrysanthe had responded to his lack of powers. Zena was equally apprehensive in her unfamiliarity of his situation, but far kinder.

Dane smiled at that, then hurried off after Quinn. He followed her out of the infirmary and down a large pearl white staircase that shone in the light of the aurora torches. They reached the bottom and entered a massive hall with a high, arched ceiling. Dozens of hanging ice-like sculptures scintillated amidst the castle light. The walls, identical to those of the infirmary, supported hundreds of aurora torches in their sconces. At the far end of the hall was a massive oak door, stretching nearly as high as the ceiling.

Quinn tapped his shoulder. Dane turned and his mouth fell open involuntarily. A giant, transparent crystal, seemingly created from pure light, towered before him, nearly scraping the high ceiling with its tapered peak. The massive gem emitted a constant dazzling array of flickering auroras into the open air of the hall, filling every dark corner with light and painting every visible surface in wondrous veils of pink, yellow, and green.

Quinn stepped toward the gem, one hand outstretched. Small tendrils of colored light licked at her palm as she sifted her fingers through the air. The lights traced her movement, enveloping her hand in their gleaming embrace.

"This is the Aurora Crystal, the energy well of Evergleam," she said dreamily. She pulled her hand away from the lights, and they receded into the Aurora Crystal, gleaming more brightly than before.

Dane looked to Quinn, then back to the massive gem.

"It's . . . beautiful."

Quinn's lips curled softly. "Isn't it? Founder Illara discovered it here on the highest peak of the Aurora Mountains. The crystal was so magnificent that she and the original Luminari built the city and this castle as a sanctuary to protect it for centuries to come." She sighed, staring pensively into the soft, soothing glow. "I like to believe part of Founder Illara's memory lives inside it, watching over the city and its people."

Dane's brow furrowed. "Why did it need protection back then?"

"There are some who do not respect the wonders of this world." Quinn shook her head in disgust. "Founder Lussiek was one of them. Shortly before the castle was built, he tried to extract the crystal's energy, steal it for himself, but Founder Illara fought him off with the help of the other founders. Lussiek was banished to the Shrouded Isle soon after, left to die for his treachery." She scoffed. "Serves him right."

Dane could feel Quinn's eyes on him, but his gaze was transfixed on the Aurora Crystal. Questions permeated his mind about the magnificent gem, about Evergleam, and about Quinn.

He opened his mouth as if to speak, slowly formulating the thoughts, when Quinn said, "Come with me. It's time for the ceremony to commence."

"Commence . . . what? Quinn?" Dane tore his gaze from the Aurora Crystal. Quinn was halfway across the hall, headed to the massive doors. He hastened after her, nearly at her side when gripped the large handles and threw the doors open.

Dane froze.

Standing in a circular courtyard on the other side of the doors were hundreds of Luminari of all ages, all waiting patiently in silence, each holding aurora torches of their own. At the forefront of the crowd, on the steps leading to the great doors, stood a dozen young men and women dressed in shimmering white robes, each wearing a nervous, hopeful smile.

Dane stood there only for a moment before he leapt to the side and slipped behind one of the doors, hidden from the crowd. He felt like an intruder. He didn't know these people. They were Quinn's people.

He stared at Quinn from behind the door. She stood in the center of the entryway, hands outstretched to address the crowd, beaming from ear to ear as she welcomed them all to the Festival of Light before leading them into the Aurora Temple—the massive hall with the Aurora Crystal. The crowd erupted into celebratory cheers as the white-robed Luminari initiates filed anxiously across the hall. People poured in around them, filling the hall with frivolous chatter and melodious song.

Despite the hordes of people flooding into the hall, despite the hundreds of excited faces and unique personalities, despite the magnificence of the entire city rejoicing with its newest members, it was Quinn who surprised Dane the most. As more and more people poured in, Quinn took the time to greet every one of them by name, offering a cheerful handshake or warm embrace. Dane struggled to name everyone in his own village, let alone each person in an entire city. But Quinn was doing so to perfection, exuding radiance and genuine happiness to each person she greeted.

Dane smiled fondly as he watched her. In spite of everything that had happened—the fear of Avon, the horrors of the Chemocyte, their near-death experience on the bridge—Quinn still managed to bless each person with her love and appreciation. The entire city was one enormous family.

"Miss Quinn! Miss Quinn!"

A squeal of delight wafted through the crowd. A young girl—no more than six years of age with curled auburn hair—emerged from the sea of legs and hurdled toward Quinn, her arms outstretched and fingers splayed.

"Agatha!" Quinn called, matching the girl's enthusiasm. She knelt to the ground and the young girl leapt into her arms, gripping her as tightly as she would her own sister. Quinn scooped up the girl in her embrace and propped her on one hip.

"It's been so long! Look how big you've grown!" Quinn gushed, crinkling her nose and rubbing it against the girl's. Agatha erupted with giggles and hugged Quinn's face.

"Do the lights, Miss Quinn! Do the lights!" Agatha squealed again.

Carefully balancing the girl, Quinn lifted her marked hand to Agatha's face and wiggled her fingers. Miniature auroras formed near her palm, twinkling and dancing in the air before the girl's eyes. Agatha clapped fervently and squealed with glee.

"Run along now, your parents are waiting inside. We'll play later, all right?"

Agatha nodded and plopped a kiss on Quinn's cheek, then wriggled free and skipped into the hall. Dane couldn't help but smile as he watched the girl disappear, infected by her unbridled, youthful energy.

Next, an elderly woman approached Quinn with a wrinkled, toothy grin. Quinn clasped the woman's hand in hers.

"How great to see you again, Lady Rivelda! These robes have been wonderful. I've never been so warm in the snow before," she said, releasing the woman's hand to pat her own fitted robes.

Lady Rivelda released a high-pitched chuckle and gently patted Quinn's cheek. "I'm so glad, my dear. I couldn't have done it without your help. Mother bless you."

Quinn stooped down to embrace her, and the woman shuffled into the hall with the same toothy smile.

After the last family entered into the Aurora Temple, Quinn stepped out from the giant doorway and into the brisk night air. She tilted her head up, watching the light snow sift down, her breath exhaling in a plume of white fog. She turned to Dane. Her cheeks were rosy from the cold, flushed with heat and color. Her eyes twinkled. Dane stared at her with newfound awe and admiration.

"What?" she asked in playful accusation, hiding a smirk. He must have stared longer than he'd thought.

"That was incredible. How do you know everyone in the city?"

Quinn's face flushed a deeper shade of red. She stared at the ground as if ashamed. "It's nothing. Part of being the Elder's daughter, I suppose."

"Really, Quinn, it is incredible," Dane insisted. "You should have seen everyone's face after you greeted them. The old woman, the little girl . . . you brought so much joy to them. And they all know you. Even the guards that found us near the bridge knew you. Everyone here loves you." His cheeks burned the instant the words left his mouth, and he hoped Quinn wouldn't notice the hidden meaning. She didn't.

Quinn sighed. "I hadn't thought of it that way before, it all comes so naturally. Evergleam isn't nearly as large as Vitalor, of course, but everyone here is so close. Luminari hardly ever leave Evergleam, and if we do, everyone knows. We watch out for each other, especially since new Luminari are becoming rarer each year. It's like one big family, really. That's why I enjoy talking with everyone, connecting with them. It gives me purpose . . ."

She looked up then, staring into Dane's eyes with a gentle smile. Dane thought he could feel a strange tension in the air, pulling at the space between them, drawing him to her. Then the background hum of voices in the hall quieted to a hushed silence, capturing Quinn's attention.

"The ceremony is starting!" Quinn hurried past the great doors and stopped at the back of the crowd, staring with the masses at the Aurora Crystal. Dane followed behind her.

Zena Evergleam stood before the Aurora Crystal, facing the crowd as it radiated light behind her. She welcomed the jubilant masses as Quinn had done, then focused her attention to the huddle of white-robed Luminari closest to her. One by one, she beckoned them forward. They each walked up to the Aurora Crystal and presented their stones while the entire room scintillated in the light of the aurora torches, appearing to float in midair from each citizen's extended arm.

Zena had just welcomed the final Luminarus to the Aurora Crystal when Dane felt Quinn edge closer to him. Her body grazed against his shoulder, a jolt of warmth sparking through him at her touch.

She leaned into his ear and whispered, "Come with me."

Her fingers wove around his and she pulled him through the crowd. It was as if he was a child again, visiting Vitalor for the first time, being pulled to the arena by the curious girl with green eyes.

Heart in his throat, a clumsy, boyish smile plastered across his face, Dane let Quinn lead him through the crowd toward the staircase, grinning all the while.

"Where are we going?" Dane asked after Quinn released his hand, starting up the staircase, taking the steps two at a time.

"You'll see . . ."

They passed the infirmary entrance and continued upward, spiraling higher and higher up the castle's central tower. At long last they reached a narrow hallway, the air chilled with the frosty, night breeze. Aurora torches lined the hallway, their heatless flickering flames unwavering against the wind.

Quinn followed the short hallway to a small balcony, not unlike the willow overlook in Vitalor—secluded, calm, and peaceful. Dane smiled fondly at the thought, how Quinn had found him there after his Trials, how she'd convinced him that, despite his failure, his life was still worth living.

From the edge of the balcony, Dane gazed out across the entire city of Evergleam glowing far below them. The city was built in a small, sloping valley nestled between twin icy slopes. Hundreds of small huts, houses, and shops filled the snow-covered space from the base of the slope all the way to the castle gates. Leading away from the castle was a single street that carved through the city, winding between buildings like a river through the landscape, its length lined with the soft glow of distant lights.

Quinn stopped beside him at the balcony's edge and turned her back, leaning against the intricate stone railing, staring at the top of the castle tower.

"Here it comes!" She pulled Dane to her side. He followed her gaze upward. The top of the tower was close enough now that Dane could see the peculiar, crystalline structure perched atop it. It looked like a small pyramid of glass and ice, its four sides sparkling in the starlight and converging to a sharp point.

The pyramid began to glow with faintly colored light that brightened with every passing moment. Dane became aware that the world around him also seemed to brighten. He peered over the balcony, craning his neck to survey the length of tower below them. A pillar of energy and light beamed up the tower from within. In an utterly magnificent display of color, the light erupted against the glass pyramid. Beautiful auroras of green, pink, and yellow sprayed from the glass, rolling into the night sky like ocean waves, showering the city below with its brilliant radiance.

"What *was* that?" Dane said incredulously.

"At the completion of the ceremony, the Aurora Crystal releases some of its energy to decorate the sky, lighting the entire city." She gazed up at the auroras. "Isn't it breathtaking?"

"Yes," Dane said, but he wasn't looking at the sky. His eyes were fixed on her. He had never seen her so happy, so carefree, so full of life. The way she swooned over the auroras, the way she had greeted everyone entering the Aurora Temple, the way she swept through the castle as if floating on a cloud; she didn't have a care in the world.

His throat tightened, his heart squeezing in his chest. He blinked several times, fighting back swelling tears, and averted his gaze to the lights above, confounded by his surge of subconscious emotion. He wanted to feel her joy and share that joy with her. More than anything, he just wanted to *be* with her. He wished he could live in Evergleam, that she'd take him through the city, introducing him to her friends, to other families, and—

"I'm sorry," she said suddenly.

Dane looked at her, brows furrowed. "For what?"

She turned to face him, her expression almost regretful. "I'm sorry I never came back. I . . . I'm sorry I broke my promise."

Dane could only stare, overcome with relief. *She felt the same way.*

"I really wanted to come see you. I wanted to watch the Trials with you, to help you, Sage, and Vilik prepare for your own Trials, but—" She let out a long, shuddering breath. "My father needed me as soon as I returned from my Trials. I tried to argue, but he said it was urgent and there wasn't any time to spare. There was a lot to do. I got distracted. Then after I met—" she shook her head. "It doesn't matter now. But I regret never telling you. You deserve better than that." Her eyes glistened and she averted her gaze, but only for a moment. "I didn't keep you waiting, did I? I hope you didn't worry."

Only every day, he thought, but he couldn't say that to her, couldn't burden her with that guilt.

"I didn't worry much," Dane said, shrugging it off. "I only thought you'd been taken to the Shrouded Isle."

"If that's all." She stifled a laugh. "But . . . thank you." An uncomfortable silence filled the air as her eyes met his. She pulled her gaze away and inhaled deeply. She leaned over the balcony, staring down at the castle gates. "Where is everyone? By now, they've usually started walking to—"

She let out a yelp of surprise as her body tilted over the balcony's edge. Dane threw his arms around her waist and pulled her away from the edge as she simultaneously braced her arms against the railing.

He released her once at a safe distance, eyeing her with concern. "Are you all right?" he said between heavy breaths. "You almost—"

Then he just stared at her, unable to hide his growing smile.

She was laughing. A genuine, beautiful sound that rolled from her throat in joyous guffaws, filling the air around them. Dane joined her, the laughter bubbling from his stomach and spilling out of him. He didn't know why he was laughing. He certainly didn't find it amusing that Quinn had almost toppled over the balcony's edge. But merely seeing her laugh, seeing her unencumbered euphoria, made him want to laugh with her all the same.

It reminded him of the Trials Festival the year before Quinn's Trials. They had just arrived at the Trials Arena, making their way to their seats, when Quinn had wanted a closer look at the arena pit. She had leaned over the railing and nearly toppled over its edge when Dane snatched the back of her robes and pulled her back to safety. Though she had almost fallen, she had burst into a fit of giggles that erupted into the same carefree laughter.

Dane's laughter heightened momentarily at the memory. But soon it receded, and all he could do was watch her and smile.

He loved the way she laughed—the way her cheeks flushed, the way her nose crinkled, the way loose strands of hair fell in front of her tightly squeezed eyes. Then came the pang of sadness; somehow, he knew she didn't laugh like that anymore, not like she had at the Trials Festivals. More than anything, Dane wanted to make her laugh again, every day, and fill her with the same joy she felt now.

"I'm sorry," she said finally, choking down the laughter and wiping at her eyes. "I don't know what came over me. But thanks for saving me." She offered a warm smile, laughter subsiding, her eyes twinkling. She sighed deeply, calming herself, and leaned on her elbows on the balcony railing, her fingers loosely intertwined as she gazed into the aurora-filled night sky.

Dane leaned on the balcony beside her. He wanted to forget everything that had happened, to forget about his Trials and his lack of powers, to forget about Cayde and the mysteries of their journey. All he wanted was her.

He looked at her on the balcony, the world quiet except for the distant whistle of the chilled mountain air, the auroras dancing in the sky. In that moment, he thought he *could* forget everything else. He felt the urge to pull her face to his, caress her smooth brown hair with his hand, cup her rouged, wind-chilled cheeks, stare deeply into her beautiful green eyes, give in to his deepest, purest emotions, and kiss her.

"Quinn, I—"

Then her hand was on his, her touch cold yet flooding him with warmth. His heart leapt into his throat. She felt the same way. Maybe she always had, and now he could finally unveil his true affections instead of letting them fester within. He could tell her he loved her.

"Look, there they are!" Quinn said, pointing down at the castle doors.

Then her hand was gone. Her head tilted downward, watching as a procession of people, aurora torches in hand, walked along the winding street before stopping at a circular courtyard in the center of the city.

Quinn watched them with a distant, dazed stare, as if she'd watched them from the balcony countless times before.

Dane hung his head. She was happy, carefree. Suddenly he felt guilty for wanting to confess his emotions. That would complicate everything. Now, she was at peace. He couldn't take that away from her.

He felt her watching him and he looked up.

Quinn was regarding him expectantly, eyes sparkling in the light of the auroras. Her eyebrows quirked up in question. "You . . . wanted to say something?"

Dane thought for a moment, his heart thumping, then diverted his gaze back to the city.

"Oh—I . . . no, I forgot."

Quinn nodded carefully, her head tilted slightly to one side as lines creased her brow, her lips slightly pursed in thought. He could see her mind working through the options, searching for something to say.

"I'm sorry for what happened—about your Trials," she said carefully. "I know there's a reason why it happened. My father will have some advice, I'm certain of it." She drew a long breath. "I can't imagine how hard it must be for you, but sometimes I— I . . . ." Her voice trailed off, her features strained as if fighting a mental battle, deciding whether or not to say what was coming next.

Finally, she submitted and said, "Sometimes I wish I could be like you."

The words hit Dane like a fist. He stared at her, eyes wide and mouth parted. Since his Trials, the thought of finding his power had lingered with him every passing moment of every day.

But the entire time, Quinn wanted to be like him.

"But . . . *why*?" he managed.

She inhaled a deep, controlled breath, looking down at the mark of faint auroras spiraling up her arm. "Being a Luminarus is part of who I am, part of my family. I love my family, and I love this city. I'm glad I can help everyone, but—" Her shoulders slumped. "Sometimes it feels like too much, like my power is a burden I'm forced to bear. Everyone expects so much from me; they expect me to be like my mother, like my father—some even expect me to be like Founder Illara, to accomplish wonders and discover new possibilities as a Luminarus." She raked her fingers through her hair and stared longingly into the sky. "But to be free from these powers, to live free of expectation and these burdens . . ."

She released a long, shuddering breath.

Dane combed through his thoughts, trying to find something to say. "But what you did back there with your powers—when we were hiding. How'd you do that? It was incredible! You *saved* us. You're already proving yourself, Quinn."

She glanced sidelong at him. "The aurora veil? It's just a veil of light to cloak our position. All that man saw was an open crevice—that's what I projected on the veil." She smiled, but it didn't reach her eyes. "But I almost lost it. I didn't concentrate like I should have. If that man hadn't left when he did, I would've—" She shook her head, her eyes shut tight.

"But you *did* save us, Quinn," Dane insisted.

She smiled again, a soft, exhausted smile, and looked out across the city.

Dane was speechless. Despite everything Quinn could do with her powers, and despite how much the people of Evergleam loved her, she still didn't feel good enough. He desperately wanted to ease her thoughts and blurted out the first thing that came to mind.

"Why didn't you tell your mother about the Chemocyte?"

He cringed. *So much for easing her thoughts . . .*

Quinn's face tensed, and her body stiffened like it had when her mother had asked about their journey.

"She has so many concerns watching over the city when my father is away. Mentioning it only would've increased her burden." She looked at Dane, her expression gentle but serious. "No one else can know what we saw out there, Dane. We have to keep this between us. Most people in the city still think Chemocytes are a myth. If word got out that there was a Chemocyte—a *real* Chemocyte—then everything we've built here would be ruined. It is our burden to bear, not theirs. Cayde and I—my father and Elder Durkanis sent us on this journey in the first place. I should have told you what we were up against, what we expected to find."

Dane's mind latched on her last words. He thought of the conversation he overheard between Elder Chrysanthe and Quinn in the Elder Temple, and what Quinn and Cayde had discussed during their argument the night before. They *were* looking for something, and this was his chance to find out what that was.

"What were you asked to do? What—"

At that moment, Sage appeared in the balcony entrance.

"Cayde's awake!" She beamed. "I helped, but Dilpha did most of the work. His wound still needs time to heal, but—" She stopped, her eyes drifting between Dane and Quinn. She leaned casually against the wall, one eyebrow cocked, and strummed her fingers on her crossed arms. "What are you two doing up here?" She flashed a coy, knowing smile.

Heat flushed to Dane's face.

"Watching the auroras," Quinn said calmly, turning to Sage.

Sage stared a moment longer, unconvinced. "Right. Well, Cayde wants to see you."

She turned back toward the tower staircase.

Quinn followed. Just before she left the balcony, she turned to Dane and said, "Are you coming?"

A pit of emptiness settled in Dane's stomach. He didn't want Quinn to leave, not yet. He wanted the moment to last forever, to stay on the balcony, stay in the serenity, watching the city and its lights flicker below them, watching Quinn's face illuminated in the bright, aurora-filled night sky.

But the moment was gone as quickly as it had come. His feelings for her were still unrequited, plastered at the forefront of his mind, trapped and yearning for escape.

The time wasn't right, he told himself. *Not yet.*

Swallowing his emotions, Dane followed Quinn and Sage back to the infirmary.

CHAPTER 12

TALES UNTOLD AND SECRETS UNFOLD

Quinn burst into the infirmary and rushed to Cayde's bedside, Dane and Sage trailing closely behind. Cayde lay still, arms limp at his sides. His head was supported by a bundle of blankets. His shirt had been removed, and a clean white cloth was wrapped around his waist and stomach. Though his eyes were closed, his chest rose and fell with the sound of his slow breaths.

Dilpha was at the foot of his bed piling excess cloth wrappings into her basket. She looked up at the sound of their nearing footsteps and adorned a wide, nurturing smile that spread across her rosy cheeks.

To Quinn, she said softly, "He'll be better come morning. For now, he needs his rest. I'll alert Lady Evergleam and prepare your beds."

Quinn cupped Dilpha's hands in hers. "Thank you, Dilpha."

"Of course, my dear."

Dilpha nodded kindly, kissed Quinn on the cheek, and waddled out of the infirmary.

Quinn's eyes glistened as she looked to Cayde. Gently, as if the movement might hurt him, she slipped her hand into his, her fingers curling around his open palm. Cayde stirred at her touch, his fingers wrapping her hand.

He cracked one eye open. The corners of his mouth twitching upward.

"You were right," he said, his voice weak and threaded. "I should've listened."

Quinn whimpered and smiled weakly. "I was so worried."

Cayde lifted her hand to his mouth and kissed it. "No need to worry any more, thanks to you." He closed his eyes, then smiled faintly. "At least we're even after the grotto."

She sniffled and laughed under her breath. "I'll come for you in the morning. Get some rest."

Cayde nodded faintly, smiling for a moment longer before his grip loosened, his breathing slow and calm.

"This way," Quinn said, lingering by Cayde's side a moment before starting toward the tower staircase. "Dilpha has prepared a guest room for you both. It's just down the hall from mine."

Quinn led Dane and Sage up the tower's spiral staircase and past the landing with the balcony until the stairs came to an end. Dilpha was waiting for them at the entrance of a long hallway, her face nearly hidden behind a stack of thick woolen blankets. Zena stood behind her with a welcoming smile, still wearing the same white sparkling robes from the ceremony.

"Here you are, dears," Dilpha said, handing them each a blanket. "The air can be rather chilly at times. These will keep you warm." Dane accepted his blanket graciously, and Dilpha, seeing his eagerness, thrust another blanket into his arms.

Zena placed a comforting hand on Dilpha's shoulder. "That will be all, Dilpha. And thank you for aiding with Cayde's healing."

"Always a pleasure, m'lady."

"And to you Sage," Zena said. "Dilpha told me you were a marvelous assistant. You're growing into a wonderful Biophage."

"Thank you," Sage said politely, hugging the blanket to her chest.

"You're very welcome," Zena said. "Now Quinn, if you'll come with me, I'd like to speak to you before bed."

"Yes Mother," Quinn said.

"Dane, Sage. Dilpha will show you to your room. You're both welcome to stay as long as you like."

Sage responded with an eager nod. Dane smiled, but there was nothing behind it, his thoughts still on the way Quinn had looked at Cayde in the infirmary.

Zena retreated down the hallway with Quinn at her side and disappeared into a doorway at the far end.

"Come, come," Dilpha said, starting toward the first door on the left. "I've prepared your beds by the fireplace."

The guest room was sparsely decorated. Each of the pearl white walls held a single aurora torch, and two beds had been made near a fireplace that crackled in one corner. Unlike the aurora torches—though glowing with the same colors—the fire exuded a pleasurable, comforting warmth that radiated throughout the room. Nearby mountain peaks, dimly lit by the glow of the auroras still dancing overhead, were visible through a lone large window at the far wall. Though the room was small and ordinary compared to the rest of the castle, it was still far and above any room Dane had ever seen in his village.

Dilpha bid good night and closed the door. Sage immediately collapsed onto the bed furthest from the fireplace. Resigned to his thoughts, Dane curled up in the remaining bed, wrapping himself in the warm blankets, his mind replaying every moment on the balcony with Quinn.

The next morning, Dane woke to a muffled sound, distant and indecipherable. Groggily, he stirred and glanced around the room. Sage lay sprawled on her bed, her blankets massed in a heap by her feet. The crisp blue of morning light shone through the lone window. He listened, and the muffled sound of voices returned, resonating through the guest room wall.

There was a knock at the door. Cayde walked in and leaned against the doorway, wincing slightly, one hand pressed to his shirt.

"Elder Yarrin arrived this morning. He'd like to speak with you both when you're ready." He gave a reassuring smile then closed the door, retreating down the hall.

"Who said what?" Sage groaned, rubbing at her eyes. She raised her head slightly, squinting through the harsh morning light as she peered around the room.

A giddy excitement spread through Dane's body as he leapt from his bed. "Get dressed. Elder Yarrin wants to see us."

Dane had held Elder Yarrin in the highest regard ever since meeting the Elder during his first journey to Vitalor. *I sense a bright future ahead of you.* The Elder's inspiring words had lingered in his thoughts since, a source of inspiration when he needed it most.

But what will he think of me now?

Dane followed the trail of voices through the hallway, Sage stumbling after him while shrugging on her clothes. He stopped at an ornate wooden door and pushed it open.

The room was similar to the guest bedroom. The white walls and lone window were the same, but instead of beds, several shelves of large, aged books lined the walls, and a glass table occupied the room's center.

Elder Yarrin stood with Quinn and Cayde near the window, deep in conversation. He looked just as Dane remembered: dark blue robes with a long, white cloak that matched those of Lady Evergleam; a dark brown beard frosted with silver framed his long, angled face. His deep green eyes, the same shade as Quinn's, peered soothingly at Dane from behind a set of dark bushy eyebrows as he strode forward.

"Dane Willows, how wonderful to see you again," he said, extending his hand, a light chuckle resonating from within. "You've certainly grown taller since we last met."

Dane smiled reflexively and shook the Elder's hand.

"And you must be Sage," Elder Yarrin said, shifting his attention. "Elder Chrysanthe has told me much about you." He chuckled again, shaking his head. "She always finds a way to mention you in a conversation. She's never spoken of an apprentice with such praise."

Sage's cheeks flushed pink. "I'm just happy to help," she said.

Elder Yarrin smiled again, then turned, addressing the whole room. "Quinn was recalling the events that took place in Vitalor before you both came in. Terrible news, especially so soon after your Trials . . ."

He faltered as the last word left his mouth. For a moment, his eyes locked on Dane, his brow etched with concern.

A lump rose in Dane's throat. *He knows.*

Elder Yarrin sighed exhaustedly. "I regret I wasn't there to help. The Trials Festival is always a wonderful experience, but I had urgent business to attend to in Mistveil."

"But Father," Quinn pressed, "why would Avon try to attack the Elderwood *now*? Why would he wait all this time? It doesn't make any sense."

Elder Yarrin stroked his beard. "There's no rationale to explain the actions of a madman. He was in hiding for so long. He must've been saving his strength, restoring his energy before attacking another energy well. But why he chose to attack now . . ."

"*Another* energy well, Elder?" Dane asked, perplexed. He looked to Sage, but her expression mirrored his own. The tale of Avon's destruction of Starspire was well known in recent Physosi history, and was often the origin of any rumors surrounding the ruined city. But not once had he heard about an attack on an energy well.

"Ah, yes, I suppose it's best you knew the whole truth of it." Elder Yarrin shared a meaningful glance with Quinn and Cayde, gave a subtle nod, then continued, "Nearly two decades ago, Avon attacked the Starforge, the energy well of Starspire, the city of the Cosmonauts. Whether he intended to or not, Avon destroyed the energy well and the entire city. Everyone in the city that day was lost. Many thought Avon too had died in the destruction, but rumors began to surface that he survived, left to lick his wounds, regain his strength before striking again. It appears the rumors were true. I believe he's found a way to damage the energy wells without expending as much energy. But if what you say is true about Vitalor, using the fires as a distraction so he could approach the Elderwood unnoticed, then he didn't plan on encountering much resistance. He couldn't have planned this alone."

"He wasn't alone," Dane interjected. "Cayde and I confronted him before he could escape. There were two other men with—"

Elder Yarrin whirled to Cayde. "YOU CONFRONTED HIM?"

Cayde's eyes fell to the ground. His shoulders slumped.

"By the Mother, *what* compelled such a rash decision?" Elder Yarrin bellowed. "If Avon has returned to full strength then he is *far* more powerful than you realize. And to bring Dane with you?"

Cayde's voice was barely audible. "I thought we could stop him . . . I thought *I* could stop him."

Elder Yarrin perched his clenched fists on his waist as if preparing for another outburst. Instead, he exhaled and looked sympathetically at Cayde.

"When will you learn, my boy? One of these days, you won't be so fortunate to emerge unscathed."

Cayde looked up from the floor. His jaw was clenched, his mouth in a hard, grim line, but his eyes were pleading.

"The greatest warriors and heroes of Physos do not seek danger, Cayde," the Elder continued. "They use their power wisely, acting only when absolutely necessary. You have exemplary talents, but you mustn't be so careless with your strength."

Cayde folded his arms, gripping his torso, unable to meet Elder Yarrin's gaze.

"But the men with Avon," Dane said, wanting to end the painful silence that had settled over the room, "they had metal swords."

Elder Yarrin turned to him, all traces of anger and sympathy gone. "They had *what?*"

"Metal swords. Avon had a weapon too, but it wasn't made of metal, more like a—" Dane stopped and stared expectantly at Elder Yarrin. The Elder's face had gone pale, his eyes staring blankly ahead.

"How'd they obtain metal?" Dane asked cautiously. "Do you know who they were?"

Elder Yarrin's voice was quiet and harrowing. "Yes . . . yes, I do." He retreated to the lone window, his hands clasped at the small of his back. Dane held his breath, simultaneously wanting and dreading the answer.

"It appears Avon has sided with the Ferrons."

The Elder's words hung in the air for a moment. Dane looked to the others, awaiting some sort of recognition in their features. But they too seemed equally perplexed.

"Ferrons, Father?" Quinn asked, her voice wavering with uncertainty.

Elder Yarrin nodded solemnly, his gaze unfaltering from the window. "Ferrons are those gifted with the power to manipulate metals—though I suppose *gifted* is far too generous a word for those of such wretched villainy."

"I don't understand. Why would they help Avon?" said Cayde.

Elder Yarrin pursed his lips into a resentful sneer. "Elder Maluin," he seethed. Dane had never heard anyone utter a word with such disgust.

"Elder? But—I thought you taught me about all the Elders," Quinn said.

"And manipulating metals?" Dane said. "That's not one of the eight powers, either."

"Correct, it is not one of the eight *blessed* powers. But Maluin was not blessed with his power." Elder Yarrin exhaled shakily. "What I'm about to tell you all must never leave this room. Ever. Some knowledge about Physos is meant strictly for elders. But if we hope to defeat this threat, then all of you must know."

"You all know the tale of the *Forces and the Founders*," Elder Yarrin began, "but there is more to this tale. When the council of Lords and Ladies met on that fateful day to discuss terms of peace in Lord Arkon's castle, one man was not invited. Pericus Gavard, Maluin's founding ancestor. Pericus was the Lord of the Midnight Mountains, a domain in the far southeast of Physos. Due to the abundance of metals there, and lack thereof in each of the other domains, Pericus monopolized the trade. He was a shrewd, spiteful man. Over time, he became wrought with greed, demanding more in return for his precious resources. When the time came to meet for a peace treaty, the other founders—wanting to reconcile their differences—offered Pericus a seat at their table. Lost in his greed, Pericus declined. He was outraged when he learned that each founder was bestowed with the powers we know today; from that day forth, he halted all trade, secluding himself and his people in their mountain fortress. No one knows how he was granted the power to manipulate metals, but the legend says he stole one of the first energy stones and forged an energy well of his own."

"What happened to him?" said Sage.

"He never amounted to much, thankfully. For hundreds of years, Pericus and the Ferrons festered in their exile from the world. But now I fear Maluin has discovered a way to harness the energy to supply his forces with the power his ancestor imagined. If that's true, there's no telling what they're capable of . . ."

Sage frowned. "The ones we saw on the mountain pass—they were strong, but they weren't—"

Elder Yarrin's eyes bulged. "The mountain pass? Here, you say? What happened?"

"We saw them coming from Evergleam," Sage said, flustered. "Dane and I fought them off. One of them fell into the ravine; the other retreated back down the mountain pass."

"These Ferrons, what did they look like?"

"Their bodies were encased in metal, except for their faces," Quinn said. "And they both wore dark cloaks, like they were trying to blend in with the mountainside."

Elder Yarrin stroked his beard furiously. "Scouts, no doubt," he murmured. "Though I can't imagine what they'd be doing all the way up here. Unless . . . no . . ."

"What, Father?"

"Unless Avon is preparing another attack. Those two men must have been scouting the city, I'm sure of it. And if he's sending scouts, his followers must be in short supply. He won't fight where he can't win, especially if he recently regained his strength. The Ferron that escaped, he'll alert Avon of what happened, just as you alerted me. But now that we're aware of his plans, Avon will stay clear of Evergleam if he knows what's best for him.

"I'm certain Elder Maluin is behind this too, scheming and plotting from the shadows. Though I must confess I don't know why he would ally with Avon."

"They both hold grudges against the world," Dane pondered, "and from what you've told us, both are hungry for power. If it's true that Avon doesn't have an army, and if Maluin lacks the experience that Avon has . . ." He paused for a long moment, searching his thoughts. "Maybe they need each other."

"Possibly," Elder Yarrin said. "But if Maluin is anything like his ancestor, he'll want the power of the energy wells for himself. Avon though . . . it appears he's trying to destroy them."

"But the two men with him in Vitalor," Cayde said, "Avon was leading them. Then those two on the bridge . . . the Ferrons are the only people who have the power and resources to manipulate metals. There has to be a connection."

Elder Yarrin said nothing for several moments, his brow creased in thought. Finally, he said, "We won't accomplish much debating possibilities. I'll alert the guards at once and send a warning to Mistveil about the Ferrons' presence. Whatever their alliance with Avon, we'll be sure to stay one step ahead. He could have sent scouts anywhere; everyone must be prepared."

At once, the tension that had settled over the room dissipated.

"Now, pardon my intrigue," Elder Yarrin said, eyes alight with curiosity, "but how *did* you all manage to defeat the two Ferrons on the pass?"

"We saw them before crossing the bridge," Quinn started. "At first we tried to hide and let them pass but—"

"But Quinn turned us invisible!" Sage blurted, then clapped her hands to her mouth. She glanced apologetically at Quinn and mouthed, *Sorry.*

Quinn smiled and waved dismissively, but Elder Yarrin looked as excited as Sage.

"The aurora veil?" he said in suspended awe. "Tell me it worked this time."

Quinn nodded, blushing slightly.

Elder Yarrin clapped his hands, creating a sound that echoed through the entire room. "Ah-ha! I knew you could do it! And *us*, was it? Don't tell me all four of you were veiled?"

Quinn nodded again, her cheeks flushing red.

Elder Yarrin let out a triumphant guffaw. "Fantastic! Simply marvelous, Quinn!"

"Are all Luminari able to do that?" asked Sage.

The Elder huffed. "Maybe to veil a foot or an arm, but to veil *four people*?" He shook his head, smiling all the while. "That's very special indeed."

"But Father, I nearly lost it again. I nearly fainted. I was barely strong enough to hold it as long as I did. We were almost seen, and I—"

"Stop right there, Quinn, I don't want to hear it. You performed exceptionally. Don't let anyone tell you otherwise, especially yourself. You simply need more practice—practice like *that*—so you can learn to control your strength."

Elder Yarrin smiled a moment longer before the corners of his mouth turned down, his thick eyebrows drawing together. "Still, none of this explains how Cayde was wounded. And I still want to know how you defeated the Ferrons."

Sage said, "The two men—the Ferrons—attacked us when we were crossing the bridge. Cayde carried Quinn safely across, so Dane and I, we held them off as long as we could before crossing the bridge—" Sage paused, her eyes glazing over. Dane guessed she was replaying her terrifying fall from the bridge, a thought that still sent shivers down his spine. She continued hesitantly, "We managed to escape in the end, but the bridge collapsed. One of the men fell with the bridge into the ravine, but . . . so did I."

Elder Yarrin glanced up and down at Sage, as if inquiring how she was standing before him.

"It turned out fine, though," she added. She patted a hand to her waist where the branch was coiled. "I would've d—well, I wouldn't be here if it wasn't for my Willow Whip."

"Your . . . what?" Elder Yarrin inquired. Sage raised the hem of her shirt, exposing the branch.

The Elder's eyes bulged.

"One moment I was falling from the bridge," Sage continued, "and then I was jerked to a halt in midair. The next thing I knew, Dane and Cayde were pulling me up. It was the Willow Whip that saved me, but I didn't tell it to. Quite strange if you ask me . . . like it had a mind of its own."

"Where did you find this?" Elder Yarrin said, his voice distant, eyes transfixed on the willow branch.

"After Avon attacked the Elderwood. I was on the willow overlook—that balcony hidden behind the Elderwood's roots—and I found it inside the burnt trunk of the willow tree. It all happened so strangely, though. The entire willow tree had burned, but this branch was completely unharmed. It was almost as if I was meant to find it, like it was a gift hidden just for me to find. I know it doesn't make sense, but how else could this have happened?"

Elder Yarrin furrowed his brow, deep in contemplation. "There are tales of similar events throughout our history—none involving a tree, mind you—but that does not eliminate it from the realm of possibility." He gestured to the branch. "May I?"

Sage uncoiled it from her waist.

"And you say it acted on its own?"

The four of them nodded.

Elder Yarrin inspected the branch further, then stopped suddenly. He cast a sidelong glance to Quinn then to Cayde, eyebrows raised in question. They both responded with a slight yet eager nod. When Elder Yarrin looked back at Sage, his eyes gleamed, looking both excited and relieved for reasons Dane didn't understand.

"I have a hunch, and if I am correct, my dear Sage, then this is a *very* special item."

Sage's eyes widened. "What is it? Why was it in the willow tree?"

"I'm afraid I can't indulge you any further at present, but I do believe it has formed a sort of connection with you. More so than a mere totem, this item seems capable of sharing your energy, allowing it to act of its own volition. Tell me, Sage, was the encounter on the bridge the first occurrence of this behavior?" Sage nodded. "Then I suppose you had yet to pledge to your power when you first handled this . . . Willow Whip?"

Sage nodded again, eyes widening with realization.

Elder Yarrin smiled. "I would imagine it required the touch of a Biophage to revitalize its own energy. As to *why* it chose you, well . . . that is a mystery of its own. I would tell you to protect it with your life, but of course, after what you've told me, it would appear that *it* is protecting you."

Elder Yarrin passed the Willow Whip back to Sage, who stared at it with newfound appreciation. She stroked a hand along its length then returned it around her waist.

The Elder straightened. "All of this *still* doesn't explain how Cayde was wounded. When Zena informed me what happened, she said it was merely a result of your travels." His eyes narrowed, locking on Cayde, "but that wasn't all, was it? There's something in your travels you have yet to mention, is there not?"

"There is, Father," Quinn said reluctantly. "In the Grove of Mist, we—we saw the Abuser's hut—something was wrong. We went to investigate. He was dead." She shuddered, as if envisioning the gruesome scene.

Elder Yarrin's expression remained unchanged.

"But it was how he died, Father. He—" Quinn opened and closed her mouth several times, but no words came out. Finally, she exhaled decisively, her breath shuddering, and said, "We think he was killed by a Chemocyte."

Elder Yarrin's inquisitive look vanished immediately. His eyes glazed over, the color draining from his face as his arms fell to his side. He looked so pale he looked to be made of stone.

"It—it cannot be," Elder Yarrin stammered. "Are—but how—are you certain?"

"We saw it," Dane said, envisioning the glowing, crimson eyes. "That night we heard something in the forest. Cayde and I—"

"We sought out the sound and a creature attacked us," said Cayde quickly. "We killed it in the end, but I was stabbed by a branch in the process." He gently prodded his wound. "I'm certain it was a Chemocyte, though. There's no other explanation for such a savage creature. And when it died, it crumbled into this . . ." Cayde reached into his pocket and pulled out the small, black shard he had gathered from the Chemocyte's crumbled remains.

Elder Yarrin took the blackened shard, turning it over in his hands. Shakily, he said, "How did you defeat it? The blade?"

Cayde nodded.

Elder Yarrin gestured to the shard. "And how long after did it turn into these?"

"Not long at all."

Elder Yarrin stared gravely ahead. "No living creature could have done this. There must be other forces present here, both creating and preserving it in a living state. Was anything else with the Chemocyte when you encountered it? Another creature? Anything out of the ordinary?"

"We did find the body of a man carrying a metal sword—a Ferron, no doubt," Dane added. "He was carrying a torch, too . . . could that have drawn the Chemocyte to him?"

Elder Yarrin shrugged. "Possibly so, but I digress. I, like everyone else in Physos, know so little about the Chemocytes. People only know what they've heard from myths and rumors. I presume you and Cayde are, in fact, the first in more than four hundred years to encounter a Chemocyte—except for that dead Ferron and Varic, of course."

"Where did the Chemocyte come from?" said Sage.

Elder Yarrin's face seized, as if those were the words he had been dreading since the first mention of the Chemocyte.

"The only possible explanation is that it came from the Shrouded Isle—there's no other place in Physos where such a creature could hide. But how it managed to reach the mainland from there . . ."

"The Shrouded Isle . . . how far is it from the mainland? Could the Chemocyte have swum to shore?" asked Dane. He felt foolish as the words left his mouth, but Elder Yarrin took no notice.

"The island is off the coast of the Aurora Mountains, far out at sea; it can only be seen from the highest peak on a clear day. But it would be impossible for a Chemocyte to swim such a distance, especially if its body is as dense as this . . ." He turned the blackened shard in his hand, then shook his head, knitted his eyebrows, and heaved an exhausted sigh. "None of this makes any sense."

Elder Yarrin stowed the shard in his robes pocket and paced to the window, hands clasped as he stared out at the city etched into the snow-capped mountainside.

"Avon . . . the Ferrons . . . a Chemocyte on the mainland . . . all of this happening so suddenly—it can't be a coincidence."

Quinn placed a comforting hand on her father's shoulder. "What do we do?"

"First and foremost, we must take every precaution to prevent further attacks from Avon. Then find out where these Ferrons have come from, and, most crucially, decipher how the Chemocyte arrived here in the first place."

He began shuffling around the room, rummaging through the rows of ancient books. He scoffed irritably and uttered something under his breath.

"Quinn, you and your friends must travel to the Grand Archive in Mistveil. Seek out Elder Erwan and tell him I sent you on urgent matters. His son, Calder, was recently appointed as the Grand Archivist, the head of the Archive." Elder Yarrin puffed an exasperated sigh. "Calder isn't the friendliest—rather presumptuous at times—but his knowledge of the Archive is unrivaled."

"What are we looking for?" Dane asked. "Should we tell Elder Erwan about Avon?"

"Search for anything that relates to Chemocytes—history, black crystals, the Shrouded Isle—whatever you can find. My library isn't large enough, but the Grand Archive has a record of every book in Physos. I imagine what you seek won't be available to the common eye, hence why you must seek out Elder Erwan. And yes, do inform him, *only* him, about what Avon has done. Though I expect he knows."

"And the Chemocyte?" questioned Sage, "Should we inform him about that as well?"

"Absolutely not!" Elder Yarrin barked. "Do not mention the Chemocyte to *anyone*. Though the evidence *seems* clear, there's no proof that this creature was indeed a Chemocyte. Erwan is a stubborn man. He won't believe anything he can't see for himself—no, talk of a Chemocyte must be kept secret. It's all we can do to prevent mass hysteria. Besides, he'll alert his guards of Avon's presence; they can protect the city from a Chemocyte as well—should such an occurrence come to pass." He brushed the frayed strands of hair from his face. "In the meantime, I will alert the guards and send patrols to intercept other potential scouts."

"Now . . ." He turned to face Quinn, a slight pained expression on his face. "I understand you have just arrived, but I hope you can see the importance of preparing as swiftly as possible. I hope it's not too much to ask that you leave as soon as—"

"Don't worry, Father, we can be ready to leave before midday," said Quinn, glancing wide-eyed at Sage and Dane, urging their confirmation. They were both quick to voice their approval.

Dane felt invigorated by the new task, excited even. There was no telling what he might find in the Grand Archive. He might even find answers to his lack of power.

Elder Yarrin nodded slowly. "Good. Yes, that will suffice. If you were to leave by midday, you'd easily arrive in Mistveil before dusk. Come to think of it, the journey is only that long if you've been carrying a child on your shoulders all day." He chuckled, gazing affectionately at Quinn, who failed to hide a knowing smile.

"Well, shall we gather our things?" Sage said, her voice laden with excitement. "I've always wanted to see Mistveil."

Elder Yarrin laughed. "I like your spirit, Sage. It's no wonder the branch chose you. And yes, go and pack, all of you. I've said all you need to hear."

Sage retreated down the hallway, Cayde hobbling out after her. Before Quinn could leave, Elder Yarrin pulled her into a firm embrace.

"Be safe, Quinn," he said. "I've missed you."

"I've missed you too, Father," she said, her voice muffled in her father's robes. "We'll return as soon as we can."

Elder Yarrin squeezed her tighter, his eyes glistening. "You make me so very proud, my daughter. You always have."

They embraced for a long moment before Quinn released her father and made for the doorway, where Dane stood waiting. They turned to follow Sage and Cayde down the hallway when Elder Yarrin called out, "Dane, there's . . . something else I must address. Privately."

Dane glanced at Quinn, eyebrows raised in question. She offered a simple shrug and walked off to join the others.

"Yes, Elder Yarrin?" Dane asked, reentering the room. The Elder stood once more by the window, back turned. His posture was rigid, unyielding.

The air in the room felt heavy. Dane's pulse quickened in anticipation.

"Dane, I'm afraid I must ask something of you that you will not want to hear, nor understand." When Elder Yarrin turned, his expression was tense, solemn, as if plagued by internal conflict. Dane shuddered inwardly, suddenly wary of what the Elder might say. The way he struggled for words sent Dane's mind into a frenzy of uncertainty.

"You must realize I would never ask this of anyone, especially of you, if it were not of the utmost importance . . ." Elder Yarrin inhaled deeply, tension hanging in the air. In a grave yet unwavering voice, he said, "Dane . . . I must ask that you do not seek the answers to finding your power."

The words pummeled Dane as if he'd been pummeled by the stone warrior. He recoiled, his mind a whirling haze of confusion.

"You . . . what?" Dane managed. He must have heard wrong, misinterpreted. What did discovering his power have anything to do with the task at hand? Finding his power was all he'd wanted since his disastrous Trials, the one purpose he could cling to. And Elder Yarrin wanted him to forget that ever happened, to forget he had no power?

The Elder's face fell, his expression wracked with guilt. "I know this is the last thing you wanted to hear, Dane."

Dane took a step back. Elder Yarrin was serious. He wanted Dane to abandon his search for his power, to abandon the one thing keeping him afloat. His confusion fell away as coils of anger began to burn inside him. The Elder's request was folly and unfair. He'd ignore it, simple as that. Elder Yarrin wasn't going with them to the Grand Archive. Dane would search regardless, with no one the wiser.

"You have every right to be angry with my request," the Elder continued, "But you must understand its importance, for you are the only one who *can* understand."

The Elder's last words cut through Dane's building rage. "What do you mean, *the only one?*"

Elder Yarrin breathed a sigh of relief, seemingly grateful that he was able to reach some level of understanding. "Think about what has happened. The attack on Vitalor, the emergence of the Ferrons, the Chemocyte on the mainland. Events of this magnitude are unheard of in Physos, tales of myth and legend. Yet suddenly, they come to pass in a matter of days. More so, before any of those events took place, the first initiate in history fails to find his power in the Trials.

"I can't shake the feeling this all started *because* you didn't find your power in the Trials. There are still many questions we must answer, but I fear we'll never understand if you were to find your power. That means *you* must be the one to uncover these mysteries . . . without your power."

Dane took a moment to let the words sink in, gain purchase. He tried to wrap his head around it. "Then what am I supposed to do? How do I find the meaning behind all this?"

"Go with the others to Mistveil and stay close to your friends. When you arrive at the Grand Archive, seek out books known as memory tomes. They will not be easy to find, but I believe the memory tomes could hold clues to the answers we seek, if you know what to look for." His voice grew sharp and stern. "But whatever you do, do *not* mention this to the Grand Archivist, the Elder's son. Your search will surely be compromised if he hears even the slightest mention of them."

Dane didn't fully understand, and questions percolated faster than he could process. But one thought stood out from the rest.

"Elder Yarrin?" Dane asked, "What can I do that no one else can? Why do you need . . . *me?*"

Elder Yarrin stared at him with a strange, almost paternal smile. He leaned in. His voice was barely above a whisper, but every word was weighted with complete certainty.

"You are the only one who can see this world for what it really is."

Dane's brow furrowed in confusion. "Wha—what do you mean?"

The Elder went on. "You didn't find your power in the arena, thus your thoughts have not yet been bound by everyone else's reality. Our thoughts are consumed by our powers, even if we do not mean them to be. I will always make decisions that benefit my own strengths—it's natural instinct, a subconscious process of thought that has been ingrained into every citizen of Physos. Every citizen, except *you*. You do not—*cannot*—see the world as others do.

"There is a reason you didn't find your power in the Trials—call it fate, if you will. I believe whatever force guided you there is guiding your path now, will guide your path in the days to come, leading you to the answers we all seek if we are to protect Physos from Avon, the Ferrons, and the dangers ahead. I believe the events of your Trials happened because you were meant for something greater than any of us could possibly imagine, a purpose that only the Mother could have designed."

Dane took a step away from the Elder, trying to calm his rising panic. What the Elder was saying didn't make any sense, but it simultaneously felt as though the fate of Physos had just been placed on his shoulders. The way Elder Yarrin spoke, it was as if he thought Dane had been blessed by his wretched circumstance, that failing to find his powers—failing to find his true place—was a gift from the Mother herself. Or a curse.

His head began to throb, the effort of attempted cognition starting to toll on his fragile mind. "But how—what can I do when I don't have any—" He cut the thought short and released a shaky breath. "I don't know what to do. How am I supposed to—" *What had the Elder said? You are the only one who can see this world for what it really is?*

Elder Yarrin placed both hands on Dane's shoulders, his touch gentle but firm. For a moment, Dane wondered if this was what it felt like for a father to look upon his son.

"In your life, Dane, there are only a handful of moments that truly define the person you will become. There will be unbearable hardship, there will be insurmountable sadness, and there will be ceaseless struggle. But in these moments, it doesn't matter if you are faced with overwhelming odds or feel the weight of the world on your shoulders. It only matters how you respond when it seems the world is fighting against you—that is what defines who you are.

"*This* is one of those moments, Dane. The challenges ahead will test your very being. At times they may even seem impossible. And I fear even greater challenges will come to pass in the days ahead." His grip tightened on Dane's shoulders. "I am truly sorry for the situation you have been placed in—you deserve so much better than what I'm asking of you. But you are the *only* one who can overcome these challenges."

211

Dane merely shook his head. He became dimly aware that his brow was slick with sweat, his hair clinging to his forehead. He could feel his limbs tingling. The room started to spin.

"But . . . my power," he managed. "Am I supposed to stay like—like this—forever?"

The confidence with which Elder Yarrin shook his head grounded Dane's senses once more. "I promise you, there will be an end to your struggle. You will discover your power in time. I'm sure of it. But the time isn't right...not yet."

The Elder released Dane's shoulders and stepped back, sizing Dane up. Already Dane could feel himself calming down, his mind finally starting to fathom Elder Yarrin's request.

Elder Yarrin seemed to sense Dane's bolstered fortitude. "Now go, follow the others to Mistveil, but you mustn't speak a word of this to them—especially to Quinn. She already has a monumental task at hand—I fear for her psyche were she to take on much more. It would only cloud their thoughts. They won't understand, not like you do."

"I won't," Dane said. As he made to leave, he stood in the doorway and looked at Elder Yarrin. He still had so many questions, so much he was unsure of, but he could see the hope glistening in the Elder's nurturing gaze.

The Elder believed in him, believed in what he was asking Dane to do. Elder Yarrin needed *him* for this monumental task. Not Quinn. Not Cayde. Not Sage. Him.

And for now, despite all that had happened since his Trials, being needed was enough.

CHAPTER 13

THE GRAND ARCHIVIST'S APPRENTICE

Dane ran through the winding central street of Evergleam, weaving through the scattered crowds as the castle walls receded behind him.

Elder Yarrin's parting words echoed through his mind with every step.

You mustn't speak a word of this to them . . . it would only cloud their thoughts. They won't understand, not like you do.

He still didn't fully grasp why, but the Elder was convinced that Dane mustn't seek his powers, must remain different from everyone else so he can truly see the world of Physos—whatever that meant. Small tides of rage still licked his mind at the thought, but he forced the anger down, clinging to his new purpose.

You will discover your power. I'm sure of it, the Elder had said. *But the time isn't right . . . not yet.*

"What took you so long?"

Sage stood waiting with Quinn and Cayde at the edge of the city as Dane caught up with them. He slowed to a stop and clutched his knees.

"It was . . . a lot . . . of stairs," he managed between breaths.

Sage shook her head. They had followed the path leading out of the city, nearly reaching the city limits, when Dane realized he had forgotten his Elderwood staff in Quinn's guest room. He'd run back to the castle, up the seemingly endless spiral staircase in the central tower, into the guest room to retrieve his staff, then retraced every step. The excursion left him thoroughly fatigued, an embarrassment Sage wasn't likely to forget.

Once outside the city, the path cut through the snow-capped mountains in a series of switchbacks. Quinn and Cayde walked side by side a few paces ahead of Dane, who fell in beside Sage as they pressed on.

Dane's thoughts returned to what Elder Yarrin had told him. *They won't understand, not like you do . . .*

He wanted to tell Quinn, Cayde, and Sage about what Elder Yarrin had said. Though he had been given some clarity, his mind still churned with questions. There had to be something in Mistveil that Elder Yarrin wanted him to find that aligned with the new purpose the Elder had given him. *Does it have to do with the memory tomes?*

"It's not like you to forget your staff," Sage said suddenly.

Dane's gaze lingered on the path ahead, but there was something odd in Sage's voice; it was wistful and distant, bereft of her usual liveliness. It left him with a feeling of unease.

When she spoke again, her voice was trembling, almost a whisper. "You never forget your staff."

This took Dane by surprise. He had been expecting some playful retort on how foolish he was to forget his staff, or how easily he had run out of breath. The usual quips. He hadn't expected this. Then, from the corner of his eye, he saw her wipe at her face with one hand.

"Sage . . . are you crying? Is everything all right?"

"I'm fine." She sniffled, wiping her eyes with the heels of her palms. "It's nothing. It's just—" She let out a strangled whimper. Dane's heart squeezed in his chest. Sage had been in high spirits ever since arriving in Evergleam. She had even seemed fine after their talk with Elder Yarrin that morning. But here she was, on the verge of tears.

"You know you can tell me," he said gently.

She slowed and turned to him. Her arms were folded across her midsection, clutching at her sides. Her sea blue eyes swam with longing, as if she was staring at him for the last time.

"It pains me to see you like this, Dane. You're never happy anymore. You're always lost in your thoughts, staring off as if—I don't know what—I don't want you to—" She squeezed her eyes shut and shook her head, loose strands of hair falling around her face. "I spoke with Elder Yarrin before we left, while you were packing. I asked him if there was any way I could help you find your power. He said this was something you had to do on your own." Her eyes flickered, sparkling with tears. "I want you to find your power more than anything . . . that's all you ever talked about growing up. But seeing you hurt like this, I—I—" She let out a sob, tears spilling down her cheeks. "I just feel so useless."

Dane blinked and stared at his sister. He'd been so consumed by his own thoughts—of his Trials, of finding his power, of Quinn—that he'd never once considered what Sage was feeling, how much she still cared for him.

The mere thought brought Dane to tears. He felt utterly foolish. Aside from Grandfather Horas, Sage was the only family he had in the world, the one person he trusted more than anyone else. But what happened at his Trials had affected her in a way he hadn't imagined; she was distraught. And though she'd done everything to help him, he'd done nothing for her in return.

"Sage, I—I didn't know my happiness meant so much to you."

"Of course it does, Dane. You're my brother. I don't want anything bad to ever happen to you. I just—I wish I could do more."

Dane flung his arms around her. "You've done more than enough. I could never ask anything more from you." He squeezed her tighter and she buried her head in his shoulder. "I love you."

Sage sniffled again, releasing a shaky breath. "I love you, too," she whispered. She feigned a smile. "But are you sure you're all right? You're not just saying that so I won't worry?"

"Yes, I'm fine," Dane said reassuringly. "It'll take some time, but one way or another, I'll find my power. I have to . . . but maybe it's not supposed to happen yet." The calmness and assurance of his voice surprised him. Somewhere along the path leading away from Evergleam, he'd subconsciously accepted the task Elder Yarrin had bestowed upon him. Though the others didn't know it—and if Elder Yarrin could be believed—they were counting on him to succeed. He wouldn't let them down.

♏ ♏

Quinn and Cayde stopped at the base of the mountain, where the path leading away from Evergleam converged with the lakeside road. Trees were scattered on either side, preluding the glistening canvas of water that was Mistveil Lake.

Dane inhaled deeply, breathing in the brisk lake air, which, while still rather cold, felt like a warm summer breeze compared to the harsh frigidity of Evergleam's gelid climate.

They had just started along the lakeside road when Quinn turned and asked the question Dane had been dreading since his talk with Elder Yarrin.

"I've been meaning to ask," she said, "what was it that my father discussed with you?"

Dane fought the urge to wince. *Whatever you do, you mustn't speak a word of this to them . . . they won't understand, not like you do.* The thought of lying to Quinn pained him, but her father had been adamant that Dane keep their conversation a secret. But would it be so bad if he just told her the truth?

He realized Quinn was regarding him expectantly. He wrung his hands, then said, "He asked that I—he wanted me to—"

Quinn arched an eyebrow. He sighed resignedly. "He asked me not to find my power."

Quinn erupted the instant the words left his mouth. "He said *what?*" Her face tightened, and her fists balled at her sides. For several moments she stared past him, biting into her lower lip, as if searching the horizon for her father. "What was he—how does he expect—and *you*, of all people—" She threw her hands in the air. "It's unreasonable! You can forget *everything* he said! As soon as we return from Mistveil I'll give him a piece of my mind! I'll—I'll—"

As she continued to spew curses, her words tainted with raw emotion, Dane felt a strange sense of elation. Elder Yarrin had asked Dane to forgo his search for power, but Quinn acted as if he'd asked the same of her. She still cared about him. His heart warmed at the thought.

"No, it's all right," he said, eager to soothe her rage. "I too was mad at first, but he helped me understand. He said I—"

Just then a sound resonated behind him—a peculiar sound, like that of ruffling pages. He strained his ears, trying to discern it. It sounded as if a pile of old books was speeding toward him.

Dane had only enough time to glance between the others' shock-stricken faces before Sage yelled, "Look out!"

They all dove off the path as a wooden cart barreled past them, weaving maniacally and narrowly avoiding collision.

Dane pushed himself up from the ground, spitting dirt and grass from his mouth. He stared, bewildered, as the cart sped away as quickly as it had come. A mound of old books was poised precariously on the back of the cart, whose polished wooden exterior floated atop a—

Dane blinked, certain he'd been imagining things. He stared at the cart again, but it wasn't his imagination. The cart rolled atop a giant droplet of water—if he could even call it that. The water beneath was as long and wide as the cart itself—but it acted identically to that of a droplet of water, rolling effortlessly across the stone surface of the path, the cart balancing perfectly atop it.

"Watch where you're going!" Sage yelled after the strange cart, snapping Dane out of his bafflement. He glimpsed the driver: a scrawny young man with a tangle of wiry black hair, mussed and frayed as if he'd been lost for days traversing the wilderness. Yet the man wore seamless robes of pearly white that belied the entire scene.

As the cart crested a short incline in the path, the man turned and shouted back, "I'm terribly sorry but I'm in a real hurry and I couldn't stop since there's no time and I have to get back to—" His shouts turned to indiscernible mumbles as the cart sped out of view heading toward Mistveil.

Dane stood speechless. For a moment, he thought he'd merely dreamt of the odd encounter, but quickly dismissed the idea. He couldn't possibly have made up such an encounter in his wildest dreams.

Sage squinted at the spot where the cart disappeared, her mouth agape. "Did a boy . . . hauling old books . . . in a cart balanced on a big dewdrop . . . just try to run us over?"

Quinn grumbled, vigorously patting loose dirt from her robes. "That was rude. I never thought an Aquadorian could be so careless with their dewcart. Not that I'm surprised . . ."

"What did you call it?" Dane asked.

"A dewcart," Quinn said nonchalantly. She exhaled and turned to face him. "They're wooden carts Aquadorians use to transport goods to and from Mistveil. The water beneath acts as a wheel. It's far more durable since the water won't break—if controlled correctly."

"How do they work?" asked Sage. She pursed her lips in thought. "Can . . . I use one?"

"Ah, yes," responded Cayde, his interest peaked. "They're fascinating. For steering and control, one only has to place their hand on a panel at the front of the cart."

"So it's like a totem?" Dane asked.

"Essentially, yes. But that's the drawback. The carts only respond to the touch of an Aquadorian—that's why they're rarely seen beyond Mistveil. Other cities have their own unique methods of transportation too—the Tempi use gliders to traverse the wind currents through Alto-Baros. It's quite fascinating."

Dane raised his eyebrows, intrigued, making a mental note to visit Alto-Baros one day.

Sage didn't look convinced. "How does the water—err—stay in one piece? Why doesn't it spill all over?"

"That's why only Aquadorians can drive them," Quinn explained. "The water can't hold its form without their power. The same thing happens if the dewcarts are left unused for too long, hence why they're only seen near water."

Sage frowned. "Seems like quite the hassle for a simple cart."

Quinn shrugged. "I agree, wooden carts are much more reliable . . . and less subject to misuse." She turned and continued walking along the path. "Let's keep going. We're almost there."

More dewcarts populated the path ahead as they neared to Mistveil, though none were hauling old books. Most carried fresh crops or sacks of vegetables, toting supplies toward the city. Several small children bounced happily on the back of another cart headed into the lake. Dane smiled, youthful excitement flowing through him as he watched. The dewcarts were certainly an unexpected sight—unique and fascinating. He couldn't wait to see what other curiosities Mistveil had to offer.

Despite their progress, Dane could barely make out Mistveil beyond the boulders and dense forests lining the shore. He recalled his conversations with Vilik, when they had first fantasized about visiting the illustrious City of Fountains. Vilik had carried on about the waterfall at the edge of Mistveil Lake and how the city, supported by massive geysers, was due to topple into the sea below.

He let his thoughts wander, sifting through the fond stories they'd shared. Vilik's favorite had always been the story of Founder Rodran fighting off Lussiek's army with his shapeshifting stone blade. Vilik would ramble on how Rodran, armed solely with a hilt made of stone, plunged it into the ground and unsheathed a mighty blade, forged from the very earth itself, and struck down his hapless enemies. Dane distinctly remembered the fascination on Vilik's face every time he told the story. He smiled fondly at the memory, a tug of sadness pulling at his heartstrings. He wondered if Vilik still thought the same of Mistveil, if his musings of childhood had persisted over the years. He vowed to ask when they reunited.

Dane was pulled from his thoughts as he collided with Sage, who'd come to a stop on the path. He stumbled, recovering his balance, fully expecting Sage to offer a snide yet playful retort how he'd gotten lost in his thoughts again.

Instead, Sage stared ahead, her mouth open. Dane followed her gaze. His breath caught in his throat. They had finally reached the northern edge of the lake. Mistveil towered before them.

A massive geyser as thick as the Elderwood's trunk erupted from the lake, disappearing into an enormous earthen foundation suspended above the lake's surface. Water spilled from a ring of tunnels surrounding the foundation, pouring back into the lake. Hundreds of buildings, rising from the foundation's flat surface, stretched skyward to varying heights, held aloft by miniature geysers all across the city. Four smaller foundations circled the central one, each supported by their own omnipresent geysers, and each littered with more buildings. A network of walkways made entirely of water webbed over all parts of the city, connecting every building to its neighbor. Dane couldn't begin to count the number of levels in the city, for each building was on a level of its own, creating a mesmerizing pattern amongst the amalgamation of water and stone.

"I had the same expression when I first saw Mistveil," Quinn said.

"When did you first visit?" Sage asked, still partially dazed.

Quinn rubbed her shoulders, gazing fondly at the city. "My father, mother, and I would travel here often in my youth, much like we did to Vitalor. I'll never forget the first time I saw it. I nearly fell off my father's shoulders because I was staring up so high!" She giggled as if recalling the memory. Dane couldn't help but smile at her.

After a moment of calming silence, she pointed and said, "Look there—the tallest building on the main island." Dane followed her gesture. A towering, shimmering black spire, taller than any of the city's other suspended buildings, bloomed from the center of the main foundation. "That's the Grand Archive."

They walked toward one of two bridges—the East Bridge, as Quinn called it—that arched up from the lake shore and led to the city gates. Either side of the bridge was lined with waist-high barriers of solid, slick stone and decorated with small statues resembling miniature fountains. As they ascended toward the city gates, Cayde's expression turned sour, his eyes narrowing as he peered toward the archway that parted the stone wall surrounding the floating island. Discretely, he placed a hand on Quinn's shoulder and whispered in her ear.

Roused by a spark of jealousy of yet another shared secret, Dane blurted, "What is it? Is something wrong?"

A few passing citizens stared momentarily in Dane's direction. Once relieved of their gazes, Cayde scanned the steady stream of people. Quinn darted a hand to her mouth and hissed, "Keep quiet about any problems, remember?"

"Why is everyone whispering?" Sage whispered.

"Look up there." Cayde thumbed toward the archway. "Four guards by the entrance. Usually it's just one or two . . ."

"Why is that strange?" whispered Dane, watching the guards in his peripherals. "That's no different than Vitalor."

"They probably heard of the attack and wanted to have more guards patrol the city, right?" Sage followed.

Quinn shook her head. "That's just it, though. I didn't think they had forces to spare; there always seemed to be a need for more guards in the past. It's almost as if—" She trailed off, mumbling to herself.

"As if what?" said Dane.

"Never mind, it doesn't make sense. It's just strange that they could bolster their ranks so quickly."

"Maybe they recruited guards from the surrounding farmland?" Sage turned her palms up. "Let's not waste time on it now. I want to see the Grand Archive up close!"

"She's right," Dane said, forcing some urgency into his voice while minding the passing crowds. "We need to find out any information we can—before another attack."

Quinn nodded apprehensively. "Yes, we need to keep moving. But . . . let me do the talking."

They made their way toward the city gate. Once within earshot, a tall guard to the left of the entrance stepped into their path and thrust a hand toward Quinn. "What is your business in the city today?"

Quinn straightened, staring into the guard's eyes with a powerful elegance that reminded Dane of Lady Evergleam.

"We've come to visit the Grand Archive, by order of Elder Yarrin of Evergleam," she said coolly.

"We'll need more explanation," the guard scoffed, as if every passerby had issued the same declaration. "The city is under tight lockdown by the orders of Elder Erwan. Unless you can provide further—"

Another guard, stout but sturdy, pushed his way forward and shoved the tall guard to the side.

"My apologies, Lady Quinn. Of course, go right ahead," he said. He turned and rapped the taller guard on the back of the head, shooting him a vicious glare before turning back to Quinn. "It's good to see you again."

"Likewise, Captain Granius." Quinn dipped her head lightly toward the stout guard. She beckoned to the others and proceeded through the archway. Granius turned to the tall guard and grunted, "Don't be daft, Gerald! Don't you know who that is?" The tall guard yelped in pain as Granius slapped him again.

Before Dane could follow Quinn through the archway, Cayde stopped and turned to the stout guard. In a stern voice, he said, "Excuse me, Captain Granius, but where did you find the guards to patrol the entire city? Last I checked, you were short on representation."

Granius stared quizzically at Cayde. Just as he seemed set on dismissing Cayde's question, Gerald intervened, puffing his chest outward. "We received word of the attack on Vitalor— terrible thing, that was—so Elder Erwan ordered us guards to protect everything." He stared contemplatively into the sky and stroked his bare, frail chin. "Not that we expect anything strange soon, mind you, but there's no harm in being prepared, eh?" Gerald grinned a moment, evidently pleased with his response, then flinched as Granius shot him a penetrating stare. Gerald quickly stammered, "As for the additional guards . . . we were brought in from the surrounding area. 'Don't need more protection for the farmlands,' Elder Erwan says, 'We need to protect the Archive, the Mystic Fountain, and the city.' So here we are." He adorned a smug grin and puffed his thin chest out. Granius just stood, his arms crossed, rubbing the bridge of his nose.

Before Cayde could ask any further questions, Quinn's voice called out over the dull humming of chatter. "Cayde, Dane, let's go. We've got to get to the Archive."

Dane obeyed and Cayde reluctantly followed as they rejoined Quinn and Sage and ventured toward the towering structure in the center of the city.

Though much larger in size, Dane couldn't help but notice the similarities between Mistveil and Vitalor. One expansive street ran through the entire city—exposing the West Bridge at the far end—and was lined with rows upon rows of bustling market stands. Dewcarts floated by in a system of narrow canals—filled to the brim with water that trickled down from the hundreds of spouting fountains—that curved down every street in sight. Every so often a dewcart would roll across the wide main street, weaving between travelers to stop at market stands and gather supplies before returning to the canals, the water beneath disappearing and reforming with every transition between the flowing canals and the city streets.

Despite the intrigue of the dewcart canals, Dane's attention was quickly drawn skyward. Slender geysers spouted from behind the row of visible buildings, reaching upward and supporting houses above, just as the trees supported the huts in his village.

The entire city seemed conjured from a dream. Floating huts, walkways of water, carts that traversed both land and water . . .

all encompassed in the largest city he had ever seen. And yet, he still hadn't seen the——

Dane stopped in his tracks as a massive shadow eclipsed his vision. He craned his neck back, eyes bulging as he gawked at the Grand Archive before him. An enormous spire sheathed in sleek black stone rose from the street, its surface shimmering as if rivulets of water coated the entire exterior. Colossal oaken doors, each decorated with giant metal rings, towered above him a short distance ahead.

Those doors must be centuries old, Dane thought in awe, staring at the ancient designs on the rings. His gaze followed the seemingly endless line of stone statues and tapering parapets that bordered each of the spire's three sides and reached to the sky itself.

Dane took a moment to rub his eyes, which now stung from their prolonged exposure to the misty air. He glanced at Sage, who wore the same expression—eyes wide and beginning to tear, her jaw agape as she stared in wonder.

"Marvelous, isn't she?" a voice cooed from behind.

Dane startled and whirled around to see a tall, thin man standing behind him. His robes were familiarly elegant and colored a deep azure like the ocean depths, laced with a light pattern of narrow stripes, which, upon closer inspection, appeared to be small, encapsulated currents of water flowing through the robe's fabric.

Quinn turned as if expecting the voice, a light smile across her lips.

"Hello, Elder Erwan. How did you know to find us here?" she said.

Elder Erwan steepled his fingers under his chin, gazing at the Archive. His thin lips curled pleasantly from behind his crooked, protruding nose. He stared skyward through a pair of narrow yet brilliantly blue eyes, and his head craned so far back that Dane could see the small bald patch surrounded by his thin, wisp-like black hair.

"I heard from one of my guards that you had entered the city today," he stated. "And after my recent meeting with Elder Yarrin, it was inevitable I'd find you here soon enough." His voice hung in the air like mist, his words flowing like gentle river currents. Everything about him radiated calmness. The sentiment quickly faded as the Elder turned to Dane.

"I haven't met either of you." Elder Erwan's eyes flicked between Dane and Sage. He lofted one of his thin, bony fingers in Dane's direction. "I presume you are the young man who—well, had the *incident*, yes? Is that why you've come to the Grand Archive?"

"Actually, Elder, we came with more important matters at hand," Dane said in a low voice, pushing away thoughts of his Trials, clutching his new purpose.

He felt Quinn's gaze on him momentarily, regarding him with . . . was it admiration?

She stepped beside him and added, "It's true, we came to investigate the attack on Vitalor, and to find out more about . . . Avon."

Elder Erwan's eyes narrowed at her final words. A small, humorless smile tugged at the corners of his mouth. "Ah. I figured as much from the daughter of the esteemed Elder Yarrin. Very grave news that was to hear. But you have come precisely to the right place." He gestured his arms upward, as if supporting the Grand Archive in his grasp. "This is only the largest collection of books and historical records in all of Physos. I have no doubt that you will find the answers you seek in my collection."

"That's why we need your assistance, elder," said Cayde. "What records are there of Avon? Or information detailing what he has to gain from attacking the energy wells? If we act quickly, we can stop him before he strikes again."

Elder Erwan stared pensively at the Archive. "I do wish I had the time to aid you all, as I would indeed join you in your quest for knowledge, but I'm afraid that I have more . . . *pressing* matters to deal with. But fret not! My son, the Grand Archivist himself, is more than capable of aiding you in my stead. He can point your search in the right direction. May the Mother guide your journey."

Elder Erwan bowed gracefully and retreated back down the bustling street.

"Well . . . shall we?" Quinn said, eyeing the doors.

"We didn't come all this way for nothing," Sage said. "Let's hope this Grand Archivist knows what he's doing." She blew out a sigh, sizing up the massive building, her wide eyes matching its enormity. "Otherwise, we'll be here for a long while . . ."

They entered through the massive doors and into a vast circular hall where hundreds of ornate shelves lined the walls, each crammed full of books in all sizes. Large walkways with even more shelves lined the circular interior above the main hall, spanning up five more floors before reaching the domed ceiling. A wide dais spread across the main floor, with several neat rows of ornately carved tables and chairs.

Aside from the occasional reader buried face-deep in oversized books, the Grand Archive was sparsely populated; even the lightest of footsteps echoed off the towering stone walls. At the far end of the hall behind the rows of tables was a large circular desk where several men and women, each clad in simplistic white robes, sifted through piles of ancient books.

As Dane started toward the nearest bookshelf, still in a partial daze, he caught sight of a tall, thin man wearing identical white robes except for the bright blue sash draped over his left shoulder. It was pinned on his garment just above the chest, embroidered with two gleaming medallions.

Dane turned to Quinn and Cayde and thumbed to the man. "Is that him? The Grand Archivist?"

Quinn considered the man, then nodded. "Must be—he's the only one wearing a sash."

As if hearing their conversation, the man chose that moment to stride toward them, hands folded neatly to his chest as the delicate robes billowed around his feet. In no time at all, he was standing directly before them, a wide, toothy smile plastered across his narrow face.

"Greetings, travelers, and welcome to the Grand Archive, the single greatest wealth of knowledge in all of Physos. I am the—"

"You're Calder, correct?" Cayde inquired dryly. "The son of Elder Erwan? We don't have much time and we need your help."

The man sputtered, evidently thrown from his practiced greeting, looking as if he'd been slapped across the cheek. His twitched involuntarily, and his nose crinkled as if he had just eaten a bitter fruit. When he finally composed himself, his voice was shrill and stern. "Yes, young man, that is correct. But here, you will refer to me as the Grand Archivist, if you *please*."

Cayde dropped his voice to a hushed whisper. "Elder Erwan said you'd help us find information about the attack on Vitalor. You *can* help us, can't you?"

The Grand Archivist pondered this for several moments. Dane saw the corners of his mouth dip into a foul sneer—only accentuating his hooked nose and cold, squinting eyes—and quickly concluded that the sneer was a perpetual resident of his facial expression. The Grand Archivist stared at each of them with repugnance, as if debating the morals of helping inexperienced travelers with a task of such vital importance.

"This way," the Grand Archivist finally relented. He led them across the grand hall to a shelf tucked behind the rounded desk with the other archivists. He paused before the shelf, gesturing with his rigid, almost skeletal fingers. "I don't know the exact text you may be looking for, but you will find it here with the other historical records on energy wells and their inherent abilities." The Grand Archivist's nostrils flared. "If you require further assistance," he said forcibly, his voice controlled and monotone, "I am at your disposal. But please know I am *quite* busy." With a dismissive sneer, the Grand Archivist swept away from the shelf and back across the grand hall.

Sage leaned toward Quinn and whispered, "Your father was certainly right about him. He's a genuine ray of sunshine." Sage stared up at the shelf teeming with ancient, oversized books and added, "I'm so glad he was able to help."

Quinn ran a finger across the binding of a particularly large book. "At least he pointed us to the right shelf . . . I hope." She squinted, then drew her face closer to the book and blew hard.

A wave of dust blossomed into the air. Grimacing, she added, "I wonder if any of these books even contain the information we need."

After a meticulous scan of the shelves, it became evident that, despite the Grand Archivist's haughty conviction, he was *not* able to aid them in their search; they could find no information whatsoever pertaining to why Avon would seek to attack the energy wells. To the Grand Archivist's credit, the Archive was indeed packed full of books on every topic imaginable. One book detailed the exact layouts of each of the capital cities in the Plateau region—which, Dane deduced from a poorly drawn scribble on the first page, was the area that included Mistveil, Evergleam, Vitalor, and his own village, along with the surrounding expanses of land packed between Aurora Mountains and the mirroring Avalanche Mountains. Another book forced Dane's stomach to groan with hunger as he flipped through pages containing hundreds of recipes for cooking chickens.

Another, detailing the origins of dewcarts and their use with the systems of canals running through Mistveil, though not pertaining to the task at hand, particularly sparked Dane's interest. Further investigation yielded a book titled, *The Caves and Caverns of Alto-Baros,* which recounted the ancient storytelling of a long-deceased elder who had traversed every single nook remotely close to Alto-Baros, the City of Storms, much of which Dane found to be bland and uneventful.

The others were having no better luck. Cayde was rifling through various copies of the mindless ramblings of Elder Ignatius, the apparent former Elder of Mistveil who was obsessed with every aspect of upkeep involved with the Grand Archive, detailing even the very placement of the book itself. Sage mumbled on about the pages of *Essential Garments of the Evergleam Luminari,* which explained the finest of details required to fabricate the intricate robes akin to those of Quinn and her family.

But, despite their acquisition of the new wealth of generally unimportant information, not one text provided even the vaguest of leads as to where the Ferrons originated, how the

Chemocytes could have progressed to the mainland, or what Avon hoped to gain from attacking the energy wells.

Late afternoon shadows crept along the floor of the Archive, swallowing each shelf one by one as the day slowly dwindled away. Dane stared up at one of the many small, circular windows that peppered the stone interior. The sun would soon disappear behind the mountains. They were no closer to discovering the next course of action than when they had started. His body ached in places he didn't know could ache, the strain from the day finally catching up with him. The others looked no better off.

"We're running out of time," Quinn said as she thrust a book back onto the shelf and whisked her silky brown hair from her bloodshot eyes. Fatigue plagued her voice. "There's nothing here that can help us . . ."

The others all nodded lightly. Dane massaged the back of his neck, which had grown especially sore while unsuccessful rummaging through rows upon rows of ancient books. He wanted to slump to the floor—or any unoccupied patch of ground, for that matter—and collapse into a deep sleep.

On the brink of collapse, Sage's eyes suddenly widened, her posture straightening. "Maybe we should ask one of the other archivists? Just without Cald—I mean, *the Grand Archivist*—knowing," she said, scoffing at the mention of the unhelpful Grand Archivist. "Look there." She pointed to the long circular desk. A young man in white archivist robes, looking no older than Dane and Sage—was shuffling through a leaning stack of oversized books. "Maybe he can help us instead."

Cayde considered this, running his fingers through his curled, fraying hair. "We really don't have a better option," he said, shrugging his shoulders in a way that further accentuated his undeniable urge for slumber.

"Excuse me," Sage whispered in her most polite tone as they approached, careful to project her voice loud enough so the young man could hear them, but not so loud as to attract the attention of the patrolling Grand Archivist.

The young man poked an eye out from behind his leaning stack of books, acknowledged them with astounding disinterest, then returned to his work. Sage frowned, then persisted, "We were hoping that you'd—" Her face contorted. "Wait, do I know you?"

Dane stared at Sage quizzically. "Sage, we've never been here before. How could you possibly—"

The young man poked his face out again, and Dane's thoughts halted abruptly. He *did* look familiar. His mussed, frayed black hair gave him a slightly crazed appearance, accentuated by his dark, clouded eyes, looking as though he were thinking a thousand thoughts at once. His scrawny, rather gangly limbs made the leaning pile of books appear even larger as the young man slunk back behind cover.

Sage took another step toward him. "I remember you from somewhere, I'm sure of it," she said, scratching her white-blonde hair, which looked equally frayed after the long day of unsuccessful reading.

The young man glanced at her, donning an unsatisfactory frown. "If you can't tell, I'm quite swamped," he said shortly. He began rummaging more rapidly through his books, as if trying to look busy.

Sage ignored him and pressed her thumbs to her temples. Then she snapped her fingers, her eyes flaring with confidence. "Of course!" she said, foregoing her whisper. "You're the one who asked that ridiculous question to Elder Chrysanthe at the Trials initiation in Vitalor, before the Trials!"

The young man froze, his leaning stack of books wobbling precariously. Dane couldn't see his face, but from the new coloration spreading to the young archivist's neck, Dane presumed he remembered too.

"I—uh—I have no idea what you're talking about," he stammered. His gaze flitted over Sage. "And no, we've never met, so if you don't mind . . ." He grabbed his stack of books and made for the nearest vacant shelf. In trying to balance the books, he only managed a clumsy, sluggish pace.

Sage followed persistently, watching through quizzical eyes as he shuffled away. She tapped her fingers on her folded arms with increasing speed. Then she straightened again, her face contorting in anger.

"It was *YOU!*" She strode toward the young man and wiggled an accusatory finger. "*You* were the one who almost ran us over with that dewcart down by the lake, weren't you?"

Quinn fixed him with a petrifying glare. "It *was* you!" She declared. "How could you be so careless? You almost flattened us!"

"Look," the young archivist said, gulping loudly, "you must have me confused with some other—"

A shrill bark rang across the grand hall. "CERULIS!"

The young man released a high-pitched yelp and flung his arms wildly into the air, toppling his stack of books in a flurry of ruffled pages. The color had all but drained from his face, his pale skin nearly matching the color of his archivist robes.

The Grand Archivist was storming across the long hall, his bony hands balled into fists at his sides. His robes fluttered in his wake as he seemingly floated across the floor like a rush of frigid night air.

"It was *you* who stole the dewcart earlier?" the Grand Archivist seethed, hauling the young man down a sheltered aisle, breaking the line of sight between them and the agog onlookers. "What have I told you about using—I can't believe that—*again*, no less—it's lucky that you're the only one who can—" Dane could only hear fragments as enraged words spewed from the Grand Archivist's mouth. He almost felt sorry for the young man. Almost.

The young archivist gulped loudly, his voice small and quaking.

"Somebody had to pick up the delivery. Since you assigned all the guards in the city, there was no one else available to—"

"Enough with the petty excuses, boy! Not another word! Now pick up that mess!" He raised a bony finger to an equally tall, equally unstable pile of books. "And I want all these shelved by morning, or so help me, you'll—you'll—" The Grand Archivist threw his hands in the air, his face red and twitching violently. He whipped his sky-blue sash, now dangling below one arm, over his shoulder with exaggerated authority before marching off.

Relieved of the verbal onslaught, the young archivist bent to gather his chaotic heap of misplaced books.

Sage strutted forward and paused near the pile, staring smugly down at the young man. *Serves you right*, her eyes seemed to say.

The young man glanced up. His dark eyes were wild, almost crazed, as if he were thinking a thousand thoughts at once. He shuddered momentarily before turning back to his pile of books. "As I said," he said with dry calmness. "I'm quite swamped. If you wouldn't mind bothering someone else—"

"Look," Sage said, planting her hands on her knees and bending down to stare directly into the young man's eyes. "It's late. We're exhausted. The Grand Archivist can't help us. There's some very important information we have to find before something worse happens and we're running out of time to do it. Now, you're either going to help us find what we want, or I'll drag you straight back to Sneers and tell him that you nearly trampled us with that *stolen* dewcart!"

The young man sprang to his feet and began thumbing frantically through the nearest bookshelf, mumbling incoherently. "Important information ... *very* important information ... something worse happens ... *something worse* ... running out of time ..." He fell silent for a brief moment, then gasped loudly and turned back to them, his eyes riddled with intrigue.

"I know *exactly* what you're looking for. You're trying to find out about Av—" He straightened suddenly, smiling deviously. In a low voice, he continued, "Let's just say, 'learn more about the attack', am I right? Yes, I must be right. What else could it be?" Dane swore he saw the young man wink at Sage. "What you want is the—" He stopped abruptly and narrowed his beady brown eyes. "Wait, I can't tell you that."

Cayde rolled his eyes. "And *why* is that?"

"Can't tell you that either. It's forbidden—restricted—closed—whatever—doesn't matter, you can't go there."

"And why not?" Sage said irritably. "The Grand Archivist said the Archive contains the largest wealth of knowledge in all of Physos. It's open for everyone, is it not?"

"Well, *I* can go there, but *you* can't. Besides, I don't really want to, and I still have much, *much* more important matters to attend to." He turned back to the pile of books.

"Oh, by the Mother—" Quinn let out a long, disgruntled sigh and turned to the others. "This is going nowhere. We have to find an inn for the night. We can try again tomorrow." She thumbed in the direction of the archivist. *"Without* help from this one."

They turned to leave, making their way across the Archive floor, when the young man called out behind them. "Stop!"

Quinn rolled her head toward him, fixing him with an exasperated stare.

"Please don't go," he said, a sudden desperation in his voice. "I—I can help you, but—" his eyes shifted to the sword hilt on Cayde's back, "—is that a sword? Can I see it? Never mind, of course not." He cleared his throat, emitting a sound like that of a dying cat, then sighed an exaggerated breath. "I know what books you need—but I need your help too."

Cayde shook his head lightly, rubbing the bridge of his nose. "Go on."

"Well, I assume that the attack isn't all that you know. You see, I've been around these books for most of my life. I know almost everything there is to know about the history of Physos, former elders, other important people, other not-so-important people—anyways, I've discovered certain mysteries I didn't quite understand. Certain mysteries possibly regarding—oh, I don't know . . . Chemocytes?" the archivist whispered the final word, intently watching Cayde's expression. When Cayde's eyebrows lifted, a smile broke out across the young man's face, his eyes igniting with curious intrigue. "So, you *do* know something . . ."

Quinn hesitated, stealing a knowing glance with Cayde. *He's right, you know,* she seemed to say. *Should we just tell him?* Cayde's bleary expression was all the response she needed.

"What's it to you?" Quinn said.

"If they're anything like what I've read—you know, from the myths, legends, stories, and so on—then dangerous times lay ahead if those . . . *things* . . . return like Avon did."

Quinn peered into the young man's eyes, as if assessing his deepest intentions. She glanced to Dane and the others. He didn't quite trust this young archivist, but something told him there wasn't much choice if were to find the information they came for. The others seemed to think the same. They each nodded.

After a long pause, Quinn exhaled and said, "We've searched enough for today, but if you honor your word, then we will help you. But you have to help us first."

The young man nodded eagerly.

"And keep this quiet. There's no reason the Grand Archivist needs to know any more about our search. Got it?"

"Naturally," the young archivist said, rubbing his hands together.

Sage scrutinized the young man, clearly unconvinced. "You haven't told us your name," she said matter-of-factly. She looked over his thin, gangly frame. She crossed her arms. "I'm not sure I can trust someone who won't tell me their name . . ."

The young archivist's mouth spread into a toothy, lopsided grin. "Leon. The name's Leon."

CHAPTER 14

THE PRIVATE COLLECTION

"I can't stand that Leon!" Sage fumed as they approached the Archive the following morning. "He's simply unbearable. The sooner we can leave him behind, the better."

Quinn sighed. "It's only for a short while."

"Maybe he'll surprise us," Dane said thoughtfully, gazing up as beams of morning sunlight reflected off the Archive's sleek black exterior. He felt rejuvenated, excited even, beckoned by the mysteries hidden inside. A blissful night's sleep at a nearby inn had done wonders for his spirits. "I have a good feeling about this."

Leon was standing beside a nearby shelf as they pushed through the palatial doors to the Grand Archive. An uncomfortable grin was plastered across his face. That with his tangled black hair and oversized archivist robes, it looked as though he'd had a run-in with a Chemocyte the night before.

Dane's confidence wavered. Sage let out an audible groan. "What now?"

Leon winced, his grin faltering. "We . . . have a slight problem."

Dane could almost hear Sage's eyes roll in their sockets.

Leon held his hand up, pinching his thumb and index finger. "Just a little one," he mumbled.

Quinn cradled her forehead in her palm. "And what problem is that?"

"I *do* know where to find information that could relate to Avon or the Chemocytes, but . . . it's locked away in the private collection. For archivists only. Remember? Forbidden. Restricted. Closed—"

"I don't see why that's a problem," Sage said, glaring at Leon. "You *are* an archivist, aren't you? Just take us there yourself."

He swallowed. "I wish it were that simple. I *would* take you there, except that no one is allowed to see the private collection except for senior archivists. Hence why it's the *private* collection. And the collection is always patrolled by Senior Archivist Sylas—I swear he's older than most of the books in this place— and he only ever leaves to—"

"We'll need to see that private collection," Quinn interjected, "otherwise we're wasting our time here while Avon runs rampant across Physos. Can you help us or not?"

Leon's breathing suddenly escalated, coming in rapid, shallow breaths. He shoved his twitching fingers into his frizzled hair, exposing streaks of pale scalp beneath.

Quinn stared expectantly at him. When he remained silent, she turned to the others and said, "We can find someone else to help. If I mention my father sent us—"

"WAIT!"

They all turned. Leon held one hand outstretched toward Quinn, desperation plaguing his features.

"Take me with you," he said, his voice barely audible. His eyes were gaping wide, almost glistening. His gaunt chin trembled.

Quinn recoiled slightly, eyebrows raised. "You—what?"

"Look, I lied about wanting to know about Chemocytes—I mean, I still do . . . creepy myth creatures *are* my thing—but—"

His gaze fell to the floor. "All I do is read these books. Then shelve them, then read some more, and then shelve some more—I don't want to just read and shelve books about Physos. I want to *see* Physos. I want to *live,* not be the second kid who lived and died in the Grand Archive. I want a life that has meaning . . . like all of you. I've had nowhere to go since I lost my parents—no one to guide me or help me find where I belong." Leon's body slumped in defeat. "Please. Just give me a chance."

Sage looked at him earnestly, all traces of the previous day's resentment gone. "You lost your parents?"

Leon looked up, startled. "Oh—right—I can see how you'd think that I meant—no, see, my parents are still alive—at least, I think they are—but I can't find them. We were visiting the market one day when I was younger, and before I knew it, I was alone and they were nowhere to be found. When I returned to the house, they—you know what, I don't want to get into that now. Where was I?" Leon scratched his head. "Right. If I can get you into the private collection, will you take me with you on your journey?"

From the few interactions Dane had had with the young archivist, he didn't take Leon as someone whom he'd want as a traveling companion. With his frenzied, unkempt hair, shifty brown eyes, and incessant talking, Dane would've thought Leon lived on the streets. But in that moment, Leon's face drooping with longing, Dane couldn't help but sympathize with him; it was the same look Dane wore just before he asked Quinn and Cayde if he could accompany them to Evergleam, yearning for somewhere to belong.

Quinn's eyes narrowed on Leon. "That's all I ask," he added. "I'll get you in—briefly, at least. Just take me with you. Please." If it weren't for the other archivists—and the watchful eyes of the Grand Archivist—Dane suspected Leon would have fallen to his knees and groveled at her feet.

Quinn looked to Cayde, exchanged a short series of stares and glances, then turned back to Leon. "Give us a moment first, will you?" The young archivist nodded vigorously as he stepped back, his wide, timid eyes peering from behind floppy folds of hair.

"So?" Cayde whispered, lowering his voice so only Dane, Sage, and Quinn could hear. "Can he actually help us?"

Quinn's pursed her lips. "I don't completely trust him. I've heard of the private collection, but I've never seen it for myself." She gnawed her lip. "Do we have another choice?"

"Elder Erwan said the Grand Archivist would be able to help us," said Cayde. "So far that hasn't really been the case, but maybe we just have to tell him more about—"

"We should do it—take Leon with us," Dane said suddenly, surprising himself with his own confidence. "He's not too different from any of us, right? Besides, what if he knows something we don't? He could prove useful. We're going to need all the help we can get. I say we take him."

Cayde regarded Dane a moment, then the corners of his mouth tugged upward. He shrugged indifferently. "Sure. Why not. I didn't really like the Grand Archivist anyway."

Dane lifted his eyebrows in question to Quinn. "What do you say?"

Quinn hesitated, then nodded reluctantly.

Dane turned his attention to his sister, who was scowling disapprovingly at Leon. "Sage? You heard what he said about his parents. Maybe it's not the same as with our parents, but he knows what it's like . . . that has to mean something."

Sage scrunched her face, staring skeptically at Dane. He guessed she still held some resentment toward Leon for the dewcart encounter, but he saw the way she had looked at Leon when he'd mentioned his parents, with the same familiarity and sadness of losing someone they loved. The same understanding was in her eyes now.

Cayde broke the silence. "We'll only accept if we all agree."

Sage heaved a sigh. "I still don't like him," she scoffed. They all looked back toward Leon, who was conducting a grim attempt to control his frayed hair. He launched an awkward, toothy smile in their direction.

A mischievous glint shone in Sage's eyes. "But I suppose he could be useful." She rubbed a finger across her chin. "He could carry our extra food. And water. And clothing . . ." This brought a wicked grin to her face. "Fine, he can join, but *only* if he can lead us to this private collection . . . and haul our supplies."

Quinn smirked. "Then it's decided." She turned back to Leon. "Are you certain you can grant us passage into the private collection? You understand that *we* have to be in there too, right? We don't know exactly what to look for but describing it to you isn't enough."

A glimmer of hope ignited in Leon's clouded brown eyes. His body began to shake like an oversized water droplet about to burst. "Ah-ha!" he exclaimed, leaping clumsily into the air. His flailing arms nearly smacked Cayde in the face. "Yes, yes, yes, I most certainly can! As long as you are content with . . . how do I put this . . . *unsanctioned* methods of entrance, then yes, I know how to sneak you in. You'll still take me with you, right? After you find what you're looking for?"

"Yes," Sage groaned. "But you also have to carry our food and water." Leon cocked his head and stared at Sage. "And clothes," she added. "Don't forget the clothes. Part of the deal—you know, for getting us into the private collection."

"Um . . . sure? Of course . . . I guess. Why is that important?"

Sage lifted her shoulders. "If you don't want to, we have no problems leaving you behind . . ."

"Fine, fine. Yes, I'll carry your food too."

"And water and clothes," Sage added, beaming with satisfaction.

"What's your plan, Leon?" Cayde said.

"Well—hmm . . ." Leon's squinting eyes surveyed the hall. He crinkled his nose in disgust. "Not here," he whispered. "In the Archive, voices spread like—like that fire through Vitalor— oh wait, too soon. Err—like the wind through—through the— doesn't matter. Everyone can hear everything in this place." He glanced sidelong at Sage and mouthed, *I don't like you either.* "We need to go somewhere more public."

Sage raised an eyebrow. "*More* public? Isn't this supposed to be some sneaky plan?"

Leon nodded. "Of course. In a large enough crowd, all sounds—voices, rushing water, people's footsteps, even the air—merge into one indiscernible blob. It's the perfect place to hide a conversation . . . or a *sneaky plan.*"

"Won't someone notice you're missing?" Sage retorted.

Leon barked a laugh. "Oh, they won't care . . . no one likes me here anyways. They'll probably rejoice."

"Where do you want to go?" Quinn asked.

Leon's lips curled into a smile. "I know just the place."

༨ ଏ

"You've *never* seen the Mystic Fountain?" Leon gaped at Dane and Sage as they followed Leon down the street leading behind the Grand Archive.

Dane shook his head. Sage returned Leon's gaze with a complacent shrug.

"This is their first time in Mistveil," Quinn offered. "We came straight to the Archive and—well, you know the rest."

Leon's mouth hung open. "I just don't understand it," he said, throwing his hands in the air, causing a passing Aquadorian to leap away from Leon's rogue limbs. "It's the *Mystic Fountain.* Anyone who's anyone has seen it! Do you even know what energy—"

"Yes, of course we know what the energy wells are!" Sage snapped. "We just haven't seen this one yet. But I'll bet *you* weren't gifted something by *your* energy well . . ." She tossed her head to the side and clasped her hands to her waist.

"You what now?" Leon's face twisted with confusion. He shifted his gaze down to the branch coiled around her waist, then back to her eyes, then once more to her waist.

Leon squinted shrewdly. "What, *that?* A useless branch? As a gift?" He waved a dismissive hand. "That can't possibly be a thing."

Leon halted as they neared the end of the street. A massive, curved stone wall rose from the path ahead, its surface covered in writhing tendrils of water. The street forked around the wall, each identical path curving and disappearing from view.

Leon scratched his ragged folds of hair and mumbled to himself, flicking his gaze between the two paths. He lifted a hesitant finger toward the right path and opened his mouth to speak, but said nothing. He pointed unconvincingly down the left path, then steepled his hands beneath his chin, staring blankly forward.

Quinn let out an exasperated groan and pushed past him. "They both lead to the same place!"

Leon startled violently as if shaken from a vivid dream. "Right," he said, flashing a sheepish grin, "let's go left."

Dane noticed the crowd thickening as they followed the curved wall, the air growing heavy and clouding with mist. Then, for just a moment, surrounded by people on all sides, Dane realized he could no longer pick out each conversation; all he could hear was a singular, solid wall of noise. He stared at Leon walking clumsily through the crowd, feeling a newfound respect for the young archivist. As odd as Leon was, he did have at least some wits about him.

Dane turned as they reached the end of the curved wall and, despite the constant presence of saturating mist, glimpsed the shape of an enormous column of water, spouting up from a shallow pool in the center of the walled enclosure, reaching toward the sky with its glistening streams. A light breeze blew through the enclosure, whisking away the mist to unveil the breathtaking splendor of the Mystic Fountain.

A continuous geyser blasted upward, reaching nearly as high as the suspended buildings above. Dozens of kneeling Aquadorians surrounded the small pool at the base of the Fountain, all mumbling indiscernibly, each placing their hands on the rippling pool surface. A soft shroud of mist cascaded down from pluming jets. Dane closed his eyes, soaking in the cleansing beads of water flowing gently past his face.

The clashing scent of cool, lake air stole Dane's attention away from the Fountain. Behind him was a large gap in the city's exterior wall. Leon stood at the edge of a railing, peering out at the vast canvas of mist beyond.

"It's a shame the mist decided to roll in today," Leon said as they approached.

"Come again?" Quinn asked.

"Oh!" Leon shuddered and swiveled where he stood, a trace of shock plastered on his face. "I didn't know you were—never mind." He waved a hand dismissively then stared out at the misty air. "It's too bad the waterfall is shrouded by all this mist. Usually I like to stand here and watch the mountains beyond the waterfall and the sea . . ." He sighed deeply and returned his gaze to the shroud of mist.

"Mountains?" Dane said, perplexed.

Leon nodded nonchalantly. "Mhmm, floating mountains."

Dane gaped, his eyes bulging. "*Floating* mountains?"

"Yes, yes, yes, we've all seen 'em. Now stay focused, we have to go over my plan." His gaze darted to Sage's sleeved arm. "Speaking of . . . how many stones did you claim, Biophage?"

"I—I never told you I'm a Biophage."

Leon stared at her, unamused. He glanced exaggeratedly at her exposed hand.

"So?" Leon pressed. "How many stones? Can I see your mark?"

Sage clutched her arm defensively.

"I won't touch you or anything. Mother forbid I lay my hands on a girl's arm." He lifted his palms in submission. "I just want to see."

"Fine." Sage pulled her sleeve back, exposing the twisting green vines marked into her skin.

Leon's eyebrows lifted. "Two stones, I'm impressed."

"How did you—"

Leon rolled his eyes. "Puh-lease, Biophage." He hovered a finger above her arm, tracing her mark. "The twisting pattern there . . . the clumped leaves here . . . it's quite obvious, really. Myself, I claimed the Observer energy stone." He puffed out his chest with a satisfactory sigh. "It's all I need, really. I was never one for fighting anyways . . . or jumping . . . or running." He looked at Sage. "But I'm sure you understand."

Sage shook her head vehemently.

"Agree to disagree," Leon dismissed. "Well, what about you?"

There was a short pause, and Dane realized Leon was talking to him.

"How many stones did you claim?" Leon repeated.

Before Dane could open his mouth, Cayde said, "Let's hear your plan. I want to get this over with."

Leon looked genuinely shocked. "Right!" His eyes twinkled, alight with mischief. "The private collection is on the eighth floor—the highest floor. I can't sneak you in unnoticed while Senior Archivist Sylas is on patrol, and he is *constantly* on patrol. Fortunately for us, he leaves each day at high noon to collect the books stacked outside the private collection. This is when I'll attract his attention. I'll stall long enough for each of you to sneak in, find whatever it is you want to find, and leave undetected. Though I wouldn't suggest grabbing more than one book each. Sylas *probably* wouldn't notice if three or four books went missing for a short time. Beyond that and he might just have a heart attack.

"Once you've found the information, locate a table hidden behind some shelves. Few people ever walk all the way up to the eighth floor unless they know exactly what they're looking for, and trust me, no one *ever* knows what they're looking for—you won't be seen there. When you're finished, I'll slip the books back into the private collection and nobody will ever know what happened." Leon rung his hands, grinning with satisfaction as if his flawless plan required no further explanation. "Ready?"

"No, we're not ready," Quinn said. "You expect us to know what the room looks like once we're inside? How are the books shelved?"

Leon slapped a hand to his forehead. "Ah, of course! The private collection actually doesn't contain many shelves—only four or five, if I recall—they're quite tall shelves—but they're ripe with all sorts of insatiable knowledge. Any one of them could hold a multitude of wonders about our world." His eyes gleamed with intense passion. "Oh, what I would give to read them all. Someday I will, too."

"And how do you expect to distract the Senior Archivist?" Sage pressed.

Leon snorted dryly. "Oh, trust me Petals, I know *exactly* how to capture his attention."

Sage's cheeks flushed bright red. "*Petals?*" Leon flinched as she took a menacing step toward him. Quinn caught her by the shoulder and twisted her away.

To Leon, Quinn said, "We need a moment." When Leon didn't move, she flicked her eyebrows up and pursed her lips. Leon took several steps back.

"Farther!" Sage called out. Leon rolled his eyes and obliged.

Once Leon was out of earshot, Sage shrugged out of Quinn's grasp, expelled an infuriated breath, then calmly patted her clothes down. "I'm fine, I'm fine." She shot a glare over her shoulder and mumbled, "I'll get him for that one."

"Is everyone comfortable with this?" Quinn said. "I think it could work. Do you all know what to look for? There won't be much time. We'll have to think quickly."

"I think I'll manage," said Cayde playfully. Quinn narrowed her eyes and wrinkled her nose at him, a slight smile on her lips, as if to say, *I know you know what to do.*

Cayde grinned in response.

"Ferrons, Chemocytes, energy wells," said Sage. "Got it."

"Dane?"

His mouth a hard line, Dane nodded. Quinn offered a light smile, then continued on in a whisper.

But Dane wasn't listening. The past few days had been a blur of information, excitement, and intrigue upon arriving in Evergleam. He had momentarily forgotten about Cayde's relationship with Quinn—at least, he'd chosen to ignore it—until now. He chided himself, wishing his mind wouldn't latch to the simplest of affectionate displays between them. But he couldn't help it. His heart constricted every time he watched them, his mind replaying all the moments he'd shared with her before his

Trials, before he'd failed. He could have done more for her, could have traveled to Evergleam, find her, and tell her how he felt. But despite everything they'd been through, all the hardships and struggles, Quinn and Cayde seemed truly happy together.

A solid lump lodged in Dane's throat, nearly bringing tears to his eyes. No matter how much it hurt, no matter how much he wished Quinn loved him in return, he couldn't take that feeling away from either of them.

Dane's thoughts were brought to a halt as Leon cleared his throat with exaggerated loudness and glanced skyward. The sun peered through the mist directly overhead.

"Not to rush your decision or anything," he called out, "but it's almost midday. Unless we want to do this tomorrow . . ."

Quinn's eyes blared open. "By the Mother—we've wasted too much time. We can't afford another day of waiting!" She spun around and sped back down the narrow street. Dane and the others hustled to her side while Leon, who had still been staring at the misty sky, wheeled around and clumsily threaded through the crowd behind them.

∾ ∾

"Has he come out yet?" Quinn whispered. "Did we miss him?"

They were peering from behind a shelf on the eighth floor of the Grand Archive, staring at the entrance to the private collection.

Leon shook his head. "Not yet . . . I think."

"You *think*?" Sage hissed. "You mean we could be waiting here for nothing—"

The sound of a creaking door silenced her. Leon straightened his robes and stepped out of concealment. "Don't worry, I've got this whole situation under control," he whispered. "And remember, stay out of sight. The door locks from the inside, so you'll have to keep it open once I've got him distracted. Then you can sneak in undetected."

"What happens if we're caught?" Sage asked.

"Let's say they don't take kindly to trespassers," Leon said. He drew his thumb across his neck.

Sage clutched her throat. "They'll have us *killed*?" she gasped.

"What? No! Why did you—I meant we'd be done for, thrown from the Archive, expelled for the rest of our mortal eternity!"

Sage's shoulders relaxed. "Oh. That's a relief."

"A *relief*?" Leon shrieked. "Life without the Archive would be a *relief*?"

Sage shrugged indifferently. "I've lived this long without it."

Leon clutched his heart. "Your words pain me so."

"Now would be a good time for your distraction," Quinn prodded.

"We could toss him over the balcony," Cayde offered. "That'd create quite the distraction."

Quinn slapped Cayde's arm and glared at him. Cayde turned his palms up.

"You can't possibly think that would help," Leon said. "Right?"

"Leon, the door—" Quinn started.

"*Right?*"

Sage tapped a finger to her lips and eyed the balcony in consideration. "Well . . ."

Leon sucked in a startled breath. "Now that's just rude."

Dane glanced over Leon's shoulder. An elderly man emerged from the private collection and, back hunched, shuffled toward the books piled outside. "Err—Leon?"

"Seems as good an option as any," Cayde said.

Leon looked to Cayde with a dull expression. "What, I suppose you'd be the one to toss me over? You won't do it."

Cayde folded his arms and arched an eyebrow.

Leon bristled and took a step back. "I didn't think so."

The man gathered the books and set them inside. He turned and reached for the handle.

Dane's pulse quickened. "Leon—"

"At least we'd accomplish something," Sage mumbled.

Leon grabbed a book from the nearest shelf and waggled it in Sage's face. "I've got my eye on you, Petals. So help me if—"

"The *door*!" Quinn hissed.

Leon straightened his robes, slicked back his unruly black hair—accomplishing nothing—and strode forward. He called out, "Oh, Senior Archivist Sylas!"

The man stopped with his hand on the handle. His head was cloaked in a thin, white hood, and he was hunched over so far that his ancient, graying beard nearly grazed the floor.

Leon hastened into a brisk, purposeful walk, flicked his hand as if gesturing to the door, then said, "Do I have a scholarly pondering for you!"

Sage pinched the bridge of her nose. "This can't end well."

The Elderly man turned at the sound of Leon's voice, his wandering eyes glazing past where Dane and the others remained hidden. Leon intercepted the senior archivist's gaze and wrapped his arm around the man's hunched back, leading him in the opposite direction.

"I've been wondering," Leon began, "let's say—in theory, of course—that two elders, one Gravitus and one Tempus, both used their powers on the same person and pulled in opposite directions. How far would said person be launched when flung by their competing energies? I know what you're going to say, but hear me out. What if—" Leon's voice trailed off as he accompanied Senior Archivist Sylas around a curve and out of view.

Dane released a breath he didn't know he'd been holding. "That was close." His gaze shifted to the door . . . the closing door.

Before he could even speak the words, he and the others surged from hiding. Cayde reached the door first, his hand outstretched and curled, poised to summon a gravity well and pull the door back open. Instead he stopped, shaking his head, staring at the ground. Dane edged forward for a closer look. Lodged between the door and the wall, keeping the door ajar, was the book Leon had grabbed not a moment earlier.

Sage's mouth dropped. "How did he—" She tried to form another word but resigned to silence.

Cayde's mouth curved into a smile. "He's a crafty little bastard, I'll give him that." Then, silently and swiftly, he removed the book, parted the door, and slipped into the private collection, Quinn and Sage following hastily. Dane snuck in last, easing the door shut behind him.

The private collection was just as Leon had described. Several massive pillars erected from the tiled floor, staircases spiraling around them, each stuffed with ancient books. Spindles of light shone down from windows set high above, cutting through the thick, musty air.

Dane ran to the nearest pillar and up the stone steps encircling it. He traced his fingers along the bindings, scanning for the slightest indication of Avon, Ferrons, or Chemocytes. His mind was a blur as he mumbled the title of every massive book, searching almost blindly, sifting through the plethora of untapped knowledge. His feet slowed as he climbed higher. The books seemed to pull him in, whispering in his ear, pleading to be read. There was so much he wanted to know, so much he *could* know—and it was all right there at his fingertips.

Dane swallowed down the temptation. The others were counting on him. Elder Yarrin was counting on him. He couldn't fail them . . . not again.

As if by some fabled stroke of luck, his fingers caught on the book directly in front of him: *A Complete History of Elder Lineage.*

Dane nearly shouted aloud. The book was sure to detail the history of Ferron elders—maybe even Chemocyte elders. And it was enormous, nearly twice as thick as any other in his view.

The soft patter of footsteps drew his focus, and a sense of urgency swept over him as he glanced around the room. Quinn, Cayde, and Sage were all descending to ground level, making their way back to the door.

Dane hefted the book from the shelf. He tucked it under one arm and retreated down the steps.

Just as his foot hit the solid, tiled floor, a croaking voice resonated from outside.

Dane froze. Quinn was at the door, hand outstretched toward the handle. None of them moved; they had heard the voice too. Quinn, Cayde and Sage leapt to the side and pressed their bodies against the wall. But Dane stood rooted in place, halfway between the door and the pillar behind him, nowhere to hide. His stomach plummeted.

The door creaked open. Senior Archivist Sylas stood in the doorway.

Through the swamp of fear that had cemented in his mind, Dane slowly realized the archivist wasn't actually staring at him. His head was turned to one side, as if listening for something in the distance.

"You're thinking about it all wrong," came Leon's voice from behind. "Sure, a mountain is a bit of a stretch, but think about the *energy*! Releasing that all at once could *easily*—"

Attention recaptured, the old man released the door and shuffled away, the door shutting behind him.

For several moments, Dane simply stood there, his fluttering heartbeat enveloping his senses. *Too close. Much too close.* When the feeling had returned to his legs, he stumbled toward the others.

"He didn't see you, did he?" Quinn whispered.

Dane shook his head, eyes wide. Fear had escaped him, but he still marveled at his good fortune.

Cayde pressed his ear to the door. "I think we're clear." He nodded to Quinn, "Stay here, I'll make sure they're gone."

Before she could refuse, Cayde edged the door open just enough to peer out with one eye. The only sound was that of distant voices—presumably Leon's and the senior archivist's.

"Now's our chance." Cayde cracked open the door and ushered Dane, Sage, and Quinn back into the Archive, closing the door behind him with complete silence.

Walking purposefully and slowly, as not to arouse suspicion, they returned to their hiding place behind the nearest shelf just as a hoarse, elderly voice echoed behind them.

"—To conclude, said person would not *fly* at all. They would dissipate into nothingness."

"Do you really think so?" came Leon's voice, sounding crest-fallen. "I was certain they'd fly from here all the way to Stone-helm." He sighed heavily. "Oh well, thank you for your time, Sylas. I'll let you return to your collection."

"Any time, Leon," the Elderly archivist said, bowing his aged head ever so slightly before disappearing behind the door. Leon waited a moment, then, with a smug grin, strode back to the others, his oversized archivist robes billowing gallantly behind him.

"See?" he said. "I told you I had it under control."

After finding a secluded table at the far end of the top floor, Cayde set his hefty book on the table and asked, "What did the rest of you grab? Between the lot of us, I'm certain we'll find something about the Ferrons, Avon, or the Chemocytes."

Quinn was already buried in her book, flipping wildly through the thick, tattered pages, as Dane took a seat beside Cayde. Leon slumped into a chair at the table's end, still wearing that smug grin.

"What did you find?" Dane asked her, intrigued both by the allure of secret knowledge and the speed at which she was de-vouring its contents.

Without lifting her gaze, Quinn said, "A full historical record of Founder Arkon's defeat of Founder Lussiek." She sounded breathless, her eyes wide with curious hunger. "If I had more time—there's so much in here about what happened—perhaps later . . ." she trailed off, stopping on a text-filled page, tracing her finger over the writing. "Look here, it says that after Lussiek was defeated in a failed attempt to seize the Aurora Crystal for himself, the other seven founders gathered and agreed upon his punishment: four votes for exile, three for execution." She pe-rused further down the page. "This is fascinating. Listen to this: 'After deciding on the punishment of exile, the founders agreed on banishing Lussiek and all his followers to the Shrouded Isle to live out the rest of their days.'" She skimmed down the page. "It says here the island was largely uninhabitable, the surface being covered in jagged rock formations, except for a network of underground caves beneath the island. Though I don't know how the island could support any life without native food or water—"

"You mentioned Lussiek *and* his followers?" Dane interjected. "I thought the island was out at sea. How could the other founders transport so many people?"

Quinn's eyebrows knit together. She ran her finger to the bottom of the page. Then her eyes widened in amazement. "I don't believe it . . ."

"What?"

"The founders . . . they all worked together, worked as one. Founder Cyndus gathered his Aquadorians to create a vessel of solid ice large enough to transport Lussiek and his followers; Founder Rodran and his Geomancers encased the betrayers' hands and feet in solid stone; Founder Aoric and his Tempi directed the wind currents to sail the vessel across the sea."

"And Lussiek?" Dane said, seized by insatiable curiosity. "What became of him and his followers?"

She flipped through several more pages. "The rest contains tales from other warriors during the battle, but . . ." She frowned. "Nothing more on Lussiek—"

"I think I know why," said Sage suddenly, her voice low and wavering. She nudged the book she'd found to the center of the table; it was small, palm-sized, with tattered, fraying pages. Its leather-bound cover was warped and crinkled, a casualty of age and time. She pointed to the open page. "Look."

On the open page was a smeared, hastily drawn image surrounded by dozens of frantic scribblings. At the top was a rough sketch of an island with steep, black cliffs. Below, the drawings continued, winding back and forth in a twist of lines and circles that all connected to a large circle at the bottom of the page. Drawn over the circle was a pair of bright, crimson eyes.

"I believe it's a—a map . . . of the Shrouded Isle," Sage continued. "Up here—" she gestured to the top of the page "—that must be the island itself . . . but what about the rest of this?"

"It could be anything," Cayde said. "A chamber of some sort? Maybe a cave? That next page, there, what's it say?"

"The rest of it appears to be journal entries. Barely legible." Sage thumbed through several pages at once, fanning the air with the ancient pages.

"Read one," said Dane, completely mesmerized. "It could help."

Sage looked to Dane and shrugged, as if uncomfortable with the idea, but equally curious. "I will," she resigned. She thumbed back to the beginning. "Listen to this."

Day the second: These creatures took me beneath the surface. Deep into a tunnel. Deeper and deeper underground. For once, I am glad to be a Biophage. Without my trusted luminescent torch . . . well, I don't know what I'd do. I am surrounded by darkness . . . darkness everywhere. I don't know how much longer I will last. The creatures seem to want something from me. They don't speak, but if they wished me dead, I would not still be their captive. They're saving me for something. I have to escape. Only time will tell my fate. May the Mother guide me . . .

Dane's stomach knotted. "Chemocytes?"

"I'm not sure." Quinn rubbed a finger across her pursed lips. "This book said Founder Lussiek was banished there with his followers . . . but if it's true they were corrupted, turned to Chemocytes like the one you saw . . ." Quinn shook her head in dismissal. "We don't even know when this happened. The journal could be hundreds of years old by now."

"Are there more entries?" asked Cayde.

Sage flipped through more pages of identical scrawlings. "Dozens . . . hundreds, maybe. They all look the same, though."

"Skip to the last one, what does that say?"

Sage gulped and read aloud:

Day the . . . : Light. There is no light. There is the red glow. Eyes . . . eyes everywhere. Red, glowing eyes. From the walls. From the ceilings. From the floor. Peering . . . watching . . . endless watching. Energy . . . gone. Power . . . failing. Life . . . life . . . no, there is no life here. Not anymore. There is only . . . him.

Sage flipped the page over, then back again, her face contorted in puzzled fixation. "That's it? What does it mean?"

But her question was met with blank stares.

After a moment's silence, Leon said, "Well, I may not know much about this Shrouded Isle, but I know this: you do NOT want to go there. If it was me stuck in—" he stared cock-eyed at the drawing "—wherever that is—I'd be a lost cause from day one."

"Something's not right about that entry—about all of it," Dane said. He looked at Quinn. "I thought you said that no one had ever been to the Shrouded Isle and lived?"

Quinn nodded apprehensively.

"Then how—" But he didn't need to finish the sentence; the looks on the others' faces said enough. Somewhere in Physos, possibly still alive, was someone who had ventured to the Shrouded Isle, retrieved the journal, delivered it to the Grand Archive, and lived to tell the tale.

There was no further discussion about the mysterious journal entries. Dane delved into his book, Cayde and Quinn following suit, joining him in silent study. Sage stared blankly at the small, tattered cover of the journal, as if held in a trance by their recent discoveries.

Leon, meanwhile, darted in and out of cover from behind neighboring shelves. He'd told them he'd watch for any archivists that might wander in their direction, but Leon's erratic head movements and skulking only seemed to increase their chances of garnering unwanted attention. Dane had wanted to mention as such on several occasions but decided against it. At least Leon was being quiet.

After some time in silence, Sage abruptly snapped out of her mental stupor and ordered Leon to sit.

"But see—I was just thinking, if we—rather, *you*—get caught with a book from the private collection, and they see you with *me*, then *I'll* be the one who pays for it." Leon pulled frantically at his already frenzied hair, murmuring to himself between breaths. "Disregard what I said earlier—I actually really like it here. You don't know what'll happen if they catch us with those. I still have so much to live for—Mother help me, what have I gotten into—surely they'll banish me to the Shrouded Isle for this—"

"Calm down, will you?" Sage snapped. She gripped his robes in one fist and thrust him into the chair beside her. "No one is going to *banish* you for reading some books. If anything, your apprenticeship will be revoked and you'll be kicked out of the Archive."

Leon let out a small whimper. Sage moved her face closer to his and added, "But that's not going to happen, because we're not going to get caught, are we?" She tilted her head, pinning him with her gaze.

"Right, right, of course not . . ." he murmured. He slumped further into his seat until only his head remained above the table.

"Then how about you stop being so suspicious and act like a normal archivist!" Sage hissed.

"Fine! Fine." Leon straightened, body rigid, hands poised neatly in his lap. With startling poise, he tilted his head toward Sage and uttered, "I am calm. I am not suspicious. I am a normal archivist."

Sage rolled her eyes at him. "Yes, now just—stay like that—*quietly*—so we can finish and get out of here."

A smile played across Dane's face as he watched Sage with Leon. She talked to him just as the mothers in their village had with their small children, scolding them for poor behavior. He found it amusing, albeit peculiar, that she was using the same tone of voice with Leon. More amusing, it actually worked.

Despite his seemingly genuine intentions, Leon didn't hold his formal composure for long. He began to twitch in his seat, craning his neck toward the books strewn across the table. With almost comedic slowness, he eased closer to Sage, attempting to peer over her shoulder.

"Mind if I take a look?" Leon whispered, edging his seat even closer to Sage, hand already outstretched toward the journal.

Sage said nothing, planting her hand firmly on the cover and pressing it into the table, her eyes still fixed in the unwavering trance of deep thought.

"What did I say?" she scolded.

Leon frowned. "I won't take it or anything. I just want to see if—OUCH!"

He recoiled with a shriek of pain, gripping his upper leg.

Quinn and Cayde glowered at Leon. Dane anxiously scanned the vast array of shelves, hoping Leon's yell hadn't attracted the attention of everyone in the Grand Archive. Leon was right. If someone saw them with books from the private collection—

To his relief, no one appeared to notice. He blew out a sigh.

"What'd you do *that* for?" Leon hissed. "I was only trying to *look*!"

"I did tell you to sit quietly," Sage said.

"But why'd you have to *pinch* me?" He lifted his robes and turned his leg toward her. "It still stings! Am I bleeding? Please tell me it's not bleeding."

"Oh, get over it," she scoffed. "I'm sure it didn't mean to actually hurt you."

"I most certainly will not—wait, *it?*"

Sage nodded innocently, and Leon's gaze shifted to the willow branch coiled around her waist. When nothing happened, Leon glared at Sage, his lips curled. "You mean to tell me," he said flatly, "that this—this—*twig* pinched me?"

"You're making such a big deal over a little pinch."

Leon's face contorted, flushing red. He scooted closer to Sage.

"Look here, Biophage, *I'm* the one who hustled all of you into the private collection out of the goodness of my heart," he said, his voice hardly passing for a whisper, "so it's about time you show me a little—"

This time there was no denying what caused Leon to lurch backward. He leapt from of his chair, gripping his thigh with one hand and pointing in accusation at Sage's waist. But there was no screech of pain or barrage of insults. His frustration had all but washed away, replaced with a look of complete incredulity. He looked from Sage, to the whip, and then back to Sage, then back to the whip, mouthing fruitlessly like a fish gulping for food. After several moments of stunned silence, Leon collapsed back in his chair, gaze unbroken from the whip.

"It just pinched me," he stated matter-of-factly. "That twig reached out and pinched me." He spoke as though saying the words aloud would make it more believable. His expression said otherwise.

"I don't know what else you expected," Sage said, suppressing a laugh. "It probably didn't like you being so close." Her voice returned to that of a scolding mother. "And I don't think it likes being called a twig."

Leon stared viciously through his dark, narrowed eyes. "Just—don't do it again, all right?" he said, jostling his accusatory finger between Sage's face and the Willow Whip.

"Maybe if you let us finish reading, it would be more inclined to leave you in peace . . ."

Leon threw his arms in the air. "Fine!" He pushed away from the table. "I'll be over here. Let me know when you're done." He leaned against the nearby railing and peered at the ground floor below, mumbling under his breath.

They read quietly for a few moments before Leon began pacing once more, circling the table quietly and cautiously, purposefully veering away from Sage and the whip. After several laps around the table, he paused to peer over Cayde's shoulder, head tilted to one side, brow furrowed. He looked both thoroughly perplexed and genuinely intrigued; clearly, he was preparing another ridiculous question.

"Why are you interested in the Praetorian Ar—"

Cayde's hand shot upward. He clasped Leon's mouth, masking the bottom half of Leon's face with his cupped palm. Leon mumbled something incoherent. Cayde removed his hand, sending Leon a wide-eyed glare before wiping his palm on his shirt.

"What did we say about keeping quiet?" Cayde said, voice hushed.

"That word . . . Praetorian," Dane said. He looked to the page he'd been reading before Leon's distraction. "It's listed here next to each of the founders' names and a few others, but that's it. What does it mean?"

Leon made a snorting sound, chuckling to himself. His laughter ebbed a moment later. "Oh, you're serious?" He looked to Cayde. "You mean they don't know?"

Dane looked up from the page. Quinn and Cayde were exchanging glances, holding yet another silent conversation. But from the nature of their exchange, it had to be important. *Is this what they've been hiding?*

Cayde nodded subtly after the exchange, as if submitting to Quinn's thought. They both turned to face him. Quinn spoke first, her voice resigned and wary.

"Praetorians were the first people to ever harness their powers," she confessed. "There were only a handful of them—the founders, most notably—and their first followers. Praetorians had such strong connections to their energy wells that their powers were unnaturally strong, supernatural even. Legends say that Founder Celosia used her power to grow the Elderwood herself, and that Founder Rodran created all of Stonehelm with nothing but his bare fists—that's how powerful they were." She shuddered and stared at the table. "I don't care to imagine what would happen if there was a Praetorian still alive today . . ."

"But . . . why? Why would it be so terrible to have a Praetorian among us now?"

Quinn held her unflinching gaze on the table. Cayde turned to Dane and said, "Remember that story I told you in the Grove of Mist, about the Tumulus brothers, Varic and Atax? How

Varic tried to conjure a maelstrom to destroy the city? Imagine if his powers had been enhanced a hundred-fold. If someone like Varic had the power of a Praetorian . . ." Cayde released a deflating sigh, his face stricken with worrisome awe. "No, we're very fortunate the Praetorians all died long ago."

"How do you know all of this?" Sage asked, gaping in bewilderment. "I know Dane and I had limited exposure to the rest of the world when growing up, but what you're saying can't be common knowledge to everyone, can it? Grandfather surely didn't mention anything about Praetorians . . ."

Cayde cocked one eyebrow and nodded to Quinn. "One of the benefits of having this one with us," he mused, gazing fondly at her. She flashed him a subtle smile. "Elder Yarrin has an archive of his own," he continued. "It's small, mind you, but he told us everything he thought necessary for—" Cayde hesitated for a moment.

"For what?" Dane asked quickly.

"Err—let's just say for the journey ahead."

"Does it have to do with your mission?"

Cayde hesitated again. "In a way—"

"Can't you tell us?"

Cayde let out a long sigh and shook his head. "I will . . . but not today. We need more time, and right now we don't have much." Cayde gestured to Dane's open book and said, "What else is there about the Elders? Anything that could give us a better idea as to why Avon attacked Vitalor?"

Dane frowned inwardly, unsatisfied with Cayde's quick dismissal, but he knew now wasn't the time to question Cayde about his and Quinn's mysterious true motive.

"Nothing out of the ordinary," Dane said, returning his gaze to the sea of knowledge before him. "Though, there's loads of information on the Elders of old here: family trees, how they used their powers, what they specialized in—the information is endless." He scanned the page further, skimming past each of the undoubtedly important—though meaningless to his eyes—list of elder lineages. His focus waned. The information was endless, but none of it drew any hints about the Chemocyte or the

Ferrons. And there was nothing to explain why Avon would want the energy wells destroyed.

Dane pounded a fist into the book and shifted his gaze to the barren, archive wall, his mind drifting back to Avon's attack on Vitalor. *How* can *Avon attack the energy wells?* He thought. *Surely, the amount of energy needed to do such a thing would be too strenuous for one person . . . unless—*

Then he had a horrifying thought. "Is Avon a descendent of a Praetorian?" he said in a low mumble.

At once the others fell silent.

"What did you say?" Quinn asked, leaning toward him.

"Avon," Dane repeated. "Is he a Praetorian descendent?"

Quinn sat back in her chair. "I—I don't know. I never considered—" She pinched her lower lip between her fingers, gaze falling to the table. "I suppose it's possible, but—"

"How else could he be so powerful?" Dane said. "Maybe he wants to destroy the other energy wells and increase his own power to *become* a Praetorian." His words started coming faster, picking up momentum. "He didn't attack Vitalor by himself; he needed help. He only recently emerged from hiding. Maybe he's weak. That's why he needs the Ferron leader—Maluin—and his forces to help him attack the energy wells. I'll bet that's why the Ferron soldiers were with him that day in Vitalor. Avon is working with Maluin to destroy all the energy wells so they can have that power for themselves and become Praetorians!"

Dane felt as though his heart was about to burst out of his chest. Saying it all aloud made perfect sense, a jumble of tangled roots finally unraveling.

The others only stared at him for a long moment in stunned silence, realization slowly creeping across their features. Finally, Cayde gasped and said, "Dane, that's brilliant!" He clapped Dane on the back, filling Dane with a pride he hadn't felt since before his Trials. Cayde leaned for a closer look at Dane's book. "Does it mention anything about the Ferrons? Their whereabouts and history?"

"That's just it—there's nothing about them. There's only one part about the Ferrons, the same information Elder Yarrin told us. But they have no history of Elders, no city history, no important names or stories . . . nothing. How can that be?"

Cayde shook his head and looked to Quinn for support, but she wore the same stupefied expression.

"The only logical reason I can think of is that someone eliminated all traces of their history from the Archive," she said. "But as to how or why . . . I just don't know."

"Erased from the Archive?" Leon mumbled. "I wish I'd thought of that."

"What should we do then?" Sage said urgently. "How do we stop them before they attack another energy well? And where—and when—is Avon attacking next?" She shared a vacant stare with Quinn and Cayde, who both shook their heads. Then she turned to Dane. "When Elder Yarrin talked with you in private, did he mention anything else about how to stop them? Can you remember?"

Dane seized his hair between clenched fists. He held his gaze on the worn surface of the table, but he could feel the other three pairs of eyes burning into him, pleading for an answer. Why were they looking to him for answers? He didn't know any more than they did, and Elder Yarrin hadn't told him anything more about Avon or the Ferrons.

He gripped his hair harder. Pain radiated through his scalp, but it was nothing compared to the incessant throbbing in his head.

There has to be something, he thought through gritted teeth, *something I'm missing.*

Sage's voice echoed through his mind. *Can you remember?* He repeated her words like a chant as he searched the chaotic confines of his memory. *Can you remember? Can you remember? Can you . . . remember.*

The faintest trace of hope sparked within. There *was* something he knew that the others didn't, something Elder Yarrin had mentioned only to him, something he only had to remember.

He looked up. His gaze swept across the others' expectant faces, their eyes matching the glimmer of hope in his own.

Then he turned to Leon. The young archivist had been standing idle near the end of the table, staring blankly down at the main hall before turning to the others, looking wrought with boredom.

"I'm going to take this long silence as a sign that you're finished with these books. You don't mind if I sneak in here and take them back to the private collection before—"

Dane stared into the archivist's shrewd, brown eyes. *I have no idea if this is going to work,* he thought. *But I know there's something you haven't told us yet, something you've withheld beyond the private collection.* Even now he could see it behind Leon's gaze, some untamed knowledge lurking behind those dark, wild eyes. *I think you know more than you let on. Maybe this is what you know, what Elder Yarrin needed me to do. So tell me, Leon, what other secrets are you hiding?*

Leon stared back, one eyebrow raised. He eased his hands away from the scattered books. His face contorted while holding Dane's stare. He seemed to squirm in his own skin.

"What—what's going on? Why are you staring at me like that? It's creepy. Stop it."

Dane rose from his chair and sucked in a deep breath. Maybe it was just a hunch. But maybe it was something more.

"Leon," he said, "show me the memory tomes."

CHAPTER 15

LOST MEMORIES

All eyes turned to Dane.

Cayde cocked his head to one side, as if unsure he'd heard correctly. Sage's mouth fell ajar, failing to hide her confusion. Quinn stared with penetrating intensity, as if analyzing a dozen different questions simultaneously.

All of this Dane noticed in a heartbeat, scanning their faces in his periphery. But his focus was on Leon. He watched the archivist's face with practiced precision, scouring every feature and surface like he'd done countless times while crafting totems for Duxor, searching for the most minute of flaws, the most imperceptible of errors.

Then he saw it, not a moment after he'd mentioned the memory tomes, the chink in Leon's mental armor.

Much like the others, Leon had been staring at him, stricken with bewilderment. Unlike the others, Leon's eyes briefly widened beneath his furrowed brow. His nostrils flared with the speed of a blinking eye. It was not a look of innocent ignorance, but one of befuddled vexation, as if to say, *how do* you *know?*

Dane forced down a smirk, eyeing Leon shrewdly. *I knew there was something else.* His mind whirred into action, plotting Leon's next move. Leon could lie and feign ignorance. Dane would have to press him further, press him with information Dane didn't know. That wouldn't end well. Or Leon could stand there like the uncharacteristic mute he'd suddenly become, and Dane would have to repeat the question, likely with the same results. Then, of course, especially for someone so absurdly peculiar and completely unpredictable, Leon could run for it. Even with a head start, Dane would catch Leon easily, but Leon surely wouldn't reveal anything else if Dane were to tackle him to the ground in the middle of the Grand Archive.

It was a game of wits and deception, a game in which Leon seemed to thrive. Dane's only hope was that—

"How do you know what the memory tomes are?" Leon asked, peering at Dane through his narrowed eyes.

—he'd say the wrong thing. Dane couldn't conceal his smirk any longer.

"How do *you* know what the memory tomes are, Leon?" he countered. "I know there's something you haven't told us, something you're hiding."

At this, the inquisitive expression abruptly vanished from the archivist's face. His eyes darted wildly. His face flushed to a sickly pale, evidently aware of the other three pairs of judgmental eyes awaiting an explanation. For a long moment, he said nothing, arms plastered to his side.

"Well?" said Sage suddenly. She glared at him, demanding a response.

It was too late for Leon to evade an answer; he'd stalled too long. Any attempt at a lie would instantly arouse suspicion. It was clear Leon was reluctant to part with whatever knowledge he held, but as evidenced in their recent days with the young archivist, Leon was no match for Sage's piercing, will-bending gaze.

"I—er—well, you see—I thought—" he sighed in exasperation and hung his head in defeat. "Fine. I'll tell you, I will. But not here."

Without another word, Leon gathered the prized books from the table and walked off toward the private collection. But Dane could tell he had no intention of running off. While Leon had been reluctant to divulge, Dane had seen something else in the archivist's eyes—Leon needed them.

He reemerged from the direction of the private collection not a moment later, arms empty.

"We need to go somewhere private," Leon said. His eyes darted around as he said it, as if dozens more were watching from every corner.

Sage frowned, unamused. "What, do we need to return to the Mystic Fountain?"

With a straight face, Leon replied, "No, this is far too important to mention in public."

Dane dismissed it at first, but there was a subtle hint of something strange in his voice. Not defeat, frustration, or sadness, but . . . excitement?

What is Leon hiding?

Leon ushered them across the floor, down the spiral staircase to the main hall, and toward the Archive's magnificent doors, all the while fleeting through the shadows like a leaf on the wind, pausing in each of his temporary shrouds to ensure his next step would go unseen by observing eyes.

They had almost reached the doors when Sage whispered to Leon, "Wait, aren't you supposed to be working? Won't someone notice your absence again?"

Leon replied, "Don't be absurd. I have the utmost confidence that every other archivist secretly dreams I'd disappear from this place just like my fam—no, no, Leon, we're not going there again." He paused, took a calming breath, then returned leaping toward the next shadow like a child through puddles after rainfall.

The sky was baked in the familiar warm, orange glow of the setting sun as they emerged from the Grand Archive. The light reflected across the city, refracting through the water columns supporting the network of floating walkways overhead. Dane smiled fondly, thinking how similar the water columns were to the tree trunks sprouting from the forest floor of his village. They'd only been gone a matter of days, but he was surprised to find how much he missed home.

Quinn turned to Leon and said, "I know you don't want to mention it until we're in private, but need I remind you that we don't have time for distractions. These memory tomes . . . will they help us stop Avon? Or does telling us merely fulfill one of your ridiculous fantasies?"

"Don't worry, the tomes will indeed prove useful," Leon said. He flashed an awkward grin, then added, "And it fulfills one of my ridiculous fantasies."

Quinn pursed her lips but said nothing. Sage flicked her gaze upward and sighed heavily. Leon, seeming quite pleased with himself, continued his slow, aimless march through the street.

"I don't suppose you could tell us where you're going?" Sage said.

Leon spun in place, beckoned them to follow, then continued marching onward, weaving through the crowded city streets; it reminded Dane of the young children in Vitalor who'd strut around pretending to be guards, arms pumping, chins held high, looking rather ridiculous.

After deviating from the bustling market streets, their path vaguely leading toward the city's southeast edge, Dane recalled the four other foundations of suspended rock, and their clusters of layered buildings, that circled the central foundation of Mistveil. Those buildings had been small, possibly residential, especially on the foundation nearest the East Bridge, the same direction they were heading now. *Leon must live somewhere,* he thought, though he had difficulty envisioning Leon living anywhere but in the Archive.

"You're taking us to your house, aren't you Leon?" Dane called out over the dull roar of the fleeting crowds. "On one of those—er—"

"Islands?" Leon responded cheerfully. "I sure am!"

"You couldn't have told us that in the first place?" yelled Sage. When he said nothing, still smiling and now humming a melodious tune, she added, "And by the Mother, *why* are you so cheerful? It's maddening!"

"You'll see," Leon nearly sang. He halted before a small archway that split the monotony of the city's looming stone wall. He turned, his white archivist robes billowing in the breeze that siphoned through the archway. "This way."

He thumbed over his shoulder to the walkway extending out from the gap in the wall—only, the walkway was unlike anything Dane had ever seen. Suspended in the air, just like the houses held overhead like drops of mist, was a bridge made entirely of water. Attached to the other end of the water bridge was the island that Leon had referred to, which looked like a smaller, more compact version of the central island of Mistveil. From where he stood, Dane could see rings of streets circling a fountain at the island's center, each tightly packed with houses of all shapes and sizes.

"Follow me," Leon said. Without hesitation, he strode across the walkway, small splashes of water erupting underfoot as he went. Quinn went next, her steps rigid and methodical. Cayde proceeded behind her with ease, following the trail of puddles.

Dane looked to Sage and was relieved to see her staring back with equal apprehension and fascination.

"I suppose it's safe, right?" Dane said.

Sage looked back at the walkway and gave an unnerving smile. "I'll bet it holds itself together using the energy from the Mystic Fountain, just like the Elderwood back in Vitalor." Her smile wavered as she glanced over the edge, glimpsing the lake far below. "What's the worst that could happen?"

She grinned at him, and Dane couldn't help but grin back. It was as if they were traversing the treetops for the first time again, reliving one of his happiest memories, exploring the majesty of their world with his sister by his side.

Dane stepped to the edge of the walkway. Inhaling a deep breath of fresh, misty air, he closed his eyes, launched a foot forward, and planted it firmly where the bridge should be.

For a moment, he felt his weight carrying him forward as his foot hit the watery surface and sunk inward. His first reaction was to leap back for fear of plummeting to the lake's surface. Then his foot stopped. He cracked one eye open and peered down.

His booted foot had compressed the surrounding water ever so slightly, like that of damp soil after a soaking spring rain. He wriggled his toes from within his boot, tilting his foot to either side. The water around it sloshed back and forth, but otherwise proved a secure foothold.

Dane turned and watched as Sage planted her foot behind him, her face transforming with the same wave of emotions he'd just experienced. Dane's confidence grew with each successive step, and soon they bounded across the walkway of water toward the others.

The bridge opened onto a modest street on the smaller suspended island, which paled in comparison to the complexity and awe on the central island of Mistveil. The street struck Dane as nothing out of the ordinary—assuming it was ordinary for the city's foundation to be suspended above a lake by a massive, ever-present geyser.

They followed the street to a small central plaza where a fountain erupted from a large pool; it looked like a miniaturized version of the Mystic Fountain, except for the beauty and extravagance that could only come from the energy well itself.

Sage stopped at the pool's edge and gazed into its bottomless waters, droplets spraying into her hair. "Where does this water come from?" she asked, grabbing Leon's sleeve and pulling him beside her, nearly sending him sprawling into the pool.

"It comes from the lake—the water, that is. If you could jump in and swim down—which you can't, by the way, trust me—then you'd eventually be swimming in the lake. But honestly you're better off trying to swim up a waterfall." Leon stared unappreciatively at the fountain and shook his head in mock disappointment. "I've resigned to watching the fountain instead."

Sage glanced sidelong at him and thumbed toward the pool. "Who would be dumb enough to try and swim down there?"

Leon looked like he was about to say something, then threw his hands in the air and walked off in silence. Sage smirked, watching as he left. "Oh, he definitely tried," she whispered. Dane cracked a smile.

They wound through the narrow streets until Leon paused at the end of a long, deserted path, nestled between the island's high stone wall and the backside of tall, narrow houses.

Leon stood before a lone waterfall that spilled from an unusually small and unwelcoming stone slab at the path's end. He pulled back his right sleeve, exposing his Aquadorian mark, and waved his hand through the small waterfall.

As if reacting to his touch, the thin veil of water subsided to a trickle, exposing a dimly lit room resembling a damp cave. Leon ducked under the trickling water and disappeared. The room flooded with the natural, orange glow of sunset. He reappeared a moment later.

"Come on in," he said, his voice coated in uncharacteristic warmth. He'd taken off his white archivist robes and now donned muddy brown pants cinched with a rope-like belt and an off-white tunic that swallowed his thin body. His chaotic strands of fleeting black hair remained unchanged. "But quickly, the door's about to close."

They all hastened into the room as the miniature waterfall spouted back to life behind them.

"Is this . . . where you live?" Quinn asked, pity evident in her voice.

"Sure is," Leon said proudly, thrusting his fists triumphantly to his side.

Sage wrinkled her nose. "What's that smell?"

"Oh, that's the clay. Most of the buildings on the main island are made with stone and solidified with clay deposits—the stuff's everywhere around the lake—but they must've run out of stone when they made this place. I've grown accustomed to it though." He patted the wall next to him. A damp, gray chunk slipped from the wall and plopped onto his boot.

"I just patched that," Leon mumbled, hefting the chunk back into place, smearing it with both hands. For a moment, nothing happened. Then the clay slid again, landing on his other boot. His shoulders slumped, and he laughed uncomfortably. "Who am I kidding, the place is falling apart." Even as he said this, his mouth still curved in a slight, admiring smile. "But . . . it's home."

Dane glanced around the room. The walls were all the same dull, blotchy gray. A small wooden table sat in the center of the room, positioned near the dying embers of a fireplace. He felt a tinge of sadness as he noticed the five chairs surrounding the table. Leon seemed to live alone, yet there were five chairs, pulled back, inviting company. *They're for his family,* Dane thought. *He still thinks they're coming back.*

Sage shifted uncomfortably beside him. "It's—umm— smaller than I expected." Then she noticed the chairs and amended, "But it looks wonderful."

Leon arched his shoulders in a humble gesture, still smiling. "I think so too," he beamed.

"So," Cayde said after a long pause, "let's hear it, then. What are memory tomes?"

"Ah, yes . . . one moment."

Leon disappeared into an adjoining room. He reappeared a moment later holding two books: one a journal, by the look of it, the other an incredibly thick book nearly bursting at the seams. Leon dumped the thick book onto the table with a grunt and thrust it open, spewing a frenzy of dust from the ancient pages. He flipped through the journal to a page filled with non-sensical scribblings.

"Here's how we'll sneak inside. All we have to do is wait for—"

"Stop," Quinn said exhaustedly. "Sneak in where? You haven't told us anything yet. And *what* are memory tomes?"

Leon glanced up from his journal, looking offended, as if Quinn had just rudely interrupted his brilliant plan. Then he gasped and raked his fingers through his hair.

"Oh! Right! Just—err—forget about this for now," he said, gesturing to the etchings and scribbles in his journal. He mouthed, *We'll get to this later,* heaved the massive book closed, then began dusting off the intricate, leather cover with slow, calculated precision.

"The memory tomes?" Sage prompted, unable to mask the irritation in her voice, strumming her fingers along her crossed arms.

"The what now?"

Cayde slapped the back of Leon's head.

"Right, right, right," Leon stuttered, rubbing the back of his neck. He opened his mouth, then stopped. His eyes narrowed. "What if I decided not to tell you?"

Cayde rolled his eyes and made for the doorway.

"WAIT!" Leon pleaded. "Fine, I'll tell you—I was going to tell you anyways—I was just musing. Besides, I still might need your help . . ."

Cayde turned back to Leon, his expression dull. He looked about ready to leap off the floating island. "You're on thin ice, archivist."

Leon kneaded the floor with his feet. "Actually, it's hardened clay."

Cayde glared at him.

"Memory tomes!" Leon exclaimed. He stroked a hand through his hair. "Let's see, where to begin, where to begin . . . you've never heard of the memory tomes before? Ever?"

"Hence why we're here," Quinn stated matter-of-factly. "Now please, what are they?"

Leon took a deep breath, "From the beginning, then. To get straight to the point, memory tomes are books that harness a person's memory after they've passed—usually in the form of an image—sometimes stationary, sometimes moving, though always brief. I think they're supposed to be a person's most valued memories—or maybe their final memories?" He waved dismissively. "Whatever the case, these memories are captured by the memory tomes somewhere in the Grand Archive. As far as I know, only the oldest, most trusted archivists are allowed to see them. Though I'm not entirely certain why—with all the people who've died over the years, I can't see how most of the memory tomes aren't useless."

"You—you're serious?" Quinn stammered.

"Crystal—err—dead."

Quinn's mouth fell open. "How is this possible?"

"That . . . I don't know," Leon admitted. "But I *do* know memory tomes absorb memories from the energy flowing into the energy wells—like a wet cloth absorbing a puddle of water." He clenched his fist in demonstration. "Apparently there's only one blank page in each memory tome, but when you place your hand on the page, the energy in the tome binds with your own." His eyes widened with hunger. "You can *see* someone else's memories."

"Apparently? You mean you've never actually seen one?" Dane asked.

Leon winced as if he had just dropped the enormous book on his bare foot. "Not exactly . . ."

"Then how do you know any of this? Why should we even listen to you?" Sage blurted. She thrust her hands on her waist and glared at Leon, her blue eyes gleaming.

"I only know what they are, and that there might be a memory tome out there that could provide more information about whatever it is you wanted to find," Leon retorted defensively. "Hold on." He jabbed an accusatory finger at Dane. "*He* knows about memory tomes too! Why didn't you just ask him?"

Dane felt the others watching him, but he merely smirked and said, "I don't know anything about them."

Confusion slapped Leon across the face. "Then how—"

"I only knew they carried significance, that we'd need to find them to further our search. I didn't know where to look, so I didn't mention it. But when we found you, I took the risk."

Leon said nothing. He only stared, mouth agape, with an expression akin only to one who'd just been thoroughly bested and humiliated.

Now Dane could feel Quinn's gaze on him harsher than before, demanding an answer. He turned to her and said, "That's what your father said to me before we left. He said to search for the memory tomes, that they could hold the answers we seek."

Part of what he said, he wanted to tell her, but he held his tongue. *They won't understand, not like you will.*

She flashed him a smile. "That's genius," she said. But her enthusiasm waned as quickly as it had come. Her gaze fell to the floor. She slid her hands to her shoulders, squeezing tightly. "I . . . I'm glad he told you."

Leon emerged from his defeatist's stupor and said, "So . . . you didn't know what they were when you asked me?"

Dane shook his head.

"You had no idea whatsoever?"

He shook his head again. "No clue."

Leon blew out an exasperated sigh. "Now I feel sheepish." He laughed under his breath, a slight smile playing at his lips. "Well played, Dane. Well played indeed."

Sage cleared her throat. "You still haven't answered my question," she stated.

Leon stared blankly at her.

"How is it that you know all this?" Sage repeated dully.

At this, he gave a mischievous, knowing smirk. "Let's just say being an archivist has its benefits."

"And what benefits are those?" Cayde prompted.

"I'll tell you all about it sometime, but right now—assuming you still need to find the information you seek, and fast—we don't have the time."

Cayde rolled his eyes but resigned. "Let's say we believe you. Memory tomes contain the lost memories of people who have passed, so some of them may hold insight regarding the Ferrons or the Chemocyte. Meaning, if we could find the right tome— say, that of a Ferron soldier—we could discover more about them and possibly put an end to Avon's attacks?"

"Potentially, yes," said Leon.

"Where can we find memory tomes?" asked Quinn.

The knowing smirk returned. "That's where I need your help."

He thrust the thick book into the center of the table and flung it open, sending another cloud of dust into the air.

Through a fit of wheezing coughs, he fingered through the pages, pausing on a page with a folded corner.

"There," Leon said, pressing his finger into the ancient page. "What does that look like to you?"

They all leaned in and examined the page, which, from the familiar sketches of streets and buildings, appeared to be an old map.

"That's Mistveil, isn't it?" said Dane.

"Yes. More precisely, it's a map of every street, path, house, walkway, and crawl space—the entire city mapped on one page. Now, look at this here." He flipped through the book and stopped at a different page, noticeably less worn than the first. "What do you see?"

No one said anything for a long moment. Sage eyed Leon with concern and said, "It's . . . the same map."

Leon shook his head. "Look closer. There." He pointed to a spot along a thick line—designating the city wall—near the West Bridge.

Sage shrugged. "It's the same map, but made more recently?"

"No," he said, his frustration rising. "Look harder. What do you see *there*?"

"Nothing out of the ordinary," said Quinn. "Why? What's so important about that spot?"

Leon flipped violently back to the first page, pointed to the same spot on the city map, and remained silent.

Dane stared for a moment, seeing nothing. Then he saw it— a small gap just above Leon's finger. He flipped to the newer page. No gap. He flipped back.

"Is that . . . a secret passageway?"

Leon smiled triumphantly. "It most certainly is."

"That's impossible," said Quinn. "I haven't seen every part of this city, but there can't be a secret passageway on that street. If these memory tomes are kept under discretion, they surely wouldn't be displayed on a common street."

"How do you know it's even there?" asked Cayde.

"Because I've seen it. With my own eyes—I've seen it. That's where we have to go," Leon's eyes shone with fierce determination.

"But where you're pointing . . ." Quinn stared at the page, brows furrowed, "there's nothing there." Her eyes widened in sudden realization. "You don't mean it's—"

Leon's lips curled into a confirming grin. "Under the main island? Oh yes, yes I do. And that's where we need to go."

"*Under* the island?" asked Sage. "But how—"

"That's where you come in. There's a breach in the city wall right here." He gestured to the thick line closest to the supposed secret passageway. "You crawl through here—*very* carefully, mind you—the ledge on the other side of the wall is barely wide enough to stand on. From there, you have to lower yourself and—how do I put this—ah yes, scale down an inverted slope to reach a hidden landing . . . using only your hands."

"That sounds extremely dangerous," Quinn said hesitantly.

"Oh, it is." Leon rubbed his lower back. "It's a very long fall. Trust me."

"Let me get this straight," said Cayde. "You expect all of us to squeeze through a hole in the wall without falling off the other side, then climb down, *while* hanging, to reach a ledge we can't even see? And for what? How do you know this passageway is even down there?"

"It's there, trust me. I told you, I've seen it. And no, all of us don't have to climb down while hanging—only one of us does."

"And who would that be?" Sage said. "It'd better be you."

Leon waved his hands dismissively. "Not important—we'll figure that out later. But once said person climbs down, we'll use your whip thing to ease ourselves down, then swing toward the ledge underneath until the first person can pull us to safety. See? Easy."

Dane tried to envision Leon swinging on a branch, swaying his body back and forth as he dangled helplessly over the edge of the city. His confidence in Leon's plan wavered.

Quinn eyed Leon skeptically. "I don't think it's going to be that simple. What if someone sees us?"

"I'm glad you asked. Conveniently—well, conveniently for us—Mistveil will be hosting the pledge ceremony for all the new Aquadorians traveling from the more distant cities: Stonehelm, Alto-Baros, and Katovela. If my predictions are correct, most of the population will be gathered at the Mystic Fountain, except for maybe a guard or two. That's when we'll go."

"And when will this ceremony be held?" Sage asked.

"Tomorrow afternoon."

Quinn nodded reluctantly. "Fine, we'll wait until tomorrow."

"And if we time it right, the sun will align with the Archive's spire, casting a shadow directly over the spot we need to crawl through. No one will even see us leave."

"You've given this some thought, haven't you?" said Sage.

"Oh, Petals, you have no idea . . ."

Sage recoiled sharply, blood rushing to her cheeks. "*Petals*? Again? What did I—the nerve of—you'd better watch yourself, Leon, or by the Mother, I'll start calling you Dewdrop!"

Leon let out a genuine, hearty laugh. "Maybe you should . . . that's not half-bad."

"Oh? Well, how about I take my Willow Whip and give you a fresh crack on the a—"

"Sage, that's enough!" shouted Quinn, barely able to contain her own swelling laughter. When Leon returned his attention back to the thick book, Quinn smirked and whispered, "Maybe later." Sage smiled deviously, her anger ebbing.

"Before I was so rudely interrupted," Leon continued, "I was going to ask if there were any more questions, because I'm getting rather tired and would like a good night's sleep before—"

"I do have one more question," said Sage, her arms folded tightly across her chest. "Why do they even keep you around the Archive? You said yourself that no one likes you there."

Leon gave her a sharp glare. "Someone has to sort the heavy books." His voice turned high and squeaky. "'It always helps to have a strapping young lad around.' That's what they all say."

"Yes, I'm sure the other archivists can't say enough about 'Leon, the *most* strapping of strapping young lads,'" she mocked.

She clasped her hands together, batting her eyes in feigned admiration. "'Leon, oh, Leon, come stack these books for me, Leon. I couldn't have done it without your positively *marvelous* skills!'" She delved into derisive snorts of laughter.

Leon's pride took a visible blow. His body seemed to deflate, and his proud grin slumped into a hard line. "Yes, you're quite hilarious, aren't you?"

After calming herself, Sage, still smiling and recovering her breath, shifted her gaze to the massive book still open on the table. "Where did you find this anyways? And why is it in your house? And how did—" She sighed and raised her hands in mock surrender. "Never mind, I don't want to know."

"That's probably best," Leon said.

"So . . . let's imagine, for a moment, that everything goes as planned and we all enter this secret passageway," mused Cayde. "Where will we find the memory tomes?"

Leon's pursed lips twisted to one side. "I'm not entirely sure, but I have a few ideas . . ."

☙ ❧

This'll never work, Dane thought.

The sun burned brightly overhead as Leon led Dane, Quinn, Sage and Cayde through the winding streets on the central island of Mistveil the next morning. They followed narrow side roads, away from foot traffic, heading vaguely toward the west end of the city.

Leon stopped behind a lonely building near the gap leading outside the city wall. He pressed himself against the building, shrinking into the shadows. The others did the same.

But something wasn't right. People still milled about, not to mention the several guards stationed on patrol; the city was as busy as ever. But Leon took no notice as he poked his head out from cover and peered down the street.

As if reading Dane's thoughts, Quinn whispered, "You said the street would be deserted. There are people everywhere."

"You'll have to trust me," said Leon, his gaze unyielding from the crack in the wall. "Wait just a little longer, you'll see."

Quinn looked unconvinced. She muttered, "I'd better not have to use another aurora veil to cloak us . . ." then fell silent as she too peered down the street.

Dane looked to the sun then at the shadow cast by the spire of the Grand Archive as it slowly eased up the street toward the city wall. Just as the shadow settled over the gap, a distant voice penetrated the perpetual murmuring that hung over the city, calling all citizens to convene at the Mystic Fountain to celebrate the arrival of the newest Aquadorians.

Dane nearly laughed aloud. Leon had planned it to perfection.

"That's our cue," said Leon. "Follow me."

In an uncharacteristically coordinated display of graceful agility, Leon fleeted through the street, now deserted and shrouded in shadow, and disappeared into the small crack in the city wall.

"Here goes nothing," said Quinn, then followed Leon's path before she, too, vanished into the gap.

Dane took a deep breath and charged after her. He sprinted through the darkened street and squirmed through the crevice. The next moment, he found himself leaning over the edge of a narrow cliff, staring straight into the swells of Mistveil Lake far below him. He flailed his arms, trying to prevent the inevitable fall into the looming waters, his body already tilting away from the ledge. A hand grabbed his collar and thrust him backward against hard stone.

"I thought that might happen," said Leon. "As I said before, it's quite a long way down."

Dane could only stare, careful not to part his body from the safety of the wall. "Thank you," he managed.

"Don't mention it."

A moment later, Sage scrambled out of the gap just as Dane had done, but before Leon could reach a hand out to prevent her fall, the tip of the Willow Whip released from her waist and clung to the wall, anchoring her where she stood.

"Think I can't handle myself?" Sage scoffed.

Leon opened his mouth in retort, but cleverly advised against it.

Cayde was next to emerge from the crack, doing so with practiced ease and stability.

"Now that . . . you've convinced us . . . onto this ledge . . . what's next?" said Quinn between shallow breaths, her eyes locked skyward. Despite the growing howl of wind, the anxiety in her tone was unmistakable.

"Now," Leon shouted, "Someone must climb down to the platform underneath this ledge. Then the others will use Sage's whip to lower down and swing to it."

Before Dane could take another breath, Cayde said, "I'll do it."

"You can't!" Quinn said immediately, tearing her fearful gaze from the sky.

"Be reasonable, Quinn," he said. "We both know I'm the best choice for this. I can use my power to pull you all in once I'm down there. Sage has to stay to control the whip. I don't trust Leon to push a door open—" he gave Leon's scrawny limbs a once-over "—and I wouldn't dare put you or Dane in this situation when I know I'm capable. I couldn't forgive myself if something were to happen to any of you."

"What about *you?*" She cried, her eyes welling with tears. "What if you slip or fall or—"

"Nothing will happen to me."

"How can you be so certain?" she pleaded.

Cayde's hand fumbled against the wall, his fingers curling into hers.

"Because I have to succeed," he said.

Quinn nodded and flashed a nervous, unconvincing smile. "Please be careful, will you?"

"Always," Cayde said. He turned to Leon. "Is there anything else I should know?"

"There should be some worn handholds in the rock," Leon shouted back. "Appears to be the work of a Geomancer. They'll be sturdy."

Cayde closed his eyes and inhaled deeply, carefully turning in place until his back was facing the exposed air. Slowly, with unrivaled strength and control, Cayde lowered himself over the ledge until only his fingers remained. Then, he was gone.

Dane peered as far over the ledge as his balance permitted. His heart pounded in his throat. Cayde's confidence had been unwavering, but there was still the possibility he could slip, and Dane would have to watch helplessly as Cayde tumbled into the lake far below. He didn't want to look, but he couldn't tear his gaze away.

A sudden pain shot through his hand. He looked down to see Quinn squeezing his hand in hers, gripping so tightly her knuckles had turned white. Under any other circumstance, Dane would have rejoiced at her holding his hand, but he knew her thoughts were only of Cayde.

After a long moment, Cayde's voice penetrated the monotonous drone of the rushing winds.

"I'm all right!" he shouted. "Send someone down!"

Quinn jolted at the sound of his voice. She blew out a deflating sigh, her grip loosening on Dane's hand.

Leon nodded to Sage, who uncoiled the Willow Whip from her waist and guided the tip toward a rock jutting from the wall. The small vine-like tendrils anchored themselves to the rock, failing to budge when Sage gave several swift tugs.

"Don't let go," she said.

"I won't, but I appreciate your concern," said Leon, glancing momentarily over the ledge.

Sage looked at him strangely. "Not you."

Leon frowned and diverted his gaze as Sage lowered the rest of the whip over the ledge, letting it dangle at full length.

After a long, silent pause, it dawned on Dane that someone else would have to descend the cliff next. Quinn was to his right, the whip to his left, Sage crouched beside it, Leon on her left. His spine stiffened. He forced down the fear clawing into his mind and said, "I'll go."

Before the others could respond, he grabbed hold of the whip and slowly lowered himself over the edge. He glanced up at the last moment to see Quinn peering down at him. The fear and worry had left her face, but she was unable to hide her growing unease.

"I'll follow," she said shakily. "Just—you be careful too, Dane."

Dane swallowed hard and nodded. He lowered himself over the ledge. Hand over hand he eased himself down until his feet had nearly reached the end of the whip's length.

Cayde called out, "Dane! Get ready! Start swinging and I'll pull you closer!"

He looked up to meet Cayde's concentrated gaze. Both of Cayde's hands were outstretched toward him, as if trying to grasp an invisible boulder. Clutching the end of the Willow Whip between his feet, Dane began to swing his legs back and forth, timing each motion with the swaying branch. Despite his efforts, the whip gained speed faster than it should have, and Dane felt himself being pulled closer to Cayde with every passing instant.

Just when Dane thought he could reach out and touch Cayde's hand, Cayde drew back, bracing one hand on the low-hanging cliff ceiling and stretching the other outward. As Dane sailed backward for the last time, Cayde shouted, "This is it! REACH!"

Dane forced his entire body weight into the whip, carrying it forward with as much speed as he could muster. The rough branch scraped and burned his palms, his grip slipping. *Not again,* he willed himself, memories of his Trials resurfacing. *This time I won't fail.*

With every bit of strength left, he released the whip and flung himself blindly toward Cayde.

Their hands met mid-air and the next moment Dane was sent sprawling to safety on the rocky platform behind Cayde.

"See? That's how it's done," Cayde whooped. "I'd like to see someone do that *with* powers, let alone without."

Dane let out a nervous laugh, mostly due to the delayed hysteria of dangling off the edge of a cliff supported by nothing but an immortal willow branch.

Still, he managed a grin. "Thanks."

Once the whip had returned to its stationary, hanging state, Quinn's legs appeared from the ledge above. With the same apparent ease, Cayde concentrated his focus once more on the whip. Quinn began to sway. She picked up speed much faster than Dane had, and in two fewer swings, she leapt from the whip and soared into Cayde's firm embrace. He swept the hair from her brow as she buried her face into his chest to calm her shaking limbs.

"You made it," he said. "You're safe now."

"Remind me . . . never . . . to do that again," she said between breaths.

Quinn released Cayde from her clutches as Leon's dangling feet protruded from the ledge. His grip slipped during his descent, and Dane's breath hitched as Leon narrowly managed to regain a hold on the whip before plummeting into the churning waters. Weakly, he began to swing, but when he barely moved, it became evident that Cayde would have to garner even more strength to pry Leon's icy grip from the hanging branch.

After setting Leon in motion, Cayde summoned a final surge of power, sending Leon and the whip soaring through the air toward the platform. Cayde grabbed Leon by the collar and, with a cry of exertion, wrenched him from the whip.

Leon landed face-first on the platform. He spread out on the cold rocky surface and lay motionless for a moment. After several quick, shallow breaths, he muttered, "Made it this time." He pushed himself into a sitting position. "Now we just have to wait for Pet—"

"Look out below!" came Sage's voice. A moment later, Sage leapt off the edge of the cliff, both hands fastened around the whip's handle. She twisted her body midair as the whip pulled taut, arcing toward the platform. Once past the nadir of her swing, she tucked her outstretched legs to her chest. She flicked her wrist, the whip releasing from the fastening rock above and, with the smoothest of grace, soared through the air and planted both feet firmly on the rocky platform.

"That was incredible, wasn't it?!" She shrieked excitedly. "Let's do that again!"

Leon, now on his feet and gaping like a fool, stared in a frozen daze as Sage strutted past him.

She playfully flicked her hair in his face and, as if she hadn't just achieved partial flight, said, "Where do we go now?"

Leon stumbled to the rock surface at the back of the platform, stealing a glance at Sage between words. "Well—I think—there should be—it has to be somewhere around here—"

"Don't tell me you don't know where it is," said Quinn, tension returning to her voice. She stole a quick glance over the platform. "There has to be a hidden door to this secret passageway, right?"

"I know where it is." Leon fumbled against the stone surface where the platform merged with the rocky underside of Mistveil. "A-ha!" He pressed both hands to the surface. "Here it is."

With a crumbling shudder, the stone groaned, separating ever so slightly from the rest of the rock. Leon heaved again, but nothing happened. He wiped his brow and stepped back to examine the stone with pursed lips.

"This path hasn't been used in decades, I'm sure," he said. "The stone's probably—"

Cayde pulled Leon aside. "Allow me." He pressed his body weight into the stone. With little effort, it rolled to the side to reveal a wide, dark tunnel carving deep into the city's foundation.

Leon's mouth fell open. "By the Mother," he breathed, "it does exist."

CHAPTER 16

THE CAVE OF FOUNTAINS

"Leon, wait—"

Quinn's warning fell on deaf ears as Leon stepped blindly forward, leg outstretched into the dark tunnel, and plunged his foot—and entire leg—into a trough of water.

He shrieked and stumbled, nearly submerging himself before falling back onto the platform.

Sage made a tutting sound. "An Aquadorian afraid of water. That has to be a first."

Leon shot her a disgruntled look and swatted at his dripping leg. "Surprised me, that's all," he said dryly.

Quinn examined the tunnel, frowning at the knee-deep layer of water. "We'll have to wade through."

"You heard her, back in you go," Sage jeered.

Leon scowled. "If you're so adamant about it, why don't you go first?"

"Fine." Sage tightened the straps on her carrying sack, fastened the Willow Whip, and made a two-footed leap into the water.

Before Leon could retort, Quinn followed behind her. The water sloshed and rebounded off the tunnel walls, forming a miniature tidal wave that crashed into Leon, dousing his tunic. He grumbled to himself, patting the water uselessly, and trudged in behind them.

Seeing no other alternative, Dane shrugged and sunk his feet into the water. It poured into his boots, soaking his feet instantly. He began following the others deeper into the tunnel when he realized he hadn't heard the splash of Cayde entering behind him. Careful not to disrupt the delicate balance of his foothold, he twisted to see Cayde supporting himself against the removed stone. Cayde had one hand clutched to his side, the same spot he had been injured and healed only a few days before.

"Is something wrong?" Dane called out to him.

Cayde looked up, startled, as soon as the words left Dane's mouth. He put his hand to his side and eased into the water.

"Cayde?" came Quinn's voice from further down the tunnel. The subtle hint of worry plagued her tone as her voice reverberated off the tunnel walls. "Is everything all right?"

"I'm fine . . . just catching my breath," Cayde said with a warm smile that quickly ebbed Quinn's worried grimace. "Swinging everyone took more effort than I thought."

"I thought your wound had healed," Dane said as Cayde fell into stride beside him.

"I must have strained myself," said Cayde dismissively. "The exertion of climbing down and using my power like that didn't help the healing, either."

Dane lowered his voice to a whisper. "Why did you hide it from Quinn?"

"She doesn't need to know," Cayde said. "I'm fine, really. I don't want her to worry more than she should—she carries enough burdens as it is."

Though still unconvinced of Cayde's quick dismissal of pain, Dane let his thoughts drift away from Cayde's condition. The way forward had grown very dark; the only light was that from the tunnel entrance, which was now no brighter than a star in the night sky.

Dane squinted through the thick layer of shadow obscuring his vision. Leon, leading the way and closely flanked by Sage and Quinn, had come to a halt before two identical, diverging tunnels.

"Which way do we go?" he heard Quinn whisper, followed by Sage's perfunctory addition, "And why are there two tunnels anyways? Nothing else could possibly be down here."

"I don't know," Leon responded hastily. "I could tell you if we had any light in this place, but as is, I couldn't see Old Man Calder sneering at me if he was standing in my face!"

Dane heard the mild lapping of water around Quinn as she fished something from around her waist. A moment later, the tunnel was flooded with a dim, glowing light. The walls of the cave danced with dim white auroras, emanating from the orb in Quinn's palm and illuminating both passages in front of them.

Leon grinned sheepishly. "Right . . . you're a Luminarus."

"Just find out which tunnel we're supposed to take," said Sage.

Dane trudged to Quinn's side as Leon began inspecting the two paths.

"I didn't know that orb could produce its own light," he said, staring in fascination. "I thought Luminari needed a source to control light, not create it from nothing . . ."

"That's not wrong," Quinn said slowly, "but this orb is . . . well, it's different. It contains a small piece of the Aurora Crystal inside, always emitting a faint spark to light my way even in the darkest of nights. My father gave it to me the day I pledged as a Luminarus, but the orb has been passed down through each generation of my family." She gazed into the orb, a soft smile touching her lips. "I like to think I'm carrying a small part of them—my father and mother, and the rest of my ancestors—with me wherever I go, and it's their light that comes to my aid when I need it."

"That's beautiful," said Sage.

Quinn's smile wavered, the weight of duty pulling at her features. "I only hope I can make them proud someday . . ."

"If you're done reminiscing about your parents that *didn't* leave you for dead," Leon called out from the tunnel on the left. "I think I found the right tunnel—rather, the correct tunnel. See, the right tunnel is actually the *left* tunnel, not the right tunnel, which is the wrong tunnel. We want the left tunnel, because that's the right tunnel to take if—"

"Enough, we get it," barked Cayde. "Just lead the way."

Leon aptly obeyed and marched down the dimly lit tunnel on the left, the others following in his wake.

"Are you sure this is the right tunnel?" asked Sage, inspecting the damp earthen walls and ceiling. "They all look the same to me."

"Technically, it's the—"

"The *correct* tunnel," she amended.

"Right—err—correct. If you look closely, the walls glow a particular way in the light, which means air passes through this tunnel and not the other."

"I . . . don't think that's right," said Quinn skeptically.

"Correct," said Leon.

"Then why did we take this tunnel?" said Sage, irritation rising in her voice. "Did the water whisper its secrets to you? Did you have a *gut feeling*?"

"Sure did." He slapped his gaunt midsection. "I looked at the right tunnel and said to myself, 'Leon, that doesn't look right,' and here we are."

Sage huffed her disapproval and scowled at Leon but said nothing. A tense silence ensued, disrupted only by the lapping waves around their wading bodies. Dane took the moment to examine the surrounding walls, running his hand along the coarse, damp surface and extending his arm to full length to graze the rocky ceiling with his fingers. The air was now heavy with the musty scent of wet stone.

"Why are these tunnels here anyways?" he postulated, rubbing the wall's grain-like residue between his fingers.

Leon stopped abruptly and examined the walls as if for the first time.

"You know . . ." he said, speaking with the same scholarly voice he had used when conversing with the other archivists, "some of the original archivists—the ones who maintained the Grand Archive shortly after its completion—were thought to be a cautious and profoundly mistrusting group, always weary that the Grand Archive, holding the massive wealth of knowledge that it does, was highly sought after by others of questionable integrity. If the original archivists were the ones who discovered whatever is down here, or were the ones who created the memory tomes, it wouldn't surprise me if they also created an escape route . . . just in case."

"In case of what?" Sage asked.

Leon shrugged and uttered a sound that confirmed his uncertainty. "Can't think of any other reason these tunnels would exist," he said. "But while we're on the topic of scholarly discussion . . ."

Maintaining his forward progress, Leon turned, his face half-cloaked in the shadow battling against Quinn's light, and looked to Cayde with intrigue. "I have a scholarly pondering for you, my Gravitus friend."

"Not again," Sage grumbled.

Leon cleared his throat and asked, "Do you think you could conjure a gravity well strong enough to lift a person off the ground and suspend them midair?"

"And why would I want to do that?" said Cayde.

"Oh, I was thinking about how you swung us on the branch—err, whip—earlier," Leon said, stealing a suspicious glance toward Sage's waist. Curiosity sparkled in his dark eyes. "Don't get me wrong, I know my stuff about Gravitus powers—you know, reading and all—but the way you used your power in such quick succession . . . well, it got me thinking. If you focused all of that energy on one person, *could* you lift them?"

"You do understand how difficult it is to lift the entire weight of someone, don't you?" Cayde said, almost jokingly. When

Leon stared back with genuine interest, Cayde's expression turned hard and unreadable. "But no, I couldn't. I'm not—I wouldn't be strong enough." There was a long pause, then he added, "Even if I could, I'd probably overexert myself with the effort."

Dane shuddered momentarily, remembering Varic the Abuser's desiccated skin in the Grove of Mist.

A disappointed frown carved into Leon's face. Clearly unsatisfied, he pressed, "Let's assume for a moment that you *could* lift someone—say, oh, I don't know . . . someone like me. Does that mean, if you had enough power to sustain it for long periods of time, you could potentially hold me midair and transport me anywhere in Physos like my own personal floating dewcart?"

Cayde exhaled an exasperated sigh, as if his pride had taken a physical blow from the mere idea of becoming Leon's personal mode of transportation.

Leon didn't take the hint.

"Just think of the possibilities!" he exclaimed, "I could—"

"Leon, look." Quinn extinguished the orb's soft glow and gestured down the tunnel. Ahead, a ghostly blue light cut through the monotonous sheet of blackness, flickering like a luminescent fish beneath a lake's surface.

"The end of the tunnel . . ." she said, almost in disbelief. The light in her orb pulsed back to life.

Leon shrugged out of her grip. "Told you I knew what I was doing."

"I was beginning to think we'd be stuck in here forever," said Sage, forcing a laugh. "Let's see what it is. These tunnels are starting to creep me out."

As they neared the end of the tunnel, the pinhole of blue light widened, revealing a massive cave. Hundreds of rock pillars erupted from the ground like tree trunks, merging with the jagged cave ceiling partially cloaked in shadow. Dane stared at the nearest pillar to see dozens of alcoves carved into its rocky exterior, the backs of which had eroded away, exposing a constant stream of glowing liquid coursing up the pillar's length and disappearing into the ceiling. The same ghostly blue he'd seen from the tunnel emanated from the inside of each pillar, painting the cave with its hue like the sun shining through a leafy canopy.

Leon exhaled and mumbled, "It can't be . . ."

"Wha—what is this place?" Dane stammered, trying to take in the vastness of the cave.

"I knew it. I knew it was real," said Leon in a misty, faraway voice. "The Memory Archive."

Sage looked at him with a mixture of awe and confusion. "Wait, so . . . the memory tomes are down there?"

Leon nodded without lifting his gaze from the cave.

"Somewhere down there . . ." he repeated in a whisper.

A small alcove in one of the pillars illuminated with a warm, yellow light, then extinguished as quickly as it had appeared. For a moment, Dane thought he saw something where the flash had been. Quinn had seen it too.

"Is that . . . a book? In the alcove?" she said, pointing toward the location of the flash. "A memory tome?"

"I'll bet it is," Cayde said. "Let's find a way down."

Dane, nearest to the tunnel's edge, hauled himself from the water-filled trench onto a small overhang jutting from the cave wall. He squinted to survey the surroundings.

"Do you see a path?" asked Quinn. When he didn't answer right away, she added, "Here, this will help." She held her orb at arm's length, illuminating the surrounding cave walls. Upon re-investigation, Dane could see an unnatural set of rocks protruding from the cave wall on his left, descending evenly from the overhang to the cave floor.

Dane pointed to the rocks, "There's a path down here."

Cayde leaned his head out, scanning the steps. "You go first, we'll follow."

After securing a foothold on the first rock, Dane proceeded down the rock steps with caution, keeping mindful of the damp surface beneath his sopping boots, all the while keeping his body close to the cave wall.

Upon reaching ground, Dane took in the full grandeur of the cave. From where he stood, the rock columns appeared twice as large, looming overhead in the soft glow of blue light. The cave floor, while as solid as the rock steps, was covered in a thin layer of stagnant water.

As Dane inhaled a deep breath, he noticed the unseen weight of the air, hanging like an everlasting fog, consumed with the fresh, residual moisture of the rushing water inside the rock pillars. When he took another breath, inhaling the thick, hazy air, he was reminded of the Grove of Mist. He shuddered at the thought, but his unease soon dissipated. The memory tomes had been stored here for a reason. He doubted some tome-guarding creature lurked in the cave's shadowed recesses, waiting for an innocent intruder to indulge themselves too deeply.

Quinn, Sage, and Cayde started toward the nearest pillar, only a short distance from the makeshift steps. Dane followed eagerly, trotting toward the others, water from the cave floor sloshing underfoot. He stopped before the alcove, staring at the object inside.

It was a book—rather, it appeared to be a book, like the ancient, tattered ones he'd seen in the Grand Archive. The thick, leather-like cover seemed hundreds of years old, cracks spreading from its edges, colored a dull gray-brown akin to the cave walls. Behind the tome, a small chunk of rock had eroded away, exposing the glowing water within.

"What should we do with it?" asked Sage intently, taking a curious step forward. "Can we touch it?"

Leon, who had been tiptoeing delicately across the cave floor, finally reached the alcove, raised a solitary finger, and poked the tome's cover. When nothing happened, he smiled proudly and turned to Sage. "Yes, I do believe we can touch it."

Exasperated, she amended, "I *meant,* can we pick it up? To examine it?"

Leon shrugged as if to say, *why didn't you say so?*

Quinn huffed and lifted the book from its misty shelter. She thrust it into Dane's hands. "Here. See what's inside."

"Wait, why me?" said Dane, suddenly wary of the memory tome. Its surface felt cold and clammy, and it weighed far less than a book of its size suggested. He held it at arm's length, unable to look away from its cover, as if doing so might cause it to spontaneously combust.

"Wait, why him?" Leon retorted defensively, planting clenched, accusatory fists on his waist.

"Dane was the one who mentioned the memory tomes to begin with," Quinn explained evenly. "We wouldn't be here if it wasn't for him, so it's only fair that he opens it first. And besides," she added rather bitterly, "I doubt you would've brought it up if Dane hadn't asked you."

"Fine," Leon grumbled, rolling his eyes with exaggeration. "But I get to see the next one."

Quinn turned back to Dane, evidently noting his unease. Gently, she said, "I doubt it'll be of any harm. It's just a book, after all."

Cautiously, Dane tore his gaze from the cover and said, "What should I do with it?"

"Open it and place your hand on the page," she offered, lifting her shoulders lightly. The excitement in her eyes was palpable. "See what's inside."

Dane's entire body tingled with excitement. Despite the tome's seemingly pedestrian appearance, he now thought better than to judge it by its cover. Something about the memory tomes warranted their secrecy in the first place. He was about to discover why.

Sucking in a deep breath of the coated, misty air, Dane gripped the tome with both hands, forced his thumbs between its pages, peeled it open, and lowered one hand onto the blank page.

Instantly a torrent of muddled, streaking colors seized his vision, blinding him to all other sensation. He heard one of the others call his name, but the sound was sucked away. His head throbbed. He could no longer see the others beside him, feel their presence. He felt as though he were being pulled into a dream.

He clenched his jaw tight, fighting back the urge to scream as the colors whipped by like a whirlwind, wreaking havoc through his mind. Then the barrage of colors ebbed and his senses cleared.

He was running through an open field of tall green and gold grasses that swayed like waves. He looked around and realized he was running along the edge of a cliff, overlooking massive ocean swells far below. He knew it was a memory, but it all felt real. He could feel the wind across his face, the grasses licking his fingertips, the smell of the misty ocean air. It was as if he was living in the memory unfolding before him.

His vision swiveled involuntarily to his right. A girl ran beside him. She was noticeably taller than he was, which felt strange, but even stranger was the surge of warmth that spread to his face as he stared at the girl. She was strikingly beautiful for a girl trapped in a memory. Her pale blue eyes shone like the bright winter sky after fresh snowfall. Her wavy, sunset orange hair streamed behind her as she ran, whipping past her soft freckled cheeks.

His gaze dropped and the warmth in his face doubled, his pulse racing. He was holding the girl's hand, running by her side along the cliff. He started to look away but stopped when he noticed the hand holding the girl's wasn't his own. He chided himself and instantly felt foolish, remembering that it couldn't possibly be his hand—it belonged to whoever memory he was experiencing.

But something about the hand was disconcerting. The fingers were short, thin, and small, and the hand nearly disappeared in the girl's grasp.

Dane's throat went dry as the realization hit him. It was the hand of a child.

A hand grabbed his shoulder. His vision was once again barraged by chaotic color as his mind was torn from the memory and thrown back into the dim blue glow of the cave.

Cayde stood over him, memory tome in hand. He snapped it shut and shoved the book back into its rocky alcove.

"What happened?" Dane breathed, bright spots of color still dancing in his vision.

"You weren't listening to us," came Leon's voice. "Quite rude, you know."

"You were unresponsive," Cayde said. "I thought you'd been petrified."

"But how? It all happened so quickly, I—" Dane paused to look at his surroundings, his brow furrowed. "Where are Quinn and Sage?"

"We heard a noise deeper in the cave. They went to investigate," said Cayde. "That's when I took the tome from you."

Before Dane could reply, Leon was in his face, scrutinizing him. He shook his head, tutted, and said, "By the Mother, you look awful. Maybe I don't want to see a memory tome."

"What happened in there?" said Cayde. "What did you see?"

Dane told them about the field, the girl, and the hand.

"That's it?" said Leon. He sounded disappointed. "Just a cliff and some girl?"

Dane nodded speculatively. "I thought you said memory tomes held someone's final memories. Was this someone's final memory?"

"Or their most cherished," Leon corrected. "Though I may just be spouting nonsense. Even *I* don't know what I'm saying sometimes."

"I didn't recognize that place," said Dane. "Do you know where they are?"

"Where they *were*, not where they *are*. Do you listen to anything I say? Memory tomes absorb memories. You can't take memories from those still living." Leon paused to let his words sink in. "The child whose memory that was—and maybe even that girl—are both dead now." He shook his head solemnly. "Such a shame. The child must have been young, too, if that was his most cherished memory. Not that it was a bad one, mind you, but *something* interesting would have been nice." Leon thumbed toward Cayde. "As to where they *were*, I'd ask him. I'm the one stuck in the Grand Archive all day."

"Does that place sound familiar?" Dane said, turning to Cayde.

But Cayde didn't answer. His mouth was set in a hard, grim line. Despite the dim glow of the cave, his dark gaze was distant, clouded in thought.

Concern etched Dane's brow. *Was there something I missed? Did the memory tome mean more?* A new thought occurred to Dane as he stared at Cayde's blank, sullen expression. It was as if the memory had awakened a deeper sentiment in Cayde, something forgotten, repressed, almost as if—

"Oh Cayde, anyone there?" Leon snapped his fingers in Cayde's ear. "Don't you go all unresponsive too."

Cayde inhaled a quick breath. His eyes widened briefly, the cloudiness subsiding from his gaze. He looked as if he'd been torn from a memory of his own.

"We should find the others," he said quietly.

Leon cradled his head in his palm. "Not quite the answer we were looking for."

As if on cue, he turned to see Sage and Quinn emerge from the shadows behind them.

"Glad to see that memory tome didn't eat you alive," Sage said, offering a relieved smile.

"What'd you find?" Cayde asked.

"You'll never believe this," Quinn said in a hushed voice. "We heard voices, those of the Grand Archivist and—"

"What?! Old Man Calder's down here?" Leon nearly shrieked. He slunk against the nearest pillar, eyes darting wildly. "Where is he? Can he see me? How'd he get in? Oh, I can't get away from him!"

"If you'd let me *finish*," Quinn hissed back, "we heard the Grand Archivist, and, we think, Elder Erwan."

"The Elder?" Dane exclaimed before clasping his hands to his mouth, realizing how easily voices echoed in the cave. "What's he doing here now? Isn't he supposed to be at the Aquadorian pledge ceremony?"

"We couldn't hear what they were saying," Sage said. "I'm certain one was the Grand Archivist, but I don't know who he was speaking with. It definitely sounded like Elder Erwan, though."

"There must be another entrance," said Cayde. "A path that leads back into the Archive—they certainly couldn't have entered the same way we did."

Leon scoffed. "That's for sure. I'd banish myself to the Shrouded Isle for a chance to see Old Man Calder try and climb his way under the city—figuratively speaking, that is."

"Did you see anything else in the cave?" Dane asked. Despite the threat of others lurking in the cave, his mind yearned for the chance to experience another memory tome.

Quinn's eyes widened. "There are at least a dozen alcoves in each pillar—most filled with tomes—and we lost count of how many pillars we passed. I wish we had more time, but if Elder Erwan and the Grand Archivist are down here with us, then time isn't on our side. We certainly can't let them find us."

"What should we do?" said Dane.

Quinn tapped a finger to her lips and gazed into the deep recesses of the cave. "Sage and I will return the way we came and see what we can find." She turned to Cayde and pointed behind him. "You, Dane, and Leon search that way. If anything happens, we'll all meet back at the tunnel."

Cayde nodded in agreement. He gripped Quinn's shoulder. "Be careful, all right? Both of you. These memory tomes are deceiving. If you both use one at the same time—"

"I know," Quinn said, her voice calm and soothing, "you be careful too." She gently brushed Cayde's cheek with her hand, then turned and retreated into the shadows with Sage.

Once they'd disappeared, Cayde faced Dane and Leon and said, "I don't like being down here with the Elder, so—"

"That's only if the others were telling the truth," Leon said, panic rising in his voice. "What if Old Man Calder was just talking to himself—I've heard him do that, you know—quite odd if you ask me—"

"If Quinn said she heard Elder Erwan, then he's down here too," Cayde said sternly. "She knows what she's doing. I'd trust her with my life."

Leon raised his palms in submission. "Fine, fine, I believe you."

A sense of urgency swept over Dane as they ventured deeper into the cave. Memory tomes were tucked into similar alcoves, but they all bore the same resemblance to the tome he'd already seen. Each step forward was taken in agonizing silence as he strained for the faintest sign of voices.

"These all look the same," Dane whispered as they passed yet another series of standard-looking tomes. "There has to be some way to tell their importance, right? Some must look different than others."

"That would make the most sense," said Leon. "But archivists don't always make sense."

"Someone has to sort through them, though," Cayde said. "There must be hundreds of memories that pass through here every day, maybe more. I guarantee a collector like Elder Erwan has saved the most valuable ones."

"Unless we can solve the mystery as to where his special hiding place is, we'll either be stuck down here forever or Old Man Calder is going to carve me up for dinner!" hissed Leon. "What would this special hiding place even look like? It's not like Elder Erwan has a giant sign somewhere in this cave that says, *Special Memory Tome Hiding Place.*"

"When I apprenticed for Duxor in Vitalor," Dane started, "he fastened his most valuable items and tools on the back wall. No one could use them without his permission. What if Elder Erwan did the same thing? What if he locked up the most valuable memory tomes so only he could access them?"

"You mean like those?"

Leon had stopped between two pillars and was pointing toward a pulsating glow coming from the center of the cave. Circled around a large pillar—nearly four times as large as any other—was an earthen table. In the dim blue glow of the cave, Dane could see several tomes spread about its surface.

"Well I'll be damned," Cayde breathed. "Spot on, Dane."

"I was the one who found it," Leon grumbled.

Dane's stomach sank a little as they approached the table. Each tome was secured with thick leather straps. And fastening the straps together, in the center of each tome's cover, was a large, metal lock.

"Metal locks?" Leon said in a panic once within arm's reach of the tomes. "How do they have *metal* locks?"

Dane inspected the locked memory tome in front of him. "These locks must be ancient," he said, recalling the refined gleam of the Ferron swords. He rubbed his fingers over the lock's discolored, gritty surface, tracing his thumb around a keyhole in its center.

An idea came to him, one that set his nerves on end. He mumbled, "Elder Erwan must have the key . . ."

Dane closed his eyes, listening for the faintest trace of voices in the cave, searching for the voice of the Elder. "Maybe if we can distract him long enough, then—"

"The Elder? You want to steal the Elder's key?" Leon said flatly. He scoffed as if the very idea disgusted him. He shouldered between Dane and Cayde. "Allow me."

"You mean to tell me you *don't* want to steal something?" Cayde said, almost amusedly. "You are truly a man of mystery."

"Don't get me wrong, I'm not above petty thievery. How do you think we found this place to begin with?" He rummaged for something at his waist. His hands closed around a small pouch hanging from his belt. He flashed a devious smile. "But why risk capture when I can do *this* instead."

He pulled the pouch free and dumped—rather, poured—the contents into his cupped palm.

Dane stared curiously at the fluid pooled in Leon's hand. "What is *that?*"

Leon didn't respond. He slipped the pouch into his pocket and began rolling the fluid in his hands, kneading it like fresh dough. Once the fluid was thin and threadlike, Leon felt for the keyhole on the lock and carefully inserted the molded fluid. He slowly pressed it further until it seemed to fill the entire keyhole.

Dane watched, dumbfounded, as the portion of fluid in Leon's hand crystallized. At first, it reminded Dane of the ice that would form in shallow puddles during the cold of winter.

But as he examined closer, he realized the fluid wasn't *like* ice at all. It *was* ice.

"How'd you do that?" Dane blurted out once Leon had finished.

"Oh, this?" Leon said, feigning surprise, but not without a hint of hubris. "It's a special concoction I made—it's nothing, really—but since you asked, it's only fortified water taken from the Mystic Fountain and mixed with, shall we say . . . a little something special." He made an exaggerated show of cracking his knuckles. "Damn, it feels good to be an archivist."

"An ice key that will fit any lock?" said Cayde, almost sounding impressed. "Clever. I haven't known an Aquadorian to use their power that way before."

Leon gave him a toothy smirk, shrugging innocently. "I try."

He began to twist the makeshift key when a lone, monotonous voice rose above the misty silence of the cave.

Dane's heart leapt into his throat. While he'd been distracted by Leon's key, he'd forgotten about the others in the cave.

"I thought I heard something . . ." the voice came again from behind the giant pillar, louder now. It was shrewd, unforgiving, and surely masked by a perpetual sneer.

"We have to get out of here!" Cayde hissed, nearly inaudibly. "To the shadows—this way!"

Dane registered Cayde's words immediately and crept backward with Cayde, taking shelter behind the nearest pillar.

"Where's Leon?" Cayde asked once they had disappeared into the blackness.

Dane felt the blood drain from his face. He swiveled in place to see Leon standing before the table, still attempting to twist the key. He hadn't heard the Grand Archivist's voice.

"LEON!" Dane urged, barely holding his voice to a whisper.

But Leon continued to fiddle with the memory tome, unaware.

"What is he *doing*?" Dane whispered frantically. "He'll be seen!" The Grand Archivist was just around the corner. At any moment, Leon would be caught, their chances of finding answers in the memory tome ruined. But despite his mind's incessant pounding, Dane couldn't move. He could only watch the scene unfold before him.

Then, from the darkness, Cayde spoke with pure heroic determination.

"Not if I can help it."

Just as the Grand Archivist's foot stepped into view, Cayde, still cloaked in shadow, thrust his arms forward, hands tensed and aimed directly at Leon. The next instant, Leon's body lifted from the cave floor. The key handle broke in his hand as he rose to the ceiling and disappeared, his entire body cloaked in darkness, suspended by Cayde's gravity well.

Not a moment later the Grand Archivist strode from behind the large pillar and paused in front of the ring of locked memory tomes, scanning the vicinity. His scrutinizing gaze swept past Dane, but his eyes showed no sign of recognition.

Elder Erwan emerged from the shadows. "Don't you see, Calder? There's nothing else down here but your ridiculous paranoia."

"Don't mock me, Father!" the Grand Archivist spat. "I heard voices. Someone is in here with us."

Elder Erwan clasped a palm to his forehead and said, "To think someone else could have possibly found a way into this cave is mockery in itself. There's a reason the secrecy of the Memory Archive has persisted for so many generations; there's no other entrance. My precious memory tomes have never been in *any* sort of danger, I assure you."

"These tomes contain nothing compared to the collection of the Grand Archive. They're too abundant; there are so many *useless* memories. I don't see why we can't abandon—"

With a surge of unfamiliar speed and aggression, Elder Erwan gripped the Grand Archivist's spotless white robes and dragged him closer until their shapes, outlined by the blue glow behind them, molded into one.

"Do you dare challenge *my* authority?" Elder Erwan seethed. "Challenge *my* reasons for preserving such—such—*perfection*?"

He raised one hand, encompassing the cave's entirety before returning his menace to his sniveling son.

"You'd be a *fool* to deny the unlimited knowledge the memory tomes possess! With these, I have access to every piece of knowledge in all of Physos." The Elder, scowling viciously, threw the Grand Archivist to the ground. He let out a feeble whimper as Elder Erwan continued. "If you do not wish to obey my will, then I will find someone else who can. The *only* reason I haven't stripped you of your title is because you are my only son and heir. Don't make me regret my decision."

A growing realization struck Dane as he watched the Elder and the Grand Archivist. His gaze faltered and he turned, his expression a mixture of worry and awe, and stared at Cayde.

His outstretched arms trembled with strain, veins rippling and bulging from his skin. His face was contorted in pained concentration, beads of sweat dripping from his quaking brow. His legs quivered, looking as though he might collapse at any moment. But instead he held firm, silent and resolute, unyielding as he fought through the pain of sheer overwhelming fatigue to keep Leon from being seen.

Dane watched with newfound admiration. Cayde would risk his own life to protect the lives of others, of those in need. He had been the first initiate in years to collect all energy stones in his Trials. Instead of using his power for his own gain, to assert himself into Physosi hierarchy, he had chosen this path, to stop the forces of evil spreading across the lands. He was truly selfless, a beacon of light when others needed him most.

Dane's heart twisted with sudden sadness, but he also felt a relieving, freeing clarity. *This is why Quinn loves him,* he thought. *Cayde would give everything for her . . . even for Sage, for Leon . . . for me.*

Dane thought of all the times Cayde had helped him during their journey: how Cayde had stopped the stone warrior's finishing blow, how Cayde had practiced with him in his moment of weakness after the Trials, how Cayde had saved him from the Chemocyte's fatal claws. Despite all Cayde had done for him, Dane had only resented Cayde every time he showed the slightest affection toward Quinn, some adversary standing between

Dane and the girl he once saw a future with. The mere thought brought tears to his eyes. *If Cayde doesn't think he's good enough for Quinn, after all that he's done . . . how can I ever hope to be?*

Wiping his stinging eyes, Dane returned his focus to the memory tomes. The Grand Archivist was rising clumsily to his feet, attempting to straighten from his cowardly huddle.

"Yes, father," Calder submitted. "I will obey."

"Good," Elder Erwan said coldly, returning to his usual placid demeanor. "Now, come. We have work to do. And since you're so insistent on your paranoia, we'll cleanse the Memory Archive for good measure."

"But father, the tomes?"

"Don't worry, water won't affect them in the slightest . . ."

The Elder's final words faded into the thick air as he and the Grand Archivist disappeared once more into the shadows. Dane remained in silence, waiting, until their footsteps retreated deep into the cave.

Once certain they were gone, Cayde's arms fell to his side. Leon yelped as he plummeted to the ground with a suppressed thud, splashing in the thin veil of water on the cave floor. Cayde fell to his hands and knees, his whole body shaking as he sucked in several rasping breaths.

"You could have lowered me down gently," Leon grimaced, clutching his lower back as he climbed to his feet. He laughed uncomfortably, then rubbed his neck and said, "Thank you, though. If you hadn't done that, I—"

"Don't . . . mention it," Cayde rasped.

Dane moved to help as Cayde struggled to his feet, but Cayde waved him away. "No, I'm fine." He gestured to the pillar. "The memory tome . . . we don't have much time."

Nodding his agreement, Dane trotted to the memory tome as Leon refitted his makeshift key. Surprisingly, after jostling it mildly, the lock broke free, releasing the leather straps and freeing the memory tome. Leon retrieved his prized concoction and deposited it back in his pouch.

Dane made to grab the tome but hesitated and looked at Leon. The archivist shook his head slowly and said, "It's all right, you open it."

"But you haven't seen—" Dane started. "But we came all this way. You lead us here. Discovering this place was your dream. This might be your last chance."

Leon let out a small whimper. "I know, I know. But at any moment, Elder Erwan will *cleanse* this place—whatever that means—and I, for one, don't want to be stuck watching some dead person's memory when that happens." He flashed a tight smile. "I'll leave that to you. Now hurry, I'll take care of my personal dewcart over there and pull you out if something goes wrong." Without another word, Leon, still holding his lower back, staggered clumsily toward Cayde.

Dane swept the leather straps to the side and lifted the tome with both hands. Elaborate, decorative markings had been engraved on the cover, but otherwise it looked and felt the same as the first one he'd seen.

But something felt unique about the tome as he positioned his hands around it. Maybe it was only the tome's perceived importance, or maybe he was suddenly aware of the adrenaline pumping through him, but for a moment, Dane thought he could feel the energy emanating from the tome, as if it was somehow calling to him, urging him to open it, wanting him to unveil its secrets.

Taking a deep breath, Dane thrust the tome open and pressed his palm to the page.

CHAPTER 17

THE MEMORY TOME

The torrent of streaking colors whirled through his mind faster than before, and soon, fighting through the mental pain, Dane found himself in a room, sitting at a long, ornately carved table. Directly in front of him was an open book.

An aged hand reached out and turned the page to display a ring of strange symbols, each drawn with immaculate color and detail. At the center of the ring was a dark circle with two yellow blotches inside.

Through the memory, Dane stared at the open page for several moments, unable to make sense of it. He looked to the set of symbols—eight, to be precise—drawn around the central one. Below each was a crudely drawn cluster of buildings—possibly depictions of cities, each the same as its neighbor, though the symbols themselves were all unique.

He started with the symbol at the top of the page, a small, orange sun. The symbol to its right was an equally small green tree. The next was a distorted red web, followed by a pluming blue fountain, a sparkling white crystal, a yellow sphere, a gray whirlwind, and a stone helmet.

Dane stared fixedly at the symbols, racking his brain for any sign of recognition. The longer he stared, the more his eyes gravitated to the symbol of the tree. It seemed familiar, as if he'd seen it before.

Then it struck him. He hadn't seen the *symbol* of the tree before; he'd seen the tree itself—the Elderwood tree. He looked to the blue fountain. If the symbol of the tree was meant to be the Elderwood tree, then that of the fountain had to depict the Mystic Fountain.

They're energy wells, Dane thought incredulously, scanning each symbol with increasing speed. *These symbols depict the energy wells of each city: the Elderwood of Vitalor, the Mystic Fountain of Mistveil—and the white crystal must be the Aurora Crystal of Evergleam.* He studied the five remaining symbols. *The stone helmet . . . that must be the energy well of Stonehelm. And the whirlwind . . . that's the Sacred Cyclone, the energy well of Alto-Baros.* His eyes glazed over the red web and the yellow sphere and locked on the symbol at the top of the page, the one that looked like an orange sun. *This one . . . it must be the Starforge, the energy well for the city of Starspire, the city that—*

Dane's thoughts stopped cold. Starspire was the Cosmonaut capital city, the city Avon had destroyed decades ago. The first city—the first energy well—Avon had attacked.

With mounting horror, Dane looked to the next symbol in the circle, the one of the Elderwood—the second symbol on the page. His breath stuck in his throat. *It can't be.* First the Starforge, then the Elderwood. There was only one conclusion he could make.

By the Mother . . . is Avon attacking the energy wells in order of their creation?

Suddenly, the entire memory shuddered and blurred, and his vision jolted forward as if he'd been struck from behind. For a moment, his vision returned to normal. Then something dark dripped onto the bottom corner of the page . . . then again . . . and again . . . then a dark, oozing liquid obscured his vision, distorting the memory.

Dane's stomach turned over. The fluid . . . there was no mistaking it now. It was blood.

The memory dissolved in a flash of light. Dane's mind was ripped from the memory's crimson tide and thrown back into the cave. He blinked wildly in an attempt to ease his throbbing head before slamming the memory tome shut and securing it with the leather straps.

Dane heard yelling in the distance, but he couldn't discern the voice over the ringing in his ears. The voice grew louder, resonating over the constant drumming all around him.

"Dane! We have to go! NOW!"

The noise pounding in his ears suddenly became clear. He frantically searched the cave. Water poured down from holes in the ceiling like dozens of miniature waterfalls. He looked down to see his legs submerged in a knee-deep tide of water, growing deeper with every passing instant.

"The cave's flooding!" Cayde's voice came again. "RUN!"

Dane shoved away from the locked memory tomes and trudged through the rushing water. Cayde was only a few strides ahead of him, still clearly inhibited by his recent exhaustion. Leon was closest to the tunnel, attempting to wade through the rising waters.

Dane's foot slipped and he exhaled involuntarily as his body sank into the water, the current threatening to sweep him deeper into the cave. He planted both feet on the cave floor and launched himself upward, inhaling a huge breath as he surged above the surface. The water was now at his shoulders; he could barely touch the cave floor beneath him.

The others had reached the overhang that preceded the tunnel. Quinn and Sage were pulling Leon up as Cayde lifted his feet. Dane could vaguely see Quinn shouting in his direction as she helped pull Cayde up, but all he could hear was the water frothing and churning around him. He didn't need to hear her to know what she was saying. The water was rising faster. Soon it would flood the tunnel too, blocking their only means of escape.

Adrenaline rushed through Dane's body. He gave up any attempt to walk across the cave floor and swam toward the ledge, silently thanking Grandfather Horas for teaching him at such a young age.

"Quickly!" Quinn yelled as he reached the ledge. "Grab hold!"

She and Cayde both extended a hand down to him. With a powerful downward kick, Dane stretched his arms up. Their hands clasped around his wrists.

Just as his hands neared the ledge, Quinn let out a strangled cry and stumbled backward into the tunnel, his slick skin slipping from her grasp. Dane's stomach lurched as his body began to fall back into the water. At the last moment, Cayde, grunting and crying out in pain, clutched Dane's other wrist with both hands, halting him midair.

"Grab the ledge!" he shouted through gritted teeth. "I can't . . . hold . . . on!"

Dane swung his free arm up and gripped the ledge just as Cayde's grip failed. With one final surge of energy, Dane hurled himself over the ledge. He wanted to give in to his exhaustion, revel in the momentary victory, but the water was still rising. He had to move.

"Hurry!" Sage shouted, already starting down the tunnel with the others.

"I'm right behind you!" Dane shouted back. He heaved several quick breaths, clambered desperately to his feet, and sprinted after them through the darkened tunnel. He could barely see the ground ahead without Quinn's light to guide the way, and soon he lost sight of the others completely. His footsteps pattered against the floor as he went, the loud claps echoing off the cave walls. He vaguely realized that the tunnel floor was now devoid of water. Briefly, he wondered if the water had been drained to aid the cave's 'cleansing', but he quickly doused the thought; it wouldn't matter if he couldn't escape the tunnel alive.

The tunnel seemed to stretch on longer than before. It had been relatively straight from what he could remember, but now he felt as though he were running in circles, lost in a maze of never-ending darkness.

He surged out of the tunnel and into a small cavern, the same one where they had stopped to choose the correct path into the Memory Archive. His stomach fluttered with relief. The end of the tunnel had to be close; he was almost out.

Behind him, the sickening roar of rushing water echoed from the tunnel. The water had flooded the cave entirely and was now racing through the tunnel toward him.

Dane glanced briefly over his shoulder, eyes wide with fear and adrenaline. In a lapse of concentration and focus, his foot slid from under him and he skidded across the slick ground and crashed against the cave wall.

His ears rang as he tried in vain to rise to his feet. White stars spotted his vision. He felt a hot jab of pain in his left hand as he slipped again, his aching, disoriented body collapsing to the ground.

He briefly envisioned the water swallowing him whole, thrashing him against the sides of the tunnel before shooting him out and sending him spiraling down to the crashing waves of Mistveil Lake.

Desperately, he wished the others would come to his aid, to pull him to his feet and drag him to safety. With mounting horror, he realized they hadn't seen him fall; the tunnel was too dark, the water blocked out all other sound. They didn't know he had fallen behind.

Tears burned his eyes. *This is it,* he thought as he lay against the wall, his body aching and exhausted, nothing but the darkness and the impending onslaught of voracious water to accompany him. He'd managed to survive everything leading up to this moment—his Trials, Avon, the Chemocyte, and the Ferrons—only to die alone in this tunnel, defeated by water and darkness.

Then, at the back of his mind, Quinn's voice parted through his despair, the last words she'd said to him after she'd found him on the willow overlook after his Trials, after she'd convinced him his life was still worth living.

They won't remember how you fell down in defeat, she'd said. *They'll remember how you rose back up.*

Almost at once, her words ignited something in him. A furious, searing rush of determination spread through his body. He wasn't alone. He had his family and his friends. They needed him and the information from the memory tomes if they hoped to stop Avon. Allowing himself to be defeated by simple exhaustion and fear was no better than letting Avon destroy another energy well or kill the ones he loved. Suddenly he realized it didn't matter that he'd failed his Trials and failed to find his power. He was a survivor, a fighter. He was needed. For the first time since his Trials, he felt valued, even loved, and the ones he loved needed him now more than ever.

"NO!" He cried aloud. His eyes burned with passion and purpose. "NOT. LIKE. THIS!"

With a mighty heave he thrust his body from the ground. He wobbled in place, his knee almost buckling under his weight, but he held firm. He got his bearings. He was in a larger part of the tunnel, where Leon had found the forking pathways.

The water was still surging toward him from the tunnel behind. He could barely make out a spot of natural light at the end of the long strip of tunnel before him.

He was close. He could still make it.

Dane took off running. All the pain in his body had dissipated, blanketed by the adrenaline burning through him. His strides lengthened, his legs becoming a blur beneath him as he focused on light growing brighter with every step.

The sound of the pursuing water echoed all around him, but now he could smell the brisk lake air. The scent breathed life into him and spurred him on faster until sunlight illuminated the tunnel walls. He could see the platform outside the tunnel. There was no sign of Quinn, Sage, or Leon, but the Willow Whip dangled down from the cliff above, wriggling slightly as a pair of feet disappeared overhead. The others had made it. They were safe. He only had to jump to the Willow Whip. Joy erupted inside him. *I'm going to make it!*

That was when he noticed Cayde standing on the platform's edge. The whip swayed in the air, seemingly inviting him to leap to it and climb to safety. But Cayde didn't budge. He only hesitated, as if preparing to jump, but unable to commit.

Now, a few mere strides away, Dane suddenly understood why Cayde couldn't move. *He can't make it.* He glanced hurriedly at Cayde's hand clutching his side and took in his slouching form. *He's too weak. The jump is too far, and he knows it.*

Then an idea came to him. It wasn't a good one, but the water was closing in fast. The platform was the water's next victim.

You've done enough for me, Dane thought, eyes locking on Cayde. *It's time to return the favor.*

Water licking at Dane's heels as he burst out of the tunnel. He ran at Cayde at full speed, arms outstretched, bracing for impact.

"Cayde!" He screamed. "JUMP!"

Cayde must have understood immediately—to Dane's great relief—and he leapt outward, hands reaching for the Willow Whip as Dane shoved his entire body weight into Cayde's back. Cayde soared through the air and fastened his hands around the branch as its tendril-like fingers fastened around Cayde's wrists.

Dane, having forfeited any hope of retaining his balance, used his momentum and leapt up from the platform, meaning to reach for the handhold in the rock above, the last of the handholds that Cayde had initially used to descend from the cliff's edge.

Incredibly, Dane's fingers closed around the rocky handhold and he lifted his knees to his chest just as a deluge of water exploded from the tunnel beneath him, narrowly evading his feet as it plunged toward Mistveil Lake far below.

He closed his eyes and concentrated all his strength into his hands, determined not to let go. The water beneath him ebbed to a trickle. Despite the burning in his hands, legs, and mid-section, a huge smile spread across his face. *I made it. I survived . . . all on my own.*

"Dane!"

Dane swiveled his head cautiously to see Sage peering upside-down at him, her blonde hair falling loosely around her head. Her expression was pure, overwhelming joy.

"Grab hold!"

She dangled her arm beside her head, Willow Whip in hand. She gave it a swift flick and the tip coursed through the air and fastened itself around Dane's waist.

Sage disappeared. The whip pulled taut, then she called out, "Let go!"

Dane released the rock, letting his body swing gently through the air. He breathed in the cool lake breeze, reveling in the wonderful, revitalizing scent.

He was immediately met with Sage's warm embrace as he clambered back onto the ledge.

"Never do that again," she scolded, holding him at arm's length, attempting to look stern. Then she beamed with relief and hugged him again.

When she finally let him go, Dane swiveled carefully on the ledge to face Quinn. She flung her arms around his neck and pressed her body into his, nearly knocking him over.

"We thought you were—I can't believe you're all right!" She drew her head back and kissed him on the cheek, flooding him with warmth despite the cool wind rushing past his soaked clothes.

Then Dane felt a hand on his shoulder. He looked beyond Quinn to see Cayde staring at him as if in awe. Dane held Cayde's gaze in silence. He could see the gratitude in Cayde's eyes, the recognition of the potential sacrifice Dane had made for him. In some ways, it was more than Cayde could have ever said in words.

"Thanks for that," Cayde finally said. Dane nodded and managed a smile.

Leon, already squeezing himself back through the gap in the city wall, let out a heaving sigh. "As fun as that was . . . let's not do it again."

They all laughed briefly, then Quinn looked to Dane, her green eyes shining. "That was quite the adventure. Are you sure you're all right?"

"I am now," Dane said, grinning in triumph. "I know where Avon will attack next."

ॐ ॐ

"Tell us, what did you see?" Quinn asked as they all huddled around the small table in the safety of Leon's house.

They'd agreed not to mention anything of the Memory Archive until they could speak in solitude, in the off chance Elder Erwan or the Grand Archivist happened to find them. Luckily, Leon's secluded clay-scented house, perched at the edge of one of Mistveil's smaller islands, was the perfect hideaway.

"I'm assuming you only had time to view one more tome, right?" Quinn asked. "We heard the Elder and the Grand Archivist arguing in the distance . . . that must have been close to you."

Dane nodded, confirming her assumption. He told them all about the ring of symbols he'd seen on the ancient page, and how the memory had come to a jarring end. Before any of them could postulate the significance of the symbols, Dane proposed the daunting theory he'd been formulating ever since.

"The symbols must represent the energy wells of each city. If that's correct, then I think Avon is somehow using these symbols to plan his next attacks."

They stared at him blankly, so he pressed on.

"The first symbol—the orange sun. That's the energy well of Starspire, the Cosmonaut capital city, the energy well Avon destroyed first. Next was the tree—the Elderwood, no doubt, which was the second energy well he attacked." He paused for effect, then looked to Quinn. "In what order were the cities built? When the founders first created them?"

Quinn stared as if unsure what point he was trying to make. "Well," she started slowly. "Founder Arkon built his city first, of course." She tapped her finger to her lips. "And I suppose that would mean Founder Celosia had Vitalor built shortly—" Her eyes suddenly widened with understanding. "You don't think—"

"Yes, I do," Dane said. "Avon is attacking the energy wells in the order they were built."

Sage let out an audible gasp. "And what was the symbol after the tree? The red web?"

"The Chemocyte energy well—the Crimson Mirror," Quinn said automatically. "It was buried somewhere in the ruins of Chyrim after Founders Arkon and Rodran banished Lussiek."

"I'll bet that's where Avon went after fleeing Vitalor," Cayde said. "It wouldn't have been protected by any means. I'm sure Avon has destroyed it by now, which means—"

"What symbol came next?" Quinn whispered, as if dreading the answer.

Dane gulped, recalling the symbols with unfaltering clarity. "The Mystic Fountain."

"It could just be a coincidence," Cayde said carefully, as if trying to convince himself otherwise. "He can't be that predictable."

"What if that's the only way he can damage them?" said Sage. She looked at Dane. "You said the memory tome was locked up—those symbols have to be important, especially if someone was killed for seeing them. What if the energy wells can only be damaged in the order they were created, if each energy well is somehow protected by the one before it?" Her eyes grew wide in terror, and she said quietly, "And the person in that memory . . . what if it was Avon who killed them?"

A ringing silence filled the air. After a long pause, Dane, unhinged by the fact that he might have seen the last memory of one of Avon's victims, looked to Quinn and Sage and said, "Did you find any memory tomes related to this?"

Quinn opened her mouth to speak, but before she could, Sage rifled through her pack, pulled out a book and dropped it onto the table.

Dane's eyes grew wide. It wasn't any ordinary book; it was a memory tome.

Leon had noticed it too. He had been conducting a futile attempt to fix another slab of loose clay when Sage thumped the tome on the table. At the sound, Leon glanced nonchalantly over his shoulder, returned to the clay for a moment, then wheeled to face Sage, his mouth agape and face stricken with horror.

"You—you—*STOLE* a memory tome?!" Leon sputtered furiously.

Sage nodded calmly, staring at its cover. "I wanted to keep it."

"You—*WHAT*?! You can't just *keep* a memory tome from the Memory Archive!" Leon paced around the room, wringing his hands. "What if someone finds out? Now it's probably broken! It'll never work again! And everyone is going to know!"

"Oh, calm down," Sage said. "I don't think *everyone* is—"

"This is a breach of all archivist laws! They'll surely banish us now!"

Sage looked at him sternly. "*Us?* They can't—"

But Leon wasn't listening. He wailed maniacally, voice cracking in frenzied hysteria. He launched into a recitation of archivist laws, flinging his hands madly into the air.

"Will someone shut him up!" Quinn shouted over Leon's delirium.

Without the slightest hesitation, Cayde swept his arm across his back, unsheathed his sword and thumped the hilt to the side of Leon's head.

Leon's eyes rolled upward. He collapsed against the nearest wall and slumped to the ground, his head lolling to one side. A slab of clay dislodged above him and splattered in his lap.

"Thank you," Quinn said, pressing her fingers to her temples. She gave a small sigh and eyed Leon with a mixture of anger and concern. "It was probably best."

"You were saying?" said Cayde calmly, returning to his chair and gesturing an open hand to Sage.

"This memory tome . . . I—" Sage dragged a hand wistfully across the thick, leather cover. "I recognized someone . . ."

"Who?" Dane asked, his mind suddenly spinning at the implications of recognizing someone in a memory tome. *Was it Grandfather?* He thought worriedly. *Old Lady Fern? Or even . . . Vilik?*

Distantly, Sage said, "I saw Elder Chrysanthe . . ."

313

Instantly, a weight lifted from Dane's chest, but then he felt a pang of guilt at his relief. By no means did he wish her dead either.

"The memory," Sage continued. "I was an elderly woman resting in a bed—her hands were spotted and frail, so she must have been quite old. The room was nothing out of the ordinary, but there were two other women looking down at me, standing by the bedside. One of them was Elder Chrysanthe, though it must have been before she was christened as elder—she looked so much younger, maybe a few years older than I am now. But the other woman . . ."

"Who was it?" Dane asked gently, sensing the pain in Sage's eyes.

"I—I don't know—not for certain, at least. But she looked familiar, like I'd seen her a long time ago." She caressed the tome's cover, staring vacantly, her brow knit as if trying to replay the memory. "She was wearing pretty green robes, similar to the ones Elder Chrysanthe likes to wear, with the twisting vines. There was a small, white rose embroidered on one side, just above her heart. And her hair . . ." Sage breathed a long sigh, fondling her own hair between her fingers. "It was the color of the spring sunlight . . . the kind that pokes through the budding leaves back home."

She broke her gaze with the tome and looked at Dane. Her eyes brimmed with tears, filled with loss and longing.

"Dane," she said, her voice trembling, "I think it was our mother."

Dane could only stare at her; it was the last thing he'd ever expected to hear her say. He'd dismissed his parents as nothing more than mere myth, strangers who had died when he was very young.

"But—how?" he asked Sage. "How do you know it was her? It's been so long—I don't even remember what she looked like . . ."

Sage shook her head. "I don't know how, but I *know* it's her. I can feel it. I know it is, Dane. It's our *mother.*"

Dane's heart ached in his chest, and his throat constricted as tears threatened to surface. The mother he never knew felt more than a mere tale from his childhood. She finally felt real . . . as did her loss.

Then anger seized him. At some point in her life, Elder Chrysanthe had known their mother, had been good enough of friends with her to stand together before the previous Elder of Vitalor. But after all this time, she'd never told them a thing.

"It's getting late," Quinn said hesitantly, breaking the monotony of silence. She peered at Leon's lone window where dim streaks of waning sunlight shone in, painting the floor and signaling the ensuing blanket of night. "It's been a long couple of days. We could use a good night's rest. I'll alert Elder Erwan in the morning of what we've learned. Besides, we should wait for this one to regain consciousness." She thumbed distastefully at Leon, who was still slumped against the wall.

After a brief meal, they all settled in for the night within the confines of Leon's house.

Dane tossed and turned through the night, thinking, for the first time in a very long time, of the mother he had never known.

Leon stirred the next morning as Dane, Sage, Quinn, and Cayde packed their belongings, preparing for the return journey to Evergleam.

"The city should be well prepared once I alert Elder Erwan that Avon is coming to Mistveil next," said Quinn. "That should make it more difficult for him. There are only two entrances into the city after all, not to mention the hidden defenses. It'd be nearly impossible for Avon to breach the confines of the wall unnoticed." She let out a triumphant sigh, allowing a small smile. "Finally, it feels like we've gained the upper hand."

"And why do we think Avon will attack Mistveil?" muttered Leon, rubbing the back of his head with both hands.

"That's what we predict he'll do next, based on the order of the symbols Dane saw in the memory tome," Sage said shortly.

She cocked an eyebrow at Leon. "And he's not attacking cities. He's attacking the energy wells."

Leon's head wobbled dazedly. He repeatedly shifted his gaze between Dane and Sage, lifting a finger as if to say something, then bringing himself to a halt each time. Frowning lightly, he gestured a wavering finger in a direction that was assumedly toward Sage.

"I'll deal with you later, Petals," he said slowly, bracing himself on a chair. He turned to Dane. "What's this about symbols?"

"The symbols I saw—in the memory tome—so far Avon has attacked each city's energy wells in the same order as the symbols. Under that assumption, he has destroyed the Chemocyte energy well by now—what was left of it, at least—and is heading toward Mistveil for the Mystic Fountain. Then, we—"

Leon broke into a sputtering, delirious laugh, which quickly subsided as he clutched a hand to the spot where he'd been struck by the sword hilt.

"What?" Quinn said tersely. "What could you possibly find amusing?"

Leon sighed with a crooked smile. "Oh, that memory tome is wrong," he said, then winced again, still cradling his head.

Quinn dismissed him and returned to her pack. "You're delusional. Memory tomes can't be wrong."

Leon shook his head rather defiantly. "Nope," he exclaimed with far greater volume than expected. Then, much quieter, "It's about time my years as an archivist paid off. I've read a lot of books over the years . . . a *lot* of books. If only you knew what I knew. And to think, you all thought—" He laughed again, a slow, high-pitched chuckle, then heaved an exaggerated sigh. "Oh, if only you knew what I was saying, then you'd know where Avon was really going next . . ."

Quinn straightened, her body rigid. She stared at Leon, unable to mask her growing unease. "What are you saying?"

"Do *you* even know what you're saying?" Sage mumbled at Leon.

"What I'm *saying*," Leon emphasized slowly, "is that Avon is on his way to Evergleam right now."

"Mistveil," Quinn corrected, but not before lines of worry spread across her forehead. "You mean he's on his way to Mistveil. That's the next symbol Dane saw—the Mystic Fountain—that's here."

Leon shook his head again.

"I once read a book about the founding of Mistveil—remember, I've read a *lot* of books. I've acquired quite the plethora of seemingly useless facts over the years." He paused, then, at no one in particular, shouted, "Not so useless now, is it!" He shook his head lightly. "Anyways, near the end of the book, it said that Founders Illara and Cyndus held a friendly competition to see who would be the first to complete the construction of their city. In the end, since Mistveil had more people to help, Founder Cyndus created the fourth city of Physos. However, even though his city was completed first, and even though it took Founder Illara and the citizens of Evergleam another year to complete their city, *they* were the first to establish their energy well, the Aurora Crystal, before constructing the city itself. It took citizens of Mistveil another year to finish carving out the canals and tunnels needed to create the Mystic Fountain that we so admire today. They *did* have to design the city to be supported by enormous geysers. That takes time, you know.

"The symbols in that memory tome must have depicted the order in which the *cities* were created, not the energy wells." Dane's stomach dropped as he recalled the small city-like drawings scrawled beneath each of the symbols on the page. "If you were to look at a page depicting the order of the energy wells," Leon continued, "then the Mystic Fountain and the Aurora Crystal would be switched."

At once, Quinn's entire complexion changed. Her face turned a ghostly pale. Her green eyes no longer held the triumph and relief that had graced her moments earlier. Now, they were wide with terror.

"What are you saying?" she croaked, choking back tears. "What does that mean?"

With gripping fear, Dane realized Quinn already knew the answer. He knew it too.

"If what you say about Avon attacking energy wells is true," Leon went on, his demeanor unchanged, "and he is attacking them in order of their establishment—which isn't unlikely, for someone of his, shall we say, *ambition*—then right now, Avon is, probably as we speak, on his way to attack the Aurora Crystal in Evergleam."

Not a moment later, a shrill, blood-curdling scream erupted through the air—sounding like that of a child—coming from the main island, near the East Bridge.

Quinn's eyes bulged. Without a moment's hesitation she flung her pack across her shoulder and sprinted out of Leon's house.

"Quinn, wait!" Cayde called. He tore out of the house after her.

Ignited by the spark of sudden alarm, Dane fastened his own pack, tied his staff to it, and sprinted with Sage after them, leaving Leon behind as he succumbed to his daze and sunk to the floor.

They tore through the streets leading toward the main island of Mistveil, the scream growing louder and more agonizing with every stride. Once crossing the water bridge and returning to the main market thoroughfare, Dane skidded to a halt behind Quinn, who stared at the East Bridge gateway only a short distance down the street.

Two guards knelt beneath the giant archway, trying to calm a small child. Her small robes and pale skin were dusted with soot. Her arms and legs were riddled with small cuts, and a red streak dripped down one side of her face.

Quinn ran forward. The child stopped wailing and looked down the street. Upon seeing Quinn, she tore away from the guards and ran into Quinn's outstretched arms.

"Agatha!" Quinn screamed. They embraced for a long moment, the child sobbing into Quinn's shoulder as Quinn stroked the hair from the child's reddened face. "What's wrong, Agatha? Tell me, please!"

Agatha didn't respond with words. She merely pointed toward the Aurora Mountains, where a massive plume of smoke blackened the sky above the very spot where Evergleam should be.

Quinn clasped her hands to her mouth in horror. She rose and wheeled to face Cayde. Her face had lost all semblance of color. Her wide, reddened eyes held the look of pure terror.

"I have to help them," she muttered.

"Quinn, I can't—"

"They need my help, Cayde, I have to go! We have to go!" She cried hysterically. "If I don't go, they'll all die! We have to do something!"

Cayde straightened, inhaling deeply, then turned to Dane and Sage. His face seemed calm, determined, but his eyes shone with agony. "Accompany her to Evergleam and do what you can to lead everyone out of there."

"I'll send them here. It's safe here," Quinn uttered, her eyes still lost in fear.

"Good, yes," Cayde reassured her. "I can't travel fast enough just yet, so you'll have to go without me. I'll stay here to help everyone."

Quinn didn't argue. She turned toward the bridge, but Cayde gripped her hand and twisted her back to him. She threw her arms around his chest. Cayde cradled her face in his hands and placed a kiss on her forehead.

"Be careful, and come back safely," he said softly, stroking a tear from her cheek with his thumb.

Quinn nodded solemnly. "You stay safe too," she whispered. "Now go."

Quinn turned, knelt to embrace Agatha one last time, then sprinted toward the gate, past the guards, and onto the bridge toward the burning Evergleam.

Sage nodded at Cayde in understanding then followed Quinn's path. Dane was about to do the same when Cayde's voice halted him.

"Dane . . . wait."

Dane turned to face him, but Cayde's eyes were not trained on his. Instead, Cayde watched as Quinn ran from view, eyes flooded with longing, as if he was watching her for the last time.

"You have to protect her," he said quietly.

"I—what?"

"Promise me you'll protect her, Dane. Keep her safe."

"Of course, but—why are you telling me this now?"

"I won't always be there to do so, especially now. I need you to protect her in my stead."

"But why can't you come with—"

A thought struck him suddenly, and he recalled the many signs he had seen over the past several days. Dane shifted his gaze to the wound Cayde had received on the night of the Chemocyte attack.

Without a moment's pause, Cayde lifted the bottom of his shirt. Surrounding the thick scar splayed across one side of his midsection were dozens of gruesome, purple tendrils. The skin around the wound had turned hard and dry, and something dark and red festered beneath the surface.

Dane felt an eerie chill trickle down his spine, the same he'd felt that night of the Chemocyte attack. "That wasn't from a branch, was it?"

Cayde said nothing as he lowered his shirt over the wound. As if fighting the full force of a waterfall crashing down on him, he tore his gaze from Quinn and turned to Dane.

"Quinn is the key," he said, his voice wavering. "I knew it from the moment I met her. She has more strength than any of us realize. Whatever you do, you *must* ensure her safety, no matter the cost. Do you understand me?" His words finished in a plea. He gripped Dane's shoulders, his eyes glistening with longing. "She has to live, and you must give *everything* to protect her. Without her, all of Physos will be lost."

"What do you mean? How—"

Cayde raised a silent hand. He straightened and, wincing at the movement, curled his arm to his back, unlatched the strap holding his sword in its sheath, and offered it to Dane.

"Take this," he said. "You'll need it more than I will."

Dane stared down at the glass sword. "But—I—"

"You'll need this if you ever hope to defeat Avon, and that moment may come sooner than you think. You are their defender now." His voice grew stern, but he was unable to mask the pain and fear in his words. "Now go, please. Remember what I said. Protect Quinn, whatever it takes. Promise me you'll protect her."

Dane fastened the sword to his back, his hands trembling as he fastened the straps. "I promise." He grabbed his staff and made for the gate. He stopped momentarily beneath the massive archway, stealing one last glance over his shoulder at Cayde's tear-stricken face.

"It's up to you now, Dane," Cayde called out behind him. "It's up to you . . ."

CHAPTER 18

AVON'S ASSAULT

Dane had never run faster in his life.

Dark clouds of smoke billowed into the sky above Evergleam as he trailed Sage and Quinn. Despite Sage's obvious physicality and natural prowess—she'd beaten Dane countless times while racing through the village in their youth—even she began to fall behind as Quinn sprinted up the winding stone path that led to her burning city.

Quinn.

Cayde's words still swirled in his head as he ran. What he'd said had taken Dane by complete surprise. And the way he spoke of Quinn . . . it was as if he'd never see her again. Dane couldn't wrap his head around it.

His thoughts shifted to the sword as it rattled in its sheath on his back. As magnificent and deadly as the sword was, Dane had never used it before. Its touch and weight had felt foreign when he had taken it, as if it didn't belong to him. If he encountered anything that required combat skills, he'd use his staff, as he always had; it felt natural, effortless.

But still, Cayde's words left him feeling uneasy, like there was something else he was missing, something Cayde hadn't told him about it.

You'll need this if you ever hope to defeat Avon . . .

Quinn and then Sage slowed to a stop at a curve in the path ahead. Dane slowed as he approached them, his unease rising. They still had a significant distance to cover before reaching the city. Something had to be wrong.

He opened his mouth to speak when the noise hit him.

The sound of muffled wails and sobs pierced the chilled air, rattling relentlessly in Dane's ears, unhinging his every nerve. He looked to the sky, trying to discern the origin of the screams. They weren't distant, as if from Evergleam. They seemed closer . . . much closer.

Dane turned to Sage and Quinn as increasing horror dawned on him.

"What is that?" Dane asked, his voice shaky.

Quinn covered her mouth with a trembling hand. She let out a muffled cry, gestured a quivering finger toward Evergleam.

Though afraid of what he might see, Dane slowly turned to look where Quinn was pointing. His legs nearly collapsed from under him.

Straight ahead of them, flooding down the mountain slopes, were hundreds of Luminari. Smoke and ash soiled their clothing and skin. Many cradled bloodied limbs and pressed seeping wounds. Others carried bodies in their arms—whether injured or dead, Dane couldn't tell—and others still nursed blackened skin and open flesh scarred by horrific, boiling burns.

They came down the mountainside in droves, pain, fear, and agony plastered on each and every face. The sight shook Dane to his core.

Quinn burst into a run toward the first survivor.

"Wha—what happened?" she cried out. Her green eyes bulged, and tears slid down her cheeks as more injured survivors passed, far too many for her to help. "Who would do this?"

"Fire—they came from—the city on fire," said the survivor, a younger man, whose bloodied face grimaced as he struggled for words. He pressed his hands tighter to a dark red stain on his clothes and let out a torturous groan. "They—they went for the castle." The man stumbled onward with another groan, leaving Quinn alone to face the horde of wounded.

"There's so many," Quinn whispered. "I can't help them all."

"Is there anywhere they can go?" Sage said, her face stricken with horror. "There has to be something we can do."

"They must find safety," Quinn muttered to herself, then to those around her, her voice growing louder until she was shouting in a desperate plea. "Please, go to Mistveil! Help each other! It'll be safe! Please, you must—"

A pained voice called out from the crowd. "Lady Quinn has returned!"

Murmurs passed through the horde, rippling away from the source until the wails and sobs turned to pleas and cries of hope.

Quinn ignored the pained voices and murmurs at first as she tended to a nearby Luminarus, but soon everyone was closing in around her in utter desperation, brushing and gripping her robes with their bloodied hands and burned limbs.

"Lady Quinn, help us! The city has been attacked!"

"We must return! We can help you!"

"Protect the Aurora Crystal!"

Quinn's breaths shortened, coming in shallow, rapid inhalations. She scanned the crowd. Her eyes locked on Dane, pleading and fearful. A lump rose in Dane's throat. She wanted to help them all; they were her people, her family. But there were too many to help.

And from the pain in her eyes, Quinn knew it too.

Quinn startled as a hand found her shoulder and turned her around. She let out a cry, then threw her arms around an elderly woman—the same elderly woman, Dane noticed, who had greeted Quinn on the night of the Festival of Light—Lady Rivelda—the one who Quinn had thanked for her robes. Her skin had been burned in several places, her clothes singed and limbs pocked with burns, but her face lit up at the sight of Quinn.

"Lady Rivelda," Quinn said, gripping the woman by the shoulders. Her voice cracked. She swallowed hard then said, "What happened? Was anyone outside the city? Is everyone accounted for?"

"I'm afraid I don't know, my dear. Dozens of men came with torches. Set the city ablaze. We barely managed to escape. But due to the ceremony, no Luminari were traveling when the fires started—everyone was safe in the city. We all fled at once, as quickly as we could." Her voice wavered. "Some have fallen already . . . their wounds were too great . . . but most survived."

"Lead the survivors to Mistveil," Quinn pleaded. "They want to help us, but they're wounded—they must find safety. The guards already know. Cayde is there; he can tend to the injured. Please . . . I can't help them all."

The woman stared lovingly into Quinn's eyes. "Of course, Lady Quinn. I will do what I can."

"Thank you." Quinn embraced the woman once more. She eyed the crowds again, eyes searching. "Have you seen my parents? Are they with you?"

A concerned look crossed Lady Rivelda's face. "I—I'm afraid not, my dear—"

Quinn was quick to notice the woman's discomfort. Her eyes darted to the plumes of smoke still rising over the city. "The Aurora Crystal . . . they need help—I need to—" She covered her mouth, shaking her head violently as a soft whimper escaped her lips.

Lady Rivelda reached a hand to Quinn's shoulder and, gazing with her into the blackened sky, said, "You've done enough for your people—there's nothing more you can do for them now." She nodded toward Evergleam, then turned Quinn's face to hers, "But there are some who do need your help. Mother bless you, dear child."

Quinn set off, weaving through the crowd of survivors toward the burning Evergleam. Dane and Sage followed closely behind, spurred faster by the horrific cacophony of desperate, miserable pleas from the wounded Luminari.

Thick clouds of ash and cinders rained from above, peppering the snow as they rounded the final turn onto the winding central street of Evergleam. Dane pulled the hem of his shirt over his mouth, careful not to choke on the floating debris suspended in the cloud of smoke around him.

Every house and market stand in sight was either engulfed in flame or had burned to the ground. Residual columns of blackened wood and stone lingered on either side of the street. Some houses still burned actively, lighting the surrounding sky with orange flames. Despite the horror and wreckage that lay before him, there were no screams in the city, no pained moans. Aside from the licking flames and the occasional settling of burning wood, there was nothing to be heard. The silence sent a chill down Dane's spine. He couldn't shake the feeling they weren't alone.

"Why's it so quiet?" Sage whispered to Quinn, voicing Dane's concerns as they slowly made their way down the street, stepping over occasional burnt rubble.

But Quinn wasn't listening. She stumbled forward as if living a nightmare. She pressed a hand to her trembling lips, slowly turning her head to survey the damage on either side, her shoulders slumped, her entire body deflated and defeated.

Quinn's pace quickened as they neared the market circle at the center of the city.

"Quinn, wait," Dane said amidst his growing unease, "something else is wrong, I think—"

A faint sound pulled at Dane's ears, coming from the castle ahead.

"Did you hear that?" he whispered. Sage shook her head beside him. Quinn turned to face him, staring blankly. Dane reached instinctively for his staff. Sage slowly brought a hand to the Willow Whip and Quinn's eyes began darting wildly around them.

Then the sound came again. There was no mistaking it this time. A faint, agonized moan that pierced the deafening silence hanging over the city.

Quinn reacted instantly and sprinted toward the castle.

Dane lurched forward, meaning to follow, but not before a hand clamped painfully on his shoulder. He wrenched himself free from his unseen attacker, losing his balance as he did so. He careened forward, nearly driving his shoulder into Sage's legs as he toppled to the ashen ground.

A wicked, rasping laugh rolled through the air.

Dane pushed himself to his feet and whirled to see three men standing on the street behind him, their menacing figures silhouetted by tall, searing flame. Two of them—one thin, his back hunched, the other stocky and brutish—were wreathed in the unmistakable metal armor Dane remembered so vividly: Ferron soldiers, similar to the ones they'd encountered on the ice bridge. But the third man . . .

Dane felt the color drain from his face. The small, beady eyes; the crooked, weathered nose; the sick, twisted grin—it was the same soldier Dane had fought before, the one who'd tried to kill him on the ice bridge, the one he'd let escape. *The metal man . . . .* He'd shown the man mercy before. And now he had to pay the price.

The metal man took a step toward Dane and unsheathed a gruesome metal blade, its jagged edges glinting in the ambient firelight. Dane flinched involuntarily, forcing the man's thin lips to curl upward.

"We meet again, *boy*," he spat. "But this time," he unleashed a low, resonating laugh, "you won't be escaping with your life."

"Dane! Sage!"

Dane risked a glance over his shoulder. Quinn had stopped at a curve in the street ahead, her face stricken with a new fear. She looked once to the three men, then to Sage before her gaze locked on Dane, her beautiful green eyes glistening with tears and pain.

Whatever you do, you must ensure her safety, no matter the cost . . .

Anger boiled from within as Dane stared at her. The pain she was feeling, the hurt in her eyes, the attack on her people, the loss of her home . . . all of it had been caused by the Ferrons, by the three men behind him.

The fear, uncertainty, and doubt that had been building inside him dissipated at once, replaced by a furious, empowering rage. He turned back and glared at the metal man and his soldiers. They would pay for Quinn's suffering.

"GO!" Dane shouted to Quinn, holding his gaze level with the attackers. "We'll handle this!"

After a moment's hesitation, he heard the fading sound of her boots on the stone street as she ran to the castle, leaving Dane and Sage alone with the three Ferron soldiers.

Dane spun his staff overhead and readied it as Sage wrenched the Willow Whip from her waist, cracking it through the air.

The men drew their own weapons. The metal man brandishing his blade, preparing to advance. His mouth parted, revealing his crooked yellowed teeth.

"How adorable," the metal man jeered. "The brave little hero thinks he can protect his friends yet again." He let out another rasping laugh. Then his features hardened. "Kill them. Kill them all."

He lumbered forward, his pace quickening with every step. The other two soldiers parted from his side, moving to flank Dane and Sage like predators closing in on their prey.

Then Dane felt Sage's firm grip on his shoulder.

"This time," she said, "we do it together."

"Together," he agreed.

The flanking soldiers charged. The brutish soldier attacked first, cleaving a downward blow at Sage. His swing was quick, but Sage was faster. She sidestepped as the soldier's blade swept through empty air. She wrapped the Willow Whip around the man's wrist and pulled. With a grunt, she twisted in place and threw the soldier into the metal man, sending them both crashing to the ground in a screech of metal and garbled cries of agony.

Dane looked away from his sister just as a sword cleaved toward him. He launched his staff upward at the last moment, intercepting the blow. The thin soldier stared at him, confusion muddling his features, his eyes flashing from Dane to the staff. Evidently, he, too, had underestimated its ability.

The corners of Dane's mouth curled upward. He seized the moment and deflected the soldier's sword, knocking the soldier's limp arms up to expose his chest, then gripped the staff and launched a two-handed swing.

The soldier recovered quickly, blocking Dane's strike with one arm as the staff smacked the soldier's metal bracing. Dane's arms shuddered at the impact. Before he could ready another swing, the soldier gripped both Dane's wrists, pulled his arms outward, and thrust his head into Dane's chest.

Pain burned in Dane's ribs as he reeled backward. He gasped for air, but the soldier was on him again, swinging wildly with furious, practiced blows.

Dane stumbled, narrowly deflecting each strike as the soldier pressed toward him. He tried to regain his footing, but the soldier's strikes were too strong.

The soldier heaved a crashing swing. Dane flung his arms up, waiting for the blade to hit the staff when the soldier swung wide, missing him completely. The next moment the soldier's metal boot plowed into his chest.

Air escaped him as Dane was lifted off his feet, crashing to the ground a moment later. The jarring impact shook the staff from his grasp, sending it spinning toward the burning house behind him. Black spots blossomed in his vision as he stared dazedly up at the scorched sky. In his periphery, he could see Sage leaping around the courtyard while fending off the other two soldiers.

The thin soldier's face appeared over him, his head cocked, his lips carved into a malicious grin. The soldier lifted his boot and pressed it into Dane's chest, pinning him where he lay, squeezing the air from his already burning lungs.

Dane stretched his arms outward, trying to reach for his staff, for anything he could use to defend himself, but his hands found nothing but embers and snow.

As the soldier bared down on him and raised his sword for one final strike, Dane was reminded of the stone warrior, poised to deliver the finishing blow. Only this time, Cayde wouldn't be there to protect him—

The sword!

Dane threw his hand over one shoulder and grasped the hilt of Cayde's glass sword as a wave of heat seared through his entire body. Powers or not, he couldn't let the Ferrons win, not when others were depending on him.

Just as the soldier's sword came swinging down, Dane wrenched the glass sword from its sheath and swept it through the air in rapid succession. Metal squealed as the tip of the soldier's sword sheared off and streaked past Dane's ear, embedding itself into the ground. When Dane swung again, there was a grisly squelch as the glass sword cut through the armor above the soldier's knee, slicing flesh.

The soldier shrieked and stumbled backward clutching his wound. Blood seeped through his clamped fingers, painting his armor in deep crimson. His face was frozen in shock, eyes darting from the blade tip wedged in the snow to the stunted remnants of his blade still clutched in his hand.

The soldier looked up. His eyes shone with a ferocious, maniacal glint. All semblance of pain was gone, replaced with murderous intent.

Dane pushed himself from the ground and lunged for his staff. The sword had bought him time, but he needed the staff to finish the soldier off.

The soldier howled and charged, seemingly blind to the pain in his knee, clutching his stunted sword like a knife. Dane's heart pounded, throat going dry in anticipation of his possible imminent demise. The soldier would kill him if he didn't kill the soldier first, but the thought of taking someone else's life, even someone as vile as the Ferron soldier, rattled Dane to the core.

But there was only one option if he hoped to survive.

The soldier barreled toward him, arm cocked, sword in hand, ready to strike. A seed of calm assurance sprouted in Dane's mind as the soldier neared. The scene reminded him of Cayde baiting the Chemocyte, moments before he'd emerged victorious. Dane grasped the staff with both hands.

The soldier stabbed with the stunted blade, aimed straight at Dane's chest. Dane twisted away at the last moment. Clutching his staff, he swung with all his strength and cracked the soldier on the back of the head.

The result was far more devastating than Dane had anticipated. The soldier, carried by his own momentum and howling in pain from Dane's strike, plowed head-first into the blackened doorframe of a burning house. It shattered and splintered upon impact, spraying wood and cinders as the soldier tumbled dazedly into the flame. The burning house groaned and cracked. The entire structure collapsed, crushing the soldier under its scorching beams.

Dane toppled backward as searing heat plumed from the entryway, unable to tear his gaze from the soldier's lifeless body.

One down . . . he thought shakily.

A shriek of agony forced Dane's gaze across the street.

The metal man, his nose now broken and dripping with blood, stood behind Sage, holding her at arm's length, both hands around her throat. The brutish soldier stalked toward her holding a long knife that gleamed orange with the fire's reflection.

Panic seized Dane. He thought of running to her, but he knew the knife would surely find its mark before he reached her.

Then he saw the Willow Whip still clutched in her hand. Without hesitation, he reached for the glass sword, clutched its hilt, and screamed, "SAGE! CATCH!"

He hurled the glass sword across the market circle. It spun end over end as it neared Sage. For a moment it looked as though she hadn't heard him; the sword was on course to land out of reach.

Then Sage screamed. She thrust her head back into the metal man's bloodied nose, stunning him momentarily. She kicked her feet off the ground, planted them firmly on the brutish soldier's chest, and pushed.

The soldier toppled backward as Sage wrenched herself free from the metal man's grasp and soared over his head. She landed expertly on her feet and flicked her whip hand to the sword still spinning toward her. The whip's finger-like tendrils sailed through the air and caught the sword's hilt. In the same continuous movement, Sage brought the whip and sword down on the dazed soldiers.

The blade whizzed through the air, narrowly missing the two soldiers as they leapt from its path, but Sage continued the onslaught with relentless abandon. The next blow caught the metal man across the chest. He reeled backward, howling in agony as red streaks doused his metal armor.

Sage turned her barrage to the remaining soldier. The soldier ducked at the last instant and the sword clattered against a stone support, tearing it free from the whip's grasp and tumbling out of view. She jerked the whip back and glared furiously at the soldier, her eyes blazing with hatred.

"You threaten *me*?" She lashed the whip at the soldier, catching him across the face. He groped for his sword but took a cautious step back.

"You threaten my *friends*?" She lashed the whip again with terrifying speed. The whip's tendrils clawed at the man's cheeks and he let out a whimper, his eyes suddenly clouding with fear.

"You threaten my *family*?!" Rage spilled from her mouth as she lashed a third time. The man shrieked in pain as the whip ripped at his nose and mouth. He abandoned his search for his sword and pedaled backward, face streaked with blood and petrified in fear.

"And for WHAT?!" Sage bellowed. She lashed again and the soldier threw his arms up in defense. The whip wrapped around his arms as Sage pulled the whip taut.

"ANSWER ME!" she screamed.

The brutish soldier said nothing, mute with fear.

Then the Willow Whip transformed. Dane watched in stunned silence as its green surface festered and bubbled, turning a sickly purple. Barbed thorns sprouted from its length, creeping away from Sage's grasp until coiling around the soldier's arms.

Sage jerked the whip back. The pale-faced soldier let out a blood curdling shriek as the thorns tightened around his arms, carved through his armor and ate into his flesh. Sage wrenched the whip harder and the thorns tore through the soldier's forearms. The barbed whip slithered back to Sage's side as two severed hands dropped to the ground, sizzling with decaying flesh.

The soldier lifted his stumped limbs, his eyes bulging from their sockets. As if trying to escape the horror, he staggered away from Sage and the gruesome sight before him, unaware of what lay behind. The soldier's agonized screams extinguished as he tumbled into the burning house behind him, his body igniting with flame.

Two down . . . Dane gulped. Then he remembered the metal man. He whirled around, scanning the street, expecting the final soldier to strike at any moment. But there was no trace of him; he'd escaped again.

Not this time, Dane thought. *I won't let you get away and cause more pain.*

Sage's trembling voice stopped him before he could take another step.

"I—I—what have I done?" she whimpered. She dropped the whip and clasped her hands to her mouth. "I—I *killed* someone."

"He would've done the same to you," Dane tried to assure her, gripping her shaking shoulders. "And it was the fire that killed him. You did what you had to do."

She looked at him, and he was surprised to see her eyes brimming with tears. "Don't you see? I *wanted* to kill him. I was so . . . so . . . *angry.* I never thought that I could take—that I—" She cupped her face in her shaking palms.

Dane found no words, so he pulled her to him. She threw her arms around him and sobbed into his shoulder. They stood for a moment, then Dane held his sister at arm's length.

"We have to find Quinn. She might need our help."

Sage took a deep breath, wiped her eyes, and nodded in understanding.

Dane gathered his staff and sheathed Cayde's sword. Sage coiled her whip, which had transformed back to its usual thornless green, around her waist.

Then an agonizing cry ripped through the air.

Dane and Sage sprinted toward Evergleam castle.

Despite the heat and smoke radiating over the city, cold sweat beaded on Dane's brow when he saw the castle gates. Though untouched by the flames that had raged through the rest of the city, the magnificent oak doors leading into the Aurora Temple clung delicately to their hinges, appearing to have been blasted open from the inside.

He bit back his fear and rushed into the temple, expecting to see Avon waiting for him, hands blazing with his cosmic flare, Quinn heaped on the ground at his side.

But Avon wasn't there.

Dane nearly breathed a sigh of relief, but his breath caught in his throat. Quinn knelt beside two figures at the end of the vast hall, surrounded by thousands of tiny crystalline shards that peppered the ground where the Aurora Crystal used to be.

"No . . ." he muttered under his breath. "It can't be . . ."

His gaze fell to Quinn and the two figures beside her. One was motionless, her body framed by the crystalline remnants, a dark red stain marring her elegant white robes. Quinn cradled the other's head in her lap, both hands clasped to his cheeks. His chest rose and fell in time with his labored breaths. His hands—gleaming and crimson—covered a dark wound in his stomach.

Dane's staff slipped from his hands and clattered to the floor as he stumbled toward Quinn and her parents.

"I—I can try to heal him. I—" started Sage, her lips trembling, but Dane shook his head. He didn't need a closer inspection to know that Elder Yarrin was beyond healing. Dane clenched his jaw as he watched Quinn, forcing back tears of his own.

"Father," Quinn sobbed, staring into Elder Yarrin's clouding eyes. She fumbled for his hand, but his hand slipped from her grasp. "Father, please don't go."

"They look to you now, Quinn," Elder Yarrin said, almost too softly to comprehend as blood trickled from his mouth. Dane could see the Elder's eyes trying to focus on his daughter, but his gaze was cloudy, his life fleeting. "Our people . . . they look to you now . . . they always have . . . you must protect them . . . you are their guiding light."

"Please, Father . . ." Quinn's shoulders shook violently. "Don't talk like that. You'll be j-just fine." Her gaze strayed to her mother's lifeless form and she choked down another sob. "Please don't leave me . . . I-I can't do this without you."

The corners of Elder Yarrin's lips curled, ruffling the edges of his beard. He raised his head ever so slightly, gazing into her eyes with blissful, composed serenity. He made a reaching gesture with his fingers and Quinn clutched his hand in hers and pressed it to her cheek, leaning into his touch.

"We are so proud of you, Quinn." Tears pooled in the Elder's misty gaze, making Quinn whimper. "Of all the wonders in our world . . . it was always you . . . who brought me the greatest joy. You are . . . my brightest star . . ."

Elder Yarrin's eyes glassed over, and one final breath escaped him.

"Father!" Quinn cried, shaking his limp hand. "*Father! FATHER!*"

The Elder's hand slipped from her grasp and fell to the floor.

Quinn screamed at the ceiling, her voice tortured with pain. She clutched at her sides, doubled over, and collapsed into tears.

Dane could only stand there, useless, as her cries echoed off the walls of the desecrated temple. It had all happened so fast—he couldn't believe what he was seeing. He had talked to Elder Yarrin—been so graciously welcomed by Quinn's mother, Zena—only days before. Elder Yarrin had given him purpose when he had none, direction when he'd needed it most.

And now he was gone.

Quinn's tears subsided. Sage knelt beside her and placed a hand on her shoulder. "Quinn, I—I'm so sorry."

Quinn sniffled and rose weakly to her feet. She wiped her father's blood from her cheek and stared blankly at the bodies of her parents, her green eyes clouded and vacant.

"They didn't stand a chance," she said flatly, her voice barely more than a whisper. "Avon was already gone by the time we arrived. He knew we'd come back if we saw the flames. He wanted us out of the city."

Dane's brows knit together. "What—do you mean Avon planned this? It was all a set-up? A trap?"

She looked once more at her parents' bodies and the shattered remains of the Aurora Crystal. Dane could see the struggle in her movements, as if she was waging an internal war, her wish to grieve overcome by her duty to continue their mission.

Finally she turned her gaze to Dane.

"Avon's already in Mistveil, I'm sure of it," she muttered, "we have to stop him before he causes more pain. We have to save Mistveil—and my people—from this same fate." She stared past the castle gates, searching the mountainous horizon. "But it might already be too late."

CHAPTER 19

CLEANSING WATERS

Adrenaline coursed through Dane's body as he sprinted with Quinn and Sage away from the dying embers of Evergleam. He could no longer feel his legs, only ran as fast as he could. In what felt like the blink of an eye, they'd reached the lakeside path.

Dane relaxed slightly as Mistveil came into view. Much to his relief, the sky above the city was still a cloudy blue, but the relief was soon swept away, replaced by a renewed fear as the sounds of distant screams split the air.

Avon . . . his attack has begun.

They raced onward until the East Bridge was in sight. Dane stared hard for a moment before an eerie tingling sensation gripped his skin. There were no guards patrolling the outskirts of the city like before. The bridge was completely deserted. There was no one outside the city walls. And the city gates—

Quinn, noticing the same, crouched behind a nearby bush, observing the entrance to Mistveil with concern.

"They've closed the gates," Dane said. He crouched beside Quinn and Sage. "But why? Aren't the gates supposed to remain open at all times?"

"I don't know," said Quinn, her voice tainted with lingering pain as another round of screams echoed across the sky. "But we have to find another way in. We have to help my people."

"Why don't we try to open them?" Sage said. "What if—"

"No. It has to be Avon," Quinn said. "He's barred the gates and locked them from the inside! They're trapped in there, they're trapped—" Her voice caught in her throat and a small whimper escaped her lips.

Sage held Quinn by the shoulders and looked deeply into her eyes. "It's all right, we'll find a way to save them." She squeezed Quinn's shoulders tighter. Tears blossomed in Quinn's blood-shot eyes. "I'm so sorry . . . for everything . . . but we'll save them. We just have to think of another way—"

"There's no time, Sage. Cayde—he'll be helping some as we speak. But the Luminari—they're in pain. I can't lose them too. I can't. We *have* to save them." Quinn's voice went flat. "It's what my parents would have wanted . . ." Though her face and features had turned hard and grim, Dane could still see the grief swimming in her eyes.

Sage motioned toward the bridge. "So we don't enter through the gates. What are our other options? There has to be another way inside."

Quinn mumbled to herself, staring fixedly at the gate. Her eyes darted wildly, scouring the landscape before them, the fingers of one hand tugging at her fraying hair. Finally, her jaw clenched, her voice frantic and panicked, she said, "No, no, no! We're running out of *time!*"

Dane turned his gaze back to the eerie outskirts. From their crouched position, he could see two of the Mistveil islands, each suspended by geysers erupting from the lake's surface. Suddenly he recalled something Leon had said while passing the small fountain on his island. *If you could jump in and swim down,* Leon had said, *then you'd eventually be swimming in the lake.*

The comment had seemed strange and insignificant at the time—like most of Leon's ramblings—but now, and only now, Dane realized the usefulness of Leon's remark.

It gave him an idea—a crazy idea—but it just might work.

Dane whirled to face Quinn and Sage and said, "Remember the fountain we passed—the day we walked to Leon's house? He said the water there was the same water coming from the lake, from the geyser holding up the island."

"What's that have to do with anything?" Sage said shortly.

"He said it was impossible to swim down the geyser, that the current was far too strong." Dane met each of their questioning stares with a level gaze, letting his idea sink in. "But what if we didn't want to go down?"

Quinn stared at him for a long moment. Then her eyes widened in realization.

"You're not suggesting we . . . swim *up* the geyser, are you?"

He nodded.

"But I—it's never been done! How do you know that'll even work?"

"I don't, but there's only one way to find out. And it's not like we have any other options . . ."

Quinn opened her mouth in retort but produced no words. She nodded weakly, swallowing hard.

"How do we do this?" Sage said. "And if this plan miraculously works and we don't end up dead, what do we do once inside the city walls?"

"Once inside . . . I don't know," Dane admitted. "But getting into the city . . ." He pointed to the island floating between the East Bridge and the waterfall at the edge of the lake. A series of rocks jutted from the water, extending from the rocky shoreline toward the island's supporting geyser. "We'll follow those rocks as far out as we can. Then we'll be close enough before we jump. From there, well . . . we hold our breath and let the geyser's current pull us in."

Sage eyed him skeptically. "And you think *that* is going to work?"

Before Dane could respond, Quinn, her voice flat and devoid of emotion, said, "There's no other choice."

She rose and ran toward the shoreline, Dane and Sage following close behind. As they passed the bridge, Dane thought he felt the sinister gaze of a Ferron soldier boring into him. The hairs on the back of his neck stood on end as he awaited a distant shout alerting their position.

To his relief, their presence went unnoticed as they approached the shoreline.

Dane gingerly maneuvered ahead of Quinn and Sage, leading the way as he leapt from rock to rock, the geyser's roar growing louder with every jump.

When he could go no further, Dane looked down into the minor swells crashing around his feet, the frothing white water masking the deep blue abyss that lurked beneath.

Carefully, he looked to Sage and Quinn on the rock behind him. Sage was craning her neck forward, trying to glimpse the sweeping current below the surface. She swallowed, her face locking in determination. She tightened the straps of her pack and gave the Willow Whip a swift tug about her waist. Quinn wrapped her orb tightly in its sling across her shoulder and fastened the straps of her own pack.

Reminded of his own spare belongings, Dane pulled taut on his own straps, securing his staff. He fastened Cayde's sword and its sheath so tightly it nearly constricted his breathing. Despite the urge to loosen it, Dane willed his hands to his sides. The sword was Cayde's gift to him; it had helped him when he needed it most. He had every intention of returning it to its rightful owner.

He locked his gaze on Quinn. Pain and grief still ran rampant behind her glassy eyes.

A renewed vigor sparked inside him. Her pain would only deepen if they failed to save her people, to stop Avon. She had already lost her parents, her home. And from the twisting ache in his heart, Dane didn't think he could bear to see her in any more pain. They had to succeed.

He glanced at Quinn and Sage, nodding decisively to pass on as much courage as he could muster. He turned and faced the geyser. He slowed his breaths, trying not to focus on his pounding heartbeat. His plan was insane. There was no way it could possibly work as he intended.

But it has to work . . .

Dane sucked in a deep breath, swung his arms back, and dove headfirst into the lake.

The cold hit him like a tangle of icy thorns, stinging every surface of his skin. He suppressed the urge to cry out in surprise. Once the sensation of the frigid water subsided, he realized he was already being pulled in by the geyser's current, toward the geyser itself.

The foolishness of his ludicrous plan finally came to fruition. What if the geyser's stream didn't flow directly upward? What if they were caught on the edge of the geyser, only to be carried into the island's rock foundation?

He vaguely heard Quinn and Sage dive in behind him. He couldn't bring himself to think about what would happen to them if his plan failed.

The current pulled him further down before lurching his body upward, sending him into the geyser. The world spun around him, distorted by the thick veil of surrounding water as he twisted higher. His pulse throbbed in his head like claps of thunder. His lungs burned. His stomach convulsed, searing his insides as he forced down the urge to gasp for air. He could feel his consciousness waning, blackness closing around his vision as he stared up as a small bead of light took form overhead.

His vision tunneled further—the light growing closer with every passing instant—until finally he was thrown into fresh air. He sucked in a huge, gasping breath and collapsed into a shallow pool.

The crisp air seared his throat and lungs as Dane dragged his body from the pool and dropped in a heap on the stone street of the island. He lay on his back, staring into the misty sky, the cloudiness in his vision dissipating.

He allowed himself a grin. *We made it . . . the plan worked.*

He forced himself up as Sage erupted from the pool. Soaking wet and showing no signs of exhaustion, she dragged a wincing Quinn from the water. Quinn's knee was bruised and swollen, faint traces of purple blotching her skin. A thin trickle of blood ran down her leg, disappearing into her sopping boot.

Quinn doubled over and wretched a lungful of water as Sage helped her to her feet.

"We made it," Quinn gasped, bracing her hands on her knees.

Sage stared at Quinn's knee with concern. "What happened?"

"I must've hit the rock . . . near the end," she managed between rasping breaths.

"I can heal it if—"

Quinn shook her head vehemently. "There's no time." She staggered upright and made for the center island, grunting in pain every other step. Her eyes burned with intensity. "We have to save them."

She clenched her jaw and hobbled forward, her pace quickening until she was running down the street. Dane set off after her as another round of screams pierced the air.

Quinn stopped once they crossed the water bridge connecting to the central island, peering cautiously at the street ahead. After a moment, she gestured over her shoulder and made for the shadows of the closest building.

"What are you doing?" Sage questioned as she pressed herself beside Quinn.

Quinn held a finger to her lips. "Something doesn't feel right." She whispered. "Where are the guards?" She stole another glance at the deserted street. A thick layer of mist had settled over the city, cloaking the ends of the street in fog, filling the air with an eerie silence.

Dane shuddered. It reminded him of the grove of mist, just before he'd seen the mangled body of Varic the Abuser. He swallowed hard.

"I don't see anyone," he whispered.

No sooner had the words left his mouth when two shapes took form in the distance, heading in their direction. Dane watched from the cover of shadow until two men, each wearing the distinct leather armor of the Mistveil guard, came into view.

"Are you sure that's everyone? We can't have them escaping this time," one voice said.

"I told you, we've found them all. The city is secure," said the other.

As they spoke, an unwelcome chill coursed through Dane's body. The men *looked* like Mistveil guards, but there was something off about them—

"They're just guards," Sage said, sounding relieved. "Did they catch Avon and the Ferrons? Maybe they know what is going on—"

Before she could take another step, Quinn flung her arm across Sage's chest, pinning her against the wall.

"Wait," Quinn mouthed, holding her gaze on the guards. "Listen."

The second voice, now sterner, continued, "You heard what he said. The Luminari aren't a populous people. I assure you they're all there. Everything is going according to plan."

"Fine . . . let's just find the others and get out of here, and fast. I bet he's already executing it as we speak."

The guards continued down the street and disappeared from view.

Inexplicably, Quinn, her body rigid and shaking, took a step forward, as if to follow the guards. Dane grabbed her shoulder before she could. She slapped his hand away and whirled to face him.

Dane took an involuntary step away from her. All traces of pain, loss, and grief in her eyes had shattered, leaving only boiling, blinding anger. She leveled her murderous gaze on him, her jaw quaking beneath the strain of her clenched teeth.

"They. Have. My. People," she seethed, her cheeks flushing bright red. Her entire body was tensed, every muscle strained, as if it took all she had to stop from screaming with rage. "We have to *stop* them!"

"I know," Dane said. "But going after those gua—" He cut himself short, knowing very well the men they'd seen couldn't have been real Mistveil guards. He amended, "Going after them now won't do anything. There are bound to be more. We have to find another way."

Quinn released several long torrents of air through her nose, her face contorting all the while, until the rage building inside her seemed to ebb—though only slightly.

"Fine," she said tersely. "But standing here isn't helping anyone. We have to keep moving."

Without another word, she turned, heading down a street that led to the Grand Archive. Sage started to follow, but stopped suddenly, peering into the mist. She grabbed Quinn's sleeve and pulled her back behind cover.

"What are you—"

"There's another guard coming," Sage hissed.

Not a moment later, another form took shape in the mist. It appeared to be another guard, alone, from what Dane could tell, wearing the standard Mistveil uniform. But something about him looked out of place. He was far scrawnier than any other guard Dane had seen, his leather straps and pads clinging loosely to his thin body. He walked backward, head swiveling in all directions, stumbling as he went. If Dane had to guess, the guard looked afraid, as if he was expecting someone—or something—to leap out at him at any moment.

Then something did.

Sage sprung from the cover of shadow the instant the guard passed into view. She grabbed both his shoulders, pulled the guard into the shadows, and pinned him against the wall.

The guard gasped and let out a small whimper as his helmet struck the cold stone.

"Please don't hurt me! I'll do whatever you need! I just want to live! I—"

Sage shook the guard's shoulders violently and slapped him across the face.

"Pull it together, Leon! It's us!" she hissed. She released him and he collapsed to the ground. He wheezed heavily, then stared up at Sage with wide, twinkling eyes.

"You . . . you came for me!" he cooed as he removed his guard helmet, uncaging his black tangle of hair. "I thought I was done for, but . . . you came back for me!"

"Save it, Dewdrop. What's going on here?" Sage demanded. She eyed his crumpled form and added, "And *why* are you wearing a guard uniform?"

Leon stared blankly into the distance. "They—they were in the city," he said mistily. "Before you even left, they were here—they were among us. Evergleam was just a diversion. He wanted you—"

"Evergleam was *not* a diversion," Quinn said, lowering her face to Leon's, anger pooling in her voice. "The Aurora Crystal is *gone*, and my parents are—" she paused and pressed a fist to her mouth, eyes closed and jaw trembling. She let out a shuddering breath. "They're gone too."

"So he attacked both cities one after the other. But this attack . . . it was *planned*."

"Get to the point," Sage said. "What are you trying to say?"

"The Ferron soldiers—I don't know how, but they were posing as Mistveil guards—must have been for several days now. Once you left for Evergleam and all the Luminari came here for shelter, the guards—err, the Ferrons—sealed the gates and corralled everyone—Aquadorians, Luminari . . . *everyone*—in front of the Archive. No one was hurt—not badly, at least, as far as I could tell—but I'll bet that was part of Avon's plan so no one could interfere."

"Avon, he—he planned this too? He's here now?" Dane asked.

"Who else could plan something so vile?" Leon retorted. "If he *is* trying to destroy all the energy wells, and if he failed to destroy the Elderwood because of *your* intervention," he waved an accusatory finger between Dane, Sage, and Quinn, "maybe he thought he needed more . . . *drastic* measures . . . to ensure you couldn't intervene this time."

"How do you know so much about this?" Sage said, eyeing him skeptically.

"Anyone with a brain could've figured that out—well, that and the knowledge that Avon is trying to destroy the energy wells . . ." he let out a nervous giggle then his face went slack, turning pale. "You would have come to the same conclusions if you saw what they did." His eyes glassed over as if replaying the memory. "Luminari poured into the city. All bloodied, injured, screaming in pain—" he shuddered, gripping his shoulders "—that's when the mist rolled in. Couldn't see a thing. Then the screaming started. Guards started pushing everyone deeper into the city, threatening them with swords—*metal* swords. It all happened so fast and I—I thought I was going to die. There were dead guards scattered across the city—the *real* guards. When I found one I—I didn't know what to do so I put on his uniform and—" His bulging, euphoric eyes lifted from the ground and looked directly at Sage. "Then *you* came . . . you came back for me . . . to *save* me." He walked forward on his knees, hands outstretched, reaching for Sage's.

Sage bit her lip, failing to mask her subtle amusement at Leon's gesture, and swatted his hands away. "You can thank me later. Right now, we have bigger problems."

Quinn bent down until her face was level with Leon's. "Where did they take them?" she demanded. "Where did the Ferrons take my people?"

"The Grand Archive, as I said. But there's something else you should—"

"There's no time."

"But—"

"We have to go!" Quinn strode down the street with renewed vigor, heading in the direction of the Grand Archive.

Leon sputtered then blurted, "He went after Avon!"

Quinn froze.

"Who?" Dane asked, confused by the sudden urgency in Leon's voice.

Leon looked frantically to Dane, then to Sage. His gaze finally settled on Quinn. Her entire body was limp. Her limbs trembled. She looked on the brink of collapse.

"Just before I found you," Leon said, gulping loudly, "I heard the guards say Avon was on his way to destroy the Mystic Fountain—I was hiding with him at the time—but he ran off after Avon. I tried calling out to him—to tell him to wait for you to come back so he wouldn't have to fight Avon alone, but—"

"Leon, what are you talking about?" Dane urged. "Who went after Avon?"

No sooner had the words left his mouth when the weight of his realization crushed him like the stone warrior's foot. Who else would go after Avon alone? Who else would do whatever it took to protect a city of innocent people? Who else would risk everything he had to protect the ones he loved?

And when Leon finally spoke, his single word cleaved through the final threads of Quinn's withered emotions like the glass sword through the Chemocyte.

Cayde.

Quinn broke into a wild sprint. She tore down the street that bordered the city wall, heading toward the Mystic Fountain.

"Wait!" Leon called from behind, trying to shrug out of his guard uniform. "I don't think—"

His voice was lost as more screams cut through the air, louder than ever. A nauseating, white-orange glow was seeping into the mist, radiating and pulsing from the street ahead. Dane had seen the same glow before, inside the Elderwood the night Vitalor was attacked—Avon's cosmic flare.

He propelled his body forward. He could now see the gap in the city wall, the overlook where Leon had detailed his plan about the private collection. They were close to the Mystic Fountain. They hadn't heard any more excruciating screams. There was still time—

Then Cayde's ragged, torturous voice tore through the air.

"COWARD!"

Quinn burst from the street, skidding to a halt near the overlook railing, and whirled in the direction of the Mystic Fountain.

Dane couldn't see the Fountain yet, but the look on Quinn's face was all he needed to fathom the horror of what was unfolding before her.

The emotional barricade she'd summoned after the loss of her parents shattered before Dane's eyes. She cupped her trembling hands to her mouth. Her eyes bulged, flooding with fresh tears, staring fixedly ahead. She shook her head violently, her dark hair fanning around her, reflecting the haunting orange glow that shone just out of Dane's view.

Dane tried to swallow, but his throat was parched. Quinn looked ready to run toward the Fountain, toward Avon's flare, but she did nothing, said nothing. She stood rooted in place near the railing, continuing shaking her head as if doing so would make it all go away.

When Dane finally reached her side and stared at the Fountain, he saw why.

A miniature pulsating maw of white energy hovered above the base of the Fountain. Water sizzled and frothed as it collided with the searing sphere, spraying steaming droplets of molten energy in all directions. It pulsed angrily, orange arcs of heat lashing outward, threatening to claim the streets with its flame. But it seemed to be restrained, trapped in its dwarfed state, unable to wreak its full havoc.

Dane's gaze slowly drifted away from the cosmic flare as Sage and Leon pulled up beside him. Avon was nowhere to be seen, but another figure stood at the edge of the pool from which the Fountain erupted, his arms outstretched, his entire body straining with fatigue and concentration.

Cayde.

Every one of his limbs was shaking to the point of collapse. Dark, jagged lines rippled up his arms and into his sleeves, making his skin look like sunbaked earth—cracked, desiccated, pale, and lifeless.

Horrific realization seized Dane as his gaze flitted between the cosmic flare and his Gravitus protector. Cayde was using his power to control the flare, conjuring a gravity well to suppress it and prevent it from destroying the Fountain. But the cracks on his arms . . . Cayde was overexerting his power, using too much energy to contain it. If he let go, the flare would engulf the Fountain and everything around it. But if Cayde held on, overexerting his energy . . .

He can't do this alone, Dane realized. *He'll die.*

The flare pulsed again and expelled a massive arc of searing energy that ripped through the air, its power seeming to multiply with each passing instant. Cayde let out another tormented cry. His entire body writhed under the strain, but he refused to falter, fighting against his failing limbs to keep the deadly flare at bay.

Dane frantically searched his mind, trying to think of some way—any way—in which both Cayde and the Mystic Fountain could be saved. But he could think of nothing—no way to save them both.

Then Dane's heart plummeted. There was only one choice if the Fountain was to be saved, and Cayde had already chosen.

Quinn suddenly whimpered beside him. She seemed to have reached the same conclusion.

"Cayde?" she said hoarsely, her tears flowing freely. "No, Cayde, not you too . . ." She held her gaze on him, wincing every time he cried out in pain.

She took a step toward him, her arms extended as if to pull him away from harm and never let go.

Dane sought her arm before she was out of reach, gripping it tightly. "Quinn, no, he—"

But she continued forward, pulling against him. Her voice rose, cracking with unbridled fear as she called his name once more.

This time, her words found their mark.

As if snapped from a trance, Cayde broke his gaze from the cosmic flare and twisted his head toward her.

Dane's hand nearly slipped from Quinn's arm at the sight of him. His eyes were streaked with lines of red. His jaw was clenched so tight his veins looked as if they'd burst from his skin. At the nape of his neck, most horrifying of all, were unmistakable dark cracks carved into his skin, slowly creeping toward his face.

It's too late. Dane thought gravely, trying to force down the lump in his throat. *He's used too much power to contain Avon's flare. He's already accepted his fate.*

Cayde looked around wildly, as if preparing for another of Avon's attacks. Then he saw Quinn. The anger, torment, and rage in his eyes instantly vanished. His face went slack and his pained grimace turned to an expression of utter devastation. He stared, his mouth parted, shaking his head as if his worst fears had just been realized, begging Quinn to stay away.

"CAYDE!" she shrieked again. She wrenched her arm free and lurched toward him, but Dane slung his arm around her waist, pulling her back to the railing. She struggled and screamed but Dane only squeezed harder; it was all he could do to stop himself from releasing her, letting her run to Cayde's aid, desperately hoping she'd find a way to save him. But even Dane knew it was too late.

Cayde shook his head more fervently as she screamed. Tears streaming down his face. The pulsating maw of cosmic energy unleashed another arcing flame, larger and brighter than before, narrowly avoided Cayde's body.

"PLEASE! COME BACK!" Quinn sobbed, her torturous wails like knives in Dane's heart. "CAYDE! DON'T LEAVE ME!"

Then Cayde's lips parted and he mouthed something that went unheard over the rising chaos. Though Dane couldn't hear Cayde's voice, could only see his lips mouth the simple words, the pain in Cayde's eyes was enough to burn this moment into Dane's memory—the last words Cayde would ever speak.

Forgive me . . .

Quinn screamed in agony.

"NOOOOOOOOOOOOOOOOOOO!!!"

Cayde spun in place, abandoning all efforts to hinder the cosmic flare, and thrust his open palms at Dane and the others. Dane felt his feet lift from the ground. His body lurched away from the Fountain, pulled by the unseen force of Cayde's gravity well.

As Dane and the others sailed over the railing—nothing but the open water of Mistveil Lake beckoning far below—Dane stole one final glance at his infallible protector.

Cayde collapsed to his knees, his arms falling limp at his sides. The cosmic flare erupting behind him, but his gaze remained solely on Quinn, only faltering as a tendril of cosmic energy sprung forth, sizzled through the air, and tore through Cayde's body.

Then, Dane fell.

As the wind whipped past his face and hair, Dane could only watch in stunned horror as his mind replayed Cayde's final breaths. He became vaguely aware that the island of Mistveil dangled tantalizingly out of reach, separating further and further from him as he plummeted toward the lake. But he didn't care. He wished he was back in Leon's house, planning the next steps to stop Avon and the Ferrons, with Quinn, Sage, and Cayde standing beside him. Everything since—the fires in Evergleam, the death of Quinn's parents, Cayde's fatal sacrifice—all of it felt like a never-ending nightmare.

To Dane's absolute horror, the nightmare had only begun.

A thunderous, earthy moan snapped him from his stupor. A haunting orange glow radiated across the misty sky. Massive slabs of rock sheared from Mistveil's foundation, plunging toward the lake. Thousands of terrified screams filled the air as people fell with the city, utterly defenseless amongst the cacophony of sudden chaos. The sound echoed through Dane's mind for what felt like a lifetime, their dying pleas forever unheard, crying out for help that would never come.

Then the flare exploded. A flash of light and heat engulfed the entire crumbling remnants of Mistveil, eviscerating everything caught in its fatal clutches, silencing every last scream.

A stinging pain surged across Dane's skin as he finally hit the water.

He sank for a moment, hoping he would wake from this nightmare, then forced his way to the surface and gasped for air. Enormous chunks of the city's foundation fell all around him; the shockwave generated by the explosion had sent debris in all directions, barraging each of the four surrounding islands as they, too, crumbled out of existence.

Dane looked up just as an enormous swell came crashing down on him and pulled his body under. As he struggled to regain his bearings amidst the ravenous vortex, he caught glimpse of a body sinking in the water, limp and lifeless. His heart sank like the rocks crashing down from above.

Quinn!

Dane fought against his deprived lungs and swam deeper, narrowly evading falling debris sinking into the lake's depths all around him. The water's pressure squeezed his head and chest, but he kept swimming, deeper and deeper, replaying Cayde's final words to him. *Promise me you'll protect her, Dane . . . . Keep her safe . . . . Quinn is the key . . . .* She was sinking faster, fading into the murky depths. He pushed himself to keep going.

I promise, Cayde.

On the brink of unconsciousness, Dane gave a final kick and thrust one arm blindly forward, his outstretched fingers closing around Quinn's wrist. He tugged her close, tucking one arm around her chest, and pulled her from the lake's clutches.

Air flooded his burning lungs as he broke the surface. He pulled Quinn up beside him, tearing up with relief as she let out a ragged, shallow breath. He hoisted her body up and cradled her head as he examined her for injuries. Her eyes remained closed, and there was a seeping bloody gash over her left eye, but she was alive—wounded and dabbling into unconsciousness, but alive.

"Dane!"

Sage's voice suddenly rose above the crashing waves. Dane twisted his body, treading in place as he tried to find her, but swelling waves obscured his view and pushed him farther from where Mistveil had been, toward the lake's edge.

"Dane!" her voice came again, but it was softer this time, drowned by the steadily growing undertone of cascading water.

"SAGE!" he called back. He waited, craning his neck in a futile attempt to search over the swells. She was nowhere to be seen. He called out again, but he couldn't hear the sound of his own voice over the crashing water, still growing louder as his body drifted further. Suddenly, he realized what the growing sound was, the horror that awaited him at the edge of Mistveil Lake.

Waterfall...

Panic seized Dane's entire body. He tried to swim away, but the current was too strong. His limbs felt useless and weak—he could barely keep Quinn's head above the surface, let alone his own—and the strength of the current was overpowering, its power doubling as they neared the roaring cascade of water.

Then, all at once, the water was gone, replaced by frigid, misty air whipping across his face as they tumbled over the edge of the waterfall.

The world slowed as they fell. Mistveil Lake disappeared from view. The air grew thick with the salty scent of the sea. Debris and shattered remnants of demolished buildings cascaded down beside him, serving as a perpetual reminder of the eviscerated Mistveil as they fell further and further into the unknown.

In fear of losing what little sanity still remained, Dane focused on his promise to Cayde. He clutched Quinn's limp body as tightly as he could, hugging her with what little strength he had left.

No more failures, he thought, replaying Cayde's final words to him. *Not again, Cayde ... I won't fail you again.*

Excruciating pain lanced down Dane's back as he hit the water. The pain was unlike any he'd ever felt, like he'd just been crushed beneath a boulder. Everything ached. Black spots blinded his vision. He could feel his body sinking yet again, Quinn's weight pressing him under despite his best efforts to stay afloat. He tried to move his legs and one free arm, urging his utterly spent limbs, but his strength was gone. His legs felt like stone, dragging him down to the seafloor.

In a final, desperate attempt, he reached up with his free hand. He could vaguely see debris floating overhead, bobbing on the surface; if he could only grab hold of something large enough, something that wouldn't sink under his and Quinn's weight, maybe they could escape their watery graves.

Inexplicably, his fingers sprouted from the water and closed on a solid surface. With renewed vigor, Dane pulled himself up. He'd grabbed hold of a large chunk of wood—the remnants of a bookshelf—wide and sturdy enough to support them both.

With a burst of energy that must have come from the Mother herself, Dane heaved Quinn's body out of the water and onto the shelf. He eased himself beside her, careful not to tip the makeshift raft. For a moment it looked as though they were too heavy, that the shelf would sink under their weight. He watched as water lapped over the robust wood, but the shelf held firm, bobbing gently on the surface.

Dane collapsed on his back, staring up breathlessly as black spots returned to his vision, clouding the sickening gray sky piece by piece. He closed his eyes as exhaustion claimed him, trying to block the recent horrors from running rampant through every corner of his mind. Then he slipped into unconsciousness.

CHAPTER 20

FADING LIGHT

Sunlight streaked down as Dane's eyelids fluttered open.

His head still swayed like the tossing waves, but his body was on firm, unmoving ground. Waves lapped at his feet and legs. He lifted his cheek from the coarse, grainy surface beneath and looked around. Sand—thick, rocky granules—stretched as far as he could see.

He pressed his palms into the sand and lifted himself onto hands and knees. His head spun, his mouth tasted of salt, his back throbbed with stinging pain, and his clothes were soaked from the seawater. But he was alive—somehow, he and Quinn had survived.

Quinn.

His mind twisted in panic. The last he'd seen of her, she'd been unconscious by his side on their makeshift raft.

Despite his weak and weary limbs, Dane forced himself upright. His whole body swayed and he pressed a hand to his head to stop the dizziness before scouring the shore. The bookshelf had run aground nearby, but Quinn no longer lay on its surface. His panic turned to dread, fearing the worst.

She couldn't have fallen off . . . she was right next to me, she couldn't have—

He glanced to his right and breathed an audible sigh of relief. Quinn knelt on the shore a short distance away, her dark hair swaying in the warm sea breeze. For now, she was safe.

An eerie silence settled over him, making his skin prickle as he searched the landscape. They'd washed up on a beach—possibly on an island—but there was no vegetation, no trees in sight, no sign of life. Treacherous black crags towered overhead not far from the desolate shore, and even those were barren, their rock surfaces teeming with shadow and mystery.

Dane stumbled again and realized his pack and Cayde's sword were still fastened tight on his back. Grimacing, he released the straps and dropped the waterlogged pack and sword to the sand before staring more intently at the foreboding island.

Despite the lack of life, he couldn't help feeling that he and Quinn weren't alone. It was as if the island—if they *were* on an island—had been devoid of life for decades, possibly even centuries. Its shores and black cliffs seemed to be hiding something, shrouding it from—

Dane's breath froze in his throat. The dreadful, yet painstakingly clear realization hit him like a physical blow. All the stories came flooding back from the deep recesses of his mind: the black cliffs, the absence of life, the horror of eternal darkness— he'd heard of it all before, the tales, the myths, the legends.

It wasn't just any island they'd washed up on . . . it was the Shrouded Isle.

He stared, rooted in place, gaping at the black cliffs, as if tearing his gaze away would unleash whatever evil lived within. He tried to swallow, to call out to Quinn, but his breaths had become shallow and ragged. He willed his feet to move, stumbling across the shore to where she was kneeling.

Quinn sat on her heels, staring out at the sea. He followed her gaze. In the distance, barely visible through the hazy sea air, was a string of mountains. A thick layer of smoke had settled over the highest peak.

Then everything came back to him: Quinn's parents, Cayde, Mistveil . . . all of it seemed like a distant memory. For a hopeful, fleeting moment, he wondered if it had even happened. But one look at Quinn's face was all the proof he needed.

Her arms dangled limply at her sides, her hands half buried beneath the rocky sand. Her back was hunched, and there was a long tear in her damp robes above her right shoulder. Her mouth was parted slightly, but her lips were no longer trembling. She only stared vacantly forward, her green, glassy, unblinking stare haunting Dane to his core.

The sight was almost too much to bear. It took all his waning strength to stop himself from collapsing beside her, immobilized by the horrors that now plagued her mind.

"Quinn?" he prodded, testing her sentience.

Quinn's spine straightened slightly at the sound of his voice, but still she said nothing, only stared blankly at the horizon.

He tried again. "Quinn, it isn't safe here, we have to—"

"It's my fault . . ." she muttered, her voice ghostly and distant.

"Your—Quinn . . . n-no, how—"

"I told them where to go . . . where they'd be safe. They trusted me. The Luminari . . . it's my fault they're dead."

Dane couldn't believe what he was hearing. "That was Avon—the Ferrons. They're responsible for this. It's not your fault—"

"My people, my family, my friends . . ." she went on. "Lady Rivelda . . . and Agatha . . . sweet, sweet Agatha —" her voice hitched in her throat and she bit back a sob "— I-I failed them." Her wall of masked emotion crumbled. Anger, fear, and grief spilled into her words as tears streaked down her pale, weathered cheeks. "I could have done more. I could have saved them. I could have saved *him*." Her fingers coiled into fists, clenching the gritty sand in her palms. "But I didn't . . . and now they're all *dead*."

Dane could barely hold back tears of his own. It wasn't true. It couldn't be. *All of them?* He didn't want to believe her. "M-maybe some of them escaped, or maybe some s-survived. Maybe—"

Quinn ripped her gaze from the sea and looked directly at him, piercing through him with her trepid stare.

What he saw terrified him. Her beautiful green eyes, once full of vigor and youthful intrigue, now opened into endless pits of misery and despair, void of life, void of joyous curiosity, void of all hope; her eyes looked like reflections of the Shrouded Isle itself.

"Don't you *understand?*" she seethed, almost pleading. "*All* Luminari were in the city when it was attacked. *Every one* of them fled down the mountain into Mistveil, where I *told* them to go."

"But—"

She lurched to her feet and threw her clenched fists at his chest. "*Everyone* was there! *All* of them, when—" She paused, her eyes widening, as if replaying the thousands of dying screams over and over in her mind. "They're *dead!* The Luminari . . . my parents . . . Cayde—" She shook her head violently and squeezed her hair in her fingers, looking like she wanted to rip it from her head.

Dane's voice trembled beyond his control. "What if s-someone survived—l-like we did—they could've—"

"THEY'RE ALL DEAD, DANE!" she screamed. She shoved him away, filling the air with her ragged cry. "ALL OF THEM! EVERYONE! EVERYONE IS DEAD! BECAUSE OF *ME!*"

Quinn's legs failed her. She collapsed to the ground, clasped her face in her hands, and shattered into racking, weeping sobs. When she finally spoke again, her voice was barely more than a whisper. "You should've let me drown . . ."

Dane felt as though his heart had shriveled up in his chest, leaving him with a pain even worse than the impact at the base of the waterfall. He opened his mouth then closed it again, unable to produce a sound as he stared at Quinn, the last remnants of her former self washing away with the ebbing tide.

Then a faint sound wafted through the air. His spirits lifted slightly. It sounded like a cry for help. *We aren't alone,* Dane thought, tears of desperate relief battling the pit of sadness within. *Someone* did *survive . . . they must have washed up on the Isle like us. Maybe there are more of them.*

The shout came again, louder this time, emanating from behind the cliffs curving to his left along the shoreline.

Dane nearly shouted aloud.

Leon!

Despite the pain still flaring in his back, Dane broke into a run toward the archivist's voice. Before, the thought of seeing Leon had left him with a sour taste in his mouth, the kind that lingered for days on end. But as he ran across the desolate beach, rounding the black cliffs, Dane wanted to hug the Aquadorian.

Dane skidded to a halt as he rounded the cliffside. Leon, with his tattered white tunic and ragged brown pants, emerged from the sea swells with Sage in tow, her white-blonde hair glinting in the sun's reflection. Dane wanted to leap to the sky.

Sage! She's alive—

Then his heart sank. She was motionless, her limbs dragging as Leon pulled her from the water. Leon dropped her to the sand and collapsed beside her.

"Stay with me, Petals," Leon shouted desperately, patting her cheeks and pressing his ear to her mouth. "Come on, quit playing games. I didn't swim all this way to have you dying on me. I've got you now, but I need you to *wake up*!"

Something in the corner of Dane's eye pulled his attention away—a movement by the cliffside not far from where Leon was kneeling. Before Dane had time to think, primal instinct took over and he leapt to the side, taking cover behind the jutting cliff nearest him. He peered out to see two large, black shapes—eerily familiar shapes—emerge from the cliffs themselves, lumbering slowly toward Leon.

Dane tried to warn Leon, but his mouth and throat had gone dry. The only sound he managed was a strangled exhalation. The black, hardened skin; the red, crystalline veins; the knife-like fingers. Chemocytes.

No, they can't be, Dane thought, perplexed. The Chemocyte he'd seen before prowled like a ravenous predator, its hunched back level to the ground, its lethal claws poised for attack. But these Chemocytes walked like someone caught in a daze, shoulders and torso slumped as they stumbled mindlessly forward with no indication of ferocity. Their movements were calm, controlled even. It was almost more haunting than if they'd charged forth shrieking, ready to kill.

They looked obedient.

With sinking horror, Dane realized Leon couldn't hear them approaching; he was still trying to revive Sage, his back turned to his pursuers.

Every bone in Dane's body urged him to run to their aid, but he fought against his own will, forcing himself to stay hidden. There might be more Chemocytes lurking in the cliffs out of view, waiting for the chance to strike. Even if there weren't, there was no telling what the two Chemocytes would do if he revealed his position. He was already weak from exhaustion. He'd left his staff and Cayde's sword on the beach behind him. He was defenseless. If the Chemocytes turned feral at his call and came at him with their savage, ripping claws, then he, Quinn, Leon, and Sage wouldn't stand a chance; they'd end up no different than Varic: mauled, bleeding, left for dead.

There was only one option. Despite how much it pained him, he had to remain hidden and hope the Chemocytes wouldn't kill Leon, a hope that waned with every step the Chemocytes took toward the archivist and his sister.

Chemocytes stopped directly behind Leon. Before Leon had the chance to spin around, one of the Chemocytes raised its mangled fist into the air and slammed it down on Leon's head.

Dane clasped his hands to his mouth to stifle a guttural cry as Leon dropped lifelessly to the ground beside Sage.

Moving as slowly and methodically as they'd come, the Chemocytes each lifted a body over one shoulder, carrying Sage and Leon as if the two were nothing more than ordinary sacks of food, and retreated into the shadows of the cliffside.

Dane pulled his eyes away from the scene and pressed his head into the cliffside, clutching his weathered hair in his fingers. He sank to his knees. He felt as if the world was closing in around him. The Chemocytes had taken Leon and Sage into their lair, deeper into the Isle. Whether to kill them, eat them, or rip the power from their bodies, Dane didn't know, but he had to do something; if he didn't, they were as good as dead.

He took a deep breath, grasping the thin hold of his mental composure that still remained. Sage needed his help. He *had* to save her, but he couldn't do it alone.

Dane rose to his feet and, cautiously, peered around the cliff one final time, checking that the Chemocytes hadn't returned. When he saw nothing, he retreated to where Quinn still lay kneeling on the shore. Her wrenching sobs had ebbed, but she looked utterly distraught, staring mindlessly at her trembling palms cradled in her lap.

"Quinn?" he prodded softly.

"I heard Leon's voice," she murmured matter-of-factly. "He called out to Sage. Then he stopped. They're gone now too . . ."

A lump lodged in Dane's throat. Tears welled in his eyes. Part of him believed her, that Sage and Leon were already beyond help, left to die somewhere beneath the Isle, lost in the Chemocytes' clutches.

But his tears weren't only for them. They were for Quinn. She was merely a shell of the girl he once knew, of the girl he loved. All hope and life had been torn from her piece by piece as those she loved had died around her. He wanted to comfort her, to wrap her in his arms while she cried and tell her things would get better. He wanted to hold her until her pain went away, to wake her from the endless nightmare that had become their reality and return to the lives they once knew.

But he knew the words would be a lie, a futile attempt to persuade them both that their world wasn't a nightmare. She needed her people, her parents, and Cayde. They were the only ones who could rebuild the pieces of her shattered spirit and give her back the hope she needed.

Dane swallowed hard, unable to quell the pain in his heart. She needed them, not him. But they were all gone, lost forever in the cosmic oblivion that had claimed their souls. He was the only one left who could help her. If he didn't, she'd soon be gone too. He had to try.

"I'm sorry about Cayde," Dane said weakly, his voice croaking from the strain of suppressed tears. "I wish he were here too. He would have known what to do."

Tears spilled down his cheeks and he dropped his gaze to the sand, ashamed to meet her tortured eyes. "I'll never be as strong or brave as he was . . . but I wish I could be. He made me promise to keep you safe no matter the cost . . . to do whatever it takes to protect you—" Dane could feel Quinn's sorrowful gaze burning into him. He swallowed again. "—But I can't keep that promise. I can't protect you like he did, because you're the one who protects me. I don't know what I'd do without you . . ."

Dane shook his head, trying to fight back his onslaught of tears.

"Sage and Leon . . . Cayde would have gone in after them. He would've given everything to save them. But he already gave his life for them—for all of us. He can't save them again." He wiped his eyes with his sleeve and took a deep breath, trying to summon what little determination and hope still sparked within. "He may not be able to save them now, but we still can—he would have wanted us to try. We can't lose Sage too. I know I don't have any powers. And I don't know what lies beneath the Isle. But I have to go after them. I don't want to do it alone . . ."

"How do you know we can save them?" Quinn whispered, her voice tremulous.

Dane breathed a long, shaky sigh. "I don't."

Her voice dipped even quieter. "What if we lose them too?"

A burning determination flared inside Dane, searing through the fear and uncertainty that had eclipsed his mind. He clenched his fists, steeling himself against his tears.

"I won't let that happen. It doesn't matter if I don't have powers, we have to go after them. They're counting on us to save them, and we're the only ones in the world who can. We have to try."

He paused for a moment, recalling something Cayde once said to him. He offered his hand to Quinn, and said, "For even when all hope seems lost, you know you'll stop at nothing to save the ones you love . . ."

Dane finally lifted his gaze from the ground. Quinn stared back at him. Her green eyes found his, still glistening and teary with irreparable remorse. But for a moment, he glimpsed the recognition in her eyes. And as he stared deeper, searching beyond her sorrow and despair, he found the faintest spark of something else . . . hope.

Wordlessly, her gaze unwavering, Quinn took his hand. She stumbled to her feet, tightly gripping him for balance.

They walked across the shore, gathered their belongings, and stopped before the dark crevice where the Chemocytes had disappeared with Sage and Leon.

"We'll find them," Dane said, squeezing Quinn's hand as he stared into the gaping maw of shadow. "They're alive. They have to be . . ."

Dane took a deep breath, filling his lungs with the fresh, salty sea air. He savored the scent, wondering when—if—he'd ever smell it again.

Then, with Quinn by his side, her hand locked in his, Dane and Quinn ventured into the Shrouded Isle.

EPILOGUE

The sun beat down with unforgiving heat as the soldier ran across the open, rocky plain.

Thick beads of sweat had formed on his brow and he wiped them away. His breaths were ragged and labored, and his sword clanged against his leg with every exhausted step. He clutched one hand to his bleeding chest, the place where the girl had cut him. The wound was nothing serious, he knew, but pushing a hand against it filled him with rage and determination, giving him the strength he needed to endure the harsh heat.

He was on a mission. He had to deliver the message.

The soldier stopped at the edge of the plain. A thin, wiry man with ornate gray and gold robes stood perched on the edge of a cliff. His pitch-black hair remained plastered to his head despite the rising winds. His hands were folded neatly at the small of his back as he stared down the precipice into the vast desert sea of sand and rock far below.

The soldier slowed as he neared the man and dropped to one knee, in part out of respect for his superior, part from the pure exhaustion of running through the night.

"My Lord," the soldier said, bowing his head level with the ground, "the Mystic Fountain . . . it is destroyed."

The man said nothing in response, only scoured the landscape with his piercing, unyielding stare. Despite the man's calm appearance, the soldier knew what lay within. He dreaded what he had to say next.

"But . . . there was a problem."

"Oh?" the man said, with a hint of intrigue.

"Avon, my Lord, he—" the soldier's tongue was sand "—he destroyed the city too . . . Mistveil is gone."

The man whirled on him.

"He—*WHAT*?" he hissed, his lips curling into a vicious snarl.

The soldier's eyes widened and he bowed his head even lower, not daring to break his gaze from the ground.

After a long pause, the man straightened, patted his robes, and stroked his hands through his thinning hair. "Forget it," he snapped coldly, his face contorting with restrained anger. He breathed an exasperated sigh then returned his scrutinizing gaze to the desert wasteland. "He is of no concern. I will deal with his . . . *insolence* later. Now . . . "

He reached out his bony, long-fingered hand, beckoning the soldier.

Reluctantly, the soldier obliged and took his place beside the man, following his gaze across the desert below.

A massive cliff loomed in the distance, parting the endless sea of sand and stone that stretched below. A narrow crevice ran down its center, creating a gap in the rock facing that was nearly unrecognizable if not for the two huge stone statues flanking the base of the crevice, guarding an entrance.

The man's mouth coiled into a sinister grin.

" . . . I have more pressing matters to attend to."

AUTHOR'S NOTE

Thank you for reading my debut novel, Trials of Power, *book one of my new* Forces of Power *series. Above all else, I hope it was an entertaining read, and leaves you pondering and theorizing for weeks to come.*

If you enjoyed this novel and would like to show your support, please share this book with your family and friends and tell them how awesome it is (or how it's the worst thing you've ever read and it's imperative they join in the mockery). This will help reach more prospective readers, and in turn allow me to dedicate more time to preparing the next books in the series.

By the way, if you couldn't tell, I'm a huge fan of cliffhangers. Nothing like a good ol' book-ending cliffhanger to get your blood pumping. But consider yourself warned. If you thought this one was tense, you'll get a kick out of Book 2 . . .

ACKNOWLEDGMENTS

And now, the part of the book where I express my deepest gratitude to all the fantastic folk (attention leeches) to whom I owe the success of this novel. Don't worry, it's not a competition, everyone I mention is equally responsible and contributions are equally weighted.

Remember that part where I said it wasn't a competition? That was a lie. It's definitely a competition. Joseph Rodgers is the clear winner, and no, it's not close. To Joseph, my former roommate and best friend since I was a wee nine-year-old, thank you for listening to me talk and rant and complain for nights on end for the better part of two years. You are, and always will be, my first point of contact for everything conceptual about this series and those to come. You are the Watson to my Holmes, the Dr. Grant to my Hammond, the Merry to my Pippin. Your patience is legend. As thanks for your monumental efforts, I give you these words of thanks (see above). You're welcome.

To everyone involved in my Kickstarter campaign, whose faith and support in my ability quite literally allowed me to live while I battled unemployment for months before my current job. Those months were some of the best in my life. I was able to experience life as a full-time (though unpaid) writer, finish the ninth and tenth rewrites of book one, and begin the first written copy of book two. None of that would have happened if not for your support, and I don't know where I'd be today without it. You will now and forever hold my deepest gratitude.

To the Mighty Chlorians community, whose daily support during the hardest year of my life gave me purpose when I needed it and gave me the confidence to reach for the stars with this novel. You were my virtual home when I needed you, and your camaraderie and banter did wonders to lift my spirits on a daily basis. I can only hope I am able to repay your kindness and touch your lives as you graced mine. MC OP!

And now for a few honorable mentions. To Tara Halsted, whose beautiful artwork (featured on the website) gave me a much-needed glimpse into the world of Physos. To Kayla Chapman, whose editing skills and literary expertise rivaled that of professional help. And to all of my beta readers, who were suckered in to read a free novel for the low price of a barrage of detailed questions.

Also to my family, Viv, Dad, and Mom...you already received your acknowledgement. I dedicated this whole thing to you, and you still want more? Fine. Thanks again, I guess.

And to everyone else who has touched my life along the way: family, friends, coworkers, gaming community counterparts, acquaintances, random conference strangers, forum keyboard warriors, and anyone else who doesn't fit one of the aforementioned nonspecific molds of my arbitrary acknowledgement hierarchy. This book is for you (in spirit, because it's physically dedicated to my immediate family, see above) and always will be. I can't wait to see where this series takes us, and know that there is plenty more on the horizon.

This is only the beginning.

BOOK LAUNCH
EXCLUSIVE

Thank you for purchasing *Trials of Power* within the first month
of its release!

Keep reading for an exclusive look into Book 2 of the *Forces of
Power* series, *Balance of Power*.

BALANCE OF POWER

FORCES OF POWER BOOK 2

They opened into a large cavern. Quinn's grip tightened on Dane's hand and she whispered in his hear, "Look! Water!"

She held the orb out to illuminate the immediate surroundings. A short distance away, taking up most of the cavern floor, was a small underground lake, its surface spanning to the edge of the orb's dim light. Behind it, on the far side of the cavern, they could barely make out an entrance to another tunnel.

They walked over to the edge of the lake and knelt down next to the still waters. The ground dropped off immediately beneath the surface. Despite the orb's light, they couldn't see the bottom.

Dane cupped his hands and lowered them to the water but paused before touching the surface.

"How do we know it's safe?" he said.

Quinn stared into the water's depths. "It looks drinkable, but we'll never know for certain unless—" She paused and looked at Dane, sharing in the dreaded implication of her unspoken words.

Dane exhaled and said, "I'll try it first."

"No, Dane, I'll do it, I—"

He took her hands and stared into her eyes. "You're more valuable to them than I am down here—we can't see without your orb—I can't have something happen to you."

"But what if it's poisonous? What if you get hurt?"

"It'll be fine, don't worry," he said evenly, trying to convince more than just her. "What's the worst that could happen?"

Quinn opened her mouth in retort, then sighed and gave a reluctant nod. Dane shifted his gaze back to the water and cupped his hands once more. Slowly, he lowered his hands and hovered them over the surface. His heart pounded in his throat. Beside him, Quinn held her breath, watching his hands intently. Dane mustered a deep, controlled breath and submerged his hands.

"What?" Quinn said urgently when Dane winced. "What is it? What's wrong?"

Dane exhaled with relief. "The water . . . it's cold, that's all." He rung his hands shortly, cleansing them of the thin layer of dirt and grime that had built up there, then scooped up a handful of water, brought it to his mouth, and took a drink.

He nearly burst into joyous laughter. Despite a mild, earthy taste, the water was enchanting and reinvigorating on his dry lips and throat. When he scooped his hands in for another drink, Quinn let out an audible sigh and joined him.

"Let's refill the water pouches," he said, rifling through his pack after taking a few more drinks. They submerged their empty pouches, filling them to the brim before stowing them back into their packs.

Dane bent down for another drink when Quinn's hand fastened on his shoulder.

"Dane, stop," she whispered urgently. He froze, the sudden change in her voice sending an icy shiver down his back. "The walls . . ."

Slowly, Dane lifted his head and looked around. Even amidst the orb's pale light, the cavern now glowed a dull red.

He turned to see Quinn staring at the tunnel from which they'd come, her body unmoving and eyes wide. The red glow was coming from the black crystals embedded in the earthen walls, emanating from inside, pulsing like a heartbeat. It was dim at first, hardly discernable, but grew with every passing instant. Then a sound tugged at his ears—the first sound he'd heard since delving beneath the Shrouded Isle—that of slow, methodical, shuffling footsteps.

"*Something's coming!*" Quinn hissed. "We have to hide!"

She stood and spun in place, then cursed under her breath.

"There's nothing! We'll have to run for the next tunnel, that's our only chance!"

"Quinn, use one of your aurora veils! If we hide in a corner and stay quiet, they won't see us!"

Quinn turned to face him with a look of bewilderment and dread.

"No—I—I can't . . . I'm not—I'm not strong enough—"

Dane wanted to argue otherwise, but the footsteps were drawing nearer. They were running out of time. Heart pounding in his throat, Dane scrambled to his feet, making to follow Quinn to the far end of the cavern, when his gaze locked on the lake's surface.

"Quinn, wait!" he hissed. She had just retrieved her orb and pack, preparing to run, before swiveling at his call. Dane gestured to the lake, then her eyes seemed to widen with the implication.

"You don't mean—"

"It'll be safer than running through the tunnels ahead—we can hide until they pass!"

She opened her mouth, hesitated, and stole a quick glance at the tunnel they'd entered from. The lights had grown brighter, filling the cavern entrance with an ominous dim red hue. The footsteps sounded even closer.

"Fine," she relented. Dane snatched his own pack as Quinn joined him by the edge of the lake.

"Quietly now," she said. "But hurry!"

Before Dane could risk another glance behind him, he forced several short, quick breaths, and eased his legs into the water, lowering himself until only his head remained above the surface.

The water was cold, but it paled in comparison to the frigid waters of Mistveil Lake.

Bracing himself on the rocky wall beneath the surface, he looked to Quinn now submerged beside him.

"Take a deep breath," he whispered. She nodded in understanding, then they both lowered themselves deeper into the lake until the red glow was barely visible overhead.

Dane slowed his motions, relaxing as much of his body as he could as he watched the surface above them. He didn't know how long they'd have to remain hidden. He couldn't risk any unnecessary movement.

Then a shadow obscured the surface above.

ABOUT THE
AUTHOR

Ben Crow is the author of TRIALS OF POWER, the first of three books in his debut YA Fantasy series, FORCES OF POWER.

Ben graduated from Oregon State University with a degree in mechanical engineering, but after graduation he discovered his passion for creating stories and hasn't looked back since. Now he hopes to inspire the next generation of readers and all fans of fantasy with his stories.

Ben currently lives in the Pacific Northwest, working as an airline customer service lead.

For more information, visit www.benjamincrow.com

Made in the USA
Coppell, TX
18 January 2021

48360520R00229